Praise for *Long Bright River*

A *New York Times* Bestseller

"An instant sensation and the January pick for *Good Morning America*'s book club." —*Entertainment Weekly*

"Navigates assuredly between the plot twists and big reveals . . . *Long Bright River* is equal parts literary and thrilling." —*O, the Oprah Magazine*

"[Moore's] careful balance of the hard-bitten with the heartfelt is what elevates *Long Bright River* from entertaining page-turner to a book that makes you want to call someone you love." —*The New York Times Book Review*

"*Long Bright River*—a book that has garnered much prepublication buzz— nervously twists, turns and subverts readers' expectations till its very last pages. Simultaneously, it also manages to grow into something else: a sweeping, elegiac novel about a blighted city." —*The Washington Post*

"Alternating its present-day mystery with the story of the sisters' child- hood and adolescence, *Long Bright River* is at once heart-pounding and heart-wrenching: a gripping suspense novel that is also a moving story of sisters, addiction, and the formidable ties that persist between place, family, and fate." —*Good Morning America*

"Powerful." —*The Wall Street Journal*

"Moore's observations are informed and compassionate. . . . One of the love- liest things about *Long Bright River* is that it's not a literary glorification of addiction." —*The Guardian*

"Thoughtfully explores the power of nature versus nurture, the pull of ad- diction, and the lengths we go to for family." —*Marie Claire*

"An exquisite novel that dug its fingers into my heart and has refused to let go . . . I finished this novel shaken . . . by its sheer emotional resonance and also because of how clear and familiar so much of what Moore describes feels to me." —Medium.com

"Pulsating with breathtaking suspense and boundless compassion, *Long Bright River* is the kind of genre-defying novel that, once the final chapters close, you instantly implore people to read. Topical yet timeless, its page-turning narrative wrestles with the fissures and wreckage that addiction can inflict on a family—and a city. Liz Moore is a force, and *Long Bright River* should be on top of everyone's to-read list."   —*Forbes*

"This is police procedural and a thriller par excellence, one in which the city of Philadelphia itself is a character (think Boston and *Mystic River*). But it's also a literary tale narrated by a strong woman with a richly drawn personal life—powerful and genre-defying."   —*People*

"A propulsive thriller and a poignant family saga."   —*Time*

"Deftly plotted with strong, vivid characters, Liz Moore's outstanding *Long Bright River* works as solid crime fiction and an intense family thriller."
—Associated Press

"Tough, tense, and twisty—but tender, human, and deeply affecting, too . . . I don't have a sister, but when I finished the book I called my brother, just to hear his voice."
—Lee Child, #1 *New York Times*–bestselling author of *Blue Moon*

"The perfect literary page-turner. It's a brilliantly plotted crime novel, yes, but it's also a story about the complicated push and pull of family, and how much of our childhood traumas we carry forward through our lives. Anyone with a mother, a father, a brother, or a sister—anyone with a heart, for that matter—will love this book, as I did."
—Mary Beth Keane, *New York Times*–bestselling author of *Ask Again, Yes*

"A riveting portrait of so many things—of grief, of sisterhood, of a neighborhood in despair. Moore makes you care about the people society too often abandons and, in doing so, pulls off a hat trick of epic storytelling that is stigma-busting, love-rendering, and page-turning to the last word."
—Beth Macy, *New York Times*–bestselling author of *Dopesick: Dealers, Doctors, and the Drug Company That Addicted America*

"A superlative crime novel. Set against the backdrop of Philadelphia's opioid crisis, this is not just a gripping mystery but a thoughtful, powerful novel by a writer who displays enormous compassion for her characters. *Long*

RIVERHEAD BOOKS | NEW YORK

Long Bright River

LIZ MOORE

RIVERHEAD BOOKS
An imprint of Penguin Random House LLC
penguinrandomhouse.com

Copyright © 2020 by Liz Moore, Inc.
Penguin supports copyright. Copyright fuels creativity, encourages
diverse voices, promotes free speech, and creates a vibrant culture. Thank
you for buying an authorized edition of this book and for complying with
copyright laws by not reproducing, scanning, or distributing any part of it
in any form without permission. You are supporting writers and allowing
Penguin to continue to publish books for every reader.

Riverhead and the R colophon are registered trademarks
of Penguin Random House LLC.

The Library of Congress has catalogued
the Riverhead hardcover edition as follows:

Names: Moore, Liz, 1983– author.
Title: Long bright river / Liz Moore.
Description: New York : Riverhead Books, 2020.
Identifiers: LCCN 2018051652 (print) | LCCN 2018057217 (ebook) |
ISBN 9780525540670 (hardcover) | ISBN 9780525540694 (ebook)
Subjects: LCSH: Domestic fiction. | GSAFD: Mystery fiction.
Classification: LCC PS3613.O5644 L66 2019 (print) |
LCC PS3613.O5644 (ebook) |
DDC 813/.6—dc23
LC record available at https://lccn.loc.gov/2018051652
LC ebook record available at https://lccn.loc.gov/2018057217

First Riverhead hardcover edition: January 2020
First Riverhead trade paperback edition: December 2020
Riverhead trade paperback ISBN: 9780525540687

Printed in the United States of America
3   5   7   9   10   8   6   4   2

Book design by Amanda Dewey

For M.A.C.

What can be said of the Kensington of to-day, with her long line of business streets, her palatial residences and beautiful homes, that we do not know? A City within a City, nestling upon the bosom of the placid Delaware. Filled to the brim with enterprise, dotted with factories so numerous that the rising smoke obscures the sky. The hum of industry is heard in every corner of its broad expanse. A happy and contented people, enjoying plenty in a land of plenty. Populated by brave men, fair women and a hardy generation of young blood that will take the reins when the fathers have passed away. All hail, Kensington! A credit to the Continent—a crowning glory to the City.

—*From* Kensington; a City Within a City *(1891)*

Is there confusion in the little isle?
Let what is broken so remain.
The Gods are hard to reconcile:
'Tis hard to settle order once again.
There *is* confusion worse than death,
Trouble on trouble, pain on pain,
Long labour unto aged breath,
Sore task to hearts worn out by many wars
And eyes grown dim with gazing on the pilot-stars.

But, propt on beds of amaranth and moly,
How sweet (while warm airs lull us, blowing lowly)
With half-dropt eyelid still,
Beneath a heaven dark and holy,
To watch the long bright river drawing slowly
His waters from the purple hill—
To hear the dewy echoes calling
From cave to cave thro' the thick-twined vine—
To watch the emerald-colour'd water falling
Thro' many a wov'n acanthus-wreath divine!
Only to hear and see the far-off sparkling brine,
Only to hear were sweet, stretch'd out beneath the pine.

—*Alfred, Lord Tennyson, from "The Lotos-Eaters"*

LIST

Sean Geoghehan; Kimberly Gummer; Kimberly Brewer, Kimberly Brewer's mother and uncle; Britt-Anne Conover; Jeremy Haskill; two of the younger DiPaolantonio boys; Chuck Bierce; Maureen Howard; Kaylee Zanella; Chris Carter and John Marks (one day apart, victims of the same bad batch, someone said); Carlo, whose last name I can never remember; Taylor Bowes's boyfriend, and then Taylor Bowes a year later; Pete Stockton; the granddaughter of our former neighbors; Hayley Driscoll; Shayna Pietrewski; Dooney Jacobs and his mother; Melissa Gill; Meghan Morrow; Meghan Hanover; Meghan Chisholm; Meghan Greene; Hank Chambliss; Tim and Paul Flores; Robby Symons; Ricky Todd; Brian Aldrich; Mike Ashman; Cheryl Sokol; Sandra Broach; Ken and Chris Lowery; Lisa Morales; Mary Lynch; Mary Bridges and her niece, who was her age, and her friend; Jim; Mikey Hughes's father and uncle; two great-uncles we rarely see. Our former teacher Mr. Paules. Sergeant Davies in the 23rd. Our cousin Tracy. Our cousin Shannon. Our father. Our mother.

NOW

There's a body on the Gurney Street tracks. Female, age unclear, probable overdose, says the dispatcher.

Kacey, I think. This is a twitch, a reflex, something sharp and subconscious that lives inside me and sends the same message racing to the same base part of my brain every time a female is reported. Then the more rational part of me comes plodding along, lethargic, uninspired, a dutiful dull soldier here to remind me about odds and statistics: nine hundred overdose victims in Kensington last year. Not one of them Kacey. Furthermore, this sentry reproves me, you seem to have forgotten the importance of being a professional. Straighten your shoulders. Smile a little. Keep your face relaxed, your eyebrows unfurrowed, your chin untucked. Do your job.

All day, I've been having Lafferty respond to calls for us for further practice. Now, I nod to him, and he clears his throat and wipes his mouth. Nervous.

—2613, he says.

Our vehicle number. Correct.

Dispatch continues. The RP is anonymous. The call came in from a payphone, one of several that still line Kensington Avenue and, as far as I know, the only one of those that still works.

Lafferty looks at me. I look at him. I gesture to him. *More. Ask for more.*

—Got it, says Lafferty into his radio. Over.

Incorrect. I raise mine to my mouth. I speak clearly.

—Any further information on location? I say.

———

After I end the call, I give Lafferty a few pointers, reminding him not to be afraid to speak plainly to Dispatch—many rookie officers have the habit of speaking in a kind of stilted, masculine manner they have most likely picked up from films or television—and reminding him, too, to extract from Dispatch as many details as he can.

But before I've finished speaking, Lafferty says, again, Got it.

I look at him. Excellent, I say. I'm glad.

I've only known him an hour, but I'm getting a sense for him. He likes to talk—already I know more about him than he'll ever know about me—and he's a pretender. An aspirant. In other words, a phony. Someone so terrified of being called poor, or weak, or stupid, that he won't even admit to what deficits he does have in those regards. I, on the other hand, am well aware that I'm poor. More so than ever now that Simon's checks have stopped coming. Am I weak? Probably in some ways: stubborn, maybe, obstinate, mulish, reluctant to accept help even when it would serve me to. Physically afraid, too: not the first officer to throw herself in front of a bullet for a friend, not the first officer to throw herself into traffic in the pursuit of some vanishing perpetrator. Poor: yes. Weak: yes. Stupid: no. I'm not stupid.

was late to roll call this morning. Again. I am ashamed to admit it was the third time in a month, and I despise being late. A good police officer is punctual if she is nothing else. When I walked into the common area—a drab, bright space, devoid of furniture, adorned only by peeling policy posters on the wall—Sergeant Ahearn was waiting for me, arms crossed.

—Fitzpatrick, he said. Welcome to the party. You're with Lafferty today in 2613.

—Who's Lafferty, I said, before I thought better of it. I really didn't intend to be funny. Szebowski, in the corner, laughed aloud once.

Ahearn said, That's Lafferty. Pointing.

There he was, Eddie Lafferty, second day in the district. He was busying himself across the room, looking at his blank activity log. He glanced at me quickly and apprehensively. Then he bent down, as if noticing something on his shoes, which were freshly polished, somehow glistening. He pursed his lips. Whistled lowly. At the time, I almost felt sorry for him.

Then he got into the passenger's seat.

Facts I have learned about Eddie Lafferty in the first hour of our acquaintance: He is forty-three, which makes him eleven years my senior. A late entrant into the PPD. He worked construction until last year, when he took the test. (My back, says Eddie Lafferty. It still bothers me sometimes. Don't tell anyone.) He's just rolled off his field training. He has three ex-wives and three almost-grown children. He has a home in the Poconos. He lifts. (I'm a gym rat, says Eddie Lafferty.) He has GERD. Occasionally, he suffers from constipation. He grew up in South Philadelphia and now lives in Mayfair. He splits Eagles season tickets with six friends. His most recent ex-wife was in her twenties. (Maybe that was the problem, says Lafferty, her being immature.) He golfs. He has two rescued pit mixes named Jimbo and Jennie. He played baseball in high school. One of his teammates then was, in fact, our platoon's sergeant, Kevin Ahearn, and it was Sergeant Ahearn who suggested he consider police work. (Something about this makes sense to me.)

Facts Eddie Lafferty has learned about me in the first hour of our acquaintance: I like pistachio ice cream.

All morning, during Eddie Lafferty's very infrequent pauses, I have tried my best to interject only the basics of what he needs to know about the neighborhood.

Kensington is one of the newer neighborhoods in what is, by American standards, the very old city of Philadelphia. It was established in the 1730s by the Englishman Anthony Palmer, who acquired a small tract of nondescript land and named it after a regal neighborhood—one that was, at the time, the preferred residence of the British monarchy. (Perhaps Palmer, too, was a phony. Or, more kindly, an optimist.) The eastern edge of present-day Kensington is a mile from the Delaware River, but in its earliest days it bordered the river directly. Accordingly, its earliest industries were shipbuilding and fishing, but by the middle of the nineteenth century its long tenure as a manufacturing hub was beginning. At its peak it boasted producers of iron, steel, textiles, and—perhaps fittingly—pharmaceuticals. But when, a century later, the factories in this country died in great numbers, Kensington, too, began a slow and then a rapid economic decline. Many residents moved farther into or out of the city, seeking other work; others stayed, persuaded by allegiance or delusion that a change would come. Today, Kensington comprises in nearly equal parts the Irish-Americans who moved here in the nineteenth and twentieth centuries and a newer population of families of Puerto Rican and other Latino descent—along with groups who represent successively smaller slivers of Kensington's demographic pie: African-American, East Asian, Caribbean.

Present-day Kensington is shot through by two main arteries: Front Street, which runs north up the eastern edge of the city, and Kensington Ave—usually just called *the Ave*, an alternately friendly or disdainful appellation, depending on who's saying it—which begins at Front and veers northeast. The Market-Frankford elevated train—or, more commonly, *the El*, since a city called *Philly* can't let any of its infrastructure go unabbreviated—runs directly over both Front and Kensington, which means both roads spend the majority of the day in the shadows. Large steel beams support the train line, blue legs spaced thirty feet apart, which gives the whole apparatus the look of a giant and menacing caterpillar hovering over the neighborhood. Most of the transactions (narcotic, sexual) that happen in Kensington begin on one of these two roads and end on one of the many smaller streets that cross them, or more often in one of the abandoned houses or empty lots that populate the neighborhood's side streets and alleys. The businesses that can be found along the main streets are nail salons, takeout places, mobile phone stores, convenience stores, dollar stores, appliance stores, pawnshops, soup kitchens, other charitable organizations, and bars. About a third of the storefronts are shuttered.

And yet—like the condos that are sprouting, to our left now, from an empty lot that has lain fallow since a wrecking ball took out the factory it used to house—the neighborhood is rising. New bars and businesses are cropping up on the periphery, toward Fishtown, where I grew up. New young faces are populating those businesses: earnest, rich, naive, ripe for the picking. So the mayor is getting concerned with appearances. *More troops*, the mayor says. More troops, more troops, more troops.

It's raining hard today, and this forces me to drive more slowly than I normally would when responding to a call. I name the businesses we pass, name their proprietors. I describe recent crimes I think Lafferty should know about (each time, Lafferty whistles, shakes his head). I list allies. Outside our windows: the usual mix of people seeking a fix and people in the aftermath of one. Half of the people on the sidewalks are melting slowly toward the earth, their legs unable to support them. The Kensington lean, say people who make jokes about that kind of thing. I never do.

Because of the weather, some of the women we pass have umbrellas. They wear winter hats and puffy jackets, jeans, dirty sneakers. They range in age from teenagers to the elderly. The large majority are Caucasian, though addiction doesn't discriminate, and all races and creeds can be found here. The women wear no makeup, or maybe a hard black ring of liner around their eyes. The women working the Ave don't wear anything that shows they're working, but everyone knows: it's the look that does it, a long hard gaze at the driver of every passing car, every passing man. I know most of these women, and most of them know me.

—There's Jamie, I say to Lafferty as we pass her. There's Amanda. There's Rose.

I consider it part of his training to know these women.

Down the block, at Kensington and Cambria, I see Paula Mulroney. She's on crutches today, hovering miserably on one foot, getting rained on because she can't balance an umbrella too. Her denim jacket has turned a dark upsetting blue. I wish she'd go inside.

I glance around quickly, checking for Kacey. This is the corner on which she and Paula can usually be found. Occasionally they'll get into a fight or have a falling-out, and one or the other of them will go stand someplace else for a while, but a week later I'll see them there, reunited, their arms slung about one another cheerfully, Kacey with a cigarette hanging out of her mouth, Paula with a water or a juice or a beer in a paper bag.

Today, I don't see Kacey anyplace. It occurs to me, in fact, that I have not seen her in quite some time.

Paula spots our car as we drive toward her and she squints in our direction, seeing who's inside. I lift two fingers off the steering wheel: a wave. Paula looks at me, and then at Lafferty, and then turns her face slightly upward, toward the sky.

—That's Paula, I say to Lafferty.

I think about saying more. I went to school with her, I could say. She's a friend of the family. She's my sister's friend.

But already, Lafferty has moved on to another subject: this time it is the heartburn that has plagued him for the better part of a year.

I can think of no response.

—Are you always this quiet? he says suddenly. It's the first question he's asked me since determining my ice cream preferences.

—Just tired, I say.

—Have you had a lot of partners before me? says Lafferty, and then he laughs, as if he's made a joke.

—That sounded wrong, he says. Sorry.

For just long enough, I say nothing.

Then I say, Only one.

—How long did you work together?

—Ten years.

—What happened to him? says Lafferty.

—He hurt his knee last spring, I say. He's out on medical leave for a while.

—How'd he hurt it? asks Lafferty.

I don't know that it's any of his business. Nevertheless, I say, At work. If Truman wants everyone to know the full story, Truman can tell it.

—Have any kids? Have a husband? he asks.

I wish he'd go back to talking about himself.

—One child, I say. No husband.

—Oh yeah? How old?

—Four years old. Almost five.

—Good age, says Lafferty. I miss when mine were that age.

When I pull up to the entry point to the tracks that Dispatch indicated—a man-made opening in a fence, something someone kicked out years ago that's never been repaired—I see we've beaten the medical unit to the scene.

I look at Lafferty, assessing him. Unexpectedly, I feel a twinge of sympathy for him, for what we are about to see. His field training was in the 23rd District, which is next to ours, but much lower in crime. Besides, he would mostly have been doing foot patrol, crowd control, that sort of thing. I'm not sure if he's ever responded to this type of call before. There are only so many ways you can ask someone how many dead people they've seen in their life, so in the end I decide to keep things vague.

—Have you ever done this before? I ask him.

He shakes his head. He says, Nope.

—Well, here we go, I say, brightly.

I'm not certain what else I can say. There is no way to prepare a person sufficiently.

Thirteen years ago, when I first started, it happened a few times a year: we'd get a report that someone had fatally overdosed, had been deceased so long that medical intervention was unnecessary. More common were calls about overdoses in progress, and typically those individuals could be revived. These days, it happens frequently. This year alone the city is on track for 1,200, and the vast majority of those are in our district. Most are relatively recent ODs. Others are bodies that have already started to decay. Sometimes they're inexpertly hidden by friends or lovers who witnessed the death but don't want to jump through the hoops of reporting it, don't want to answer to anyone about how it happened. More often they're just out in the open, having nodded off forever in a secluded place. Sometimes their family finds them first. Sometimes their children. Sometimes, we do: out on patrol we simply see them there, sprawled out or slumped over, and when we check their vital signs they have no pulse. They're cold to the touch. Even in summer.

From the opening in the fence, Lafferty and I walk downhill into a little gulch. I've entered this way dozens or maybe hundreds of times in my years on the force. It's part of our patrol, in theory, this overgrown area. We find someone or something every time we go in. When I was partnered with Truman, he was always the one to go in first. He was senior. Today, I go in first, ducking my head uselessly, as if this will somehow keep me drier. But the rain isn't letting up. The splattering sound it makes on my hat is so loud that I can barely hear myself speak. My shoes slip in the mud.

Like many parts of Kensington, the Lehigh Viaduct—mainly called the Tracks now—is a stretch of land that's lost its purpose. It was once busy with cargo trains that served an essential purpose in Kensington's industrial heyday, but now it's underused and overgrown. Weeds and leaves and branches cover needles and baggies scattered on the ground. Stands of small trees conceal activity. Lately there's been talk, from the city and Conrail, of paving it over, but it hasn't happened yet. I'm skeptical: I can't imagine it being anything other than what it is, a hiding place for people in need of a fix, for the women who work the Ave and their customers. If it gets paved over, new enclaves will sprout up all over the neighborhood. I've seen it happen before.

A little rustle to our left: a man emerges from the weeds. He looks spectral and strange. He stands still, his hands down by his sides, small rivulets of water trickling down his face. In fact, it would be impossible to tell if he was crying.

—Sir, I say to him, have you seen anything around here that we should know about?

He says nothing. Stares some more. Licks his lips. He has the faraway, hungry look of someone in need of a fix. His eyes are an unnaturally light blue. Perhaps, I think, he's meeting a friend here, or a dealer: someone who will help him out. At last he shakes his head, slowly.

—You're not supposed to be down here, you know, I tell him.

There are certain officers who wouldn't bother with this formality, deeming it futile. Weed whacking, some say: they sprout right back up, in other words. But I always do.

—Sorry, the man says, but he doesn't look as if he's about to leave anytime soon, and I don't take the time to haggle with him.

We keep walking. Large puddles have formed on either side of us. The dispatcher indicated that the body was a hundred yards straight back from the entrance we used, slightly off to the right. Behind a log, she had said. The RP, she added, had left a newspaper on the log to help us find the body. This is what we're looking for as we walk farther and farther from the fence.

It's Lafferty who spots the log first, veers off the path—which isn't a path, really, just the place on the Tracks where people have tended to walk the most over the years. I follow. I wonder, as always, whether I'll know the woman: whether she'll be someone I recognize from picking her up, or from driving past her, over and over, on the street. And then, before I can stop it, the familiar chant returns: *Or Kacey. Or Kacey. Or Kacey.*

Lafferty, ten steps ahead of me, peers over the log to inspect the far side. He says nothing: just keeps leaning over, his head cocked at an angle, taking it in.

When I arrive I do the same.

She's not Kacey.

That's my first thought: Thank God, I don't know her. Her death was recent: that's my second. She hasn't been lying here long. There's nothing soft about her, nothing slack. Instead she's stiff, lying on her back, one arm contracted upward so that her hand has become a claw. Her face is contorted and sharp; her eyes are unpleasantly open. Usually, in overdoses, they're closed—which always gives me some measure of comfort. At least, I think, they died in peace. But this woman looks astonished, unable to believe the fate that has befallen her. She's lying on a bed of leaves. Except for her right arm, she's straight as a tin soldier. She's young. In her twenties. Her hair is—was—pulled back into a tight ponytail, but it's been mussed. Strands of it have been pulled out of the elastic that holds it in place. She's wearing a tank top and a denim skirt. It's too cold to be dressed this way. The rain is falling directly on her body and face. This is bad, too, for the preservation of evidence. Instinctively, I want to cover her, to bundle her up in something warm. Where is her jacket? Maybe someone took it off her after she died. Unsurprisingly, a syringe and a makeshift tourniquet are on the ground next to her. Was she alone when she died? They usually aren't, the women: usually they're with boyfriends or clients who leave them when they die, afraid of being implicated, afraid of being caught up in some business that they want no part of.

We're supposed to take vital signs upon arrival. Normally I wouldn't, not in a case as obvious as this one, but Lafferty's watching me, so I do things by the book. I steel myself, climb over the log, and reach toward her. I'm about to take her pulse when I hear footsteps and voices nearby. *Damn,* the voices are saying. *Damn. Damn.* The rain is falling even harder.

The medical unit has found us. They are two young men. They're in no rush. They know already that they can't save this one. She's gone; she has been. They need no coroner to tell them this.

—Fresh one? calls one of them. I nod, slowly. I don't like the way they—we—talk about the dead sometimes.

The two young men saunter toward the log, peer over it nonchalantly.

—Jeez, says one—Saab is his last name, there on his name tag—to the other, to Jackson.

—She'll be light, at least, says Jackson, which feels like a hit to my stomach. Then collectively they climb over the log, skirt the body, kneel down beside her.

Jackson reaches out to place his fingers on her. He tries a few times, obligingly, to find something, then stands up. He checks his watch.

—As of 11:21, Jane Doe pronounced, he says.

—Record that, I say to Lafferty. One nice thing about having a partner again: someone else to fill in the activity log. Lafferty's been keeping his inside his jacket to preserve it from the rain, and he takes it out now, hovering over it, trying to keep it dry.

—Hang on a second, I say.

Eddie Lafferty looks at me and then the body.

I bend down between Jackson and Saab, looking carefully at the victim's face, the open eyes cloudy now, nearly opaque, the jaws clenched painfully.

There, just beneath her eyebrows and sprinkled over the tops of her cheekbones, is a splattering of little pink dots. From far away they just made her look flushed; up close, they are distinct, like small freckles, or the marks of a pen on a page.

Saab and Jackson bend down too.

—Oh yeah, says Saab.

—What, says Lafferty.

I raise my radio to my mouth.

—Possible homicide, I say.

—Why, says Lafferty.

Jackson and Saab ignore him. They're still bent down, studying the body.

I lower the radio. Turn to Lafferty. His training, his training.

—Petechiae, I say, pointing to the dots.

—Which are, says Lafferty.

—Burst blood vessels. One sign of strangulation.

The Crime Scene Unit, Homicide, and Sergeant Ahearn arrive not long after that.

THEN

The first time I found my sister dead, she was sixteen. It was the summer of 2002. Forty-eight hours earlier, on a Friday afternoon, she'd left school with her friends, telling me she'd be back by evening.

She wasn't.

By Saturday, I was frightened, telephoning Kacey's friends, asking them if they knew where she was. But nobody did, or no one would tell me, at least. I was seventeen then, very shy, already cast in the role I've played my entire life: the responsible one. *A little old lady,* said my grandmother, Gee. *Too serious for her own good.* Kacey's friends no doubt thought of me as parental in some way, an authority figure, a person from whom to withhold information. Over and over again, they apologized dully and denied knowing anything.

Kacey, in those days, was boisterous and loud. When she was home, which she had been with less and less frequency, life was better, the house warmer and happier. Her unusual laugh—a silent, open-mouthed trembling, followed by a series of sharp, high, vocal inhalations, doubling her over as if they caused her pain—echoed off the walls. Without it, her absence was noticeable, the silence in the house ominous and strange. Her sounds were gone, and so was her smell, some terrible perfume that she and her friends had begun using—probably to mask what they were smoking—called *Patchouli Musk.*

It took a whole weekend for me to convince Gee to call the police. She was always reluctant to involve outsiders: afraid, I believe, that they would take a hard look at her parenting and deem it unfit in some way.

When, at last, she agreed to, she fumbled the number and had to call twice on her olive-green rotary phone. I had seen her neither so frightened nor so mad before. She was trembling with something when she hung up—anger or sorrow or shame. Her long ruddy face moved in unsettling and novel ways. She spoke softly to herself, indiscernible phrases that sounded something like a curse or a prayer.

It both was and was not surprising, Kacey's disappearing like that. She'd always been social, and had recently fallen in with a ragtag group of friends who were benevolent but lazy, well liked but never taken seriously. She had a brief hippie phase in eighth grade, followed by several years of dressing like a punk, dying her hair with Manic Panic and getting a nose ring and an unfortunate tattoo of a lady spider in a web. She had boyfriends. I never did. She was popular, but generally used her popularity for good: in middle school she effectively adopted a sorrowful girl named Gina Brickhouse, a girl so badly teased for her weight, her hygiene, her poverty, the misfortune of her name, that she'd gone silent at age eleven. That's when Kacey took an interest in her; and under Kacey's protection, she blossomed. By the end of high school, Gina Brickhouse was named Most Unique, an award reserved for quirky but respected iconoclasts.

Lately, though, Kacey's social life had taken a turn. She had regularly been getting into the kind of serious trouble that threatened to get her expelled. She was drinking a lot, even at school, and using various prescription drugs that, in those days, nobody knew to be scared of. This was the first part of her life that Kacey ever tried to keep hidden from me. Prior to that year, she had confided everything to me, often with an urgent and pleading note in her voice, as if she were seeking absolution. But her new attempts at secrecy were ineffective. I could sense it—of course I could sense it. I calculated a change in her demeanor, her physicality, her gaze. Kacey and I shared a room, and a bed, for the duration of our childhood. At one time we knew each other so well that we could predict the next thing the other would say before she said it. Our conversations were rapid and indecipherable to others, sentences begun and abandoned, lengthy negotiations conducted exclusively in glances and gestures. So when my sister began sleeping over at friends' houses more and more, or coming home in the small hours of the morning, smelling of things I couldn't, then, identify, it is safe to say that I was alarmed.

And when two days went by without my hearing from her, it wasn't her disappearance that was surprising, or even the idea that something was going terribly wrong with her. The only thing that surprised me was the idea that Kacey could leave me so completely out of her life. That she could hide, in this way—even from me—her most important secrets.

Shortly after Gee phoned the police, Paula Mulroney paged me, and I called her back. Paula was a great friend of Kacey's in high school, and the only one, in fact, who deferred to me, who understood and respected the precedence of our familial bond. She said she had heard about Kacey, and she thought that she knew where she was.

—Don't tell your grandmom, though, said Paula, in case I'm wrong.

Paula was a pretty girl, strong and tall and tough. She reminded me in certain ways of an Amazon—a tribe I first encountered when I read the *Aeneid* in ninth-grade English, and next in the DC comic books I fell in love with at fifteen—though the one time I mentioned the resemblance to Kacey, meaning it to be complimentary to Paula, she said, Mick. Don't ever tell anyone that. In any case, although I liked Paula—like her still— I also realized even then that she was probably a bad influence on Kacey. Her brother Fran was a dealer, and Paula worked for him, and everyone knew it.

That day, I met Paula at the corner of Kensington and Allegheny.

—Follow me, said Paula.

As we walked, she told me that she and Kacey had gone together two days ago to a house in this neighborhood that had belonged to a friend of Paula's brother. I knew what this meant.

—I had to leave, Paula said, but Kacey wanted to stay for a little longer.

Paula led me up Kensington Ave to a little side street that I can't, now, remember the name of, and then to a tumbledown rowhome with a white storm door. On the door was a black metal silhouette of a horse and carriage, only the horse's front legs were missing: I got a good look at it, because it took five minutes of knocking for anyone to open up.

—Trust me, they're home, said Paula. They're always home.

When, at last, the door opened, on the other side of it was a ghost of a woman, as thin as anyone I'd ever seen, with black hair and the flushed face and heavy eyes I would later come to associate with Kacey. I didn't know then what they meant.

—Fran's not here, said the woman. She was talking about Paula's brother. She was maybe a decade older than we were, though it was difficult to tell.

—Who's she, said the woman, before Paula could reply.

—My friend. She's looking for her sister, said Paula.

—No sisters here, said the woman.

—Can I see Jim, said Paula, changing the subject.

July is often brutal in Philadelphia, and the house was incubating the heat, baking beneath its black tar roof. Inside, it reeked of cigarettes and something sweeter. It was very sad to me to think of that house as it had been when it was first built: home to a functioning family, maybe, a factory worker and his wife and children. Someone who went to work each day in one of the colossal brick buildings, abandoned now, that still line Kensington's streets. Someone who came home at the end of each workday and said grace before supper. We were standing at that moment in what was maybe once a dining room. Now it was empty of all furniture except some metal folding chairs, leaning against a wall. Out of respect for the house, I tried to picture it as it might have been a generation ago: an oval table covered in a lace tablecloth. Plush carpet on the floor. Upholstered chairs. In the windows, curtains that somebody's grandmother made. On the wall, a picture of fruit in a bowl.

Jim, the house's owner, I supposed, came into the room in black T-shirt and jean shorts and stood looking at us. His arms hung loosely by his sides.

—You looking for Kacey? he said to me. At the time, I wondered how he knew. Probably I looked innocent, like a rescuer, like a guardian, like somebody who searched, rather than fled. I have had this look my whole life. In fact it took me quite a while, after I joined the force, to develop certain habits and mannerisms that successfully convinced those I detained that I was someone to be taken seriously.

I nodded.

—Upstairs, said Jim. She hasn't been feeling good, is what I thought he was saying, though I didn't hear exactly, and he could have said any number of things. I was already gone.

Every door on the upstairs hallway was closed, and behind them, I thought, might lie unknown horrors. I was, I admit it, afraid. For a little while I stood still. Later I would wish that I hadn't.

—Kacey, I said, quietly, hoping she would simply emerge.

—Kacey, I said again, and someone's head appeared from behind a door, then disappeared again.

The hallway was dim. Downstairs, I could hear Paula making small talk: about her brother, about the neighbors, about the police who'd lately been working the Ave in great numbers, to everyone's dismay.

Finally, summoning my courage, I knocked lightly on the door closest to me and, after a pause, opened it.

There was my sister. I knew it first by her hair, which Kacey had recently dyed fluorescent pink, and which was now spread out behind her on a bare mattress. She was on her side, her back to me, and in the absence of any pillow her head was tilted at an odd angle.

She wasn't wearing enough clothing.

I knew she was dead before I reached her. Her pose was familiar to me, after a childhood spent sleeping next to her in the same bed, but that day there was a different kind of limpness to her body. Her limbs looked too heavy.

I pulled her onto her back by her shoulder. Her left arm flopped over onto the bed. A strip of cotton T-shirt hung, loosened now, around her lower biceps. Below this makeshift tourniquet: the long bright river of her vein. Her face was slack and blue, her mouth open, her eyes closed but for a sliver of white that showed beneath the lashes.

I shook her. I shouted her name. The syringe lay beside Kacey on the bed. I shouted her name again. She smelled like excrement. I slapped her across her face, hard. At the time, I had never seen heroin. I had never seen anyone on heroin.

—CALL 911, I shouted—which, in retrospect, is quite funny. There was no possibility, ever, of authorities of any stripe being called to that home. But I was still shouting it when Paula arrived in the room and clamped a hand over my mouth.

—Oh, fuck, said Paula, looking at Kacey, and then—I marvel now at her bravery, her levelheadedness, the swiftness and sureness of her movements—she put an arm under Kacey's knees and an arm under her shoulders and brought her up off the bed. Kacey was plump in high school, but Paula seemed unfazed. She scooped her athletically and trotted down the stairs with her, her back to the wall, careful not to trip, and then out the front door. I followed.

—Don't you call from nearby, said the woman who'd opened the door.

She's dead, I thought, she's dead, my sister is dead. I had seen Kacey's dead face before me on that bed. Though neither Paula nor I had checked to see if Kacey was breathing, I was convinced that I had lost her, and my mind cut forward quickly through a future without my sister: my graduation, without Kacey. My wedding. The birth of my children. Gee's death. And it was out of self-pity that I began to cry. To have lost the only other person capable of shouldering all the weight that had been assigned to us at birth. The weight of our dead parents. The weight of Gee, whose occasional kindnesses we clung to dearly, but whose cruelties were routine. The weight of our poorness. My eyes filled. I lost sight of the ground. I tripped over a piece of sidewalk that had been forced upward by a searching root.

———

Within seconds we were spotted by a young policeman, newly on that beat: part of the influx of officers that Jim and Paula had been complaining about. Within minutes an ambulance arrived, and I rode with my sister in the back of it, and watched as she was Narcanned, raised from the dead, violently, miraculously, crying out in pain and nausea and despair, begging us to let her go back.

This was the secret I learned that day: None of them want to be saved. They all want to sink backward toward the earth again, to be swallowed by the ground, to keep sleeping. There is hatred on their faces when they are roused from the dead. It's a look I've seen dozens of times, now, on the job: standing over the shoulder of some poor EMT whose job it is to reel them back in from the other side. It was the look on Kacey's face that day as her eyes opened, as she cursed, as she wept. It was directed at me.

NOW

afferty and I are dismissed from the scene. It will fall to Sergeant Ahearn, now, to close it, to oversee the medical examiner, the East Detectives, the Crime Scene Unit.

Lafferty, next to me in the car, is quiet at last. I relax, just a little, listening now to the thwack of the wipers, to the low crackle of the radio.

—All right? I say to him.

He nods.

—Any questions?

He shakes his head.

Again, we lapse into silence.

I consider the different kinds of quiet that exist: this quiet is uncomfortable, tense, the silence of two strangers with something unsaid in between them. It makes me miss Truman, whose silences were peaceful, whose steady breathing reminded me always to slow down.

Five minutes pass. And at last, he speaks.

—Better days, he says.

—What's that? I say.

Lafferty gestures around us.

—I said the neighborhood's seen better days, right? It was decent when I was a kid. Used to come up here to play baseball.

I frown.

—It's not bad, I say. It has good parts and bad parts, I suppose. Like most neighborhoods.

Lafferty shrugs, unconvinced. He's been on the job less than a year, and already he's complaining. Some officers have the ugly and destructive habit of criticizing, at length, the districts they patrol. I have heard many officers—including, I regret to say, Sergeant Ahearn himself—referring to Kensington in terms unbefitting of anyone whose role is to protect and uplift a community. *Shitsville,* Sergeant Ahearn says sometimes, at roll call. *K-Hole. Junktown, USA.*

—I need a coffee, I say now to Eddie Lafferty.

Normally, I go to a little corner store for my coffee, the kind with glass pots on burners and the smell of cat litter and egg sandwiches seared into its walls. Alonzo, the owner, is by now a friend. But there's a new place I've been eyeing, Bomber Coffee, part of the wave of businesses that have recently opened on Front Street, and I suppose it's Lafferty's disdain for the neighborhood that makes me suggest it.

There's something about these new places—Bomber in particular—that draws me to them every time I pass. Something about their interiors, made of cool steel or warm and resonant wood. Something about the people inside, who seem to have been dropped into our sector from a different planet. What they're thinking and talking and writing about, I can only imagine: books and clothes and music and what plants to put inside their houses. They're brainstorming names for their dogs. They're ordering beverages with unpronounceable names. Sometimes I just want to be off the street for a second, to be around people with worries like these ones.

When I pull up in front of Bomber Coffee, Lafferty looks at me. Skeptical.

—You sure about this, Mike? he says. It's a reference to *The Godfather.* One that he probably doesn't expect me to recognize. What he does not know is that I have seen the entire *Godfather* series several times, not by choice, and that I have disliked it profoundly each time.

—You ready to pay four dollars for your coffee? he says.

—I'd be happy to treat you, I say.

I'm nervous when we walk in, and I'm annoyed with myself for feeling this way. In unison, everyone inside pauses briefly to note our uniforms, our weapons. An up-down glance I've gotten very used to. Then they return to their laptops.

The girl behind the counter is thin and has bangs that go straight across her forehead and a sort of winter hat that holds them in place. The boy next to her has hair that's dark at the root and dyed a faded platinum toward the end. His glasses are large and strigine.

—Help you? says the boy.

—Two medium coffees, please, I say. (I note with some satisfaction that they're only two dollars and fifty cents.)

—Anything else? says the boy. He has his back to us now, pouring the coffee.

—Yeah, Lafferty says. Throw some whiskey in there while you're at it.

He's smiling as he says it, waiting for recognition. It's a particular brand of humor I recognize from my uncles: corny, expected, harmless. Lafferty is tall and mildly handsome and probably used to being liked. He's still grinning when the boy turns around.

—We don't sell liquor, says the boy.

—It was a joke, says Lafferty.

The boy hands us our coffee solemnly.

—Do you have a restroom I could use? says Lafferty. He's dropped his friendliness by now.

—Out of order, says the boy.

But I see it there, a door along the back wall of the place, clear as day, with no sign, nothing indicating it's in disrepair. The other employee, the girl, won't meet our eyes.

—Is there another one? asks Lafferty. With many places, members of the PPD have an understanding: we don't have an office, and we're in our vehicles all day. Public restrooms are an important part of our routine.

—Nope, says the boy, and he hands us the cups. Anything else? he asks again.

I proffer my money silently. I leave. We'll go back to Alonzo at the corner store for our afternoon coffee. Alonzo lets us use his dim, filthy little restroom even when we don't buy anything. He smiles at us. He knows Kacey. He knows my son's name and he asks after him.

—Real nice kids, says Lafferty, outside. Sweethearts.

His voice is bitter. His feelings are hurt. For the first time, I like him.

Welcome to Kensington, I think. Don't pretend, yet, that you know anything about it.

At the end of our shift, I park our vehicle in the lot—I inspect it even more thoroughly than I normally would, making sure that Lafferty is watching—and the two of us walk into the station to turn over our activity log.

Sergeant Ahearn is back in his office, a tiny closet of a space with concrete walls that sweat whenever the air-conditioning is on—but his own, something that belongs to him. He has a sign on the door that says *Knock First*.

We do.

—Inside, he's sitting at his desk, looking at something on his computer. Wordlessly, he accepts the log, not looking at us.

—Night, Eddie, he says as Lafferty leaves.

I linger for a moment on his threshold.

—Night, Mickey, he says. Pointedly.

I hesitate for a moment. Then I say, Can you tell me anything about our victim?

He sighs. Looks up from his screen. Shakes his head.

—Not yet, he says. No news.

Ahearn is a small slight man with gray hair and blue eyes. He's not bad looking but he's insecure about his stature. At five-eight, I look down on him by at least two inches. The difference sometimes sends him up on his toes, hovering there while he talks to me. Today, sitting at his desk, he is preserved from this humiliation.

—Nothing? I say. She hasn't been IDed?

Again, Ahearn shakes his head. I'm not sure if I believe him. Ahearn is strange: he likes to keep his cards close to his chest, even when he has no reason to. A habit meant mainly to emphasize the relatively insignificant amount of power he wields over us, I believe. He's never liked me. I attribute this to a mistake I made once, shortly after he was transferred into this district from another one: he gave out some misinformation during roll call about a perpetrator we were looking for, and I raised my hand to correct the record. It was a silly, thoughtless move on my part—the kind of thing, I realized too late, I should have told him after the fact, to preserve order and rank—but most sergeants would let this small infraction slide, would say thank you and perhaps make a joke about it. Ahearn, on the other hand, gave me a look I will not soon forget. Truman and I used to joke that Ahearn had it out for me. Beneath the lightness of these exchanges, I believe that both of us were actually concerned.

Now, I say to Ahearn: I'd never seen her working before. Just in case you were wondering.

—I wasn't, says Ahearn.

You should have been, I want to say. It's important information. It means, perhaps, that she was either new to our district or simply passing through. Patrol officers are the ones who know our sectors best: we're the ones on the streets, getting to know every store and residence, getting to know the citizens who populate them. The East Detectives who came out to the scene did ask me that question, at least, and several other questions as well that mollified me with their specificity.

I say none of this. I tap once on his doorframe. Turn to leave.

Before I can, Ahearn speaks. He's looking at his computer, not at me.

—How's Truman? he says.

I pause. Taken aback.

—Fine, I assume, I say.

—You haven't heard from him lately?

I shrug. It's difficult to figure out Ahearn's agenda sometimes, but I've learned he always has one.

—That's funny, says Ahearn. I thought you guys were close.

He holds my gaze for just a moment longer than I'd like.

On the way home, I call Gee. We speak only rarely, these days. We see each other even less. When Thomas was born, I made the decision to give him an entirely different sort of upbringing than the one I experienced, and this means avoiding Gee—avoiding all the O'Briens, really—as much as possible. Begrudgingly, out of some unshakable sense of family obligation, I perform the perfunctory ritual of bringing Thomas to visit Gee sometime around Christmas, and I phone her once in a while to make sure she's still alive. Although she complains about it on occasion, I don't think she's actually bothered by our absence. She never calls me. She never offers any help with Thomas, though she's able-bodied enough to work her catering job all right, and to put in her hours at Thriftway, too. Lately, I've developed the conviction that if I stopped contacting her we'd never speak again.

—Go ahead, says Gee, after several rings. The same way she always answers the phone.

—It's me, I say, and Gee says, Me who.

—Mickey, I say.

—Oh, says Gee. Didn't recognize your voice.

I pause, letting the implication settle. The perennial guilt trip. There it is.

—I was just wondering, I say, whether you'd heard from Kacey lately.

—Why do you care, says Gee, warily.

—No reason, I say.

—Nope, says Gee. You know I steer clear. You know her shit don't fly with me. I steer clear, she says again, just for emphasis.

—All right, I say. Will you tell me if you hear from her?

—What are you up to, says Gee. Suspicious.

—Nothing, I say.

—You'd stay away too, says Gee, if you knew what was good for you.

—I do, I say.

After a brief pause, Gee says, I know you do.

Reassured.

—How's my baby, says Gee, changing the subject. She has always been kinder to Thomas than she ever was to us. She spoils him when she sees him, produces from her purse mountains of ancient, half-melted candy that she unwraps and feeds him with her hands. I see, in these small charities, an echo of the way she must have been with her own daughter, our mother, Lisa.

—He's very fresh these days, I say. Not meaning it.

—You stop, says Gee. Very faintly, at last, I hear a smile in her voice. You stop that. Don't talk about my boy like that.

—He is, I say.

I wait. There is a part of me that hopes, still, that Gee will come around first, that she'll ask me to bring Thomas by, that she'll offer to babysit, that she'll ask to come see our new place.

—Anything else? Gee says, at last.

—No, I say. I think that's it.

Before I can say anything further, she's hung up the phone.

The landlady, Mrs. Mahon, is raking in her front yard when I pull into the driveway. Mrs. Mahon lives in an old two-story colonial with a haphazard apartment built above it as a third-floor addition. The apartment—ours, now, for the better part of a year—is accessed by a rickety staircase up the back of the house. The lot is small, but there's a long backyard behind the house that Thomas can use, and an ancient tire swing that hangs from a tree. Aside from the backyard, the apartment's main appeal is its price: five hundred dollars a month, utilities included. I found it on the recommendation of another officer's brother, who was moving out of it. It's not much, the brother said, but it's clean, and the landlady gets stuff fixed fast. I'll take it, I said. That same day, I listed for sale my house in Port Richmond. It pained me to; I loved the house. I had no other choice.

Out the driver's-side window, now, I wave quickly at Mrs. Mahon, who pauses when she sees me, stands with an elbow on top of the wooden handle of her rake.

I get out. Wave once more. There are groceries in the backseat, and I occupy my hands with them, making small noises to indicate my great and perennial haste. I have always sensed, from Mrs. Mahon, a needfulness that I do not feel prepared to examine. For one thing, she is almost always standing in the front yard, waiting to engage anyone who might pass by (I have noticed that the postman, too, wears a wary expression as he approaches); and to me she always looks simultaneously worried and hopeful, as if wishing to be asked what's concerning her, so that she may expound upon it for a while. Unbidden, she dispenses advice—about the apartment, about the car, about our choice of attire, which is generally incorrect for the weather, according to Mrs. Mahon—with the kind of urgency one might typically reserve for medical emergencies. She has short white hair and soft ropes of flesh between her chin and her collarbones that sway when she moves her head. She wears seasonal sweatshirts and loose light blue jeans. I have heard from the next-door neighbors that she was once married, but—if this is the case—nobody seems to know what happened to her husband. When I am feeling unkind, I imagine he might have died of annoyance. Whenever Thomas has a moment of bad behavior getting into or out of the car, I can count on Mrs. Mahon to be gazing at us from her window, a referee watching a play. Occasionally she has even emerged to get a better look, arms crossed in front of her, displeased.

Today, when I straighten up from the backseat, holding my groceries, Mrs. Mahon says, Someone stopped by for you.

I frown.

—Who? I say.

Mrs. Mahon looks very gratified to be asked this question.

He didn't leave his name, she says. Only told me he'd come by another time.

—What did he look like? I say.

—Tall, says Mrs. Mahon. Dark hair. Very handsome, she says, conspiratorially.

Simon. A little pang in my abdomen. I say nothing.

—What did you tell him? I say.

—Said you weren't home.

—Did he say anything else? I say. Did Thomas see him?

—No, says Mrs. Mahon. He just rang my bell. He was confused. I think he thought you lived in my house.

—And did you correct him? I say. Did you tell him we lived in the apartment upstairs?

—No, says Mrs. Mahon. She frowns. I didn't know him. I didn't tell him anything.

I hesitate. It goes against every one of my instincts to let Mrs. Mahon in on any part of my life, but in this case, I believe I have no choice.

—Why, says Mrs. Mahon.

—If he stops by again, I say, just tell him we moved out. Tell him we don't live here anymore. Whatever you want to say.

Mrs. Mahon stands a bit taller. Proud to be given an assignment, perhaps.

—Just so long as you're not bringing any trouble around here, she says. I don't want any trouble in my life.

—He's not dangerous, I say. I'm just not talking to him. We moved here for a reason.

Mrs. Mahon nods. I am surprised to see something like approval in her eyes.

—All right, she says. I'll do that, then.

—Thank you, Mrs. Mahon, I say.

Mrs. Mahon waves me off.

Then, unable to restrain herself a moment longer, she tells me, That bag is going to break.

—I'm sorry? I say.

—That bag, says Mrs. Mahon, pointing at my groceries. It's too heavy, and it's going to break. That's why I always ask the girl to double them.

—I'll make sure to do that in the future, I say.

When I first went back to work after Thomas was born, I used to physically yearn for him toward the end of each day. It was something akin to hunger. Racing to pick him up from daycare, I would picture a string connecting the two of us that retracted, like a yo-yo, as I approached. The feeling has softened as Thomas has grown, morphed into a milder version of itself, but today I still take the back stairs two at a time, picturing his face, his wide grin, his arms outstretched to me.

I open the door. There he is, my son, bounding toward me, shadowed by the babysitter, Bethany.

—I missed you, he tells me, his face an inch from mine, his hands on my cheeks.

—Were you good for Bethany? I say.

—Yes, he says.

I look to Bethany to confirm, but she's looking down at her phone already, eager to leave. For months, it has been clear to me that I need to find a different, and better, arrangement. Thomas doesn't like her. He talks every day about his old school in Fishtown, his old friends there, his old teachers. But it's nearly impossible to find someone who can switch back and forth from days to nights with me every two weeks, and Bethany—twenty-one, a part-time makeup artist—is both cheap and available at almost any hour. What she offers in flexibility, however, she lacks in dependability, and lately she's been calling out sick so often that I've spent every personal day that I have. On the days that she does show up, she's regularly late, which makes me regularly late, which makes Sergeant Ahearn more and more unfriendly each time we cross paths at the station.

Now, I thank Bethany and pay her. Silently, she leaves. And instantly the house feels lighter.

Thomas looks at me.

—When can I go back to my school, he says.

—Thomas, I say. You know your old school is too far away. And you start kindergarten next September, remember?

He sighs.

—Just a little longer, I say. Less than a year.

Another sigh.

—Is it so bad, I say to him.

But of course I feel guilty. Every evening after A-shift, and often in the mornings, too, I try to make it up to him: I settle right down on the floor next to him and play with him until he's tired of playing, trying to teach him everything he needs to know about the world, trying to stuff him so full of knowledge and fortitude and curiosity that these qualities will sustain him even during my long stretches away from him, the endless B-shift weeks, during which I'm not even able to put him to bed.

Now, he shows me excitedly what he's constructed in my absence: a whole city of train tracks, wooden ones I bought secondhand, with construction-paper balls meant to represent boulders and mountains and houses, and cans and bottles that he's fished out of the recycling bin to stand in for trees.

—Did Bethany help you with this? I ask him, hopefully.

—No, he says. I did it all by myself.

There is pride in his voice. He doesn't realize—how could he—that I wish the answer had been yes.

Thomas, at almost five, is tall and strong and barreling, and already too smart for his own good. He's handsome, too. As smart and as handsome as Simon. But unlike his father, so far, he is kind.

Homicide doesn't contact us the next day, or the next day, or the next. Two weeks go by. Ahearn keeps partnering me with Eddie Lafferty. I miss Truman. I even miss the solo duty that succeeded his leave. It's unusual, these days, to be partnered long-term—the budget is tight, and one-man cars are becoming increasingly common—but Truman and I made a compelling case as a pair. We worked so well together that our responses were practically choreographed, and our productivity was unmatched in the district. I doubt very much that Eddie Lafferty and I will be able to duplicate that rapport. Every day, now, I listen to him tell me about his food preferences, his music preferences, his political affiliations. I listen to him rant about ex-wife number three, and then about millennials, and then about the elderly. I am, if it is possible, even quieter than I was to begin with.

We switch over to B-shift, working four p.m. to midnight, tired all the time.

I miss my son.

Several times—possibly too many—I ask Sergeant Ahearn about the woman we found on the Tracks. Has she been IDed, I want to know. Has a cause of death been declared? Does Homicide want to speak to us further?

Again and again, he shakes me off.

One Monday, mid-November—it's been nearly a month since we discovered the body—I walk up to Ahearn at the start of my shift. He's inserting paper into the copy machine. Before I can say anything, he whirls on me and says, No.

—I'm sorry? I say.

—No news.

I pause. No autopsy results? I say. Nothing?

—Why are you so interested? he says.

He is looking at me with an odd expression, almost a smile. As if he's teasing me, as if he has something on me. It's very unsettling. Except with Truman, I never talk about Kacey at work, and I have no intention of starting today.

—I just think it's strange, I say. It's been so long since we found the body. Just very strange that there's nothing on her, don't you think?

Ahearn lets out a long breath. He places his hand on the copy machine.

—Look, Mickey, he says. This is Homicide's territory, not mine. But I did hear that the autopsy results came back inconclusive. And since the vic is still unidentified, I imagine it's probably not top of their list.

—You're joking, I say, before I can stop myself.

—Serious as a heart attack, says Ahearn. A saying he likes and uses often.

He turns back to the copy machine.

—She was strangled, I say. I saw it with my own eyes.

Ahearn goes quiet. I know I'm pushing him. He doesn't like to be pushed. He stands there for a while with his back to me, hands on hips, waiting for his copies to finish. He says nothing.

Truman would tell me, in this moment, to walk away. Politics, he used to tell me. It's all politics, Mick. Find the right person and buddy up to them. Buddy up to Ahearn if you have to. Just protect yourself.

But I have never been able to do this, though several times I have tried, in my way: I know that Ahearn very much likes coffee, and so once or twice I've brought coffee for him, for example, and once, for Christmas, even a bag of beans from a local shop next door to Thomas's old nursery school.

—What is this, Ahearn said.

—Coffee beans, I said.

—They make you grind them yourself these days? Ahearn said.

—Yes, I said.

—I don't have one of those, said Ahearn.

—Ah, I said. Well, maybe for next Christmas.

He had smiled, stiffly, and said not to worry about it, and thanked me politely.

Unfortunately, those efforts did not seem to thaw relations between us. And Ahearn is the leader of my platoon, and as such he rotates with me from A-shift to B-shift and back again, and is generally the sergeant I report to nine times out of ten. The officers he favors are people who buddy up to him, mostly men, people who ask for his opinion or advice and then listen carefully, nodding while he dispenses it. I have seen Eddie Lafferty doing this very thing, actually. I can picture them both on their high school baseball team: Ahearn the leader, Lafferty the follower. At work, this is a dynamic that seems to suit them both. So maybe Lafferty, actually, is smarter than he seems.

When the copies are done, Ahearn takes them out and drops the edge of the stack against the copier a few times, evening the pile.

I'm still standing there, silent, waiting for a response. *Walk away, Mick*, I hear Truman saying in my ear.

Ahearn turns, abruptly, toward me. His face is not happy.

—Talk to Homicide if you have any more questions, he says, and strides past me.

But I know what will happen if I do. No concerned telefriendly parents means no media coverage. No media coverage means no case. Just another dead junkie hooker on Kensington Ave. Nothing to worry about too much for the folks on Rittenhouse Square.

All shift, I'm upset, and quieter than ever.

Even Lafferty notices something is off. He's drinking a coffee in the passenger's seat. He keeps glancing at me out of the corner of his eye.

—You okay? he says to me, eventually.

I look straight ahead. I don't want to speak badly about Sergeant Ahearn to him. I'm still not certain how close they are, but their history together makes me tight-lipped when it comes to my feelings. I decide, instead, to frame things more generally.

—Just frustrated, I say.

—What's up? says Lafferty.

—That woman we found on the Tracks last month, I say.

—Yeah?

—The autopsy results came back for her.

Lafferty sips from his coffee. His lip curls at the heat.

—I heard that, he says.

—Inconclusive, I say.

He says nothing.

—Can you believe that? I say.

Lafferty shrugs.

—That's above my pay grade, I guess, he says.

I look at him.

—You saw her too, I say. You saw what I saw.

Lafferty goes quiet for once, looking out the window. Two minutes go by in silence.

Then he says, Maybe it's not a bad thing.

I pause. I want to make sure I understand him correctly.

—Don't get me wrong, he says. It's a shame when anyone dies. But what kind of life.

I freeze. I don't trust myself to respond yet. I focus on the road ahead of me for a while.

I consider, briefly, telling him about Kacey. Embarrassing him, perhaps. Making him feel bad. But before I can, he begins shaking his head slowly from side to side.

—These girls, he says. He looks at me and puts one finger to his right temple, taps it twice. *Stupid,* is what he means. *No sense.*

I set my jaw.

—What do you mean by that, I say quietly.

Lafferty looks at me, eyebrows raised. I look back at him. I can feel my face getting hot. It's been a problem of mine my whole life. My face turns bright red when I'm angry or embarrassed or sometimes even pleased. It's an unhappy trait in a police officer.

—What do you mean by that? I say again. You said, *These girls.* What does that mean?

—I don't know, says Lafferty. Just.

He gestures around with his hands, surveying the landscape. I just feel bad for them, that's all.

—I don't think that's what you meant, I say. But all right.

—Hey, says Lafferty. Hey. I didn't mean to offend anybody.

THEN

When we were small, there was a field trip for certain fourth- and fifth-graders to see *The Nutcracker* in Center City. I was eleven then, old for my grade, and Kacey was nine.

In those years, I was almost silent in school. When I did speak, it was at a very low volume, such that Gee used to tell me, with frequency, to talk louder, as did most of my teachers. I had few friends. At recess, I read. I rejoiced when inclement weather forced us to stay indoors.

Kacey, conversely, made friends every place she went. She was little and fierce then, light-haired, with strong limbs and a brow she mainly kept lowered. She had buckteeth that she often strained to cover with an upper lip. Around friends, she was affable and funny. Generally, our peers were drawn to her. But she also made enemies: mainly those who targeted the weak, who swapped cruelty to others for social cachet, a bargain that, from a young age, Kacey disdained. She had a habit, therefore, of pointing out these injustices where they occurred, and then rising ardently and often violently to the defense of those in her class who were lowest in the pecking order—even, her teachers argued, when it wasn't warranted, or when those classmates didn't want or need Kacey's protection. It was for this reason that Kacey had recently gotten kicked out of Holy Redeemer (the irony of the name was not, even then, lost on me), which meant that both of us were kicked out, because Gee didn't want us in two separate schools.

This was, for me, a misfortune. I had liked Holy Redeemer. I had advocates there: two teachers, one a layperson and one a nun, who had taken a particular interest in me and my abilities, who had cut through my shyness and seen something in me that they had painstakingly drawn out over the course of several years. And who had, separately, of their own volition, told Gee that they thought I was gifted. Though I was gratified by this—though it justified for me the mild vanity I have always possessed about my own intelligence—there was also a part of me, at that time, that wished they hadn't. Because to Gee, gifted meant *uppity*, and if I wasn't punished for it, well, I was certainly looked at askance for a while.

When Kacey got into her final fight, the one that got us expelled, Gee had stood in front of us, glowering, as we sat on the couch.

—*You*, she said, nodding toward me, need to keep an eye on *her*, she said, nodding toward Kacey. So we both went to the local public school on Frankford instead, with all the children whose parents were too poor or dysfunctional to keep them in parish schools. Maybe, I supposed, this meant that Gee was, too.

In our new grade school, Hanover, Kacey was immediately and unsurprisingly adopted by a group of other outgoing students, and I was immediately forgotten about. There, shy children went through their days unexamined. Any student who didn't make the life of her teacher more complicated was generally praised once or twice for good behavior and then allowed to fade quietly to the back of the classroom. It was, no doubt, not entirely our teachers' fault. Our classrooms were full to capacity, thirty generally rowdy students in a small space. It was all they could do to survive.

Still: being at Hanover was the only reason we were going to see *The Nutcracker*. Sometimes Philadelphia's public school students had things given to them in a way that parish school children did not. The city bestowed upon its public schools charity of various kinds: coats, meant to keep us warm in winter; school supplies, meant to keep us engaged in our classwork; cultural outings, meant to allow us a few hours to ponder the large questions of life that are usually reserved for the idle rich. In this case, the outing was a prize awarded to students who sold the most wrapping paper in an annual fund-raiser—a challenge Kacey and I had taken very seriously, going door to door every weekend all fall. In fact, we had come in first and second place.

I, for one, was delighted.

I had worn a dress that day, my only dress, which Gee had brought home from Village Thrift in a rare moment of frivolity. The dress was beautiful, I thought: a blue cotton summer dress with white flowers on the bodice. But it was two years old by then and far too small, and over it, Gee had forced me to wear a boy's blue parka that had belonged to Bobby, a cousin of ours on our mother's side. It hadn't ever been washed, this jacket. It was salt-stained and slightly acrid-smelling, like Bobby himself. Beneath it, the dress looked stupid: I knew this even then. But I had never been to a ballet before, and I don't know why, but I wanted to demonstrate my respect, to acknowledge in some way the gravity of the occasion. So I wore it, and I wore the blue parka on top of it, and after lunch I waited in a long school hallway for the buses to arrive, standing in line with everyone else, reading my book.

Kacey, just ahead of me, was as usual surrounded by friends.

When it was time to board, I followed my sister up the steps of the vehicle, and then followed her toward the back of the bus, and sat down one seat behind her. It was a choice meant to assure my peers of my independence and myself of Kacey's proximity. Her presence in any situation, familial or educational, tended to reassure me.

There was a bright and funny music teacher that year, Mr. Johns, who had orchestrated the whole thing. He was young—probably younger than I am today—and the next year he was snatched up by a better school in the suburbs. As the buses approached City Hall, he stood up at the front of ours and clapped his hands twice and then held his right hand up in the air, two fingers extended, the sign that was supposed to mean

Quiet. Everyone was then obliged to return the salute. As usual, I waited until someone else did it first, and then raised my hand into the air, relieved.

—Listen up, said Mr. Johns. What are the rules we talked about in class?

—Don't talk! someone shouted.

—One, said Mr. Johns, holding up a thumb.

—Don't kick the seat in front of you! said the same person.

—Okay, said Mr. Johns. Not one of the ones we mentioned, but true. Tentatively, he held up a second finger.

—Anyone else? he said.

I knew an answer. It was *Wait to clap until you hear others clapping*. I didn't say it.

—Wait to clap until you hear others clapping, said Mr. Johns.

—Number four, sit still, said Mr. Johns.

—Number five, no whispering with your friends, said Mr. Johns. No giggling. No squirming around in your seat like a kindergartner.

He had told us all the story of the ballet in music class the week before. In it, a little girl lives in a mansion, he said. This is in the olden days, he said, so everyone onstage will be wearing old-fashioned clothes.

He paused to think.

—Also, the men wear tights, he said, so get over it in advance. The little girl's parents have a Christmas party and invite her spooky uncle, who's actually a good guy, and he gives her a doll. It's called a nutcracker, and you can go ahead and get over that too. That night she falls asleep and has a long dream and that's the rest of the ballet, he said. The nutcracker doll comes to life and becomes a prince and he fights off giant mice, takes her to a land of snowflakes, and then takes her to a place I forget the name of. It's like Candy Land. The little girl and the prince watch while a few different dances are performed. The end, said Mr. Johns.

—Does she go back to real life after that? asked a boy in my class.

—I forget, said Mr. Johns. I think so.

We had grown up less than three miles from the center of Philadelphia, but we only went there once a year, on New Year's Day, to watch a dozen of our cousins and uncles and uncles' bosses and uncles' friends march in the Mummers Parade. It is possible, therefore, that I had laid eyes on the Academy of Music before—it's right on Broad Street, part of the parade route—but I had certainly never been inside it. It's a pretty brick building with high, arched windows and old-fashioned lanterns that burn unflaggingly near its front doors.

As we filed off the bus, our teachers lined up along the edge of the sidewalk, inserting themselves between the students and the traffic, ushering us with mittened or gloved hands into the lobby.

Again, I trailed Kacey, who, I noticed, was scuffing her feet: I could hear it on the sidewalk. Gee would be mad at her later. Kacey was like this, always: doing what she shouldn't do, demanding a rebuke, daring the adults in her life to come down harder and harder on her, testing the limits of their anger. Whenever I could, I tried to distract her from this pursuit, hating to watch the punishment she inevitably received.

We entered the lobby and were stopped by the crowd. Today, what I remember most is the number of little girls who were there with their mothers, right in the middle of a school day. They were the same age as us, or a little younger. Every one of them was white. In comparison, our school group looked like the United Nations. They'd come in from the Main Line: I knew this even then. They were wearing beautiful knee-length coats in bright colors and, beneath them, dresses that looked like they were made for dolls: frilled, satin, silk, velvet, lace-trimmed and puff-sleeved. In them, they looked like jewels or flowers or stars. They wore white tights and black, polished, patent-leather Mary Janes, all of them, as if they were following some rule that only they knew about. Many of them had their hair pulled back tightly into buns, the kind I would later see the ballerinas wearing.

There were sixty or eighty Hanover grade school students in the lobby. We were clogging it. We didn't know where to go.

—Go on ahead, said Mr. Johns, but he, too, looked uncertain. Finally an usher came over to him, smiling, and asked if he was from the Hanover grade school, and he looked relieved and said yes.

—Right this way, said the usher.

We filed by those girls and their mothers, who stared back at us, open-mouthed, even the grown-ups. They stared at our puffy down jackets, our sneakers, our hair. It occurred to me that the mothers, too, must have taken the day off from their jobs. What did not cross my mind then was the possibility that they did not work at all. Every grown woman I knew had a job—or, more often, multiple jobs. About half of the men did.

I will never forget the moment the curtain rose. From the start, I was transfixed. There was snow—real snow, it seemed to me—falling onto the stage. Nothing could have prepared me for this. The exterior, and then the interior, of a large and beautiful house was shown, and inside that house were well-dressed children who were tended to by well-dressed adults. The children were given beautiful presents and then entertained by a series of life-sized doll-dancers. When the children fought, they were lovingly and carefully separated by parents more bemused than angry. There was a real orchestra playing in the pit. I felt in my own body the beautiful alien movements of the dancers on the stage, and in the music I heard strains of melody that revealed to me secrets I had never known about the world. I was, in fact, so moved that I began to cry: a fact I tried to keep hidden from the children around me. I let my tears fall silently down my face in the darkened theater. I tried not to sniff.

Soon, though, it became difficult to concentrate, for in the rows full of Hanover students, a mutiny was beginning.

To be fair, none of us had ever been taught to sit still for so long. Even at school there were breaks, many of them, from all this stillness. The other Hanover students knew they were supposed to be grateful, and they wanted to be good for Mr. Johns, but they didn't know how to be. They fidgeted and whispered and broke every rule. Mr. Johns and the seven other teachers there leaned forward, often, to turn and glare. They pointed to their eyes and then at their students. *I'm watching you.* All of us had been taught many things in our lives: to do as we were told, to entertain ourselves, to shut up, to be absent. But never to sit in one place and watch something slow and abstract for three hours. It wasn't a skill that most of us had.

Kacey, next to me, was losing it. She was squirming. One moment she hugged her knees, and the next she dropped her legs down against the chair with a thump. She lolled her head from side to side. She poked my shoulder, idly, and I elbowed her. *Ow,* Kacey whispered. She yawned with vigor. She pretended to fall asleep and wake up several times in a row.

There was a girl our age in front of Kacey, one of the ones we had seen in the lobby, her hair in a neat bun, her red dress coat folded tidily over the back of her seat. Her mother's perfume had wafted back toward us when we first sat down. After a particularly violent motion from Kacey, the little girl glanced back at her, just once, and then whipped her head toward the stage once more.

Kacey leaned forward.

—*What are you looking at,* she whispered, right into the girl's ear. I froze, watching as the girl edged nervously toward her mother, pretending not to have heard; then watching as Kacey, behind her, formed a fist and raised it. And for a strange and perfect moment, I thought that she would strike: I could see it happening, my sister's hand colliding with the tense muscles at the back of the girl's neck. Quickly, I reached out my hand to stop her. But the girl's mother turned around at that moment, and—upon seeing Kacey's pose—her mouth opened into a horrified O; and then Kacey, ashamed, lowered her hand. Then she settled back into her seat, tired, helpless. Resigned to something that neither of us, before that day, had understood.

Today, I'm not certain whether it was that girl's mother who got us kicked out, or whether our teachers collectively decided to remove us. All I know is that, at intermission, we were herded back through a crowded lobby, back past those girls and their mothers, who were now waiting in long lines for sweets, back to our yellow buses, our furious teachers beckoning us along.

I had been wearing my cousin Bobby's jacket the whole time, but at the last minute I removed it. As an adult, I am able to understand that this didn't make sense: we were exiting into the cold. But I think, as a child, I wanted to signal to the other balletgoers in the lobby that I understood, that I had dressed up for the occasion, that I belonged there. That I was one of them. I'll be back, I was saying, with my too-small cotton dress. Someday I'll be back.

This small act of apology, however, failed to reach its targets, and instead was pounced upon by two Hanover fourth-graders, a boy and a girl, who burst into laughter.

—Why is she wearing that ugly-ass dress, said the boy, very loudly, earning the cheap laughter of a few other students around us. And like clockwork, Kacey—slightly ahead of me—turned on him.

She had been waiting for an excuse. She wore a painful smile on her face, in fact, almost as if she were relieved to have someplace obvious to land the punch that she swiftly and accurately launched in his direction. She'd been holding it in for so long. For most of her life, maybe.

—Kacey, no, I said, but it was too late.

NOW

After what Lafferty says, *These girls,* I feel I have no other choice than to tell Sergeant Ahearn that I don't wish to be partnered with Eddie Lafferty anymore. I am willing to explain myself; I have even prepared a speech about our differences in style that would leave us both looking all right, in the balance, but before I can continue, Ahearn exhales, lengthily.

—Fine, Mickey, he says. He doesn't even look up from his phone.

For a week, I work solo. I'm relieved to be alone again. I'm relieved to be able to stop when and where I choose to, to select which calls I respond to. And I'm especially relieved, now, to be able to call Bethany, the babysitter, and ask to speak to Thomas. Over the course of each long call, I tell him stories, or narrate what I'm passing, or tell him about my plans for our future. And I tell myself that, while it may not be the same thing as my physical presence, at least I am able to provide him with some intellectual stimulation, in this way. Besides, he's becoming a very good conversationalist. It almost reminds me of having Truman next to me in the car.

One morning, at the start of an A-shift, I walk into the common area where roll call is conducted and notice a stranger in the room. He is young, sharply dressed in a gray suit. Serious-looking. Right away, I like him. He has one arm crossed around his insubstantial waist. In the other hand he holds a manila folder. A detective, I think. He says nothing to anyone. He is waiting for a sergeant.

When Ahearn arrives, he asks for everyone's attention, and the young man introduces himself. He is Davis Nguyen, he says, from the East Detectives. He has some news.

—Overnight, says Nguyen, we had two homicides in the district.

I am relieved to hear that they have already been identified. One is Katie Conway, a Delco girl, seventeen years old, white, reported missing one week prior. The other is Anabel Castillo, an eighteen-year-old home health aide, Latina.

Both, says Nguyen, were found in similar locations and were similarly arrayed: Conway was found in an empty lot off Tioga, uncovered and visible from the street; Castillo was found in an empty lot off Hart Lane, her legs obscured beneath a burned-out car, her head and shoulders exposed and in plain sight of passersby.

Both, he says, were most likely engaged in sex work. Both, he says, were most likely strangled. And both bodies had gone unreported for hours. (The unconscious, in Kensington, are such a common sight that they often don't receive a second glance.)

Nguyen puts pictures of Katie and Anabel up on the computer display on the wall. For a few long seconds, everyone in the room stands still, looking at the victims as they smile back on us from happier times. There is young Katie, at a party, her sixteenth birthday party, maybe, standing by a pool. Anabel is hugging a child I hope is not her son.

—All of this information, says Nguyen, is confidential. We haven't released the names or descriptions to the media, though the families have been notified.

After a moment, he continues. Additionally, he says, we've reopened the case of a young woman found on the Gurney Street tracks in October, though initially her autopsy was inconclusive.

I glance at Ahearn. He won't meet my eye.

Nguyen continues.

—She's still unidentified. But given the events of last night, we have reason to reconsider that assessment.

Ahearn isn't looking up. He's still on his phone.

—What this means, says Nguyen, is that there may be a single perpetrator of multiple homicides at large in your district.

No one speaks.

—Anything you hear, says Nguyen, take a report or send them directly to us. We've got a couple of leads but nothing credible. We're asking for your help.

For a while after roll call, I sit alone in my vehicle and contemplate my cell phone. The oaks that overhang the asphalt parking lot are moving wildly in a sudden strong wind. Thomas's favorite tree.

A slow, uneasy feeling has been building inside of me ever since we found the woman on the Tracks. The fact is that I haven't seen Kacey anyplace in the neighborhood since then. And I suppose, if I'm being honest, that I have been casually looking. It's not uncommon for a month to go by without a sighting of my sister—sometimes, in fact, this means she is actively trying to get into recovery—but the timing of her absence from the Avenue gives me a certain amount of pause, and causes within me the same low hum of anxiety that I had as a very young child when our mother was gone from the house too long.

Officially, Kacey and I no longer speak to one another. We haven't for five years. There have been rare occasions since then—three, to be precise—when I have been required to interact with her at work, in my capacity as an officer and in her capacity as a suspect—and during each of those times I have conducted myself with dignity, as any professional would, either processing her or releasing her, as I would do for any offender. To her credit, she, too, has conducted herself respectfully. When it is necessary to do so, I gently place handcuffs on the wrists of my sister, and I tell her the particular offense for which she is being arrested (usually, solicitation and possession of narcotics, one time with intent to sell), and then I narrate her rights to her, then I place a gentle hand on the crown of her head to ensure that she doesn't obtain an injury as she enters the backseat of our vehicle, and then I quietly close the door, and then I drive her to the station, and then I book her, and then the two of us sit silently across from one another in the holding cell, not speaking, not even looking at each other.

Truman was with me each time, and each time he, too, remained silent, watching the two of us guardedly, his eyes darting back and forth from me to Kacey to me again, waiting to see what would happen.

—That was the weirdest thing I've ever seen, he said, as we were driving away after the first of these episodes. I shrugged, and didn't reply. I suppose it would look 'weird' to someone who doesn't understand the particulars of our history and the tacit agreement we've come to in recent years. I've never tried to explain it to Truman or anyone else.

—You look out for her, he said another time.

When I demurred, he continued:

—You would have been done with patrol years ago if you weren't out here keeping an eye on your sister. You would have taken the detective exam.

I told him that this was not, in fact, true: it's just that I've grown fond of the neighborhood, and have grown to care a great deal about its well-being, and also I find the history of the neighborhood interesting, and I like to watch it as it grows and changes. And, lastly, it's never boring. On the contrary: it's exciting. Some people do have trouble with Kensington, but to me the neighborhood itself has become like a relative, slightly problematic but dear in the old-fashioned way that that word is sometimes used, treasured, valuable to me. I am invested in it, in other words.

—Why haven't *you* taken the exam? I said to Truman, at the time. Truman is one of the smartest people I know. He could easily have been promoted, and could easily have transferred elsewhere if he wanted to. When I said this, he laughed.

—Same reason as you, I guess, he said. I can't bring myself to miss any of the action.

———

Ten minutes have gone by, and I'm still gazing at my phone, when I realize I'm the last car in the lot. God forbid Sergeant Ahearn come outside and see me idling there. In the last year—between moving to Bensalem, swapping Thomas's reliable nursery school for the unreliable Bethany, and losing my longtime partner—my productivity has decreased dramatically, a fact about which Ahearn likes to regularly remind me.

I back out and drive toward my assigned PSA.

On the way, however, I make a detour toward Kensington and Cambria. If I can't find Kacey, at least I might find Paula Mulroney there.

Paula is not, when I arrive at said intersection, immediately evident. Alonzo's convenience store is on the same corner, though, so I stop in on Alonzo and on his favored cat, Romero, named after a long-gone Phillies pitcher. From the front window of the store, it is usually possible to see Paula and Kacey.

For this reason, Alonzo knows my sister fairly well. Like me, she is a regular customer, and has been since before we stopped talking. I know her order by heart: Rosenberger's iced tea and Tastykake Krimpets and cigarettes, the same treats she has enjoyed since our childhood, excepting the cigarettes. On the occasions when we accidentally find ourselves inside Alonzo's store at the same time, we studiously ignore each other. Alonzo glances back and forth between us, curious. He knows she is my sister, because if I'm being honest, I do often ask Alonzo about how Kacey has seemed lately, or if he has noticed anything, from his vantage point behind the cash register, that he thinks I should know about. This is not out of concern for her so much as out of a professional concern for the neighborhood and for Alonzo himself. Do you ever want them off your corner? I often say to Alonzo, about Kacey and Paula. Just let me know, and I'll make sure to get them off your corner. But Alonzo always says no, he doesn't mind them there, he likes them. They're good customers, he says. They don't give me any trouble.

Sometimes, in the past, I have made it a habit to linger inside the store for a while with my coffee, watching Kacey and Paula as they work, or sometimes as they pray for work, as they begin to look sicker and sicker from withdrawal, as they become desperate. From this position, too, I can watch their customers. I see them every shift, sidling by in their cars, all kinds of men, keeping their eyes straight ahead, on the road, when they notice me or my vehicle. Keeping their eyes on the women and girls on the sidewalk when they don't. There is something wolfish about these men, low and mean, something predatory. There is no type—or if there is, there are enough outliers to complicate it. I have seen men with children in the backseat driving slowly up Kensington Avenue. I have seen scumbags in Audis, in from the Main Line. I have seen men of all ages and races come to the Ave: men in their eighties and teenage boys in groups. I have seen heterosexual couples looking for a third. Once or twice I have seen women alone: on rare occasions, women are customers too. I don't like them any better, though I imagine Kacey and her friends might. Or are, at least, less scared of them.

I can muster sympathy for almost any type of criminal except for johns. When it comes to johns I am not impartial or objective. Quite simply, I hate them: their physicality repulses me, their greed, their willingness to take advantage, their inability to control the basest of their instincts. The frequency with which they are violent or dishonest. Is this wrong of me? Perhaps it is my weakness as an officer. But there's a difference, I believe, between two consenting adults making a thoughtful transaction and the kind of bargain that happens on the Ave, where some of the women would do anything for anyone, where some of the women need a fix so badly that they can't say no or yes. People who target these women send me into a state of hot, quick rage that makes it difficult for me to look them in the eye when I have to interact with them. On many occasions, I have been rougher than I have needed to be when cuffing them. I admit this.

But it's difficult to be levelheaded when one has seen what I've seen.

Once I encountered a woman, red-haired, fiftyish, weeping on a stoop with no shoes on. She was not hiding her face: instead she had turned it upward, toward the sun, and her eyes and her mouth were open, and she was inconsolably crying. This was when I worked with Truman, and the two of us stopped to check on her. His idea. He was always kind in this way.

When we approached her, however, she put her head down on her arms so we couldn't see her face, and another voice called out a front door nearby: *She don't wanna talk to you.*

—Is she okay? Truman inquired.

—She was jumped, said the voice, female, gravelly. We could not see its owner. The house was dark inside.

This meant different things. Usually it meant she was raped.

—Four of them, said the voice. Guy brought her to a house, three of his buddies were there.

—Shut up, shut up, said the red-haired woman—the first noise she made aside from her sobs.

—Can we make a report? Truman asked her. His voice was gentle. He was good at this, interviewing women. Sometimes, I will acknowledge, better than I am.

But the red-haired woman turned her head back into her arms and said nothing more. She was crying so hard that she could not catch her breath.

I speculated about what had happened to her shoes. Imagined she might have been wearing high heels, might have abandoned them so that she could flee. Her toenails were broken and dirty and painful-looking. There was a little patch of blood on the sidewalk next to her right instep, as if she might have cut it.

—Ma'am, said Truman, I'm going to leave my number right here for you, okay? In case you change your mind.

He handed her his card.

Down the block, another car slowed for another woman.

From Alonzo's window, I have watched Kacey make her deals. I have watched her lean down as a slow-rolling car comes to a stop. I have watched these cars turn down side streets, and I have watched my sister follow them, disappearing around the side of a building heading toward any number of possible outcomes. This is her choice, I tell myself; this is the choice she has made.

Sometimes, looking down at my watch, I find that I have been standing there, unmoving, for ten or fifteen minutes, waiting for her to return.

Alonzo doesn't object: he leaves me alone, lets me watch, lets me sip quietly from my styrofoam cup. Today he is busy with another customer, and so I assume my regular position in front of the cold window, gazing through it, waiting for Alonzo to be free.

I'm still lost in my thoughts when the other customer in the store opens the front door and leaves, sounding the three silver bells that Alonzo has hung on it.

Once the store is empty, I approach the counter to pay for my coffee, and it's then that Alonzo says, Hey. I'm sorry to hear about your sister.

I look at him.

—I beg your pardon? I say.

Alonzo pauses. A look comes over his face: the distinct look of someone afraid he has just revealed too much.

—What did you say? I ask Alonzo now, a second time.

He begins shaking his head.

—I'm not sure, he says, I probably have the wrong information.

—What information is that, exactly? I say.

Alonzo cranes his head to the right, looking around me to where Paula normally stands. Noting her absence there, he continues.

—It's probably nothing, he says. But Paula was in here the other day telling me Kacey's gone missing. Told me she's been gone a month, maybe longer. Nobody knows where she is.

I nod, keeping my mouth straight, my posture upright. I make sure my hands are resting lightly on my duty belt, and that my expression projects an air of calm collectedness.

—I see, I say.

I wait.

—Did she say anything else? I say.

Alonzo shakes his head.

—Honestly, he says, Paula could be wrong. She's been bad lately. Ranting. Going on and on. Crazy, says Alonzo, whose face has now become sympathetic, who seems to be thinking of doing something disastrous, like patting me consolingly on the shoulder. Fortunately, neither of us moves.

—Yes, I say. She could be wrong.

THEN

There are some people who ascribe to their suffering the particular cause of a difficult childhood. Kacey, for example, one of the last times we spoke, had recently come to the conclusion that her troubles began first with our parents, who abandoned her, and then with Gee, who, she said, never loved her, and may in fact have disliked her.

I looked at her, blinking, and said to her as levelly as I could that I grew up in the same household as she did. My implication, of course, was that it is the decisions that I have made in life that have placed me on my specific path—decisions, not chance. And that although our childhood may not have been idyllic, it sufficiently prepared one of us, at least, for a productive life.

But when I said this, Kacey only buried her head in her hands and said to me, It's different, Mickey, things have always been so different for you.

To this day, I don't know what her meaning could have been.

In fact, it is possible to argue, I believe—if we were to evaluate who had the more *difficult* childhood, whatever that may mean—one might find the balance tipped toward me.

I say this because, of the two of us, I am the only one with memories of our mother, and very fond ones at that. Therefore, the loss of our mother was difficult for me in a way that it would not have been for Kacey, who was too little, while our mother was alive, to recall her.

She was young, our mother. Eighteen years old at the time of her pregnancy with me. She was a senior in high school—a good student, Gee always said, a good girl—and she had only been dating our father for a few months when it happened. As the story goes, it took everyone by surprise, and no one more than Gee, who to this day narrates the shock of the news with urgency and grief. *No one believed it*, she says. *When I told them. They all said, not Lisa.*

Gee was just religious enough to make an abortion out of the question. But she was also religious enough to be enraged by the pregnancy, ashamed of it, to see it as something to hide. The year was 1984. Gee herself had been married at nineteen and had had Lisa at twenty, but times were different then, Gee liked to say. Gee's husband died very young in a car accident—I wonder, today, if he had been drunk, since Gee often mentions his drinking—and she never remarried.

I used to imagine that things would have gone differently for Gee if her husband, our grandfather, hadn't died. So much of her life has been governed by the need to simply keep her head above water: to put food on the table, to pay bills, to pay down the debt that she constantly incurs. If she had had a partner in these endeavors—someone to add a paycheck, someone to mourn alongside when her only daughter died—perhaps her life, and ours, might have been better. But this sort of idle speculation might be pure sentimentality, for to this day Gee claims she has no use for men: thinks of them only as obstacles in her path, nuisances who are only occasionally necessary for the propagation of human life. She mistrusts them implicitly. Avoids them when possible.

The only thing she really got out of her union, it seems, was the ability to say that she had been married when her daughter was conceived—*married*, she explained, often, thrusting a finger into an invisible chest. She had done things correctly.

When Lisa delivered the news of her pregnancy, therefore, Gee had insisted on a wedding. Gee had met this Daniel Fitzpatrick (*this* Daniel Fitzpatrick was how Gee permanently referred to our father) only once before, but now she sat both of them on her sofa and insisted they see the priest at her parish and formalize their vows. Our father himself was the offspring of a single mother who was notoriously irresponsible: a floozy, Gee often said, who had *not* been married when her son was conceived, thus sealing forever in Gee's mind the firm line between the two of them, where respectability was concerned. Worse, in Gee's estimation: the son was a charity case at the school. Someone who raised tuition, Gee lamented, for other working people. What our father's mother thought about all of this—the baby, the marriage, Gee herself—is lost to time. I cannot, in fact, ever recall meeting her. She did not attend our mother's funeral: an offense that Gee will take to her own grave.

In Gee's telling of things—the only version of events that I have ever heard—Lisa and Daniel, our parents, got married in private at Holy Redeemer, on a Wednesday afternoon, with Gee and the deacon as witnesses. Then Gee took Dan in, giving her daughter and her new son-in-law the middle bedroom in the house, taking rent whenever the young couple could give it, and telling the rest of the family the news as slowly as she possibly could. Head held high. Defiant.

Five months later, I was born. Kacey a year and a half after that.

Four years later, our mother was dead.

Of the years in between my birth and my mother's death, there are memories, still, if I quiet my mind sufficiently. It is rarer and rarer, these days, that I can. On a shift, sometimes, inside my patrol car, I remember being in the backseat of a car that my mother was driving. No car seat, in those days. No seat belt either. In the front seat, my mother was singing.

From time to time it happens, too, when I'm at the refrigerator, any refrigerator, at home or at work: a quick vision of my young mother complaining to Gee, in Gee's kitchen, that there's nothing inside. *Oh really,* says Gee, in another room. *Then why don't you put something in it.*

And a pool. Someone's pool. Rare to be at a pool. And the lobby of a movie theater, though I'm not sure where it was, and every movie theater is in Center City, now, and the others are closed or converted to concert venues.

I remember my mother's youth, the way she seemed like a child herself, or a peer, her skin clear and smooth, her hair still the shining hair of a child. I remember, too, the way Gee softened around her, became stiller, stopped moving, for once in her life. She laughed in spite of herself, put a hand over her mouth at her daughter's antics, shook her head in disbelief. *You're nuts. She's nuts. This must be the nuthouse,* Gee said, looking at me, grinning, proud. Gee, in those days, was kinder, bewitched by her funny, irreverent daughter, unaware of the fate that would befall her, and all of us.

Harder still to recall are the memories that come to me in the still dark of my bedroom. Whenever Thomas is in close proximity to me, little-boy head right next to me, whenever I am close enough to his skin to breathe its scent—there—just there—is a flash of my own mother beside me in my childhood bed. My mother's face, young face, my mother's body, young body, covered in a black T-shirt with writing on it that I cannot read. The arms of my mother around me. My mother's eyes closed. My mother's mouth open. Her breath the sweet breath of a grass-eating animal. I am four and I put one hand on her cheek. *Hello,* says my mother, and she puts her mouth on my cheek, talks into my face, and there are the teeth and the lips of my mother. *My baby,* said my mother, over and over, the phrase she used most in the world. If I try very hard, I can still hear her saying it in her high, happy voice, which sometimes carried inside it a note of surprise: that she, Lisa O'Brien, had a baby at all.

What I do not recall is anything to do with my mother's addiction. Perhaps I repressed it; or perhaps I simply didn't know what it was, what it meant, didn't recognize the signs of addiction or its trappings. My memories of my mother are warm and loving and made all the more painful by the fact of their happiness.

Similarly, I do not recall my mother's death, nor do I recall being informed of it. I have retained only its aftermath: Gee pacing our house like a lion, tearing at her hair and shirt. Gee hitting her own head with the hard palm of her hand as she spoke on the phone, and then biting the back of her wrist, as if to muffle a cry. People speaking in whispers. People stuffing the two of us, Kacey and me, into stiff dresses and tights and too-small shoes. A gathering in a church: tiny, subdued. Gee sinking down in the pew. Gee grabbing Kacey's arm to stop her making noise. Our father, on the other side of us, useless. Silent. A gathering at our house. A great sense of shame. The knees and the thighs and the shoes and the suit jackets of adults. The rustle of fabric. No children. No cousins. The cousins kept away. A long winter. Absence. Absence. People forgetting us, forgetting to talk to us. People forgetting to hold us. People forgetting to bathe us. To feed us. Then: foraging for food. Feeding myself. Feeding my sister. Finding and smelling what our mother left behind (her black T-shirt, still unreadable to me; the sheets on the bed in our parents' room, in which our father still slept; a half-empty soda in the fridge; the insides of her shoes) until Gee had a daylong fit of finding and purging her things. Then finding and smelling her hairbrushes, tucked at the back of a drawer. Wrapping the strands of my mother's hair around my fingers until the bulbs of them turned purple.

All of these memories are fading, now. These days, I bring forth each one only sparingly, and then place it carefully back in its drawer. I ration them. Preserve them. Each year they become slighter, more translucent, fleeting shards of sweetness on the tongue. If I can keep them intact enough, I tell myself, then one day I might pass them on to Thomas.

Kacey was only a baby at the time of our mother's death. Two years old. Still in diapers that often went unchanged for too long. Wandering around the house, lost, climbing stairs she shouldn't have been climbing, hiding in small places for too long, in closets, under beds. Opening drawers with dangerous things inside. She seemed to like being at eye level with adults, and regularly I rounded a corner to find her sitting on a countertop in the kitchen or the bathroom: tiny, unmonitored, alone. She had a ragdoll named Muffin and two pacifiers, never washed, that she stashed carefully in hiding places where nobody else could find them. Once both of them were lost, that was that: Gee wouldn't replace them, and Kacey cried for days afterward, missing them, suckling frantically at fingers and at air.

It was not an intentional decision on my part to begin to take care of my sister. Perhaps recognizing that nobody else would be stepping in to do so, I silently volunteered. She was still sleeping, in those days, in a crib in my room. But it didn't take her long to learn to climb out of it, and soon she did so every night. Stealthily, with the skill and coordination of an older child, Kacey would spider her way out of the wooden crib and toddle into bed with me. I was the one who reminded the adults around us when Kacey needed to be changed. I was the one who, eventually, potty trained my sister. I took my role as her protector seriously. I bore the weight of it with pride.

As we grew, Kacey begged me to tell her stories about our mother. Each night, in our shared bed, I was Scheherazade, recounting all the episodes I could recall, inventing the others. Do you remember when she took us on a trip to the beach? I'd say, and Kacey would nod eagerly. Remember the ice cream she bought us? I'd say. Remember pancakes for breakfast? Remember her reading us stories at bedtime? (This, ironically, was a parental activity very frequently mentioned in the books that we read to ourselves.) I told her all of these stories and more. I lied. And as Kacey listened, her eyes closed slightly, like the eyes of a cat in the sun.

I do admit, with great shame, that being the bearer of family history in this way also gave me a kind of terrible power over my sister, a weapon that I wielded only once. It was at the end of a long day, and a long argument, and Kacey had been hounding me about something I can no longer recall. Finally I let out, in a fit of rage, an atrocity that I regretted at once. *She told me that she loved me more,* I said to Kacey. To this day, it remains the worst lie I ever told. I took it back right away, but it was too late. I had already seen Kacey's small face turn red and then crumble. I had seen her mouth open, as if to respond. Instead, she let out a wail. It was pure grief. It was the cry of a much older person, someone who'd already seen too much. Even today, I can hear it if I try.

There was some talk, after the funeral, of our father taking us else-where to live. But he never seemed to have the money or the initiative to make this happen, and so instead we stayed there, the three of us, all together under Gee's roof.

This was a mistake.

Our father and Gee had never gotten along, but now they fought con-stantly. Sometimes the fights had to do with her suspicion that he was using in her house—on this question, I assume Gee's instincts were correct—but more than that, they were about his being late with the rent. I can still remember some of those fights, though Kacey, last I spoke to her, could not.

Soon, the tension between them grew unbearable, and our father moved out. Abruptly, we became Gee's responsibility. And about this, Gee was not happy. *I thought I was done with all this,* she said to us often, mostly when Kacey had gotten into some nonsense or other. When I picture her face, I mainly recall that her eyes were always elsewhere: she never looked at us, but above or beside us, glancingly, the way one might look at the sun. As an adult, I have, in more generous moments, won-dered whether the loss of her daughter, whom she clearly loved fever-ishly, caused her to hold us always at a distance. To her we must have been small reminders both of Lisa and of our own mortality, the poten-tial we held for the infliction of further pain, further loss.

If Gee often seemed annoyed at us, most of her emotion was in fact directed away from us, at our father, for whom she reserved a kind of incredulous, powerful rage, a disbelief at the depths to which he could sink when it came to shirking his familial responsibilities. I knew it the first time I saw him, she told us, in a monologue that she delivered once a month when the child-support payment failed to come. I told Leese that I never saw a shadier character in all my life.

The other thing that I knew about our father also came from Gee. *He* got her hooked on that shit, Gee said—never directly to us, but frequently on the phone, loudly enough so that we would be certain to hear. *He ruined her.*

After our mother died, *this Daniel Fitzpatrick* became *Him* and *He.* The only *He* in our lives, aside from a few uncles and God. When we saw him, we called him *Daddy*, which seems unthinkable to me now: almost like a different person was saying it. Even at the time, it felt strange to use the word if he hadn't been by in a while. But he called himself that too. *I'm their daddy,* we heard him say to Gee, often, arguing a point. And Gee would say, *Then act like it.*

Eventually, he disappeared completely. We did not see him for a decade. Then, when I was twenty, a former friend of his told me casually that he had died, the same way everyone does in the northeast quadrant of Philadelphia. The same way I thought Kacey had died, the first time I found her. The second time. The third.

My father's friend thought I'd known already, he said, noticing my reaction.

I hadn't.

As for our mother: after her passing, Gee referred to her only infrequently. But sometimes, I caught her looking at our mother's smiling and gap-toothed grade school photograph—the only whisper of her that remained in the house, one that lives, still, on the wall of the living room—for longer than she ever would have, if she'd known she was being watched. Other times, in the middle of the night, I thought that I heard Gee crying: a hollow, eerie wail, a stuttering childlike keen, the sound of endless grief. But in the daytime, Gee gave no indication that she felt anything, aside from resignation and resentment. She made bad choices, said Gee, about our mother. Don't you go choosing the same old shit.

In the absence of our parents, we grew.

Gee was still young when our mother died, just forty-two, but she seemed to us much older. She worked constantly, often multiple jobs: catering, retail, house cleaning. In the winter, her house was permanently cold. She kept the heat at fifty-five, just barely warm enough to keep the pipes from freezing. We wore our jackets and our hats indoors. *Are youse gonna pay the bill?* Gee asked us, when we complained. The house seemed ghostly when she was gone: it had been in her family since 1923, when her Irish grandfather bought it, and then her father inherited it, and then Gee. It was a little rowhome, two stories, three tiny bedrooms in a line off an upstairs hallway, a downstairs that ran straight through from front to back. Living room, dining room, kitchen. No doors between them. Halfhearted thresholds here and there to designate the purported boundary of every room.

Back and forth and back again, from the front of the house to the back, we moved, generally as one unit. If Kacey was upstairs, so was I; if I was downstairs, so was Kacey. *McKacey*, Gee often called us, or *KaMickey*. We were, in those days, inseparable, shadows of one another, one of us taller and thinner and dark-haired, the other small and round and blond. We wrote notes to one another that we secreted in backpacks and pockets.

In one corner of our bedroom, we discovered that the wall-to-wall carpeting could be lifted to reveal a loose floorboard, and beneath it, a hollow space. In it, we left secret messages for one another, and objects, and drawings. We constructed elaborate plans about the way our lives would go in adulthood, after we'd escaped that house: I would go to college, I thought, and get a good, practical job. Then I would get married, have children, retire someplace warm, but only after seeing as much of the world as I could. Kacey's ambitions were less reserved. She'd join a band, she sometimes said, though she never played an instrument.

She'd be an actress. A chef. A model. Other days she, too, talked about going to college, but when I asked her what college she wanted to go to, she named schools she had no chance of getting into, ever, colleges she'd heard mentioned on television. Colleges for rich people. It wasn't in me to disillusion her. Today, I wonder if perhaps I should have.

In those years, I watched over Kacey as a parent would, trying unsuccessfully to protect her from danger. Kacey, meanwhile, watched out for me as a friend would, drawing me out socially, coaxing me toward other children.

At night, in our shared bed, we put the crowns of our heads together and held hands, an A-shaped tangle of limbs and loose hair, and bemoaned the indignities of our schooldays, and named every crush that we had.

Our sharing of the back bedroom persisted, out of habit, into our teenage years. We could each have taken our own bedroom at some point, since there were three in the house. But the middle one—*Mom's room*, we called it, long after she died—seemed haunted by her memory, and so neither of us claimed it. Besides, it was very often occupied by someone coming or going, an itinerant uncle or cousin who needed a place to stay and was willing to pay Gee a meager sum in monthly rent. Gee herself moved into it for a spell when one of the panes in her front bedroom window fell out after she removed the window-unit A/C. Instead of paying anyone else to fix it, she taped some plastic over the opening, and then she closed the door and taped the door up, too, but the drafts that came from that bedroom in December were enough to have all of us walking around the house wearing blankets like togas.

The question of childcare was always a pressing one for Gee. There was no after-school care at the Hanover grade school, which put her in a pinch.

Eventually, Gee heard about and enrolled us in a free, nearby program run by the Police Athletic League. There—in two large, echoing rooms and on one picked-over outdoor field—we played soccer and volleyball and basketball, urged on from the side of the court by Officer Rose Zalecki, a tall woman who'd been a standout player in her younger days. There, we listened to admonition after admonition to stay in school, to stay abstinent, and to stay away from drugs and alcohol. (The formerly incarcerated stopped by, with some frequency, to drive these points home via slideshows that ended with cookies and lemonade.)

Every PAL officer at the facility was a pleasing combination of authoritative, funny, and kind: a change from most of the other adults in our lives, around whom we were mainly expected to stay silent. Each child had a favorite officer, a mentor, and small lines of children could often be found trailing after their chosen idol like ducklings. Kacey's was Officer Almood, a small and perpetually bemused woman whose irreverent, wild sense of humor—centered benevolently on the fools around her, the foolishness of the world, the damn foolishness of these kids— sent those in earshot of her into paralyzing fits of laughter. Kacey picked up her mannerisms and style of speech and boisterous laugh and brought them home, trying them out, until Gee admonished her to keep it down.

My favorite was quieter.

Officer Cleare was young when he arrived at the PAL, twenty-seven, but his age seemed to me then to be very adult, a good solid age, an age that carried with it the implication of responsibility. He had a young son already, about whom he spoke fondly, but he wore no wedding ring, and he did not ever mention a wife or girlfriend. In one corner of the large cafeteria-like room in which we did our homework, Officer Cleare read books, glancing up occasionally at his charges to make sure we weren't distracted, and then back down at what he was reading, his legs outstretched and crossed at the ankles. Every so often he stood up and made his rounds, bending down over each child, asking them what they were working on, pointing out mistakes in their thinking. He was stricter than the other officers. Less fun. More contemplative. For these reasons, Kacey didn't like him.

But I was drawn to him forcefully. Officer Cleare listened carefully when anyone spoke to him, for one thing, maintaining eye contact, nodding slightly to show he understood. He was handsome, for another: he had black, combed-back hair, and sideburns just slightly longer than the rest of the male officers, which in 1997 was quite fashionable, and dark eyebrows that inched together minutely when he read something he found particularly interesting. He was tall and well built and had an air about him that felt to me then vaguely old-fashioned, as if he had been dropped in from another time, from an old movie. He was extremely polite. He used words like *diligent* and *transcendent* and once, while holding a door open for me, he said *After you,* and swept his hand outward, bowing his head slightly, which struck me at the time as unthinkably gallant. Each day, I positioned myself at tables in closer and closer proximity to him, until at last I was seated directly next to him. I never spoke to him: only did my homework ever more quietly and seriously in the hope that, one day, he would notice my dedication and comment on it.

Finally, he did.

It was on a day when he was teaching us chess. I was fourteen years old and in my most awkward phase: mainly silent, going through a struggle against bad skin, frequently unshowered, dressed in raggedy clothes, always two sizes too big or too small, hand-me-downs or thrift-store finds.

But if I was self-conscious about my appearance, I was proud of my intelligence, which I thought of, in secret, as something that rested quietly inside me, a sleeping dragon guarding a store of wealth that no one, not even Gee, could take away. A weapon I would one day deploy to save us both: myself and my sister.

That day, I concentrated hard on each match in front of me until, at the end of the afternoon, I was one of four players remaining in the impromptu tournament Officer Cleare had staged. Soon, a crowd was watching, and he was among them. I was aware of him, though he was standing behind me, out of sight: I could feel his size, his height. I could feel his breathing. I won the game.

—Nice work, he said, and my shoulders hunched in pleasure, and I lowered them again, saying nothing.

Next, and last, I played against an older boy who was the other finalist in the room.

The boy was good: he had been playing for years. He made quick work of me.

But Officer Cleare paused, his hands on his waist, assessing me even after everyone else had gone away. Under his gaze, I reddened. I didn't look up.

Slowly, he righted my capsized king, and then he knelt down next to the long cafeteria table at which I was still sitting.

—Have you played before, Michaela? he asked me quietly. He always called me this: another thing I appreciated about him. My nickname, Mickey, was given to me by Gee, and it has always seemed to me a little undignified, but somehow it stuck. In the memories I have of my mother, she, too, always called me by my real name.

I shook my head. No. I couldn't speak.

He nodded, once. Impressive, he said.

He began to teach me. Every afternoon, he spent twenty minutes with me separately, coaching me on opening gambits and then game-length strategies.

—You're very smart, he said, appraisingly. How do you do in school?

I shrugged. Reddened again. Around Officer Cleare, I was perpetually flushed, my blood beating through my body in a way that reminded me I was alive.

—All right, I said.

—Do better, then, he said.

He told me his father, who had also been a police officer, was the one who first taught him chess. He died young, though, said Officer Cleare.

—I was eight, he said, moving a pawn out and back again.

At this, I glanced up at him quickly, and then back down at the board. So he knows, I thought.

He began to bring me books to read. True crime and detective fiction, at first. All the books his own father had loved. *In Cold Blood*. Raymond Chandler, Agatha Christie, Dashiell Hammett. He told me about films: *Serpico* was his favorite, but he also liked the *Godfather* trilogy (everyone says the second is the best, he informed me, but actually the first is) and *Goodfellas* and older ones, too. *The Maltese Falcon* (even better than the book, he said), and *Casablanca*, and all of Hitchcock's thrillers.

I read every book and watched every movie he recommended. I took the El down to Tower Records on Broad Street and, using my hard-earned babysitting money, bought two CDs by the bands he loved, Flogging Molly and Dropkick Murphys. He had described them as Irish bands, which made me imagine songs full of fiddles and drums, but when I put them on I was surprised to hear men shouting at me over aggressive guitars. Still, I stayed up late into the night, listening to these songs on my Discman, or shining a flashlight on the pages of the books he had named, or sitting on the sofa in the living room, watching classic movies on TV.

—What did you think? Officer Cleare asked me, about every recommendation that he made. And I told him that I loved them, always, even when I didn't.

He wanted to be a detective. He'd be one someday, he said, but while his son was young he had requested a PAL assignment so that he could have more regular hours. Several times, he brought the boy in. His name was Gabriel, and he was four or five years old then, a small reflection of his father, dark-haired and lanky, his ankles showing beneath his too-short pants. His father picked him up and carried him around, introducing him, proud of him. Perversely, against my will, I looked at the father and the son and felt a pang of jealousy. I was not certain what I wanted, but I knew it to be connected, somehow, to the two of them.

Then Officer Cleare put the boy down next to me.

—This is my friend Michaela, he said to his son. And I looked up at the boy's father slowly, awestruck, the phrase echoing in my mind for days afterward. *My friend. My friend. My friend.*

t was around this time, unfortunately, that Kacey was beginning to get into serious trouble. Today, I am disturbed by the possibility that this was linked, directly or indirectly, to my distractedness. For before Officer Cleare entered my life, I was devoted entirely to my sister: helping her with her homework; counseling her on her behavioral issues—the ones that I knew about, at least—and on how to better communicate with Gee; combing and arranging her hair in the morning; packing our lunches each night. In turn, Kacey revealed to me the parts of herself that she did not share with others: the small injustices that befell her each day at school, the deep sadness that sometimes came over her with such power that she felt certain it would never recede. But as I became closer to Officer Cleare, I became, I imagine, wistful and remote, my thoughts and my gaze turned away from my sister.

Kacey, in turn, withdrew. At thirteen, she began regularly skipping out on the PAL's after-school program. Gee received a phone call anytime she did, and for a while she tried unsuccessfully to punish Kacey, but soon her groundings piled up on one another, and eventually Gee gave up the chase. She's old enough to watch herself, I guess, said Gee, dubiously. I was already fifteen then, and years before she had given me the same option that Kacey now had, which was to entertain myself after school each day—or, better yet, to get a steady job. Instead, I elected to participate in a PAL teen group that was meant to provide mentorship and oversight to the younger students.

My choice—though I wouldn't have admitted this to anyone—was largely motivated by wanting to remain close to Officer Cleare.

By ninth grade, Kacey was generally spending her afternoons with a group of friends headed by Paula Mulroney.

Already, they were distracting her from her schoolwork. They wore mainly black, and smoked cigarettes, and dyed their hair, and listened to bands like Green Day and Something Corporate—music that, though I couldn't abide it, though it prevented me from studying, Kacey began playing loudly in our house whenever Gee wasn't home to stop her. She began smoking, too, both cigarettes and marijuana, and she kept a small supply of each in the hollow spot beneath the floorboards of our room—the place we had formerly used for more innocent purposes.

It felt, to me, like a slap.

I remember, with clarity, the first time I found pills in that space. There were perhaps six of them, small and blue, contained in a small Ziploc bag. Incredibly, I recall holding them up and feeling a certain amount of relief that they seemed to be professionally made, imprinted with two neat letters on one side and with a number on the other, well formed and sincere-looking. When I asked Kacey about them, she was reassuring: they were something like extra-strength Tylenol, she told me. Very safe. A boy named Albie had a father who had a prescription for them. A lot of fathers in our neighborhood did: they were construction workers, or ex-longshoremen, or laborers of other kinds who had used their bodies hard all their lives, had ground bones and twisted muscles into painful nubs and knots. It was the year 2000. OxyContin was a four-year-old medication, doled out liberally by doctors, received gratefully by patients. It was purported to be less addictive than prior generations of opioid medication—and therefore nobody knew, yet, to be afraid. Why do you even want it? I remember asking Kacey, and she said, I don't know. For fun.

What she didn't tell me was that they were snorting it.

The other activity Kacey was getting into, at this time, was sex. This I found out secondhand, from a cruel tenth-grader I overheard bragging about it to his friends. When I confronted my sister, Kacey simply shrugged it off, saying nonchalantly that he was telling the truth.

At that time, I had never even been kissed.

The two of us pulled farther and farther away from one another. Without her, my loneliness became outrageous, a low hum, an extra limb, a tin can that dragged behind me wherever I went. I missed Kacey, missed her presence in the house. Selfishly, I also missed the efforts Kacey made to draw me out socially. To bring me to parties. To invite me along with her to friends' houses. *Mickey was just saying,* Kacey used to begin, when we were younger, and then would accredit to me some witticism or observation that she had actually come up with herself. Now, when Kacey saw me at school, she just nodded. More often, she wasn't at school at all.

On several occasions, I hopefully placed messages for my sister in our hiding place. I knew it was childish, even as I did it, and yet I persisted. Small notes containing anecdotes about my day, about Gee, about some other member of our family who had done something or other I found amusing or annoying enough to recount. I longed for her to notice me, to come back, to reverse her course and return to the childhood activities we had once enjoyed together.

But each time, the note I left for her went unreturned.

The only occasions, in those days, on which Kacey seemed truly to notice me were when I spoke of Officer Cleare.

Kacey didn't like him.

He's full of himself, was how she phrased it, or sometimes she called him stuck-up, but I knew even then that her real criticism of him was darker, that my sister sensed something in him that she couldn't, or wouldn't, name.

Ew, Kacey said when I talked about him, or anything he liked, which I did with some frequency. In fact, I began so many sentences with

Officer Cleare said that finally Gee and Kacey eliminated the phrase from my vocabulary by mimicking me so mercilessly that I became self-conscious. My fascination with him prompted, for my sister and me, a brief role reversal. For once in our lives, it seemed to me that it was Kacey who was concerned about me, and not the other way around.

The first time Kacey overdosed, at sixteen, in that house full of strangers in Kensington, it was Officer Cleare to whom I turned for help and advice.

It was the summer between my junior and senior years of high school. I was seventeen years old at that time, and by then he and I had become very close. Our conversations had expanded: in addition to making recommendations to me and instructing me in various ways, he now also confided in me about problems he himself had faced as a child, problems he was facing in the department, colleagues who were causing him trouble, problems he had with his family. His mother, he feared, had developed a drinking problem after his father died, and she had recently fallen and broken her hip. His sister was a busybody who was always advising him about his life. I listened carefully, nodding, mainly staying quiet. I hadn't, yet, told him much about my own family. I still preferred listening to talking. Unlike Gee, he seemed to like how serious I was, how thoughtful. He complimented me frequently on my intelligence, on how observant I was, how sharp.

I had recently graduated from being an unpaid member of the PAL's teen program to a paid counselor in the organization's summer program for neighborhood kids—which made me, I told myself, an equal to the officers, in certain ways, anyhow. Along with a dozen other employees, I shepherded day-campers from room to room, planning activities, coaching them halfheartedly in sports that I myself didn't know much about. Really, though, I used the time to talk to Officer Cleare.

The day after the episode in question, I was distraught. I wandered through the PAL building, pale and abstracted, uncertain whether I should be there at all. Maybe, I thought, I should be at home with Kacey, who was in very serious trouble with Gee, and who was probably in withdrawal.

I was standing in the largest room at the PAL, my arms crossed around myself, lost in thought, when I saw Officer Cleare looking at me across a dozen cafeteria tables. There was enforced silence that afternoon because of too many behavioral infractions, and everyone had been instructed to read or draw quietly.

He walked slowly toward me, glancing at children whose heads popped up to look at him, directing them back to their tasks.

When he reached me, he inclined his head toward me, inquisitively. He looked at me from under his handsome lowered brow.

—What's wrong, Michaela? he said, with so much tenderness that it surprised me.

Unexpectedly, quickly, my eyes filled with tears. It was the first time in many years that I'd ever been asked. It opened something in me, some chasm of longing I would have trouble closing ever again. It made me remember my mother's smooth hands on my face.

—Hey, he said.

I kept my eyes on the floor. Two hot tears spilled down my cheeks and I swiped at them furiously. I rarely cried, and I especially avoided crying around adults. When we were smaller, if we cried, Gee often warned us that she'd give us a reason to. Sometimes, before we grew bigger than she was, she made good on this threat.

—Go out back, Officer Cleare said to me, too quietly to be heard by anyone else. Stay there, he said.

It was 90 degrees that day. The outdoor area behind the building consisted of a basketball court with rickety bleachers and a half-dead field that could be used for soccer or football. The surrounding streets were similarly dead. No passersby, no bystanders, no windows to the inside of the building. Flies buzzed lazily around my head, and I swatted them as I walked.

I found a shadowed spot and leaned against the brick building that housed the PAL. My heart was pounding. I wasn't sure why.

I was thinking of Kacey: of the hospital bed she'd been put in after her arrival at Episcopal Hospital. Of the silence between us. *I don't understand this,* I had said, and Kacey had said, *I know you don't,* and that was all. Kacey had looked to be in pain. Her eyes were closed. Her complexion was very, very pale. Then the ward doors swung open and through them stormed our grandmother, her face steely, her hands clenched. Gee has always been a thin woman, full of nervous energy, the kind of person who never stops moving. That day, though, she had stood frighteningly still as she whispered to Kacey through clenched teeth.

—Open your eyes, she had said. Look at me. Open your fucking eyes.

After a pause, Kacey complied, squinting, turning her face away from the fluorescent lights above her.

Gee waited until Kacey was focused on her.

Then she said, Listen to me. I went through this once with your mother. I'll never go through it again.

She was holding a tight finger out toward Kacey. She took her by the elbow and dragged her from the bed, so that the IV attached to her arm was ripped painfully out, and I followed. None of us had stopped when a nurse called after us that Kacey wasn't ready to be discharged.

At home, Gee had slapped Kacey once, hard, across the face, and Kacey had run up to our room, slamming the door and then locking it.

After a while I followed, knocking softly, saying the name of my sister over and over again. But there came no answer.

The brick of the PAL building was so warm that it was uncomfortable to lean against, and so I stood upright again. I had my back to the door I'd come out of, and when I heard it open and close quietly behind me, I didn't turn around. The air was thick with humidity. Trickles of sweat ran down my sides, beneath my shirt. I looked straight ahead as Officer

Cleare approached me. I could feel him stop and pause behind me, perhaps to think. I could hear his breathing. Then, swiftly, he put his arms around me. I had reached my full height several years before, and there were not many boys in my school who towered over me the way that he did. But when he enfolded me, he outsized me so completely that he was able to rest his chin on the top of my head.

I closed my eyes. I could feel his heart beating against my back. Ever since my mother died, I had had the same recurring dream: in it, some faceless figure cradled me in its arms, one arm behind my back, one beneath my legs, both hands clasped together on the other side, so that I felt that I was tight inside a little case. And in its arms this figure rocked me back and forth. It's been years since I have had this dream, but I can still recall the feeling I had whenever I awoke from it: I was comforted. Pacified. Lulled.

Encircled in this way by Simon Cleare, I opened my eyes. Here he is, I thought.

—What's wrong, said Simon, again.

This time, I told him.

NOW

regret to say that it takes me quite a while to compose myself after my conversation with Alonzo. I sit in the car for ten minutes and then begin, distractedly, to patrol my assigned sector. The people on the sidewalk are a blur to me. Every so often I think I see my sister, only to discover that it isn't her, and that it actually looks nothing like her. Although it's very cold outside, I roll the window down to let the air cool my face.

Several calls come in but I am slow to respond to them.

Enough of this, I tell myself, finally, and I pull over again—too abruptly; a civilian car screeches to a halt behind me—and I ask myself how I would approach the case of a missing person if I were, in fact, a detective.

Hesitantly, I touch the MDT fastened to the center console of my vehicle. It's something like a laptop, and I'm fairly good with computers, but these systems are notoriously terrible and sometimes even broken. Today, the one in my assigned vehicle is working, but only very slowly.

I'm going to look up Kacey's name in the PCIC database.

I'm not supposed to: technically, we are required to have a valid reason to search for any individual, and my log-in credentials will reveal what I've done to anyone who cares, and I dislike violating protocol in this way—but today, I'm banking on the idea that no one actually does care. No one has time to, in our district.

Still, my heartbeat quickens slightly as I type.

Fitzpatrick, Kacey Marie, I enter. *DOB: 3/16/1986.*

An arrest record a mile long is displayed. The earliest one I can see—the others, presumably, expunged due to her then-status as a juvenile—is from thirteen years ago, when Kacey was eighteen. Public intoxication. It seems almost mild now, almost funny, the kind of escapade on so many people's records.

But the kind of trouble Kacey was getting into got quickly more serious, after that. An arrest for possession, an arrest for assault (an ex-boyfriend, if I remember correctly, who used to hit her and then called the police the first time she ever retaliated). Then solicitation, solicitation, solicitation. The most recent item on Kacey's record is from a year and a half ago. That one is for petty theft. She was convicted; she spent a month in prison. Her third period of incarceration.

What I don't find—what I was hoping to find—is any indication that she's been brought in more recently than that. Any indication, I suppose, that she is still alive.

There is a natural next step. Any detective on any missing persons case would, of course, interview the missing party's family members as soon as possible.

And yet, as I consider the phone in my hands, I am stopped by the same queasy feeling of unease that overtakes me anytime I contemplate getting in touch with the O'Briens.

The simplest explanation is this: They don't like me, and I don't particularly like them. My whole life, I've had the uncomfortable feeling that I am in some way a black sheep in my family—as is, I should add, anyone who evinces signs of wanting to productively participate in society. Only in the O'Brien family would a young child's good grades in school, or her reading habits, or her eventual decision to enter law enforcement, be looked at with suspicion. I've never wanted for Thomas to experience the very lonely feeling of being an outsider in one's own tribe, or to be influenced in any way by the O'Briens—who, in addition to dabbling in petty criminality, have a tendency toward racism and other charming forms of prejudice as well; and so I made the decision, after he was born, not to inflict the O'Briens and their strange set of ethics upon him. My rule is not hard and fast—occasionally we see one of them on our annual or biannual visit to Gee's house, and occasionally we run into an O'Brien on the street or in a store, and on these occasions I have always been cordial—but largely, I avoid them.

Thomas doesn't, yet, understand why. Not wanting to frighten him, or to overwhelm him with information he cannot, at this age, process, I have told my son instead that our limited contact with my family is mainly a product of my work schedule. Lacking a better reason than this, he often asks after them, asks to see the ones he knows, asks to meet the rest. Once, when he was enrolled in his last school, all the children were given the assignment of constructing a family tree. When Thomas asked somewhat breathlessly for pictures of various members of ours, I was forced to confess that I had none; so instead he drew illustrations of what he imagined everybody looked like, sad smiley faces with mops of curly hair on top in a variety of colors. He has this diagram hanging, now, on the wall of his bedroom.

Sitting in my patrol car, I prepare to put aside my pride: to extend a hand to my extended family.

First, I generate a list of people to contact. This time, I do take out my notebook, and find a blank page at the very back, and rip it out. On this page, I write down the following names:

Gee (again)

Ashley (a cousin of ours, around our age, to whom we were very close when small)

Bobby (another cousin, less likable, who is himself mixed up in the business, and who used to deal to Kacey until I found him one day and threatened him with arrest, and more, if I ever caught him doing so again)

Next I move on to others:

Martha Lewis (at one time, Kacey's parole officer, though I believe she has since been assigned a new one)

Then a few bus acquaintances. Then some of our neighborhood friends. Then some of her grade school friends. Then some of her high school friends. Then some of Kacey's current friends, who may, for all I know, be enemies by now. One can never be certain.

Sitting in parked patrol car 2885, I go through everyone in turn.

I call Gee: no answer. No answering machine either. When we were younger, this was probably to avoid creditors. Now, it's out of habit, and probably a certain amount of misanthropy. People want to get ahold of me, says Gee, they can keep trying.

I call Ashley. I leave a message.

I call Bobby. I leave a message.

I call Martha Lewis. I leave a message.

Finally it occurs to me that almost nobody listens to voicemails anymore, and so I begin to text everyone instead.

Have you heard from Kacey lately? I type. *She's been missing awhile. If you have any information please let me know.*

I watch my phone. I wait.

Martha Lewis is the first to respond. *Hi Mick, sorry to hear that. That's a shame. Let me research a little.*

Then my cousin Ashley. *No, I'm sorry.*

A few old friends text that they haven't seen her lately. They wish me luck. Send me condolences.

The only person who doesn't text back at all is our cousin Bobby. I try him once more, and then I text Ashley again to make certain I have the right number.

That's the one, she replies.

Then, quite suddenly, an idea occurs to me. Today is Monday, November 20—which means that Thursday is Thanksgiving.

Every year since I was small, the O'Briens—Gee's side of the family—have come together for the occasion. When I was younger, Thanksgiving took place at the house of Aunt Lynn, Gee's younger sister. These days, Lynn's daughter Ashley typically hosts, but I haven't been in many years—since before Thomas was even born.

I've made the same excuse, over and over again, for missing the O'Brien Thanksgiving: that I have to work. What I don't tell anyone is that, even in years when I have had the option not to, I have elected to do so for extra pay.

This year is a rare one in which I happen to have Thanksgiving off. I had planned to spend it alone with Thomas. I was going to buy canned sweet potatoes and instant mashed potatoes and a rotisserie chicken. I was going to light a candle in the middle of the table and tell my son the true story of the first Thanksgiving, which I first learned from my favorite high school history teacher, Ms. Powell, and which is much different than the version that is typically taught in schools.

But it occurs to me, now, that attending an O'Brien family Thanksgiving might be a way to ask after Kacey—and, more specifically, to inquire about her with Cousin Bobby, who still has not responded to my texts.

I phone Gee once more. This time, she answers.

—Gee, I say. It's Mickey. Are you going to Ashley's for Thanksgiving?

—No, she says. Working.

—But she's hosting?

—According to Lynn, says Gee. Why?

—I was just wondering.

—Tell me you're thinking of going, she says, incredulously.

—Maybe, I say. I'm not sure yet.

Gee pauses.

—Well, she says. I'll be damned.

—I just have the day off for once, I say. That's all.

—Don't tell Ashley yet, I say. In case I can't make it.

Before I hang up, I ask her once more.

—No word from Kacey, right? I say.

—Goddammit, Mickey, says Gee. You know I don't talk to her no more. What's going on with you?

—Nothing at all, I say.

I spend the rest of the day fruitlessly scanning the sidewalks for anyone I might talk to. I check my phone compulsively. I manage to respond to only a handful of calls, cherry-picking ones I know will be easy.

That night, when I go home to Thomas, he seems worried about me. In fact, he asks me if something is wrong.

I want to tell him, everything is wrong except for you. These days, you are the only great pleasure of my life. Your small presence, your small observant face, the intelligence within you that grows unceasingly, each new word or turn of phrase that enters your vocabulary, that I take stock of, that I store like gold for your future. At least I have you.

I say none of this, of course. I say to him, Nothing's wrong. Why?

But I can tell by his expression that he doesn't believe me.

—Thomas, I say. How would you like to spend Thanksgiving at Cousin Ashley's?

Thomas leaps to his feet, his hands clutched to his chest, dramatically. His hands are boy hands, ragged cuticles, strong fingers, palms that smell always of the earth, even when he has not dug in it that day.

—I've been missing her so much, he says.

Against my will, I smile. I think the last time we saw Ashley was two years ago, at Gee's house, when she stopped by on Christmas; I doubt, therefore, that he actually remembers her. He knows about her because of the homemade family tree on his wall, which he traces sometimes with a finger, chanting every name. Cousin Ashley, he knows, is married to Cousin Ron, and is the mother of his other cousins, Jeremy, Chelsea, Patrick, and Dominic. Cousin Ashley's mother, he knows, is Aunt Lynn.

Now, Thomas raises his hands into the air in victory, and asks me how many days until we go.

I put him to bed. The weeks I'm home for his bedtimes, our routine never varies: bath, books, bed. We are frequenters of our local libraries—first in Port Richmond and now in Bensalem. Each librarian there knows Thomas by name. Each week we choose a stack of books to enjoy together, and every night I let Thomas select as many as he would like to read. Then, together, we sound out the words and describe the pictures, inventing scenarios, speculating about what will happen next.

The weeks I'm on B-shift, when Bethany puts Thomas to bed, I am under the impression that she does not read to him much, if at all.

Once he's tucked in, I linger in his dim and peaceful room, thinking how nice it would be to let myself lay my head next to his on the pillow, to drift to sleep there, just for a little.

But I have work to do, and so I rise, and kiss my son's forehead, and quietly close the door.

In the living room, I open my laptop—an ancient one of Simon's that he gave to me, years ago, when he bought a new one—and open an Internet browser.

I have always resisted 'social media.' I don't like being connected to anyone at all times, let alone relative strangers, people from my past with whom I have no reason to remain in touch. But I know that Kacey uses it—or at one time used it—frequently. So I enter *Facebook* into the search bar, and click on the link, and try to look for her there.

And there she is: *Kacey Marie.* The main picture on the page is of my sister holding a flower in her hand, smiling. Her hair looks the same as it did the most recent time I saw her on the street, so it must be at least somewhat up-to-date.

Below, on the page itself, I don't expect to find much. I can't imagine updating her Facebook page is at the top of Kacey's list of daily to-dos. But I am surprised to discover that her page is littered with posts. Many are pictures of cats and dogs. Some are pictures of babies. Strangers' babies, I presume. Some are vague rants about loyalty, or fakery, or betrayal, that look as if they have been created by others for the purpose of mass-marketing. (Reading them, I am made aware, again and again, of how little I know, today, about my sister.)

Some—the important ones—are by Kacey herself, and these are the ones I scroll through most avidly, looking for clues.

If at first you don't succeed . . . says one from last summer.

Anyone have a job for me??

I want to see Suicide Squad!

Rita's!!! (Here, a picture of Kacey, grinning, holding a water ice in a cup.)

I love love, says one from August. Attached to it is a picture of Kacey and a man, someone I don't recognize, someone skinny, white, short hair, tattoos on his forearms. He and Kacey are gazing into a mirror. He has his arms around Kacey.

He's tagged in the photo: *Connor Dock Famisall.* Beneath it, someone has written, *Lookin good Doctor.*

I squint at him. I click on his name. Unlike Kacey's, his page is marked private. I think about sending him a friend request, and then decide against it.

I enter *Connor Famisall* into Google, but there are zero results. I'll run a search on his name in the PCIC database tomorrow, when I'm back in a police vehicle.

Finally, I navigate back to Kacey's page.

The post at the top, on October 28, is by someone named Sheila McGuire.

Kace get in touch, it says.

There are no comments beneath it. In fact, the last time Kacey seems to have posted at all is a month ago, on October 2. *Doing something that scares me.*

I click on the *Message* button. And, for the first time in five years, I contact my sister.

Kacey, I write. *I'm worried about you. Where are you?*

The next morning, Bethany is early, for once. I've recently resorted to bribing Thomas to let me leave in the morning without a scene: stickers that, when a count of ten is reached, lead to a coloring book of his choosing. Today, therefore, I get to work early, and head to the locker room. I'm wiping my shoes with a paper towel when something on the little TV mounted in the corner catches my attention.

—A wave of violence in Kensington, says the anchor, solemn, and I straighten up a bit.

The media, it seems, has finally picked up the story. If these murders had been happening in Center City, we would have heard about the first one a month ago.

There's only one other officer in the room, a young woman who started not too long ago. Today, she's getting off C-shift. I don't remember her name.

—The bodies of four women have recently been discovered in separate incidents initially believed to be overdoses. But new information is causing police to question whether foul play might have been involved.

Four.

I only know about three: the woman we found on the Tracks, still unidentified; seventeen-year-old Katie Conway; and the eighteen-year-old home health aide, Anabel Castillo.

I sit down on one of the wooden benches that run between the lockers. I wait, closing my eyes, suddenly imagining my life divided sharply: before this moment and after it. It's how I've felt every time I've ever received bad news. Time slows in the breath people take after saying, *I have something to tell you.*

They give out the names, beginning with Katie Conway. Her mother is interviewed, distraught, a mess, almost certainly intoxicated. Her voice is too slow. She was a good girl, says the mother, about Katie. Always a good kid.

I'm waiting, breathless. It can't be Kacey, I think. It can't be: someone would have told me, surely. I don't talk about her at work, but we do share the same last name—Fitzpatrick, our father's—if nothing else. I check my cell phone. No calls have come in.

Next, the anchor moves on to Anabel Castillo, the home health aide, and then to the unidentified woman Eddie Lafferty and I located on the Tracks. No picture, of course, is available for her. But I can still see her clearly in my mind. I've been seeing her behind my eyelids every night before I fall asleep.

I know they will move next to a discussion of the fourth victim, the one I haven't heard about yet. Slowly, and then quickly, my vision dims.

—This morning, says the anchor, a fourth and possibly related victim was discovered in Kensington. She has been identified, say the police, but they're waiting to release her name until her family has been notified.

—Are you okay? says my companion in the locker room, and I nod, but it's not true.

When I was a child, I used to have episodes. A doctor once told me that they were 'panic attacks,' though that's a term I dislike. They consisted of minutes or hours in which I thought I was dying, in which I counted every heartbeat, certain that it would be my very last. I haven't had one of these episodes in years, not since high school, but suddenly, in the locker room, I recognize the signs of one approaching. The world darkens at the edges. I feel as if I can't see, as if the information my eyes are receiving no longer makes sense to my mind. I try to slow my breathing.

Sergeant Ahearn, ruddy and impassive, is standing over me. Alongside him is the young female officer. She's got blond hair and a slight build. She's pouring water on my forehead in a slow trickle.

—My mom told me to do this once, the rookie is saying to Sergeant Ahearn.

—She's an EMT, she adds, for emphasis.

A deep sense of shame comes over me. I feel as if a secret about me has been revealed. I wipe the water off my forehead. I try too quickly to sit up, to laugh, to make light of what has happened. But I catch a glimpse of myself in the mirror, and my face is gray and grim and frightening. I feel light-headed again.

Sergeant Ahearn, despite my protests that I am fine, insists I take a sick day. We're in his office. I'm sitting in a chair across from him, trying to will myself to feel better.

—Can't have you fainting on the job, he says. Go home and rest.

Fainting. An embarrassing word—one Ahearn seems to relish saying aloud to me. Is he hiding a smile? I imagine him retelling the episode at roll call, and shudder.

Then I pull myself together and rise from my chair. Before I leave, though, I gather my wits and my courage and ask him.

—I heard they found another body in the district, I say.

He looks at me. Only one? he says. Lucky us.

—Not an OD, I say. A woman. Another strangulation.

He says nothing.

—The news picked it up, I say.

He nods.

—Do we have a description? I ask him.

He sighs. Why, Mickey? he says.

—It's only that I was wondering if I knew her. If I'd ever brought her in, I mean.

He picks up his phone. He looks something up. He reads aloud to me.

—Christina Walker, according to her ID. African-American, twenty years old, five-foot-four, one-fifty.

Not Kacey.

Someone else's Kacey.

—Thank you, I say to Ahearn.

Through his window, I regard for a while several oak trees that have almost fully shed their leaves for the season. I recall learning, in a course I took in high school, that the majority of Pennsylvania is covered by Appalachian oak forest, which seemed to me to be strange at the time, *Appalachian* being a word I associate with the south, and *Pennsylvania* with the north.

—Mickey, says Ahearn, and it's only then that I realize I have been standing still too long.

—You sure you haven't talked to Truman lately? he says.

I don't answer right away.

Then I say, Why?

He smiles again, not kindly.

—In the locker room, he says. You were calling his name.

Truman Dawes.

Outside, I pull up his number. I look at my phone for a while, contemplating the name, imagining how many times, in the past decade, I have said it aloud.

Truman Dawes. My most important mentor. Some years, my only friend. Truman, whom I worked alongside for the better part of a decade. Truman, who taught me all that I know about policing: who taught me that respect for a community begets respect; who frowned whenever anyone maligned or insulted his district; who was quick with a word of consolation or a joke when the occasion called for it, even in the middle of an arrest—Truman, whom I miss every day. There is no one whose counsel, at this moment, I need more.

The truth is that I've been avoiding him.

I've had a certain bad habit ever since I was a child. I duck what I can't bring myself to acknowledge, turn away from anything that causes me to be ashamed, run away from it rather than addressing it. I am a coward, in this way.

In high school, I had a favorite teacher—a history teacher—Ms. Powell. She was not old, though she seemed so to me at the time. With other students, she was not popular. She did not earn anyone's admiration easily or cheaply, like some teachers—I am thinking here of mainly young, white, male teachers who played sports themselves in high school and who joked around with their students as if they were their peers—no. Ms. Powell was different. She was perhaps thirty-five, African-American, the mother of two young children. She wore jeans every day, and she wore glasses, and she generally did not try to be funny, which meant that the students she attracted were more serious, and these students she addressed with real gravity, and for them—for us—she had real ambition. I recall that she gave us her own phone number, her home number, and instructed us to telephone her anytime for extra help. Though I only took her up on this offer one time, I liked knowing that I had the option, that I had a way to reach at least one responsible adult outside of school hours. It soothed me.

Ms. Powell was supposed to teach us two years of AP U.S. History, with an emphasis on the history of Pennsylvania, but she taught a great deal more than that to students who paid attention. In her class I learned the fundamentals of philosophy and debate, and some interesting information about both geology and dendrology—the oak tree being a particular favorite of hers, and now mine, and now Thomas's—and I also listened to Ms. Powell describe, off script, the imbalances of power in this country that have resulted in institutionalized forms of prejudice—though when she approached this territory, she was delicate, aware always of the groups of Polish and Irish and Italian boys and girls in the back of the classroom who, with a complaint to their parents, could make her life and work more difficult.

So dedicated was I to Ms. Powell and her teaching that there was a time, in fact, when I believed I wanted to follow in her footsteps and become a high school history teacher myself. Even today I wonder about this other life. Thomas has begun to ask questions about how various things got to be the way they are, and I find myself racking my brain, trying to remember what Ms. Powell taught me all those years ago—or, when I can't, researching Thomas's questions on my own, and then presenting him with the answers in a way that I hope is engaging. Just as Ms. Powell herself was.

The point of all of this is to say that I was so fond of Ms. Powell and of the material she taught me, so admiring of her, that when I ran into her in a supermarket several years ago, in uniform, I froze.

It had been a very long while since I had seen her. The last she had heard of me, I was applying to colleges.

She was holding a box of cereal over a full shopping cart. Her hair had new gray in it.

She opened her mouth. Took in my attire. (I remembered, in an instant, a special lecture she had devoted to the L.A. riots, and the expression that she wore when explaining their cause.) She hesitated. Then I saw her eyes shift to my name tag, *M. Fitzpatrick*, which seemed to confirm the truth for her.

—Michaela? she said, tentatively. Is that you?

Time slowed.

After a pause, I replied, No.

Like I said: a coward. Unwilling to explain myself, to stand by my own decisions. I had never before been ashamed of being an officer. In that moment, for reasons I find difficult to explain, I was.

Ms. Powell hesitated for a moment, as if deciding what to do. Then she said, My mistake.

But in her voice I heard her disbelief.

In the parking lot, now, remembering that small undignified moment, that small failure of character on my part, I summon my courage, lift my phone once more, and dial Truman.

The phone rings five times before he answers.

—Dawes, he says.

I find, suddenly, that I don't know how to begin.

—Mick? he says, after a pause.

—Yes.

I have a lump in my throat, and it embarrasses me. I haven't cried in years, and certainly not in front of Truman. I open my mouth and a sort of horrible clicking sound comes out. I clear my throat. The feeling passes.

—What's going on? says Truman.

—Are you busy? I ask.

—No, he says.

—Can I come see you?

—Of course, he says.

He gives me his new address.

I drive toward him.

Here's how it happened. The attack. It came from nowhere and seemed to be unmotivated, unless the motivation was simply the fact of our uniforms and our work. Seconds before, Truman and I had been facing one another, standing outside of our assigned vehicle, on the sidewalk. In the background, behind Truman, I saw someone approaching. A young man. He was wearing a light jacket that, zipped all the way up, partially obscured his face, and a baseball cap that was pulled down over his brow. It was a chilly day in April, and his attire made sense to me, didn't cause me any alarm. He was wearing athletic pants, and he had a baseball bat casually slung over one shoulder, as if he was walking home from practice.

I barely glanced at him. I was laughing at something Truman was saying, and Truman was laughing too.

Unswervingly, almost gracefully, the young man swung his metal bat around as he passed Truman, cracking him vigorously across his right kneecap. Truman fell to the ground. Just as quickly, the young man stomped once on the same knee, and then took off at a run.

I believe I shouted, *Hey*, or *Stop*, or *Don't move.*

But my overwhelming sensation was one of being, myself, frozen: my partner was on the ground, writhing in pain, and suddenly my instincts failed me in a way they hadn't since I was a rookie. I hated seeing him that way: out of control, in agony. He was always in control.

I took one or two faltering steps—first in pursuit of the perpetrator, and then back to Truman, not wanting to leave him unattended.

—*Go*, Mickey, said Truman, through gritted teeth, and at last I sprinted in the direction of the vanishing man.

He rounded a corner. I followed.

I was met, on the other side, with the barrel of a small pistol—a pocket pistol, a Beretta with a wooden grip—and, beyond them, the gaze of the young man who'd attacked Truman. His face was now fully obscured but for his eyes, which were blue.

—Back the fuck up, said the young man, quietly.

Without hesitation, I complied. I took several steps backward, and then ducked back around the side of the building, breathing hard now.

I looked to my right: Truman on the ground.

I peered around the building: the perpetrator was gone.

I played no part in the young man's arrest. For an agonizing month, he was on the loose. During that time, Truman underwent the first and second of the several surgeries he has had while on medical leave. When the perpetrator was, eventually, apprehended, it was not due to any usefulness on my part, but rather to the discovery of video footage from a storefront a few blocks away that revealed the face of a known offender.

I was glad to know he was off the street—for a long time, too.

But I took little further comfort in his arrest, because it did nothing to assuage my guilt, my sense of shame. My conviction that, in not acting quickly enough—in retreating, when commanded to by the man in question—I had failed my partner.

I visited Truman only once, in the hospital. I kept my head down. I kept my condolences brief.

I couldn't look him in the eye.

Truman's new house is in Mount Airy. I've never been. I make several wrong turns along the way, which adds to my nerves.

I didn't go frequently to his last place, in East Falls—with few exceptions, my relationship with Truman took place at work—but I knew it, at least; I dropped him off and picked him up there, over the years, and once or twice attended gatherings there. His daughters' high school graduation parties; his wife's birthday. That sort of thing. But two years ago, he announced, with forced casualness, that he was getting a divorce from Sheila, after more than two decades of marriage, and that he would be moving out. The girls were in college now, he said, and there was no point pretending any longer that he and Sheila had anything in common. If I had pressed him, I believe he would have acknowledged that the divorce was her idea, not his—a particular sadness, an unusual flatness to his affect, convinced me of this, along with the many years he had spent before that lighting up whenever he spoke of her—but I did not ever press Truman for personal details he didn't volunteer, and he returned the favor to me. (This was, I believe, one of the main reasons that we always got along so well.)

Mount Airy represents a section of the city I'm not familiar with. When I was growing up, the Northwest might as well have been in a different state from the Northeast. The Northwest does have its own problems, a few high-crime pockets, but it also contains within its borders great stone mansions with long stone walls and rolling lawns, the sorts of homes Philadelphia was known for back when a mention of the city's name conjured Katharine Hepburn rather than crime statistics. Most of what I know about the history of the Northwest Ms. Powell taught me: it began as a settlement for twenty German settler families and was called, appropriately, Germantown.

At last, I find Truman's street. I turn onto it.

From the outside, the house looks charming: detached from its neighbors, just barely, a tiny stretch of grass on either side. It's narrow across the front but appears to be deep, with a short front lawn that slopes steeply down to the sidewalk, a front porch with a swing on it, and a driveway running up the side. Truman's car is parked there. There would be enough room for my car, too, but I hesitate and then park on the street.

Truman opens the door while I'm still walking up the front steps. He ran cross-country in college and ran marathons after that. His father, he has told me, was an internationally competitive track star in Jamaica before emigrating to the United States, hanging up his cleats, earning his master's in education, and then, sadly, dying too young. Before he did, though, he passed on what he knew about speed and endurance to Truman, and in Truman one can still see the vestiges of his own athletic career: he's tall and thin and ropy. He's always walked on his toes, as if ready to spring. On the many occasions I saw him take off after some perpetrator, I almost felt bad for the runner. Truman had them on the ground before they took five steps. Today he's wearing a brace on his right leg, outside his jeans. I wonder if he'll ever run again.

He doesn't greet me with anything aside from a nod.

It's calm inside the house, pale walls, neat to the point of absurdity. His last place was neat, too, but still contained within it the trappings of family life—shin guards in the foyer, scribbled notes on a bulletin board. Here, an old radiator coated in thick white paint occupies a space near an interior wall. One lamp lights up a corner of the room, which is otherwise dim. The house is shady, the front of it overhung by the ceiling of the porch, the sides devoid of windows. As if he, too, has suddenly noticed this, Truman walks to a corner and turns on the switch to an overhead light. There are built-in bookshelves everywhere, which is perfect for Truman. A major topic of conversation between us was always what we were reading. Truman, unlike me, was raised in a functional and affectionate home; but he was a shy only child, and a speech impediment that he's since outgrown made it difficult for him to speak up without getting teased. Books, therefore, were great friends to him. Today, one is open on the coffee table in the living room: *The Art of War.* Sun Tzu. A year ago I might have teased him lightly about this, asked him whom he was planning on fighting. Now the silence between us feels syrupy, tangible.

—How have you been? I ask him.

—Pretty good, he says.

He makes no move to take a seat, nor does he offer me one.

I'm still wearing the uniform I put on earlier, in the locker room, and I wish, now, that I hadn't left my duty belt in the car. Without it, my hands don't know what to do. I scratch my forehead.

—How's the knee? I ask.

—Okay, he says. He looks down at it. Straightens it.

I gesture weakly around at the room, the house.

—I like it, I say.

—Thanks.

—What are you doing these days? I ask him.

—This and that, he says. I've got my garden going in the back. I read. I do the Co-op now.

I don't know what this is. I don't ask.

—It's a cooperative grocery store, says Truman, reading my mind. It's one of the things he used to rib me about: my reluctance, at times, to admit to deficits in my body of knowledge.

—The girls are good? I say. There's a small family portrait standing upright on an end table, something taken when his daughters were young.

I notice that the portrait includes his ex-wife, Sheila. Something about this embarrasses me. It feels undignified. He's been lonely, perhaps. Missing her. I don't like thinking about it.

—They are, says Truman, and I don't know what to say after that.

—Tea? Truman asks, finally.

I follow him into the kitchen: newer than the rest of the house, something he's had redone. Perhaps, I imagine, something he redid himself. He's always been handy. Regularly, he teaches himself to do new things. Just prior to his injury, he bought and restored an old Nikon camera.

I stand and watch the back of him as he works, taking a small empty tea bag from a box, portioning loose tea leaves into it.

Without his gaze directly on me, I find it easier to think.

I clear my throat.

—What's up, Mickey, says Truman, not turning.

—I owe you an apology, I say. The words are too loud for the room. Too formal. I often misjudge these things.

Truman pauses, just for a moment, and then continues, pouring steaming water into a teapot.

—For what? he says.

—I should have had him, I say.

—I didn't act fast enough, I say. I flinched.

But Truman is shaking his head.

—No, Mickey, he says.

—No?

—Wrong apology, he says. He turns around, facing me. I can barely meet his gaze.

I wait.

—He got away, says Truman. It happens. It's happened to me more times than I can count.

He looks at me, then at the steeping tea.

—You should have come around sooner, he says. There. That's your apology.

—But I backed down, I say.

—I'm glad you did, says Truman. No point getting shot. I survived.

I'm silent for a moment.

—I should have come around sooner, I say.

—I'm sorry, I say.

Truman nods. The air in the room changes. Truman pours the tea.

—Are you coming back? I say.

The question sounds needy.

Truman is fifty-two years old. He looks about forty. He has the kind of unharried, calm demeanor that has somehow crystallized his youthfulness, preserved it. I only found out his age a couple of years ago, at a fiftieth-birthday party that some officers threw him. Because of his age, if he wanted to retire now, he could. Already, he'd get a pension.

But he only shrugs.

—Maybe I will, he says. Maybe I won't. I've got some things to think over. The world is weird.

He turns around, finally, and looks hard at me for a while.

—I know you didn't come just to apologize, he says.

I don't protest. I look down.

—Why else are you here? he asks me.

When I have finished speaking, Truman walks to the door off the kitchen. He looks out at his garden, asleep for the winter.

—How long has it been since anyone's heard from her? he asks.

—Paula Mulroney said it's been a month. But I'm not sure whether she has a particularly good handle on time.

—Okay, says Truman. He has a look on his face I've seen before: the one that used to come over him before he sprang into action, pounding after a runner. A coiled look.

—Do you know anything else at this point? he asks.

—I know she was last active on Facebook on October 2, I tell him. Also, she might be dating a person named Dock. D-O-C-K. I saw someone on her Facebook page with that name.

Truman looks skeptical. Dock, he says.

—I know, I say. Know anyone with that nickname in Kensington?

Truman thinks. Then shakes his head.

—What about Connor Famisall? I say. I think that's his actual name.

—How do you spell that? asks Truman. And I hear something silly entering his voice. A smile.

I spell it for him, reluctantly. I dislike being on the outside of others' jokes. A leftover from my childhood.

—Mick, Truman says. Did you get that off Facebook?

I nod.

Truman is laughing now. Fam is all, Mickey, he says. Fam is all.

Something about the way he says it—kind smile, kind eyes—loosens what's tight in my sternum. As if a knob were being turned there, just so. And suddenly I am laughing too.

—All right, Truman, I say. All right, you're smarter than I am, I get it.

Then Truman turns serious.

—Have you reported her missing yet? says Truman.

—No, I say.

—Why not?

I hesitate. The truth is, I'm embarrassed. I don't want everyone knowing my business.

—They'll take a look at her record and put it on the bottom of the stack, I say.

—Make the report, Mick, he says. You want me to tell Mike DiPaolo?

DiPaolo is a friend of his in the East Detectives, someone he grew up with in Juniata. Unlike me, Truman has friends in the department, allies. It's always been Truman who pulls me into things, shows me how to get what I need.

But I shake my head.

—Then tell Ahearn, says Truman.

I frown. The thought of telling Sergeant Ahearn anything about my personal life makes me stubborn. Especially after my episode from earlier. The last thing I want is for him to imagine, falsely, that I'm having some sort of breakdown.

—Truman, I say. If I can't find her, who can?

And it's true: patrol officers are the eyes. More than detectives, certainly more than sergeants or corporals or lieutenants. On the streets of Kensington, patrol officers are the ones families ask to find their missing children. We're the ones children ask to find their missing mothers.

Truman shrugs. I know, Mick, he says. But just tell him. Can't hurt.

—Fine, I say.

I might be lying. I'm not sure.

—You're lying, says Truman.

I smile.

Truman looks at the floor.

—I've got someone I think I can ask about this Dock character, he says.

—Who? I say.

—Never mind. Let me make sure I'm right. It's a place we can start, anyway, says Truman.

—We? I say.

—I've got time at the moment, he says, gazing down at his brace.

But I know he has another reason, too.

Like me, Truman loves a good case.

try to follow Truman's advice. I do.

Ahearn doesn't like to be bothered before roll call, but I get to work early the next morning and tap softly on his doorframe anyway.

He looks up, annoyed at first. His face changes just slightly when he sees me. He actually smiles.

—Officer Fitzpatrick, he says. How you feeling?

—Great, I say. All better. I'm not sure what happened yesterday. I think I was dehydrated.

—What'd you do, go out partying the night before?

—Something like that, I say. I want to add, *Just me and my four-year-old.* But it wouldn't surprise me if Sergeant Ahearn has forgotten I even have a son.

—You scared me, he says. That ever happen to you before?

—Never, I say, lying only slightly.

—Okay, he says. He looks down at his paperwork. Then looks up again. Anything else? he says.

—I was wondering if I could speak with you briefly, I say.

—Real quick, he says. Roll call in five. I still have to put out a dozen fires.

—All right, I say. The thing is.

Suddenly I am tongue-tied. I have never known how to tell the story of Kacey—let alone quickly.

—You know what? I'll just send you an e-mail, I say.

Sergeant Ahearn looks at me impassively. Whatever you like, he says. Relieved.

Walking out of his office, I know I never will.

All morning, I'm agitated. My brain keeps sending signals to my body: *Something's wrong. Something's wrong. Something's wrong.* Subconsciously, I am expecting Dispatch to come through with a call about another body. And on some level, I am expecting that body to be Kacey. It is difficult, in fact, *not* to picture Kacey dead, when I think of her: I've seen her close to death so many times.

I jump, therefore, every time a crackle comes over the radio. I turn it down slightly.

The good news: it's freezing outside today, and that means less activity. I stop and get a coffee from Alonzo at the corner store. I scan the *Inquirer* on a stand, procrastinating, but I see no sign of either Kacey or Paula.

For some reason, Alonzo has the music off, and for a moment I let myself be lulled by the calm interior of the store: the buzzing of a fluorescent light, the hum of refrigerators, the yowling of Romero the cat.

It's so quiet in here that when my cell phone rings, I jump.

I look at the caller ID before answering. It's Truman.

—You working? he asks me.

—Yes.

—Listen, he says. I'm at K and A. I'm with someone who says he knows Dock.

I tell him I'll be there in ten, and pray nothing comes through over Dispatch.

When I arrive at Kensington and Allegheny, Truman is standing on the sidewalk with a coffee, looking very casual. For just a moment, I watch him. The women who pass him stop to speak to him—making him an offer, no doubt. Truman is a handsome man, and I know that people often tease him about being well liked by women—a subject he assiduously avoids speaking about—but his looks have never concerned me. I have always seen him mainly as my respected teacher. And I have always been very careful to avoid any suggestion that Truman and I were anything more than work partners. Still, anytime a male and female officer are partnered, it is inevitable that one or two sophomoric rumors will be spread about them, and I regret to say that it has been no different for the two of us, despite the fact that, for years, Truman was married. In fact, on at least one occasion, I have overheard a joke made at our expense. But largely, I believe that our professionalism has put to rest any ridiculous notions about what I will term 'extracurricular activities.'

I exit my vehicle and approach him. He holds up a hand in greeting. Then, wordlessly, he tilts his head toward a doorway a few storefronts down, and I follow him.

There is no sign out front. It's a sort of a catchall shop: everything from kitchenware to dolls to rolls of wallpaper in its front window. A little dusty placard rests askew in front of these objects. *Supplies,* it says, as if that explains everything. I must have passed it thousands of times, but somehow I've never noticed it.

Inside the store, it's warm. I stamp my feet on a dingy mat, ridding my shoes of the wet that has accumulated on them. The shelves in this store are so crowded with merchandise that the aisles are barely visible. At the front, behind a counter, an old man in a winter hat is reading a book. He doesn't look up.

—Here she is, says Truman.

The old man slowly puts down his book. His eyes are wet and ancient. His hands shake slightly. He says nothing.

—Kacey's sister, says Truman. Mickey.

The old man looks at me for a while, until I realize that it's my uniform he's staring at.

—I don't talk to the police, says the old man. He could be ninety. His voice has the faintest trace of an accent: Jamaican, maybe. Truman's father was Jamaican. I squint at Truman.

—Ah, come on, Mr. Wright, says Truman, cajoling. Now, you know I'm a police officer too.

Mr. Wright gazes at Truman. But you're different, he says, at last, to Truman.

—Mr. Wright knows this guy Dock, Truman says to me. He knows everyone in the neighborhood.

—Isn't that right, Mr. Wright? says Truman, louder. The old man doesn't look persuaded.

I walk toward him and he sits up, defensive. I very much dislike this part: the discomfort on people's faces as I approach.

—Mr. Wright, I say, I wish I could have changed before I met you. I'm asking you for a personal favor, something that has nothing to do with my work. Do you know where I can find this person? Dock?

Mr. Wright considers this for a moment.

—Please, I say. Any information would be helpful.

—You don't want to find him, says Mr. Wright. He's not a good person.

A shiver runs down me. I don't like the sound of that, but it doesn't surprise me. Kacey has never exactly picked choirboys to date.

My radio crackles suddenly and Mr. Wright tenses. I turn it down completely, praying that a priority call doesn't come over the air.

—Mr. Wright, I'm looking for my sister, I say. The most recent information I have is that she was dating this person. So, unfortunately, I do want to find him.

—All right, he says. All right. He glances left and then right, as if to make sure no one is eavesdropping. Then he leans forward. Come back around two-thirty, he says. He's usually in the back around then. Comes in to get warm.

—In the back? I say. But Truman is already thanking Mr. Wright and dragging me out.

—And don't wear your uniform, says Mr. Wright.

Truman walks me to the cruiser.

—Who on earth, I begin, but Truman shushes me until we're inside.

—Drive, he says, and I pull away.

—He's my father's cousin, says Truman, after a beat.

I look at him, skeptical.

—He is?

—Yeah, says Truman.

—Your father's cousin, good old Mr. Wright?

Truman laughs. We're formal, he says.

—I never knew you had a cousin who runs a store on the Ave.

Truman shrugs. The implication is clear: *There's a lot you don't know about me.*

We drive for a little longer. It begins to snow, and I turn the wipers on.

—What's in the back of the store? I say finally, and Truman exhales.

—Between us? he says.

—Between us.

—He lets people shoot up back there.

I nod. There are certainly places like that in Kensington. I know about most of them. The only reason I don't know about this one, most likely, is that Truman has been protecting it.

—He's a good person, says Truman. He really is. He lost two sons to it. Now he keeps Narcan and clean needles behind the counter. He's got a camera up front that shows him what's going on. He's always hobbling into the back there and rescuing some poor fool or other. Does it for free. No one pays him.

It's an improvised safe injection site. They're not legal in Philly yet, though there's talk that they will be soon. I wonder if Kacey herself has been to Mr. Wright's.

Jarringly, a call comes through: two officers are needed for a simple domestic assault.

I answer.

—Would you like to ride along? I say, when I've finished, but Truman shakes his head.

—I'm on disability, remember? he says. Officially laid up. Can't have anyone seeing me around here.

—What will you do now?

Truman points to a building ahead of us. I'll jump out there by the library, he says. My car's nearby. Call me, okay? Let me know how it goes.

I pause.

—You don't want to come with me? To Mr. Wright's store? I say.

I suppose, on some level, I'd been relying on the idea that he would.

Truman shakes his head. Better not, he says.

He must notice the look of disappointment on my face, because he says, Mickey. You might need me to do something for you down the line. And you might not want this guy to recognize me.

A fair point. I nod, and drop him at the library, as requested.

I watch him walk away. And I think of all the things I've missed about him, in his absence: his generous laugh, low and contagious, ending sometimes in an *s*; and his steady presence when responding to calls, which steadied me in turn; and his love for his children, his pride in them, and the way he advised me on parenting concerns I had; and his concern for Thomas, for whom he brought, from time to time, thoughtful gifts, mainly books; and his privacy, and discretion, and his respect for my own in turn; and his elevated—snobbish, I told him—taste in food and drink, the wild things he bought from health food stores, kombucha, kefir, arame, goji berries; and the way he gently ribbed me about my own poor eating habits, and my stubbornness, and the way he called me 'difficult' and 'strange'—two labels I wouldn't appreciate hearing from anyone else. But from Truman I sensed an appreciation of these qualities in me; I felt understood by him in a way that, if I am being truthful, I hadn't felt since Kacey and I were allies, in our youth.

I still can't get used to seeing Truman out of uniform. In his hesitating walk now, the way he scans the Avenue to his right and left, I can suddenly see the shy child he once described to me when talking about his past. I was silent until I was about twenty years old, he said to me once.

And I said, So was I.

The other officer, Gloria Peters, has already arrived when I get to the house where the domestic assault has been reported. For the moment, things are calm. I let Gloria talk to the complainant outside while I go inside and stand in the kitchen with the perpetrator, a drunk-looking man, white, in his thirties. He glares at me.

—Would you like to tell me what happened here, sir? I ask him.

I am always very polite to the people I interview, even the worst of them. Truman modeled this behavior for me, and I have found that it works well.

But I can tell by looking at him, by the smirk on his face, that this gentleman will be intractable.

—Nope, he says.

He's shirtless. His arms are folded over his middle. He, too, is probably addicted to one substance or another, though his drunkenness is making it difficult to sort out what kind of cocktail he's on.

—You don't want to make a statement? I say, but he just laughs lowly. He knows the system. Knows he shouldn't talk.

He tries to put his hand down on the kitchen counter, wet from some earlier incident, but it slips, sending him off balance. He staggers a little, recovers.

Are there kids? I wonder. I listen. I hear the slightest sounds of movement upstairs.

—Do you have any children? I say, but he's silent.

There are not many people who alarm me, not after this many years on the job. But there is something about this person I don't like. I avoid eye contact with him, the way I might with an aggressive dog. I don't want him to feel cornered. I eye the drawers in the kitchen, wondering which of them contains knives that might be used as weapons. He's drunk enough so that if he lunged, I could probably sidestep him, maybe even knock him down.

It occurs to me, suddenly, that he looks familiar. I narrow my eyes at him, trying to remember.

—Do I know you? I ask him.

—I don't know, he says. Do you?

An odd response.

It could just be that I've seen him around the neighborhood; that happens frequently. In fact, the majority of faces I see on a given shift look familiar to me.

Gloria Peters comes back into the room, eventually, and shakes her head at me subtly. The complainant, it seems, has changed her mind, and no longer wants her husband arrested.

—Stay there, I say to him.

I've already scouted the house: there's no back door, so he'll have to walk past us if he tries to escape. We go into the little living room and speak quietly.

—Anything on her face? I ask, and Gloria says, I think so. Looks red. Too early to tell. I think she'll have some nasty bruises tomorrow, though.

—We could take him down anyway, I say.

But without physical evidence, and without a statement from the victim, there's only so much we can do.

In the end, a child tiptoes quietly down the stairs and then, seeing us, scurries away again. He's not much older than Thomas. This is enough for us: we'll book him. I volunteer to do it; Officer Peters can stay behind that way, make sure the child or children are taken care of, maybe get someone from Social Services to come out and conduct an interview.

As the husband gets into my vehicle, he never shifts his gaze. He looks up at me directly, a terrible blank stare that gives me the shivers.

All the way to the station, he's silent. I'm used to this: usually it's only the newcomers who talk, or rant, or cry, or bemoan the injustice of what is happening to them. Veterans of the criminal justice system know enough to shut up. What's different about this one is the feeling of being watched, of eyes on the back of my head.

Against my will, I glance at him, once, in the rearview mirror, trying again to figure out how I know him. And I see that he's smiling at me. Goose bumps light up my arms and neck.

I have to wait with him in a holding cell until he's processed. I look at my phone and don't speak to him. The whole time, he never averts his gaze.

Finally, as he's led from the cell, he speaks.

—You know, he says, I think I do know you.

—Do you, I say.

—Yes, he says. I think I do.

The officer leading him looks at me questioningly, wondering if he should yank this idiot down the hall and away from me.

—Give me a hint, I say. I try to include in my voice a certain sardonic inflection, but I am afraid it comes out quite differently.

The man smiles again. His name is Robert Mulvey, Jr. Earlier, he had refused to produce an ID. Officer Peters learned his name from his wife.

For a long while, he says nothing.

Then he says, I don't feel like it.

Before he's finished speaking, the officer at his elbow jerks him violently away.

A good officer never allows her emotions to rule. She should strive to be as impartial as a judge, as withholding as a priest. I am disappointed, therefore, when I find it hard to shake the sense of unease that settles onto me after my encounter with Robert Mulvey, Jr. I picture his face, his very light eyes, his smile, for the rest of my shift, which is busier than I thought it would be when I saw the weather forecast.

Normally, when it's this cold outside, people stay home.

After escorting Mulvey to the station, I respond to a call about a hit-and-run on Spring Garden, and there I find a wounded cyclist on the ground, a small crowd gathered around him.

The day goes on like this. An hour before I'm due to be back at Mr. Wright's, I intentionally slow my response to calls.

At 2:15, I park on the street near Alonzo's, a few blocks from Mr. Wright's store.

Don't wear your uniform: Mr. Wright's only instructions to me. But this is easier said than done. I can't exactly go back to the station and change into my civilian attire in the middle of a shift.

I decide, instead, to buy something to wear in the dollar store down the block.

Before I get out of the car, I contemplate my radio and my weapon. If I bring them, what's the point of changing into civilian clothes? If I leave the radio in the car, I'll risk missing something important, a priority call, which could get me in serious trouble. I have never, in all my years on the force, been separated from my radio during a shift.

In the end, I decide to leave it. For no particularly logical reason, I put it in the trunk. It just feels safer there, out of sight.

I scan the racks in the dollar store for anything at all to buy. One aisle has giant black T-shirts hanging next to men's black sweatpants. I'll be swimming in them, but I buy them anyway, and walk down the block toward Alonzo's, and ask to use the bathroom.

—No problem, he says, as always. When I emerge from it, dressed in my dollar-store purchases, my uniform now in the bag they came in, he looks at me twice.

—Alonzo, I say, I'm so sorry to trouble you, but I was wondering if I could ask you for a favor. Is there any chance I could leave this bag here briefly?

—No problem, he says again.

I hesitate, and then leave a ten-dollar bill on the counter for him.

He tries to push it back to me, but I don't pick it up.

—A tip, I say.

It's eighteen degrees out. In any other neighborhood I would look ridiculous running the several blocks to Mr. Wright's store in a T-shirt. Here, no one blinks.

When I arrive at Mr. Wright's at 2:40, I open the door, grateful for the warmth inside. A little bell rings. No one seems to be there.

I stand there silently for a while, until I hear the soft closing of a door from the rear of the store.

Mr. Wright eventually emerges from an aisle, ducking around a stack of hula-hoops to do so.

He looks at me but says nothing, and for a moment I wonder whether he even recognizes me, whether he remembers me from this morning.

He takes his time returning to his place behind the register, lowers himself painfully onto a high stool.

Finally, he speaks. Not here yet, is what he says.

—Dock isn't? I say.

He says, Now who do you *think* I'm talking about?

—All right, I say. I'm not certain, now, how to proceed.

I look at my watch. It's 2:50 now. I'm risking my job, I believe, to be here, out of uniform, apart from my radio. I wonder if I can blame it on a malfunction if it comes to that.

—May I ask you something? I say to Mr. Wright.

—You can ask me anything you want to, says Mr. Wright. I might not answer.

But for the first time there is a twinkle in his eye.

—Does this person come in every day? How certain are you that—

The door opens then, and Mr. Wright raises his eyebrows and tilts his chin, very subtly, toward the man who comes through it.

I turn.

The man is my height, maybe, and skinny. I recognize him from the picture I saw on Facebook. He wears a bright orange jacket, zipped tight, and jeans. His hair is chin length now, and so unwashed that it's difficult to ascertain its natural color. Light brown, most likely. He's very handsome. Heroin does a lot of things to a body, but one thing it can do is streamline it, knock off weight, make the features stand out sharply in the absence of flesh. Bright eyes, wet eyes, a rush of blood to the face that alters its color.

The man says nothing, but eyes me sideways as he walks over to Mr. Wright at the counter.

Then he turns around.

—Were you waiting, he says. He doesn't know me. He wants me to leave the store before making the arrangement he's here to make.

I wait to see if Mr. Wright will introduce us, but he stays out of it.

—No, I wasn't waiting, I say. And then, Any chance your name is Dock?

—No, says the man.

—No? I say again.

I'm usually better at this.

—Nope.

The man stares at me. He crosses his arms around his middle. Taps his toe a few times on the ground, making it clear that he's waiting.

—Okay, I say. It's just that you look like him in a picture I saw once.

Dock shifts. What picture? he says.

He glances every so often at Mr. Wright. At the moment, I am the one standing between him and the key that will grant him a fix. Clearly, he needs one badly. He begins to shift his weight from foot to foot.

I try a different tactic. Listen, I say. I'm looking for Kacey Fitzpatrick.

Dock pauses, finally, and puts his hand on the counter.

—Ohhhhh, he says, softly. Oh. You her sister?

I have a sudden memory of all the times I fished Kacey out of houses she shouldn't have been in, when we were younger. All the men who eyed me while asking that question. And I ask myself if the decision I have made, to do it all over again, is correct.

—I am, I say.

There's no hiding it. Despite other physical differences, Kacey and I have nearly the same face. When we were younger, people used to comment on it frequently.

—Mickey? says Dock.

—Yeah.

Mr. Wright keeps his eyes down.

—She always talked about you, he says, and my body flashes cold for a moment. *Talked* sounds like someone who's dead.

—Do you know where she is? I ask him abruptly.

He shakes his head. Nah, he says. She left me a couple months ago. Haven't heard from her since.

—So you were—I say.

He looks at me like I'm an idiot.

—You were together? I ask.

—Yeah, he says. Then: I have some business to attend to here. Let me know if you hear anything from Kacey.

—Can I have your number? I ask him.

—Sure, he says. And he gives it to me.

To make sure he gave me the right one, I call him right away. From inside his pocket comes his cell phone ring: the sound of a song I vaguely recognize, something popular when I was a child. I didn't know the name of it then, and I don't now.

—All right, I say. Thanks.

On my way out, Dock says, Hey.

—You're a cop, right? he says to me.

I hesitate. Yes, I say.

He says nothing. Mr. Wright says nothing.

—Anything else? I ask.

—Nah, says Dock.

He keeps his eyes on me until I leave the store.

So, says Truman, on the other end of the phone.

—So, I say.

I'm half walking, half jogging in the direction of Alonzo's store. I'm out of breath. I'm chattering all over in the cold. My left arm is wrapped tightly around my midsection. I want to get to my radio and my gun. They feel like children I left behind: like Thomas felt to me, when I first went back to work. I wish, now, I could sprint.

—What happened? he asks.

I tell him.

—What'd you think of him? asks Truman.

—I think he's dishonest, I say, after thinking. And untrustworthy.

Truman says nothing.

—What are you thinking? I ask him.

—Sounds about right, I guess, Truman says. He hesitates. I know why: agreeing with me too strongly means bad things for Kacey. I mean, who knows, he adds.

—Thank you again for your help, I say.

—Will you stop that, says Truman.

I return to Alonzo's, retrieve the bag from him, head into the bathroom, and get my uniform back on as quickly as I can. I check my phone compulsively, half expecting texts from other officers: *Where the hell are you? Ahearn's looking for you.* But none comes in. I thank Alonzo again and head for the door before having a second thought. I weigh the bag in my hands, full now of my civilian clothes.

—Alonzo, I say. Any chance I could leave this here for the time being? Is there someplace out of the way I could keep it?

As I run to the car, I can't shake the thought that Sergeant Ahearn will be there, waiting for me, when I turn the corner onto the little side street where I parked. Checking his watch.

But no one's there. I breathe. I open my trunk and retrieve my possessions. A call comes over the radio. Theft from auto: nothing urgent.

Gratefully, I respond.

On my way home, the gravity of what I've just done settles onto my shoulders. And I am suddenly struck by a sense of anger, the kind I used to feel with regularity, the sort of anger that led me to stop speaking to Kacey. When I made this decision, my life instantly improved. The thing is: I do have a temper. Simon used to tell me I was the calmest person he knew, until I wasn't anymore.

What is making me angriest, at present, is the fact that today's episode imperiled my profession, which I largely enjoy, and my livelihood, and my ability to earn a salary and benefits for myself and my son. Imagine, I think, if I had been caught and fired for my behavior today. Imagine if I had jeopardized everything I've built for Thomas, the modest but respectable life I have made for us both. And for what? For someone who probably does not want to be found, who has perhaps intentionally gone missing, for someone whose every decision has been a self-serving one, who has rejected out of hand every attempt others have made to set her on a better path.

Enough of this, I vow. Enough. No more. Kacey's life is her own to protect. Not mine.

And then, just as quickly, comes a vision of the woman we found on the Tracks. Her blue lips. Her hair slick against her head. Her clothes translucent. Her eyes wide-open, innocent, unprotected from the rain.

———————

In Bensalem, I pull into the driveway. As I round the house, I look up: Thomas, lately, has been keeping watch for me from my bedroom window. Yes, there he is, two hands on the panes, his face pressed to the cold glass, his expression distorted. He grins and bolts to greet me at the door.

Inside, I pay a bored-looking Bethany and ask how Thomas was today.

—Fine, she says, and no more.

When I left them this morning, I gave Bethany money to take him to a bookstore and let him choose a book. I bought her a booster seat for her to use in her car, but I have never once seen it installed.

—What did you do?

—Um, says Bethany, we read books.

—How was the store? I ask Thomas.

—We didn't go, says Thomas, darkly.

I look at Bethany.

—It was so cold out, she says. We read books here.

—One, says Thomas. We read one book.

His voice has taken on a petulant edge.

—Thomas, I say, warningly—out of obligation, not conviction.

But my heart is heavy.

When Bethany has left, Thomas looks at me, wide-eyed, his small hands at his sides, palms forward. *Look what you've done to me!* he seems to be saying, with this expression.

Thomas is very intelligent. I realize it is incorrect to say that about one's own child, but I base this on evidence: he began to speak quite young, and was putting together puzzles by one and a half, and could say all of his letters and numbers before two, and so on. He borders at times on perfectionism, a tendency I monitor to ensure it does not devolve into compulsiveness, or, worse, addiction. (Thinking about our family, I often fearfully consider the idea that addictive tendencies may be hiding someplace in his genes.) Mainly, though, I think he is simply, well, *gifted*—that word that Gee disdained so much when it was once used about me.

When Thomas was two years old, I did some research to make certain I was correct in my assessment that he was advanced for his age, and when I had confirmed it, I prevailed upon Simon to help me enroll him in Spring Garden Day School, which was close to my precinct, very well regarded, and far too expensive. It mainly serves the gentrified neighborhoods of Fishtown and Northern Liberties, and it costs so much that the entirety of Simon's monthly checks went to Thomas's tuition. But I convinced myself that I could afford it. Thomas quickly made friends there—about whom he still speaks longingly—and I took solace in the idea that he was learning things that would prepare him for a long and successful educational career that would conclude, I dreamed, only when he'd achieved a graduate degree. Medicine, maybe. Law. I had named him for Thomas Holme, the first Surveyor General of the state of Pennsylvania under William Penn, and the individual responsible for the beautiful, rational design of the city of Philadelphia, so sometimes I daydreamed that he would be a city planner or an architect. Holme was a particular favorite of my high school history teacher Ms. Powell.

When, a year ago, Simon's checks abruptly and mysteriously ceased to arrive, I struggled for a time to keep Thomas enrolled in his school, to keep paying the old part-time babysitter who stayed with him on B-shift weeks, to keep paying the mortgage on the house in Port Richmond, and to keep eating. For a brief, tense period, we held on—living on canned tuna fish and spaghetti, never buying clothing—and then in December there came a sewage leak from the basement to the street that cost ten thousand dollars to repair, and the balance tipped, and everything came crumbling down.

That was the day I drove to the South Detectives building to demand an answer from Simon, who had not only stopped sending checks but had failed to pick up Thomas on two separate occasions, and had changed his telephone number, and had even, apparently, moved. I discovered this after driving to his house in South Philadelphia and ringing the doorbell, on one of those days that he had failed to show up. Thomas, who loved his father, was bereft. The day of the sewage leak, when everything was falling apart, I decided I had no other recourse than to pay Simon a visit at his place of work. So I left Thomas with his then-babysitter and drove to the headquarters of the South Detectives. Now, this was very unusual for me. Neither Simon nor I wish to be gossiped about. We never talked about our relationship at work, probably due to its somewhat unconventional beginnings. And though my colleagues in the 24th know I have a son, they do not know who the father is; and I suppose I have always made it clear that this is a question I would consider unwelcome.

The day I went to Simon's building, therefore, I strove for anonymity: I was wearing sunglasses, and a hooded sweatshirt with the hood up.

I recognized his car, a black Cadillac sedan he had bought used and then restored, parked fifty yards away on the street, and pulled in not far from it. Then I waited for the end of his workday.

I will not recount in its entirety the ugly exchange we had when, at last, he emerged, and he spied me and tried to turn back toward the station. In brief, I got very angry, and probably shouted, and Simon put his hands out in front of himself defensively, and I told him that if he failed to send a check within one week I would take him to court, and he told me that I wouldn't dare, and asked me if I knew how many friends he had in the system, and told me if I took him to court he would take Thomas away from me like this—here he snapped his fingers—and that I was being unreasonable by keeping Thomas enrolled in such an expensive school, anyway. Who did I think I was? he wanted to know. Who did I think we were?

It was then that I made a certain decision, in my mind. I got very quiet, and I may even have smiled a little, and I said nothing further, and I walked away. I got into my car and drove north, not looking once in the rearview mirror, and then I called the realtor who sold me my house in Port Richmond, and I told her I intended to list it. Then I called the director of Spring Garden Day School and told her that, sadly, I would have to take Thomas out of school. This was, for Thomas and me both, a heartbreak.

The next day I talked to my colleague whose brother was moving out of the apartment above Mrs. Mahon's house—I had heard this colleague complaining that he had to help with the move—and I also placed an ad on a childcare website seeking a sitter near Bensalem with a great deal of flexibility.

I never told Simon where I was moving.

If he had anything new to say to me, I thought, he could locate me at the station. And if he wanted to see Thomas again, he could start sending checks.

In this way, I started our life over.

Since then I have made great sacrifices in order to retain my independence, and to protect Thomas. Largely, I think my decision has been correct.

But at the end of each workday, when I look my son in the eye, and see from his gloomy expression that he has spent another day in boredom and solitude while Bethany scrolls endlessly through her phone—I have to admit that I waver in my certainty.

Now, he disappears down the hallway while I begin to make dinner.

When it's time to eat, I find him in his room and see that he's coloring something large and bright on the back of a piece of poster board he brought home last year from school.

I watch him work in silence for a while.

—What are you making? I ask him eventually, and he regards his work.

—A picture for Ashley, he says.

—For Ashley?

—For Cousin Ashley, he says. For tomorrow.

I blanch.

Tomorrow is Thanksgiving. It crept up on me.

Thomas, perhaps sensing some hesitation on my part, looks up at me, worried.

—We're still going, he says. A statement, rather than a question.

His picture, I determine, is of a turkey and a can of something—beans, perhaps, or corn. I am embarrassed to say that most of our daily vegetable intake comes out of cans, these days.

—Of course, I say.

My voice falters, and I wonder if Thomas can sense my uneasiness.

But my son is nodding, satisfied.

—Good, he says. He is happy now. He returns to his work, relaxed for once, delighted to have something to look forward to.

Then he looks up again. I know what he will ask before he says it.

—Will Daddy be there?

The mood in the room changes quickly. And for what feels like the thousandth time this year, I must tell him no.

find, over the course of the next morning, that I am very nervous. For me, it takes an extraordinary amount of emotional stamina to go to any O'Brien family event, let alone one where I am not expected. Last night, I briefly considered phoning Ashley to let her know Thomas and I were coming, but I think an element of surprise will be useful—especially when it comes to talking to my cousin Bobby, whom I have decided, after at least five unreturned texts, is definitely avoiding me. My goal is to make some quick rounds, to ask everyone I can about Kacey, and to leave without incident.

—What's wrong, Mama, says Thomas as I tear around the kitchen.

—I can't find the beaters, I say.

I've been having moments lately where I feel that Thomas's childhood is speeding past too quickly, that it should be better in all ways than mine was. *Baking,* I will think, frantically; *Thomas has never baked anything.* And I'll run to the store.

Today, we're making brownies, but the thing is that I've never made brownies before, and the first batch is already ruined, burned to a crisp. (Dutifully, loyally, Thomas crunches one in his jaws and pronounces it good.)

The second batch is better.

But the brownie fiasco makes us late, and I hustle us to the car and then drive to Olney more quickly than I should.

Growing up, Kacey and I were very close to our cousin Ashley. Her mother, Lynn, is Gee's youngest sibling, born almost two decades after Gee, closer in age to our mother than to our grandmother. Lynn and Ashley lived right down the block from us, and Ashley went to the same parish school we did, Holy Redeemer, until Kacey got the two of us kicked out. Ashley had a baby young, at nineteen, which didn't surprise anyone except her mother, Lynn, who had blinders on when it came to the nonsense her daughter was getting into. But I give Ashley credit: She got her life together after that. She went to night school while her mother watched the baby, then got her nursing degree. In her mid-twenties, she met and married a man named Ron, who works construction, and they had three more babies three years in a row, and then moved to Olney, to a larger house with a very tiny backyard.

I don't mind Ashley. In some ways I even see in her a version of how Kacey's life could have gone: They're the same age, and have the same taste in music and fashion, and the same wicked sense of humor. They were part of the same group growing up. Of all the O'Briens, I probably miss Ashley the most, and have even tried to reach out to her on several occasions. But like me, Ashley is very busy with children and work, and mainly my calls have gone unreturned.

It's hard to find parking. When, at last, we reach the house, I can hear from the stoop a high din of voices. I picture, on the other side of the door, a living room full of people I haven't seen in years.

There is a particular insult that the O'Briens often use to describe people they don't like: *She thinks she's better than us.* Over the years, I fear that it has been used about me.

Standing there on the threshold of Ashley's house, my childhood shyness returns to me. Thomas, sensing this, clutches my leg. He is holding, behind his back, the rolled picture he made for Ashley. The tray of brownies in my hands wobbles.

I open the door.

Inside are the O'Briens, talking, shouting, eating off red plastic plates. The drinkers have beers in their hands. The sober ones have Cokes and Sprites. The house smells like cinnamon and turkey.

Everyone pauses and stares at us. Some of them nod, sort of formally; two brave souls, older cousins, come over and give us hugs. Gee's younger brother, my uncle Rich, is there. He notices me and waves. He's with a wife or girlfriend I've never met. There's my cousin Lennie, and Lennie's daughter, about ten years younger than I am. I can't remember her name. A little bunch of children runs past the doorway, and Thomas looks at them longingly but stays close to my leg.

Ashley, coming up from the basement, spots me and stops in her tracks.

—Mickey? she says from across the room. She's holding two beers in her hands.

—Hi, I say. I hope it's all right that we came. I found out at the last minute that I didn't have to work today.

I extend the brownies out to her. An offering.

Ashley recovers her manners.

—Of course, she says. Come on in.

My hands are full. With a knee, I gently nudge Thomas forward, into the house. He steps over the threshold, and I follow.

Ashley crosses the room, then stands still in front of me. She looks down at Thomas. You got so big, she says.

Thomas is silent. I see him begin to produce the poster board he is holding, and then, changing his mind, he tucks it away again.

—How can I help? I ask, at the same time that Ashley says, Is your grandmother coming?

—I don't think so, I say.

Ashley nods toward the kitchen. We're good, she says. Get some food. I'll be back in one second.

A little boy, five or six years old, comes up to Thomas and asks him if he likes army guys, and Thomas says yes, though I'm not sure he knows what they are.

Then they're gone, to the basement, where from the sounds of it a war is taking place.

Everyone else has gone back to talking.

As always, at O'Brien family functions, I am alone.

For a while, I wander through Ashley's house, trying to look casual. I see why they moved to Olney: the houses up here are older and bigger, about twice as wide as the rowhome I grew up in. It's nothing fancy, and the street it's on isn't pretty, but I can see why a family of six would want a house like this. The furniture is run-down, and the walls are mainly bare, except, surprisingly, for crucifixes above the thresholds of each room, in the manner of a Catholic grade school. It seems like Ashley's found religion in recent years.

I nod at some people and say hello to others. Awkwardly, I return hugs when they're offered. I don't particularly enjoy being hugged. When we were children, it was Kacey who kept me sane at these events. I would stick by her side as she skillfully navigated any party, fending off teasing and insults or returning them smoothly, but always with a laugh. As young teenagers, we typically found a corner and sat in it together, eating our food, making eye contact with one another whenever any one of our family members said or did something absurd, and then exploding into secret laughter. We saved up stories to trade with one another for days afterward, categorized our relatives with the cruelty and creativity unique to teenage girls.

I cannot shake a particular image as I round each corner: it's of what my sister would be like, today, if her life had gone differently. I imagine her as she has been on the rare occasions in her adult life that she has been well: drinking a soda, holding somebody's baby, crouching on the floor beside some little cousin. Petting a dog. Playing with a child.

———

I walk through a back door onto a chilly lawn, bordered by a wooden fence that separates it from adjacent lots.

And there he is: my cousin Bobby, smoking a cigarette, standing between his brother and another one of our cousins.

When he sees me, he blinks.

—Hey, there she is, says Bobby as I approach.

He's gotten heavier since the last time I saw him. He was about six-three to begin with. He's four years older than I am, and has always intimidated me. When we were small, he used to chase Kacey and me around the basements of O'Brien households with various weapon-like objects, to Kacey's delight and my terror.

Today he has a beard and wears a Phillies cap, cocked up to one side. His brother John, to his right, and our cousin Louie, to his left, regard me without much emotion. I wonder, in fact, if they even recognize me.

This morning, I carefully considered what to wear, wondering whether it would behoove me to dress up a little in order to show my respect for the occasion, or whether this would further convince the O'Briens that I'm in some way snobbish or strange. In the end, I decided on my standard off-duty uniform: gray pants that are fitted but not tight, and a white button-down shirt, and flat shoes that are good for walking. I brushed my hair into a ponytail and put on small silver earrings in the shape of crescent moons. They were a gift from Simon on the occasion of my twenty-first birthday, and for this reason I have been tempted to throw them away on a number of occasions, but they are so pretty that I never have. I don't have much jewelry. It would be a shame, I think, to throw out something I find beautiful, simply out of spite.

—How you doing, sweetie, says Bobby, when I've crossed the small lawn. His voice is sugary.

—Not bad, I say. How are you?

—Doing really good, says Bobby, and the other two murmur something similar.

Everyone drags on cigarettes.

—Can you spare one? I say. I haven't smoked a cigarette in years—not since I was with Simon, who smoked socially. Occasionally, I would join him.

Bobby fumbles with his pack, jerkily. I watch all of his movements. Is he breathing more quickly than he should be? Maybe it's just the cold. I don't know what Bobby's reasons are for avoiding my texts about Kacey, but there is something in his demeanor today that strikes me as nervous.

I consider asking him if I can talk to him in private briefly, but I fear that might put him on guard. Instead, as lightly as I can, I say, You know, I've been texting you.

—I know, says Bobby. He holds out the pack, one cigarette loose. I take it.

—I know, he says again. I'm sorry I didn't get back to you. I've been asking around.

He holds out a lighter and I stand in front of it, breathing until it catches.

—Thanks, I say. Have you heard anything about her?

Bobby shakes his head. I haven't, he says. John and Louie look at him.

—Sister's missing, he says, tilting his head in my direction. Kacey.

—Shit, says John. He's older than Bobby, smaller. I've never known him well. He seemed like a grown-up when we were kids. I've heard around the neighborhood that John's part of the same bad scene that Bobby is.

—Man, I'm sorry to hear that, John says. I study him.

—Thanks, I say again. When's the last time you talked to her? I say to Bobby.

Bobby looks skyward, miming thought. Probably . . . he says. Jeez, Mickey, I don't know. I probably seen her around the neighborhood here and there, maybe even last month. But the last time I actually talked to her has to be more than a year ago.

—Okay, I say.

We all take drags. It's cold out. Everyone's nose is red.

Historically, at O'Brien family functions, the subject of addiction is not mentioned. Many people in our family use. Kacey is an extreme example, but other members of the family partake to varying degrees. Though it's talked around—*I heard Jackie's doing better; Yeah, she is*—it is considered impolite to use specific language, reference specific problems or episodes. Today, I ignore these rules.

—Who's been dealing to her lately? I ask Bobby.

He frowns. He looks, for a moment, genuinely wounded.

—Aw, come on, Mick, he says.

—What? I say.

—You know I'm not into that stuff anymore.

—I do? I say.

John and Louie shift.

—How can I be sure? I say.

—Just have to trust me, he says.

I drag on my cigarette. I could, I say. Or I could trust your arrest record, which I can bring up on my phone right now, if you'd like.

I'm surprised at myself. I'm crossing lines left and right, now. Being reckless. A cloud passes over Bobby's face. I don't actually have access to his arrest record on my phone. He doesn't know that.

—Look, he says, but before he can continue, we hear a voice I recognize immediately. Gee used to say it sounded like a foghorn.

—Is that Mickey? asks my aunt Lynn. Ashley's mother. Is that you, Mickey?

And for a moment the conversation is derailed. I turn toward Lynn and pretend to listen while she demands to know where I've been all these years, and talks about how the world is crazy, and tells me she hopes I'm being safe at work.

—How's your grandmom? says Lynn.

Before I can respond, she continues: I saw her a couple weeks ago. She came to the birthday party Ashley threw for me. It was nice. I'm fifty-five, can you believe that?

I nod along as Lynn talks about Ashley, about how Ashley made a carrot cake that day, about how she doesn't like cream cheese frosting so Ashley put vanilla on it. But all of my senses are directed to my left, where my three cousins are still standing, shifting in place slightly, exchanging glances that I can't interpret. Louie whispers something I can't hear, and Bobby nods his head ever so slightly.

Simon used to laugh at me: he always knew when I wasn't fully listening to what he was saying, distracted by someone else's conversation going on nearby. You're so nosy, he'd say, and I never disagreed. My strong peripheral vision and my ability to eavesdrop are both skills that have served me well on the street.

Someone goes by carrying a serving platter, and Lynn departs, as abruptly as she arrived, without saying goodbye.

—Let me take that for you, she calls, in her brassy voice, and then she's gone.

Slowly, I turn back to my cousins, who have moved on to a new topic of conversation, everyone's favorite in Philadelphia: it's the Eagles' unexpected winning streak, and their odds of a shot at the Super Bowl. When I look at them, they go quiet again.

—One more question, I say. Before she disappeared, she was seeing a man named Connor. I don't know his last name. But I think his nickname is Dock.

It isn't subtle, the way everyone's expressions change.

—No fuckin' way, says Louie, under his breath.

—Are you familiar with him? I say, but the question has become rhetorical, because it's endlessly clear that they are.

Bobby is looking at me very seriously now.

—When did they get together, he says. How long were they together?

—I'm not sure, I say. I don't know how serious they were. I know they were together as of August.

Bobby is shaking his head.

—That guy is no fuckin' good, he says. He's trouble.

A little murmur of agreement from my other cousins. I pause.

—In what way, I say.

Bobby shrugs. What do you think, he says.

Then he says, Listen. I'm gonna try to find out more for you, okay? You know I'm not into that stuff anymore, he says, but I still have my people.

I nod. I see in his expression that he will take his mission seriously. That Kacey, in his mind, is family, and protecting her is his new purpose.

—Thank you, I say.

—No problem, says Bobby.

He holds my gaze meaningfully. Then turns away.

nside again, I search for Thomas for a long time—so long, in fact, that I begin to worry. Ashley walks by and I touch her shoulder, making her whirl so abruptly that she spills her wine.

—I'm so sorry, I say, but I can't find Thomas. Have you seen him?

—Upstairs, says Ashley.

I walk up the staircase, covered in thin flat carpet, and stand in the hallway for a moment. One by one, I open all the doors: a bathroom, a closet, a room with two single beds that must be shared by Ashley's two younger boys. Another, decorated in shades of purple, with an italic *C* on the wall, is for Chelsea, Ashley's only daughter. A third seems to be Ashley's oldest son's.

Ashley and Ron's room is the one I walk into last. A radiator clanks in the corner, giving off the not-unpleasant smell of warm dust. In the center of the room is a canopy bed, and on the wall next to it is a picture. In it, Jesus holds the hands of two young children. All three figures stand on a road that leads to a shimmering body of water.

Walk with me, it says, beneath Jesus's feet.

I am still contemplating this picture when I hear the faintest rustle emanating from the closet to my right.

I walk toward it and open the door. There is my son, hiding with two other boys, playing Sardines, apparently.

—*Shhhhhhh,* they say, in unison.

Okay, I mouth, closing the door, retreating quietly from the room.

Downstairs again, I make a heaping plate of food from the buffet table. Then I stand alone in the living room, eating it ungracefully, guiltily, glancing up from time to time at a TV that's on in the corner, displaying the Macy's Thanksgiving Day Parade. Around me is a din of voices I haven't heard since childhood, all of them rising and falling together. We are related, loosely, connected by limbs of a family tree that in recent years has atrophied, decayed. Near me, an older cousin, Shane, is telling a story about how much he won at SugarHouse last night. He coughs outrageously. He reaches over his own shoulder to scratch his back.

Ashley comes into the living room then with Ron. Her four children shuffle in behind her, clearly following orders.

She says, Hey, everyone? Hey!

No one shuts up, so Ron puts two fingers in his mouth and whistles.

I'm in the middle of lifting my fork to my mouth. Self-consciously, I lower it.

—Aw, here we go, says Shane. Time for church.

Ashley shoots him a glance. Now, look, she says. We won't keep you long. But we just wanted to say we love you guys. And we also wanted to give thanks for all of us being able to be together today.

Ron takes her hand and his children, behind him, join hands too.

—If you don't mind, says Ron, we're just going to say grace.

I glance around. Everyone looks skeptical. The O'Briens are Catholic, if we're anything. We're varying degrees of religious: Some of my older aunts go to mass multiple times a week. Many of my younger cousins don't go at all. I usually take Thomas at Easter, at Christmas, and whenever I'm feeling low. And at no childhood Thanksgiving, in my recollection, did the O'Briens ever say grace.

Ron is praying now, bald head bowed, and the room is silent. The substantial muscles in his arms are tense with feeling. He gives thanks for the food we are about to consume and for the family who's with us here today and the family members who have already passed. He gives thanks for their house and their jobs and for their children. He gives thanks for the leaders of the country and prays that they may continue to do their job to the best of their ability. I don't know Ron well—I've probably met him four times in the years he and Ashley have been married, including once at their wedding—but he strikes me as a firm person, hardworking, no-nonsense, someone with very definite opinions about everything that he'll share with you if you give him an opening. He's from Delco, which—though it's just over the border from Southwest Philadelphia—makes him an outsider, and lends him an exotic quality that causes the O'Briens to afford him a certain amount of respect but also, I imagine, to mistrust him slightly.

Ron concludes, finally, and there is a round of muttered *Amen*s and one wiseacre cousin who says, Good food, good meat, good God, let's eat.

Gee's brother Rich is next to me, suddenly, holding a beer. I don't know where he came from.

—Wasn't expecting to see you here, he says. He's wearing jeans and an Eagles jersey. He looks like Gee, but bigger. Like many of my older male relatives, he's a talker, a kidder, someone who elbows you to get you to laugh at his jokes.

I nod. Here I am, I say.

—Looks like you're hungry, says Rich, looking at my plate. Me, I'm watching my waistline, he says, and winks.

I laugh weakly.

—How's your new place? says Rich. Your grandmom told me you moved. Up in Bensalem now, huh?

I nod.

—With some mystery man, I bet, says Rich. Right? I bet you've got a boyfriend up there. You can't get anything past family.

He is teasing me, gently. I know this. I say nothing.

—Bring him around sometime, says Rich.

—I'm not seeing anybody, I say.

—I'm just messing with you, says Rich. Hey. You'll find someone.

—I don't want to find anyone, I say.

I return to my food. Carefully, I select a small piece of everything, so that I have one perfect bite on my fork. This endeavor takes me quite a while, because I find, suddenly, that it's difficult to focus on my plate.

For once in my uncle Rich's life, he says no more.

THEN

After I confided in Simon Cleare about the struggles my sister was having, we began to see each other outside the PAL as well.

That summer, after the end of the workday, I went to libraries or parks or restaurants, places where Simon felt we wouldn't be seen, and then he joined me. I was seventeen. (*We don't want anyone to get the wrong idea*, he told me, and at the time this actually gave me a little thrill.) Sometimes, we went to see a film at one of the independent theaters in Center City, and then he walked me all the way to the El stop at Second and Market, talking with me the whole way about the artistic strengths and weaknesses of the script and the actors. Sometimes we went to a pier that jutted out over the Delaware River. It had gone unused for decades, and by then it was decrepit and probably unsafe, but it was mainly abandoned and we could sit alone on the edge of it and look over toward Camden. To all of these places, I arrived first. Soon after, Simon would join me. He knew everything about Kacey, listened attentively to every new development as it occurred.

Not a week after her first overdose, Kacey began again to sneak out with regularity. Because we still shared a bed, I knew it every time she did. I tried, always, to convince her not to go. Sometimes, I threatened to tell Gee. But I was more afraid of what Gee would do to Kacey than I was of what Kacey was doing to herself. I was afraid, primarily, that Gee would kick Kacey out. And if that were to happen, I didn't know what would become of either of us.

—*Stay here,* I would whisper.

—*I need a cigarette*, Kacey would say. And then she'd be gone for hours.

It happened again and again. Kacey quickly got worse. Now she seemed permanently glazed over, a glossiness to her eyes, a flush to her cheeks, her speech slow, her tongue heavy, her beautiful laugh nearly gone. Seeing her this way, I often had the urge to clap my hands, loudly, in front of her face. To hug her tightly, to squeeze out of her whatever darkness was making her want to dull her life so completely. I missed my bright little sister, the quick-witted Kacey, dashing here and there, always alight with energy; the fierce small fiery version of the teenager who seemed now to exist in a world of unending, unrelenting dusk.

Though I tried very hard to keep Kacey's behavior a secret from Gee, our grandmother was sharp. She knew. She went through Kacey's things over and over again until, at last, Kacey got lazy. Then Gee found a wad of hundred-dollar bills—Kacey had begun dealing a little, on the side, with Fran and Paula Mulroney—and that was enough evidence for Gee. As I had feared, she kicked Kacey out of the house.

—Where will she go? I asked.

—You think I care? said Gee, her eyes defiant, a little wild. You think that's my problem?

—She's sixteen, I said.

—Exactly, said Gee. Old enough to know better.

A week later, of course, she was back. But the pattern continued, and Kacey got worse, not better.

All of these happenings, I related to Simon whenever I saw him. And it provided me with a certain amount of relief: to know that there was one person in the world, aside from me, who carried with him the details of Kacey's descent into addiction, who kept track of her story, who listened well and dispensed advice that seemed reasonable and adult.

—She's testing you, he said confidently. She's just immature. She'll grow out of it.

Then, inclining his head toward me slightly, he confessed: I went through a phase of it myself.

He was clean now, he said. He rolled up his pant leg to show me, on the back of his strong right calf, a tattoo of a large X that signified his sobriety. He had, by then, stopped going to meetings, but he had never stopped being wary, aware that a relapse was not out of the question.

—You can never stop being on guard, he said. That's the hell of it. To always be worried.

If I am being honest, it comforted me, this talk. To know that someone as functional as Simon, as smart and upright and worldly, a good father—to know someone like that had once been like Kacey. And had come out all right on the other side.

No one, at that point, not even Kacey, knew that I spent time with Simon Cleare in this way. On the nights Kacey was home, we two lay in the same bed, each with our own secret, a line drawn between us, a chasm that widened each week.

Kacey stopped going to high school. She didn't tell Gee. And our school, underfunded and filled to capacity with struggling students, failed to send home a notice.

I, too, said nothing. As always, my main priority was to keep Kacey under Gee's roof, and so I concealed from Gee what I knew. To this day, I don't know if that decision was correct.

But I loved her. And there were moments, still, of real tenderness between us. When Kacey was depressed, or when she was high, she came into the house wanting a hug. She came into the house wanting to sit next to me and lean against me, her head on my shoulder, as we watched television together. She used to ask me, I recall, to braid her hair into two neat rows; she would sit on the floor in between my legs as I did this, making lazy, funny commentary about whatever was on television—she could still, even then, make me laugh—her breathing slow, her head heavy against my hands. I felt for her, in those moments, something akin to maternal love—an emotion I can only name in retrospect, now that Thomas is in my life.

I pleaded with Kacey openly, in those moments, to get well again. I cried. I will, she said, or I promise, or I'll be better. But she wouldn't look at me when she replied: always, she was looking elsewhere, at the floor, out the nearest window.

In my senior year of high school, I began to narrow the list of colleges to which I would apply. The time I spent thinking about where I would go brought me some respite from the worry that otherwise constantly plagued me: At last, I thought, at last, the time has come for me to make my escape. And once I escaped, and made a good life for myself, I could rescue my sister. I'd been dreaming about it for years, ever since Sister Angela Cox, at Holy Redeemer, had told me that with my brains I could be whatever I wanted to be.

I knew enough not to go to Gee for help. Whenever anyone reported to her that I was smart, or a good student, she reacted skeptically. *They're setting you up*, she said to me once, frowning. Gee, and all the O'Briens, took pride in doing only what was practical. A life of the mind—even a profession like teaching—seemed to most of them prideful in some way. Work was done with your body, with your hands. College was for dreamers and snobs.

Still, with help from my beloved history teacher, Ms. Powell, and on the recommendation of the somewhat incompetent (or, more kindly, understaffed) guidance department at my high school, I filled out two applications to nearby universities: one to Temple, and one to St. Joe's. One public university. One private.

I got into both.

I took the admissions letters to Mr. Hill, the guidance counselor to whom I had been assigned. He high-fived me. Then he gave me a bundle of information on scholarships and a FAFSA form.

—What's this, I said to him.

—It's how you get money to pay for college, he said. Have your parents fill it out.

—I don't have parents, I said. I remember hoping that the baldness of this statement, the lack of any cushioning, would convince him that I could—would have to—do everything myself.

He looked up at me, surprised. Your guardian, then, he said. Who's your guardian?

—My grandmother, I said.

—They're for her, he said.

Already, I could feel the lump rising in my throat.

—Is there any way not to, I said.

But my voice was too quiet, or Mr. Hill was too busy, because he didn't look up from his desk.

I knew what would happen. Still, I took them to her, all the forms, cradling them lightly in my arms.

She was sitting on the couch, eating cereal for dinner, watching the local news. Shaking her head at the antics of hooligans and thugs, the words she dispensed most frequently during this part of her routine.

—What's all this? she said, when I handed her the stack of paperwork. She put her spoon down in the bowl with a high clink. Put the bowl down on the coffee table in front of her. She crossed a leg so that her ankle met her knee. She said nothing. She was still chewing as she looked through it all. She began then, quietly, to laugh.

—What, I said.

I was so ill at ease in my body, in those days. So little at home. I remember crossing my arms and uncrossing them. Putting my hands on my waist.

—I'm sorry, said Gee, laughing harder. I just, she said, putting a hand to her mouth, calming herself. Can you imagine? Kid like you at St. Joe's? You barely talk, Mickey. They'll take your money and spit you out on the sidewalk. They'll have a laugh at your expense and then get rid of you. That's what they'll do. And if you think you'll ever see a return on that investment, well. I've got a bridge to sell you.

She pushed the stack back across the coffee table. There was milk, now, on some of the papers. She picked up her cereal bowl.

—I'm not filling that out, she said, nodding at the financial aid forms. I won't help you dig yourself into debt for some useless piece of paper at the end of it.

Ms. Powell had, at the start of the school year, given us all her home phone number, telling us to call her with any questions at all. It seemed to me that, if there was ever a time to use this lifeline, it was now. I had never before phoned her, and I was painfully nervous as I dialed.

It took her a long time to answer. When she did, I could hear a child crying in the background. It was five-thirty or six at night. Dinnertime, I realized too late. Ms. Powell had two children she spoke of fondly, a boy and a girl, both very young.

—Hello? said Ms. Powell, sounding harried.

The child was wailing, now. *Mama, Mama.*

—Hello? Ms. Powell said again. A pot clinked.

—I don't know who this is, said Ms. Powell, at last, but I've got my hands full over here, and I don't appreciate the call.

It was the sternest her voice had ever sounded. I hung up slowly. I imagined what my life might have been like if I had been born into a family like Ms. Powell's.

It was not long after that that I decided to page Simon. I waited for a while by the kitchen phone, my head against the wall. Fifteen minutes later, it rang, and I lifted the receiver off the hook as fast as I could.

—Who is it? called Gee, and I shouted, Sales call.

On the other end, Simon was speaking lowly.

—What is it, he said. I have one minute to talk.

For the first time since I'd met him, he sounded annoyed. Almost angry. I began to cry. After my phone call to Ms. Powell, it was too much. I needed kindness.

—I'm sorry, I whispered. She won't fill out the forms.

—What forms? Who? said Simon.

—My college forms, I said. My grandmother won't fill them out. I can't go without financial aid.

Simon paused for a long time.

—Meet me at the pier, he said finally. I'll be there in an hour.

———

It had been autumn the last time we went, and daylight saving time hadn't set in yet. Now it was February, and brutal outside, and dark already by the time I set out for the pier. I told Gee I was meeting a friend to study. Kacey raised her eyebrows at me as I walked to the door.

It felt good to be outside, away from that house, from the dark moods of Gee, from my perpetual fear that Kacey, one day, simply wouldn't come home.

I was nervous, though, in a way I hadn't been the other times Simon and I had met. That summer and fall, we had seen each other any chance we could get, though each outing had been platonic. But winter, and my school year, had slowed down our visits. I was eighteen years old by then, but young for my age. If I was naive, I suppose, to my credit, I was at least self-aware about my naiveté. I knew that other people my age—including my own sister—were having sex, and had been doing so for years. I knew that my romantic life was limited to my imagination, to daydreams about young men on television, to journal entries in which, embarrassingly, I plotted out elaborate trysts between myself and the most current object of my desire—popular boys at my high school, various celebrities, and, most obsessively, Simon. Regarding him and his intentions, I had two dissonant beliefs. The first was that his interest in me wasn't purely the interest of an intellectual mentor: he laughed often at the remarks that I made, sometimes genuinely, sometimes teasingly, even when they weren't meant to be funny; and he grinned in response to the reddening of my face, which I thought was maybe the way that people flirted; and there was an intent and focused look he gave me as I spoke to him, scanning all the parts of my face, a small smile on his lips; and sometimes I noticed that his gaze drifted downward, to my hands, to my neck, to my breasts. Whether or not I was and am pretty, I have never been able to say. I have always been tall and skinny and I have never worn makeup. I have always dressed very plainly. I rarely wear jewelry, and I mainly keep my hair in a ponytail that, in those days, I sometimes slicked with water to keep the loose pieces from flying away. If there is anything pleasing about the composition of my face, only a few people have ever seemed to notice. But at that time I wondered, often, if Simon was one of them. The memory of his putting his arms around me produced a small thump in my abdomen, a kick in my gut, the slow warm spread throughout my body of something electric. Then, always, another voice rose up in me to tell me that everything I'd been thinking was entirely invented; that Simon saw me as a child, someone with potential, someone in whom he had simply taken a professional and perhaps an altruistic interest; that I was crazy for thinking anything else.

A stand of trees separated Delaware Ave from the pier that led out over the river. The ground was lined with weeds and refuse. It was so dark now that I kept my hands out in front of me as I walked. Suddenly, I had the notion that this was dangerous. A handful of times, there had been another person on the pier when we met there: usually someone out walking his dog. But once there had been a homeless person there, an older man who was ranting when I arrived. He had looked at me wildly and then grinned. Had made an obscene gesture with his hands. That time, I'd retreated to Delaware Ave to wait there for Simon instead.

Now, I figured it was too dark and cold out for anyone else to be there. When I emerged from the trees, I saw that I was correct. But I wasn't certain whether my solitude, and the silence of the pier, gave me more comfort or less.

I walked to the end and sat down. I drew my jacket around myself more tightly. The Ben Franklin Bridge was lit up, and its reflection shone on the water, a necklace of red and white beads.

Ten minutes went by before I heard footsteps. I turned and saw Simon, who ambled toward me, his hands in his pockets. He was out of police attire, and in a uniform of a different kind: cuffed jeans, and black boots, and a wool hat, and a leather jacket with a shearling collar. The outfit he always wore when off duty. From where I sat on the ground, he seemed taller and stronger than ever.

He joined me on the ground. Our legs dangled off the wooden pier. Before he spoke, he put his arm around me.

—How are you? he said, turning his head to look at me. I could feel his breath, the warmth of his lips, at my temple. It made me shiver.

—Not great, I said.

—Tell me what's going on, he said, and, as always, I did.

That was the night that Simon told me I should think seriously about joining the force. Today, the age requirement is twenty-two; then, it was nineteen.

—Listen, said Simon. You could fight her. You could declare yourself independent, and fill out the paperwork yourself. But that would take a while, I think.

—What will I do until then? I asked him.

—I'm not sure, said Simon. Keep working. Go to community college. You need credits under your belt either way.

—But hey, he said, continuing. I think you'd be great at it. You could be a detective. I'm always telling you you'd make a good one. I wouldn't lie.

—I guess so, I said.

I wasn't sure. I did like detective novels. I liked—some better than others—the movies Simon assigned me, many of which centered on police work. Most importantly, I liked Simon, who was himself a police officer. But I was very good in school, and I loved reading. And, thanks to Ms. Powell and her stories about the past—which had the effect of making me feel, somehow, less lonely—I had recently decided that I wanted to become a history teacher, like her.

I hedged.

—It's up to you, Simon pronounced finally. He shifted a little. He still had his arm around me. He rubbed his hand on my arm briskly, as if to keep me warm.

—What I can tell you, though, he said, is that you're going to be fine. You're going to be great at whatever you do.

I shrugged. I was looking out at the river in front of us, lit up brightly by cities on both sides. I was recalling the lessons Ms. Powell had taught us: that its fount was the West Branch River, and its outlet the Delaware Bay. That, thirty-five miles to our north, George Washington and his troops had crossed it on a similarly cold winter night in 1776. It would have been dark then, I was thinking. No cities. No lights to lead the way.

—Look at me, said Simon.

I turned my face up toward him.

—How old are you, he said.

—Eighteen, I said. My birthday had been in October. Even Kacey, that year, had forgotten it.

—Eighteen, said Simon. You've got your whole life ahead of you.

Then he lowered his head and kissed me. It took my brain a while to catch up with my body. When it finally did, I thought, *My first kiss. My first kiss. My first kiss.* I have heard from others about first kisses that were miserable, the recipient bombarded by a deluge of saliva, or forced to accept into her mouth the aggressive tongue of a similarly inexperienced teenager, or nearly swallowed by his open mouth. But Simon's kiss was, in that moment, extremely reserved, a bare brush of lips and then a drawing back, and then, in a subsequent moment, a faint clandestine touch of his teeth against my lower lip. It excited me. I had not thought of teeth as a part of kissing.

—Do you believe me, said Simon, quietly. He was looking at me intently. His face was so close to mine that my neck was bent at an odd angle to accommodate our pose.

—Yes, I said.

—You're beautiful, said Simon. Do you believe that?

—Yes, I said.

It was the first time in my life that I did.

Late that night, lying next to my sister in bed, I had the urge to tell her. Years earlier, when Kacey had had her first kiss, she had described it to me. She was twelve years old at the time, and we were still best friends. Kacey had come home from playing outside and had shouted my name once, excitedly, had run up the stairs to our room and flung herself down on the bed.

—Sean Geoghehan kissed me, she said, her eyes bright. She put a pillow over her mouth. Screamed into it. He kissed me. We kissed.

I was fourteen. I said nothing.

Kacey lowered the pillow and regarded me. Then she sat up, her face concerned, and stretched out an arm.

—Oh, Mick, she had said. It'll happen. Don't worry. It'll happen for you too.

—Probably not, I said. I forced a laugh but it sounded sad.

—It definitely will, said Kacey. Promise me you'll tell me about it when it does.

The night Simon kissed me, I wondered where I would begin. Before I could speak, I heard the soft, unguarded exhalation that meant that Kacey had drifted into sleep.

did what Simon told me to do. I graduated high school, and I continued to live in Gee's house. I moved, finally, into the middle bedroom, which still felt haunted by my mother's presence. I started part-time work as a cashier at a local pharmacy, and I began to pay Gee two hundred dollars in monthly rent. I took my sixty credits at CCP. Then took the police exam. At twenty, I became a police officer. No one came to my induction ceremony.

Kacey, meanwhile, continued to decline. She was wild and erratic by then. In her late teens and early twenties she sometimes worked as a bartender, for cash, and sometimes worked at our uncle Rich's car dealership in Frankford, and sometimes babysat for any irresponsible parents who would hire her, and sometimes still dealt, I believe, for Fran Mulroney, Paula's older brother. She lived at Gee's and with friends and on the street in equal turns. In those days she spent more time in Fishtown than in Kensington, which meant I didn't see her, yet, on my shifts. I never knew where she would be when I walked in the door at night, and I lived in anticipation of the day that she would not return at all. We rarely spoke.

Still, she was the only person who knew about my relationship with Simon. She had found a note from him among my things—it occurred to me only later that she had most likely come across it while looking for

cash to swipe—and had thrust it furiously into my chest the next time
she saw me.

—What the hell are you thinking, she said to me.

I was embarrassed. The note referenced a recent night we had spent
together in a hotel. My time with Simon was a relief to me, an escape, the
first true happiness I had ever known, and if it was a secret, well, I liked
it that way. It was mine.

I put my hand over the note protectively. I said nothing.

What I believe Kacey said next was, *He's a fucking creep.* Or, worse:
He's been trying to get into your pants since you were fourteen years old. Today
I shudder to think of it. Since I was a small child, I have always tried to
maintain my dignity in every situation. At work now, I strive to maintain my professional dignity. At home, with Thomas, I strive to maintain
a certain parental dignity, to protect him from overhearing anything
that might upset him, or anything untoward. Therefore, because it feels
undignified, I have never enjoyed the feeling of anyone else worrying
about me or being concerned for my well-being, preferring instead to
give the impression that I am in all ways fine, and that I have everything
under control. Largely, I believe this image to be an honest one.

—That's not true, I said.

Kacey laughed. It was not a kind sound.

—Whatever you say, she said.

—It isn't, I said.

—Oh, Mick, she said. She shook her head. And I saw, in her expression, something like pity.

At twenty years old, I thought what Kacey said was neither a fair nor
accurate assessment of the situation. It was I who had pursued Simon,
and not the other way around. I never thought of myself as romantic,
but I sometimes told myself that the moment I laid eyes on him was my
only experience with love at first sight; whereas Simon told me that it
had taken him years to see me as anything more than a child. Both
Simon and I were aware, however, of how our relationship might be

perceived by others who had known us when I was his charge, and so we always took pains to keep quiet about it. Simon had recently taken the detective exam, at last, and had passed, and was beginning a career with the South Detectives, and he didn't want anything to derail it. When we met, it was in hotels; he said he didn't want to risk his son, Gabriel—eleven then—learning about us, and Gabriel's mother sometimes brought him by unexpectedly, and it was all very—*complicated*, was the word he used.

—One day you'll get your own place, he told me often, and then we'll be able to stay there.

It was largely for this reason that I banked all of my money for the first two years of my career with the PPD, and used these savings on a down payment for a house in Port Richmond. I was twenty-two years old when I signed the papers. I put down forty percent of the home's price—admittedly, a small sum—but still more money than I have ever again had in my bank account at once. The realtor told me, impressed, that not many twenty-two-year-olds had the restraint to save up so much money, instead spending it on evenings out with friends. I am not like most twenty-two-year-olds, I wanted to tell her, but I didn't.

Leaving Gee's house—and the terrible fights that she and Kacey had, which now sometimes escalated into physicality—felt like escaping from a war.

I had told neither Kacey nor Gee my plan to move out in advance. There were two reasons for this: The first was that I didn't want either one to know much about my finances—Gee because she might begin to demand more in rent than what she already collected from me, and Kacey because I didn't want her to have any more incentive to solicit me for cash. (I had put my foot down, by then, but every now and again she would still come to me with a plea.) The second reason I kept my plans to myself was that I believed, truly, that neither Gee nor Kacey would care.

I was surprised, therefore, when Kacey met my announcement with sadness.

The day I moved out for good, she came home to find me moving boxes down the stairs.

—What are you doing, she said to me. She crossed her arms. She frowned.

I paused for a moment, breathing heavily. I had nothing aside from clothes and books to move, but I had too many of the latter, and was learning quickly how heavy a boxful of paperbacks can be.

—Moving out, I said.

I expected a shrug. Instead, Kacey began to shake her head. No, she said. Mick. You can't leave me alone here.

I placed the box I was holding on the stairs. Already, my back was aching; it took me days to recover.

—I thought you'd be happy, I said.

Kacey looked genuinely puzzled. Why would you think that? she asked.

You don't even like me, I wanted to say. But it felt too maudlin, too self-pitying and morose, and so instead I told her I had to get going, that my plan was to return and tell Gee that night. Somewhat formally, Kacey held the door open for me as I passed. I looked back at her, just once, searching her face for signs of the old Kacey, the ghost of the child who once depended on me so entirely. But I could find no trace of her.

The house I bought was ugly and old, but it was mine. Most importantly, there was no shouting or fighting inside of it. I came home from each shift and stood for a while just inside the front door, leaning against it, my hands on my heart, letting the peace of that house settle onto my shoulders. Telling myself, You are alone here.

The empty house had a warm and pleasing echo. I was slow to decorate, wanting to be careful in my selections, spending the first months after the move with only a mattress on the floor and several cheap chairs I picked up on the street. When I began to buy furniture, I did so carefully. I went to antique stores, to secondhand shops that would give me good deals on objects I thought beautiful. The charms of the house were beginning to reveal themselves to me. There was a strange stained-glass panel to the right of the front door, with red-and-green flowers outlined in lead, and it brought me satisfaction to know that someone else had once valued this house as much as I did, thought well enough of it to include such a small and beautiful detail. I stocked my refrigerator with plentiful, healthy food. I listened to music in peace. When I finally purchased a real bed, I spent money on it—the only luxury I permitted myself. I made it as comfortable as I could, selecting a queen-sized mattress from the Macy's in the old Wanamaker Building. From the same store I purchased bedding that a saleslady promised me was the finest I'd ever sleep on.

Simon and I now had a private place to go. At last, he sometimes stayed with me all night. When he did, a deep and pleasant calm came over me. I hadn't slept so well since Kacey and I were small. Since my mother was alive.

During the several years that followed my departure, I saw both Gee and Kacey only on occasion. Each time, Kacey looked worse and worse, and Gee looked older. I never asked Kacey what she was doing, but still, she volunteered a profusion of information that I largely took to be false: I'm going back to school, she said on several occasions. I'm going for my GED. (As far as I know, she never even took a course.) And then: I've got an interview lined up tomorrow. And then: I've got a job. (She didn't.)

What she was actually doing in those days was difficult to determine. I don't believe she had begun, yet, to do sex work; in any case, I still didn't see her on my shifts. In a moment of clarity, once, Kacey told me that time spent in addiction feels looped. Each morning brings with it the possibility of change, each evening the shame of failure. The only task becomes the seeking of the fix. Every dose is a parabola, low-high-low; and every day a series of these waves; and then the days themselves become chartable, according to how much time, in sum, the user spends in comfort or in pain; and then the months. Confounding all of this are periods of sobriety, which occur voluntarily on some occasions—when, for example, Kacey checks herself into Kirkbride, Gaudenzia, Fairmount, other cheap and local rehab facilities with dubious success rates—and involuntarily on others: when Kacey finds herself in trouble, and then in prison. These periods, too, become part of the pattern: waves of sobriety, followed by relapse, followed by larger waves of active use. Always, the constant baseline is the Ave, the feeling of family and routine that it offers.

These ups and downs might have gone on indefinitely if Kacey's poor decision making hadn't gotten in the way. In 2011, she let a boyfriend convince her to help him steal a television from his parents' place. The parents, not wanting their son to go to prison, blamed the theft on Kacey.

And Kacey took the fall. By then, she had a long track record, and the judge came down on her hard.

She was sentenced to a year at Riverside.

Some might have found this regrettable. I didn't. In fact, for the first time in a long while, I had hope for her.

NOW

The Monday after Thanksgiving, the same young detective, Davis Nguyen, comes into the common room at morning roll call, looking tired. He's wearing an expensive-looking suit today, tailored differently from the baggy suits the older detectives wear: it's slim and cut short, and beneath it his socks show, ever so slightly. His hair is cut in a style that I've seen on the kids in Northern Liberties and Fishtown, the sides buzzed to nothing, the top flipped at an angle. How old is he? Late twenties? He might even be my age, but I feel like he's from a different generation. Probably, he went to college for criminal justice. In his hand, I notice, is a cup from Bomber Coffee.

—A little news, Nguyen says. We might have a lead on the Kensington homicides.

In the room, a small murmur.

He bends over the computer. Pulls up a video on the screen in the main room.

It's footage from a private security camera set up by a homeowner, not far from the lot off Tioga where Katie Conway's body was discovered.

In it, a young girl walks, in grainy black-and-white, across the screen. Five seconds later, a man—hood up, hands in pockets—does the same.

—That, says Nguyen, rewinding to the girl, is Katie Conway.

—That, he says, pointing to the man, is a person of interest.

He pauses, zooms in. The man's face is grainy. It is difficult to discern much about it. Race uncertain, to my eyes. He seems big, though it might also just be that the girl is tiny.

His sweatshirt, the hood of it pulled up to obscure his hair, seems to give us the most information: it says *Wildwood* right across the front of it, the *Wild* on one side of the zipper, the *wood* on the other.

Wildwood, a shore town in southern New Jersey, is a common enough destination that it won't be terribly helpful. I have been there once, with Simon, one of the few weekend trips we ever took together. Almost everyone in Philadelphia, I think, has been to Wildwood. Still, the specificity of that sweatshirt offers us a glimmer of hope.

—Anyone seen this guy around? Nguyen asks. But his voice isn't optimistic. Around the room, a shaking of heads.

—We've already sent the image down to Wildwood's PD. They're asking around, says Nguyen. In the meantime, check your phones. We'll send the video to you today. Keep an eye out, ask about him whenever you take someone in.

Ahearn thanks him, and Nguyen turns to leave.

Before he goes, another cop, Joe Kowalczyk, says, Question.

Nguyen turns around.

—If you had to guess, says Kowalczyk. Race? Age?

Nguyen pauses. I almost hesitate to say, he says, because I want you guys to keep your eyes open for everyone. And that tape wasn't clear.

He looks up at the ceiling. Continues. But if I had to, he says, I'd say white guy, forties. That's the profile, anyway. That's who usually does this kind of thing.

Today, the streets of Kensington are quieter than normal. The cold spell hasn't snapped. It's freezing, and the sky is stark white, and there's a terrible wind at face level that leaves me breathless each time I have to step out of my vehicle.

Only the hardiest, or the most desperate, are outside today.

I turn the cruiser down a side street and pass six boarded-up houses in a row. Abandos, they are called here. Forgotten, condemned, some of them containing within them, no doubt, several poor souls who've made a shelter of them. I think of the drafty insides of these houses, the furniture left behind, the pictures on the walls. I think how lonely it must be for their new inhabitants to look upon these possessions, the remnants of the families who lived there in decades prior. Textile workers. Metalworkers. Fishermen, if the houses are old enough.

Two winters ago, there was a terrible fire in an abandoned factory nearby. It began when two occupants, desperate for warmth, started a blaze in a tin trash can, right there in the middle of the factory floor. A firefighter died trying to put it out. This has become the latest in the long list of things we are to be alert for on patrol: the smell of wood smoke from any unknown source.

No calls in my PSA for an hour. At ten I park the car near Alonzo's and go in for a cup of coffee.

As I come out, cup in hand, two young girls I've seen around the neighborhood, sixteen or seventeen years old, approach me, chewing gum, walking slowly. They're both wearing canvas sneakers with no socks, which makes me shiver a little in sympathy. I can't tell if they're working.

When they approach me, I am surprised. Typically, regulars simply ignore uniformed police officers, or stare at us defiantly and wordlessly.

But one of them speaks.

—Do you know anything about the murders, she says to me.

It's the first time I've been asked. Rumors are spreading, it seems.

—We're working on it, I say. We're getting close.

My standard answer whenever anyone inquires about an open case. I feel I should say this, even though I don't know much more than they do. Sometimes, at work, I feel the way I do when I'm talking to Thomas about his father: a little bit guilty for lying, a little bit noble for upholding a pretense that will ultimately preserve his feelings. I'll bear the burden of the lie, for my son, for these girls.

I remember then about the video.

—Actually, I say, could you take a look at something?

I produce it on my phone: the short clip that Homicide sent to us this morning after roll call. I play it, and then pause it on a still frame that shows the POI.

—Does he look at all familiar? I ask.

Both girls look intently. Both shake their heads. No.

I go through these motions a few more times throughout the day. But nobody seems to recognize him. A couple of women make little murmuring sounds when Katie Conway crosses the screen: recognizing her, perhaps, or recognizing their own fragility, how easily it could have been them.

Just before four o'clock, as my shift is winding down, I see Paula Mulroney for the first time in a while. She's off crutches, finally, leaning up against a wall outside Alonzo's, holding a cigarette in one hand.

I stop the car. Get out. I haven't seen her since Kacey went missing. I've been wanting to talk to her.

Paula has never let my falling-out with Kacey affect her friendliness with me. *That's between you guys*, she said to me once, confidentially. Normally, when she sees me, she greets me with a smile and with some good-natured ribbing. Here we go, she often says. Here comes trouble.

Today, she keeps her face quite still.

—Hello, Paula, I say.

She says nothing.

—I'm glad to see you, I say. I heard Kacey was missing. I was just wondering if you had any idea where she is.

Paula shakes her head. Drags from her cigarette.

—Nope, she says.

—When's the last time you saw her?

She snorts. Says nothing.

I'm confused suddenly.

—Is it true, I say, that you told Alonzo she was missing? Because—

She cuts me off. Look, she says. I don't talk to the police.

I'm taken aback. I've never before heard this from Paula.

I try a different tactic.

—How's your leg? I say.

—Terrible, says Paula.

She drags on the cigarette again. She's inches away from me.

—I'm sorry to hear that, I say.

I'm not certain how to proceed.

—Do you want me to take you to the hospital? I say, but Paula waves me off. Shakes her head.

—I was wondering if I could ask you something else, I say.

—Go ahead, says Paula. But her voice is dismissive, and her implication is clear: *You can ask anything you want. I won't answer.*

I take out my phone and play the video for her. She can't help herself: she's curious. She leans down to inspect the phone.

When Katie Conway crosses the screen, Paula looks sharply at me.

—Yeah, she says, that's Katie. I knew her.

—You did?

She nods. She turns back to me, looks at me hard.

—Little girl they found off Tioga, right? I knew her.

I consider Paula. I'm not sure why she's telling me this.

—She was such a nice girl, says Paula. She was just a baby. Such a nice kid. I knew her mom too. Her mom was godawful. She's the one turned her daughter out.

Paula is still looking hard at me. Something about her expression looks accusing in some way. The cigarette goes into her mouth. Every time I speak to Paula I recall her as she was on a particular day in high school: head held high, leading a pack of popular girls down a hallway, laughing and laughing at a joke someone told. Even now, despite how much our lives have changed, I feel a certain intimidation around her.

—Do you know anything about how she died? I ask Paula, who regards me for a moment before speaking.

—Isn't that what you should be telling me? Paula says levelly.

Again, I grasp for words. This time, none come to me.

—You're the cop, right? says Paula.

—We're working on it, I say again.

—Sure, says Paula. She squints down the Ave. Judging by the quickness of her movements, the chattering of her teeth, she's dopesick. She's stooped over slightly, her arms folded across her middle. She's nauseated.

—Sure you are, Mickey, Paula says. Well, work harder.

I know enough to know that I should leave her now, let her find her fix.

Before I do, though, I say to her, Can you watch one more time? The important part's at the end.

Paula rolls her eyes, agitated, but she bends her head toward the screen, squinting. She watches as the man crosses the screen, then grabs the phone out of my hand. She looks up, eyes wide.

—Do you recognize him? I ask.

I notice suddenly that her hands are shaking.

—You're kidding me, she says.

—You know him? I ask.

Paula begins to laugh, but there is an angry edge to her laughter.

—Don't bullshit me, she says. That's all I want in life, is not to be bullshitted.

I shake my head. I don't understand, I say.

She closes her eyes, just briefly. Takes one last drag, then throws her cigarette on the ground. She stubs it out with the toe of her sneaker.

Finally, she looks at me appraisingly.

—That's one of your guys, Mick, she says. That's a cop.

THEN

Just as I'd hoped, Kacey's yearlong incarceration at Riverside changed her.

Ask anyone who's ever detoxed in prison what it's like, and then watch her face as she recalls it: eyes closed, brow furrowed, mouth turned down, summoning the nausea and despair, summoning the feeling that this version of life might not be worth living. This, Kacey told me, was her conviction during the lowest moment of her withdrawal: that she should take her life. With her teeth, she tore her sheets into long strips. She twisted them together. She fastened this makeshift noose to a light fixture on the ceiling and then, standing on the sink, prepared to jump—but something stopped her; some force, she said, that told her something good was waiting for her if she'd only stay alive.

Shakily, she stepped down from the sink and decided, at last, to write a letter to me.

In it, she apologized for the first time: for breaking promise after promise, for lying, for failing us all, for betraying herself. She told me she missed me. She told me that I was the only person in the world whose opinion she cared about. And she couldn't stand having let me down so badly.

I responded. For a month, we wrote back and forth: an exchange that reminded me of our childhood, when we would write notes to one another to leave in the space beneath the floorboard of our room.

Soon, I decided to pay her a visit. When I saw Kacey, I barely recognized her. She was clear-eyed and sober. Her face was pale in a way it had not been in years. She lacked the flushed cheeks, described in children's books as a sign of good health, that now signify addiction to me. I began to see her regularly. Each time I went, a new version of my sister greeted me. A year is long enough for the body to begin to readjust to sobriety, for the broken brain to shakily begin to go to work, for the production lines therein to rustily churn into action, manufacturing small doses of the natural chemicals that, for years, have been artificially imported through the veins.

And so I watched as Kacey transitioned from despondent to depressed to tired to angry to, by my last visit, very tentatively optimistic. She looked determined. She knew she had work to do, and she wanted to do it.

At my home in Port Richmond, I was planning. I had weighed all my options carefully: the pros and cons of offering Kacey a place to live when she emerged. On this point, I vacillated wildly. I made capricious reversals, based largely on superstition, each time I visited her: I *will* offer her a place to stay if she's found a sponsor; I *won't* offer her a place to stay if she doesn't spontaneously express her determination to attend meetings upon her release, without my asking.

Just in case, I told myself, I would ready the house for her arrival. And then I would wait and see.

There was a small concrete patio behind the house, cracked and parched and barren when I moved in. The year of Kacey's incarceration, I restored it to glory. I built wooden planters and in them I grew herbs and tomatoes and peppers. I bought, secondhand, an outdoor dining set, and strung lights above it, and planted ivy that grew up the fence in the back.

That year, too, I made up the back bedroom in a way I knew would please Kacey. I painted the walls a soothing blue, Kacey's favorite color, and bought a dark blue bedspread for the bed, and found a pretty vanity at a secondhand store, and adorned the walls with prints that were vaguely related to Kacey's interest in the tarot. As a young teenager, she had acquired a deck and had taught herself to read them. The pictures I selected for that room included an image of the High Priestess—I was no doubt hoping, on some level, that the figure's kind, determined gaze would remind Kacey of her own dignity and wisdom and self-worth—and one of the World, and the Sun, and the Moon. I never would have chosen these pictures for myself. I do not believe in the tarot, or in astrology, or in anything of that kind. But I imagined Kacey living in that room, and as I readied it I took a sort of secret delight in the thought of presenting it all to her.

On my last visit to Riverside, Kacey was peaceful and upbeat. She was happy to be leaving but appropriately apprehensive, I thought, and reflective about the trials she would face in the outside world. Of her own volition, she vowed to stay sober, to seek out daily meetings, to find a sponsor. To leave behind, for the time being, friends of hers who were still actively using.

I determined on that day to ask her formally if she would like to stay with me, following the end of her incarceration, and, happily, she agreed.

I cannot speak for my sister, but as for me: the months following her release were the best months of my life.

The two of us were adults, finally, out from under the wary gaze of Gee. And able, therefore, to do as we pleased. I was twenty-six, and Kacey was twenty-five. In my memories of this time, it is perpetually late spring, and the air is warm and damp, and we are in the first tentative days of venturing outside without our jackets. I cannot number the evenings Kacey and I spent on the back patio, dissecting our childhood, discussing our plans. She was doing well; she stayed sober; she didn't even drink. She gained weight; she grew her hair long; on her face, old pockmarks disappeared; her complexion evened. The scars that marred the skin on her arms and neck, remnants of abscesses, lightened and faded. She found work at a nearby independent movie theater, and even started dating another ticket-taker there, a shy and somewhat awkward young man named Timothy Carey, who never went by Tim, and had no idea about Kacey's past. (If he wants to know, said Kacey, he can ask me.)

Her job at the theater suited us both: after I got off my shifts, I often went and found her there, and saw whatever film was playing at that time.

Sometimes, Simon joined me.

It was around this time that he and Kacey settled into an uneasy truce with one another.

They had little choice: it was my house, clearly, and I was the one paying the bills, and the two of them were my guests.

We had a couple of heart-to-hearts about it, Kacey and I.

—I don't trust him, she said once, and I'll never like him, but I can live with him.

Another time, she said, Mickey, you're the best person I know. I just don't want to see you get hurt.

And a third time: Mickey, I know you're a grown-up. Just be careful.

She inquired, often, about why I never went to his place.

—His son drops by unannounced sometimes, I said. I think Simon just doesn't want me to meet him until we're engaged.

She looked at me sideways.

—Are you sure that's it? she said.

But she never said any more than that. And I never answered.

Of course I sensed, even then, that Simon's behavior was unusual. But I was so happy in this moment of my life, so blissful and so calm. Several times a week, Simon knocked at my door—usually unannounced—and entered the house, and took my face in his hands, and kissed it. And sometimes we would eat dinner, and sometimes we would go instead directly to the bedroom, where he would remove whatever I was wearing, which at first made me feel deeply exposed and then became exciting to me in a way I have never since experienced, my skin all alight with being looked at, my eyes on Simon's eyes, imagining myself as he saw me. I thought of the young girl who spent so many hours daydreaming of being loved by someone, and I wished I could pay her a visit and tell her, Look, look, everything will be all right.

———

I tried hard to ignore the low noise that thrummed throughout my day, some tolling, cautionary bell. I wouldn't listen. I wanted everything to stay as it was. I was more afraid of the truth than the lie. The truth would change the circumstances of my life. The lie was static. The lie was peaceful. I was happy with the lie.

Six months went by in this way. And then, one day in autumn, I arranged to pick up an extra shift: crowd control for a special event. But when I arrived at the station, Sergeant Reynolds, who was my supervisor at the time, informed me that my services would not, in fact, be needed. Too many people had signed up, he said. And I was still junior.

Not unhappily, I left the station. It was very pleasant outside, cool and crisp, and I decided to walk all the way from the station to Port Richmond, rather than taking the bus. I was in fine spirits. I stopped along the way and bought some flowers, which was deeply unlike me. I had never bought flowers before in my life. I felt silly, holding them—the incongruity of a uniformed police officer holding a dainty bouquet was not lost on me—and I ultimately carried them down by my side as if I were attempting to dry them as I went.

When I arrived at home I found the door to my house unlocked. I am fastidious about locking the door of any house I live in, having seen too many burglaries transpire through simple carelessness on the part of a homeowner, and I had already scolded Kacey once or twice for forgetting to do so herself since she moved in with me.

That day I sighed and locked the door behind me, telling myself that I would have another talk with my sister later, when suddenly I heard movements from the second floor. Kacey, I thought, should have been at work.

I still had my weapon on me, and I kept one hand near it as I ascended the stairs. In the other, I was still holding the silly bouquet.

I tried to be quiet, but the house was old, and my footsteps caused the wooden floorboards to shift and squeak. As I went, the noises upstairs increased: I heard the sound of drawers opening and closing, and then low murmuring.

I made a quick decision. I dropped the flowers. I drew my weapon.

At the top of the staircase I nudged open the door to the back bedroom with a foot, and before I could see who was on the other side of it I said, Don't move. Put your hands up.

—What the hell, said a man I didn't recognize.

Next to him was Kacey.

The two of them were standing side by side in the center of the bedroom, a very strange place to be standing, but I could tell by the rumpled bed that they had been on it together a moment before.

They were both fully clothed; I did not believe they'd been doing anything of an intimate nature. I had the impression, in fact, that the man was probably gay. But it was clear, from Kacey's expression, that she was guilty of something.

—Mick, she said. Why aren't you at work?

Slowly, I lowered my weapon.

—I should ask you the same thing, I said.

—I was wrong about my schedule. This is my friend Lou, she said, looking at the man, who raised a hand weakly.

If this was meant to mollify me, it didn't.

For in an instant, I knew: I could easily hear, in her slow voice, and see in her flushed face the old signs that she was using.

I said nothing to her. I went instead to the dresser and began throwing open drawers. Toward the bottom, there they were: syringes, rubber tubing, lighters. Small glassine baggies with outrageous stamps. Slowly, I closed the drawer.

When I turned around again, the friend was gone, and Kacey and I were alone.

NOW

Paula is still laughing. She is wagging her head now, incredulous, disgusted.

—Tell me who, I say.

—Same cop comes around here telling girls to blow him or he'll bring them in, she says.

Then she adds, Tell me that's your suspect. Tell me that's your fucking suspect. Oh my God, please tell me you guys are looking for a cop. That would be great. That would be perfect.

I speak more quickly than I can think. A deep and uneasy confusion has settled onto me.

—No, I say. Just someone we want to talk to.

Paula's expression changes.

—Do you think I'm stupid, she says, quietly. Do you think I'm that fucking dumb.

She turns and walks away, hobbling.

—What does he look like? I call after her.

Paula's back is turned now, but I can still hear what she's saying.

—Don't bring me into this, she says again. She whips around, briefly, a dangerous look in her eyes.

She continues on her way.

—Paula, I call. Paula, will you make a report?

She laughs. No fucking way, she says, her back to me, getting smaller as she walks. Yeah, that's all I need. Make a report. Get on every cop's shit list in this godforsaken city.

She disappears around a corner. And for the first time in my career as a police officer—a profession of which I have always been proud—a sickening feeling descends upon me: that I'm on the wrong side of something important.

call Truman on my way back to the station. I want his advice. I want to know, too, if he knows anything about what Paula said.

—You okay? he says, before anything else.

—Are you busy? I ask him.

—No, I'm good, he says. What's up?

—Have you ever heard anything about an officer who wears a sweatshirt that says *Wildwood* on it?

He pauses. I don't think so, he says. That doesn't ring a bell. Why?

In the background, I hear someone speaking: a woman. *Truman?* she's saying. *Truman, who is that?*

—If you're busy, I say again.

—No, says Truman.

—What about this, I say. Have you ever heard of a cop who—I pause, trying to formulate the words—who demands *favors* from women in our sector? In exchange for letting them go?

Truman pauses for a long time.

—I mean, he says, yes. I think everyone's heard stories about that.

I haven't, I think. Until today. I don't say this.

Again, the voice in the background, serious now: *Truman.*

Does Truman have a girlfriend?

—Hang on, says Truman, and I hear muffled speaking, as if he is cradling the phone in his hands, and then he says, into the phone again, I'll call you back, okay?

—Okay, I say, but he's already hung up.

can't find Sergeant Ahearn in his office when I get back to the station.

In fact, I can't find any sergeant. And yet this is information that I need to convey, as quickly as I can.

I stand in the doorway of the ops room for a moment, until Corporal Shah notices me.

—Have you seen Sergeant Ahearn? I ask.

—He's on scene, says Corporal Shah, who, as usual, is chewing gum. He's been trying to quit smoking for what seems like the eleventh time, and therefore he's had an edge to him for a week. You want me to tell him you were looking for him? he says.

—I'll just give him a call, I say. Can you take this? I say, holding out my activity log.

I change out of my uniform and then sit in my personal vehicle in the parking lot. I bring up Sergeant Ahearn's number. I dial and reach his voicemail.

—Sergeant Ahearn, I say. It's Michaela Fitzpatrick. I have to talk to you about something that happened on my shift today. It's urgent.

I leave my number for him, though I know he has it.

I drive out of the lot, heading for home.

When I pull into the driveway, the landlady is standing in the yard, hands on hips, looking up into the sky. My car is full of junk and debris, and I wave a quick hello to Mrs. Mahon as I get out, and then I open the back door and bend in to retrieve some of it. I wish Mrs. Mahon would go inside. She is wearing another of her funny seasonal sweatshirts—this one is a wreath with three-dimensional decorations—which I imagine are meant to be conversation-opening in some way.

I gather an armful of bags and wrappers and shoes from the floor of the car. Then I stand and walk toward the backyard.

As I do, Mrs. Mahon calls after me.

—Did you hear about the snow? she says.

I stop and turn, briefly.

—What snow, I say.

—They're saying a foot overnight, says Mrs. Mahon. It's a bombogenesis.

This she says with quiet urgency, peering over her glasses, as if she is announcing a tsunami headed in our direction. Probably she doesn't expect me to know the word. I do.

—I'd better turn on the news, I say, with as much seriousness as I can muster.

I'm humoring her. Since we moved into the apartment above her, Mrs. Mahon has made apocalyptic weather announcements approximately a dozen times, including one occasion when she made us tape our windows due to what was predicted to be golf ball–sized hail. (It wasn't.) People like Mrs. Mahon clog up the grocery stores the night before storms, buying milk and bread that they won't ever consume, filling bathtubs with water that, forty-eight hours later, they will watch sadly as it disappears down a slow drain.

—Good night, Mrs. Mahon, I say.

The house seems empty when I open the door. The living room, at least, is dark, and the television is off.

—Hello? I call. No one replies.

I walk quickly toward the back of the apartment. Suddenly, my son steps into the hallway from the bathroom. He's wearing his favorite accessory: a Phillies cap that his father bought for him a year ago. He's holding one finger to his lips.

—*Shhhhh,* he says.

—What? I say.

—Bethany's taking a nap, he says.

Thomas points toward the door of his bedroom. Sure enough, there on his bed is Bethany, stretched out on Thomas's race car comforter, one hand curled under a cheek, her hair and her makeup impeccable.

I slam the door closed loudly. Open it again. On the other side of it, Bethany is rising slowly, angelically, stretching, in no particular hurry. One perfect red line bisects her right cheek: a wrinkle in the pillowcase has left its mark.

—Hey, says Bethany, nonchalantly. She glances at her phone.

—Sorry, she says, perhaps noticing at last my expression, which hovers someplace around incredulity. She adds, I stayed up late last night. Just needed a power nap.

Only later—after a short conversation with Bethany about how, even though Thomas seems mature, he's really only four, and can't be left alone; after Bethany has left, her hurt feelings conveyed by her silence and a series of baleful looks; after I have prepared dinner, and put it down on the table—do I realize I never turned on the news.

When I do, I find that I've underestimated Mrs. Mahon. She was correct: Cecily Tynan is predicting six to twelve inches of snow overnight, and more to the north and west of the city.

—No, I say softly. There are no snow days when you're a police officer. And—more thanks to Bethany—I have no more sick or personal days to expend.

—Mom, says Thomas, and I wait to be interrogated. Thomas is very perceptive, and I have no doubt that he can sense that something is awry.

But he doesn't say anything for a while, and instead sits down next to me on the couch. He has his head down.

—What's the matter? I say. What's wrong, Thomas?

I put an arm around him. His skin is warm. His hair is corn silk. He sinks into my side, and I think for just an instant of lying back with him, pulling him toward me as I did when he was an infant, his cheek to my sternum. Is there any more pleasant feeling than the weight of a baby on one's chest? But he is adamant, these days, about being *big*, a big kid, and I have no doubt that he would quickly squirm away.

—I'm lucky to have you, I say to him quietly. Do you know that?

Saying it aloud—even acknowledging my gratefulness for Thomas too frequently in my thoughts—seems to me to be a kind of jinx, an invitation, an open window through which some creature might come in the night and spirit him away.

—Thomas? I say again, and he finally looks at me.

—When's my birthday? he says.

—You know the answer to that, I say. When's your birthday?

—December third, he says. But how long is that from now?

I blink, realizing. One week from now, I say. Why do you ask?

Thomas looks down again. Bethany was talking about birthdays today, he says, and she asked me when mine was. And I told her. And then she asked me if I was having a party.

Every year prior, Simon has taken him to do something special on or around his birthday: for his fourth, they went to the movies; for his third, they went to the Franklin Institute; for his second, which he of course doesn't remember, they went to the Please Touch Museum. This year, I figured I'd take up the mantle. We'd do something similar, just the two of us. But Thomas is looking up at me hopefully. And I suppose it wouldn't be out of the question to arrange a small party with friends.

—Guess what, I say finally. If you wanted a birthday party, we could probably put one together. Maybe we could even invite a few friends from your old school.

He grins.

—No promises, I say. It depends on who's available.

He nods.

—Who would you like to invite? I say.

—Carlotta and Lila, he says, without hesitating. He's bouncing in his seat on the sofa now, his legs straight out before him.

—Okay, I say. I'll call their parents, all right? What do you want to do with them?

—Go to McDonald's, he says, unswervingly. With the playground.

I pause for just the smallest beat. Then I say, Sounds great.

He's talking about the one in South Philadelphia, the one Simon used to take him to, the one that has an indoor play space. He hasn't been there in over a year. I'm surprised he still remembers it.

He clasps his hands together tightly, bringing them up beneath his chin, the way he does whenever he can't contain his excitement.

—McDonald's, he says again. And I can get whatever I want, right?

—Within reason, I say.

He falls asleep on the sofa not long after that, and I carry him to his bed, laying him down there.

I've always been strict with Thomas about where he sleeps. He had terrible colic when he was a baby, and often cried and cried inconsolably, and hearing those sounds nearly tore me in half. There has always been a part of me—animal, feral, governed by some force that seems to be trying to claw its way out of my abdomen—that hungers for Thomas, that physically longs for him, that threatens, each time he wakes in the night, to undo all the work I did over the course of his infancy. But the sleep-training manuals I read were always very clear on one point: never let your child sleep in a bed with you, they said; not only will this imperil the life of your child, but the habit will be next to impossible to break, and will ultimately result in a child who lacks confidence and independence, a child who is not capable of soothing himself, and who is not well positioned to function in the world.

Therefore, from the time he was a few months old, Thomas has had his room, and I have had mine. When we lived in Port Richmond, this worked well. His colic subsided, as I knew it would, and soon he became a good, sound sleeper, and both of us woke each day rested and refreshed.

When we moved into this apartment, though, things changed. Now, with increasing frequency, Thomas has been begging to sleep in my room. Sometimes I even find him curled into a ball at the foot of my bed, having snuck in very quietly while I sleep. When I notice he has done this, or on the occasions when I catch him in the act, I am firm with him, and bring him back to his race car bed, and reassure him that he'll be fine, and turn on the night-light that I purchased for him for further comfort.

In general, I feel quite confident that I am correct on this point. Only one recent episode makes me waver in my certainty. It happened several weeks ago: I woke in the early hours of the morning to the sound of a whimpering the likes of which I had never heard. It was coming from the foot of the bed, and it sounded more like a puppy than a boy. And then a small voice began to chant one word aloud, over and over again: *Daddy*, the voice was saying, *Daddy, Daddy*.

Quietly, I roused myself from the bed and tiptoed to the end of it. There, in a nest of blankets and pillows, was my son. He was talking in his sleep. I watched him for a moment, uncertain whether to wake him. He pedaled his limbs wildly, like a dog chasing rabbits in his dreams. In the dim room I could only just make out his expression, which changed rapidly: he smiled, and then frowned, and then his eyebrows pinched together, and then his chin puckered. I leaned down to him, and only then did I notice he had been crying in his sleep; the pillowcase beside his face, in fact, was soaked with tears. I put one hand on his forehead, and then his shoulder. Thomas, I said, Thomas. You're all right.

But he couldn't be woken, and so, for that one night, I brought him into my bed with me, and I put my hand very lightly on his smooth forehead, the way my mother used to do for me, and stroked his eyebrows gently until he settled.

When he at last looked comfortable, I returned him to bed. And in the morning, when he recounted a memory of having seen me in the night, I told him that it had only been a dream.

Overnight, I open my eyes to find that we are in the thick of it.

Out my bedroom window, snow is falling heavily in the shaft of light sent out by the streetlamp at the foot of Mrs. Mahon's driveway.

In the morning, I wake to my phone alarm, snatch it off my bedside table, and press *Cancel*. There on the screen, unsurprisingly, is a text from Bethany, sent at six in the morning:

Roads r crazy! Can't make it :(

—No, I say aloud. I stand up and walk to the window. A thick coat of white over everything. No, I say again.

I hear Thomas's footsteps as he walks down the hall toward my room. He knocks, and then opens the door.

—What's wrong? he asks.

—Bethany can't come today, I say. She's snowed in.

Or, just as likely, she's pouting because of the exchange we had yesterday.

—Yes! says Thomas, and it occurs to me too late that he thinks this means I will stay home with him.

—No, I say. I'm sorry, Thomas. No more time off. I have to go to work.

His small face crumples, and I take it in my hands.

—I'm sorry, I say again. I'll make it up to you. I promise.

I sit down on the edge of the bed again, thinking.

Thomas puts his small chin on my shoulder, light as a bird.

—Where will I go? he says.

—I'm not sure yet, I say.

—I can come to work with you, he says. I can ride in the backseat.

I smile. I'm afraid that's not allowed, I say.

I pull him onto my lap. Together, we wonder what we'll do.

Reluctantly, I try Gee first. In the past, she's watched Thomas on a handful of occasions, true emergencies. But I'm not optimistic. Sure enough: she doesn't answer her phone.

I try Carla, Thomas's former part-time babysitter, next.

But Carla works at an insurance company in Center City these days, and she tells me regretfully that her office is open.

Ashley, I think. A last resort. I call her cell phone. No answer. I send her a text.

While waiting for Ashley to reply, I feed Thomas breakfast and gaze out the window. It's still snowing. There's the driveway to shovel, before I do anything else.

—Put on your boots, I say to my son.

Outside, the work puts me in a better mood. I used to exercise regularly when I lived in Port Richmond. I did CrossFit, very briefly. Even joined a coed soccer team. Working up a good sweat three or four times a week has always kept me calm. But recently I've had no time.

I give Thomas a trowel and tell him to help. He spends twenty minutes on the same spot, and then turns his attention to trying to build sandcastles out of snow.

I've got maybe five feet of driveway to go when Mrs. Mahon appears in her doorway.

—You don't have to do that, she calls to me. Not your job.

—I don't mind, I say.

—I can pay Chuck, says Mrs. Mahon. Usually do.

Chuck is the teenage son of our next-door neighbor. He comes around to make a buck by raking or sweeping or, I imagine, shoveling when it snows.

I keep working.

—Well, anyway, says Mrs. Mahon. Thank you.

—No problem, I say. And then I have a thought. I check my phone. No reply yet from Ashley.

—Mrs. Mahon, I say. Do you have plans today?

Mrs. Mahon frowns.

—I never have plans, Mickey, she says.

I have never once been inside of Mrs. Mahon's house. When I signed the lease, it was in the apartment upstairs. Today, when Mrs. Mahon opens the door for us, I am surprised. Somehow I was picturing something along the lines of Gee's house, knickknacks all over, old carpet that needs replacing. Instead, it's sparsely furnished and impeccably clean. The floors are hardwood except where they are covered by small rugs. The furniture is mainly well made. The apartment has modern art all over it, large abstract paintings, textured with brushstrokes. They're not bad. Did Mrs. Mahon do these herself? I can't imagine asking that question, but I'm curious.

—I like your paintings, I say instead.

—Thank you, Mrs. Mahon says, but she doesn't elaborate.

—I'm so sorry to do this, I say.

Thomas is standing very still. I can tell he is both intrigued and frightened. He leans slightly to his right, craning to look up the staircase. I imagine Mrs. Mahon's bedroom is up there.

I dig in my pocket, pull out my wallet. I open it and pray I have some cash to proffer, but all I can come up with is twenty dollars.

—Here, I say, holding it out to Mrs. Mahon. Take this. I'll get more while I'm out today.

Mrs. Mahon waves it off. Don't be silly, she says, brusquely.

—Please, I say. Please let me. I'll feel terrible.

—I insist, says Mrs. Mahon. She's standing up straight. She will not be reasoned with.

I hold out a bag I've brought down from our apartment. There's an extra change of clothes in here, I say, and some books and toys. I've packed him lunch, too, I say.

What I don't tell her: He's only four. He wets his pants still, sometimes. He gets very frightened of scary things on television, including the news. Looking at Thomas, I know he would not appreciate my saying these things to Mrs. Mahon.

—You didn't have to do that, says Mrs. Mahon. I could have made him something. Unless this young man doesn't like peanut butter sandwiches, says Mrs. Mahon, turning to Thomas. Do you like peanut butter sandwiches? she asks him.

He nods.

—All right, then. Sounds like we'll be fine.

I kneel down next to Thomas. I give him a kiss on his cheek. Be very, very good, I tell him. You know what good means, right?

Thomas nods again. Listen, he says, pointing to one ear.

He's trying to be brave now. What will he do here all day?

I write my cell number down on a notepad next to Mrs. Mahon's landline, even though I think she has it.

—Call anytime, I say. About anything. Really.

Then I walk out the front door, trying hard not to turn around and look at Thomas, whose chin was trembling ever so slightly when I kissed him goodbye: an expression that I know will haunt me as I go through the motions of my shift.

spend my commute worrying. What have I done? Whom have I left Thomas with? I barely know Mrs. Mahon. I don't know any of Mrs. Mahon's family by name, though I have heard her talk about a sister. I don't know what kind of health Mrs. Mahon is in. What if she falls down? I worry. What if she's unkind to Thomas?

And then I remind myself, as always, not to baby him. He is nearly five years old, Michaela, I tell myself. And more capable by the day.

It's warmer out today than it was yesterday, and the snow has stopped. It's already beginning to melt, forming brown puddles where the plows have come through. Bethany, if she had wanted to, could definitely have made it to our house.

Sergeant Ahearn is leading roll call this morning, and at the end of it, I go up to him and ask him if he got my message.

—Message? he says.

—I left you a voicemail last night, I say.

—Oh yeah. I got that, he says. What's up? You wanted to talk?

I glance around the common area. At least three officers are standing within hearing range.

—It's kind of sensitive, I say quietly.

Sergeant Ahearn sighs. Well, there's a ride-along getting fitted with a bulletproof vest in my office right now, he says. So unless you want to take me into the bathroom, you might as well talk to me here.

Again, I look at the other officers. Two of them fit Nguyen's prediction: white men in their forties.

—Do you have twenty minutes to meet me out at lunch today? I ask him.

—Fine, says Ahearn. Scottie's?

It's a sit-down place that's frequented by police. I want, therefore, to avoid it, and every other place we might see colleagues, as well.

—Let's meet at Bomber Coffee on Front Street, I say finally.

The morning goes by slowly. But around ten a.m., something catches my eye: a man in an orange jacket, standing under the El stop on the corner of Kensington and Allegheny, looking alert, arms crossed. He has a plastic bag dangling off one of them.

Dock.

I pull over half a block away and watch him for a while.

If he sees the cruiser, he doesn't react to it. He's too far away, in any case, to know that it is me inside. From this vantage point, visor lowered, I see that his lips are moving slightly each time someone passes him by. I think it likely that the word he's repeating is *works, works, works*: clean syringes that can be purchased for only a little money. Many people make a small living this way in the neighborhood, just enough to keep them high. Some offer more services than that: they'll help you shoot up, generally in the neck, when you've run out of other promising veins; less commonly, if the free clinic is closed or too far away, they'll try to treat infections, drain abscesses—often with disastrous results.

I take out my phone and pull up Truman's number. I hesitate for a moment, but my curiosity gets the best of me.

Are you busy? I text him. I recall the female voice in the background, the last time I phoned him. I don't want to start any trouble for him.

Very quickly, he responds. *What's up?*

Feel like a stakeout? I ask him.

———

It takes Truman half an hour to arrive. For that long, I sit still, tensely, praying that Dock won't leave the intersection, praying that no one will take him up on his offer to work them up. To my relief—to his distress, most likely—no one does.

My phone rings, finally. It's Truman.

—Look to your right, he says.

Subtly, I turn. It takes me a moment to spot him across the street, but eventually I do. There he is, Truman, dressed much differently than he was when I saw him last week: today he is wearing a backpack, baggy athletic pants, a puffy jacket, a winter cap, and a scarf pulled up around his mouth and nose. He's got on sunglasses, too. Only his runner's build gives him away.

—What do you think? he says to me. He's looking straight ahead, studiously avoiding any glance in the direction of my police vehicle.

—Where did you get that outfit, I say.

—Vice squad, he says.

Truman worked undercover for about a decade in his twenties, before I knew him. Mostly narcotics.

—See the gentleman in the orange jacket? I say.

Truman nods.

—That's him, I say.

Truman watches him for a moment. Everyone's got a hustle, huh, he says.

Two girls walk past Truman and eye him.

—All right, says Truman. I'm on it. I'll call you later.

He starts off toward our target. I recognize in his gait a familiar sense of determination. The same demeanor he always bore during our years of working side by side.

An hour later, I still haven't heard from Truman, and it's time to meet Sergeant Ahearn.

I text him to remind him, to make sure he's ready. Then I radio in my location—fudging a little, naming the Wawa next door to Bomber Coffee—and walk into the shop.

Sergeant Ahearn has beaten me here. He's sitting at a table, looking around skeptically. He has better posture than everyone else in the shop.

The table he's chosen is near the bathroom, apart from all the others.

He glances up when he sees me, but he doesn't rise. I sit down across from him.

—This your hangout? he says.

—Not really, I say. I've been here once. Just figured we'd have some privacy.

—Yeah, says Ahearn, widening his eyes. It's very fashionable.

He's being sarcastic. He shifts in his chair. He has coffee on the table in front of him. He doesn't ask me if I'd like to get one.

—So what's going on, he says.

I look around briefly. No one nearby.

I take out my cell phone and pull up the video Homicide has been distributing. I lean forward and press play, facing the phone toward Sergeant Ahearn.

As the video plays, I speak to him in a whisper.

—I spent yesterday showing this around the neighborhood, I say.

—Why? says Ahearn, before I can continue.

I pause.

—Why? I repeat.

—Yeah, says Ahearn. Why?

—Because Detective Nguyen said, I begin.

Ahearn is shaking his head.

—Who do you take instruction from? Not Detective Nguyen, he says. It's *his* job to find this guy. Not yours.

I open and close my mouth. I am trying not to get derailed.

—All right, I say. I'll remember that. The thing is—

—We have enough to worry about every day, says Ahearn.

Will he let me finish?

I wait a beat. Ahearn waits a beat.

—I understand, I say. The thing is, somebody recognized the POI yesterday. One of my regulars on the Avenue. A woman I know fairly well. She told me—here I glance over my shoulder again, lean forward—she told me it was an officer.

Ahearn sips his coffee.

I sit back, waiting for a reaction. But Ahearn looks unfazed.

—I'm sure she did, says Ahearn finally. Did she tell you his name?

—She didn't, I say.

I'm confused.

—She probably didn't know it, I say. She said the women in the neighborhood know him.

I lower my voice so that only Ahearn can hear it.

—She said that he, I say.

Again, I don't know how to phrase it. The technical term sounds so cold.

—That he demands sexual favors, I say. Threatens to bring them in if they say no.

Ahearn nods calmly.

—Listen, I say. I didn't want to go straight to Detective Nguyen with this information because it felt sort of sensitive. I wanted to start with my supervisor.

Is Ahearn smiling?

There are many reactions I pictured him having. None of them was this. He lifts the lid off his coffee, puts it carefully down on the table. Letting it cool. Steam shimmers off it.

—Is this, I say. Is this something you knew about?

Ahearn brings the coffee to his lips, blows on it a little before slurping it. Well, he says to me thoughtfully. I can't tell you everything. But I can tell you we're aware of these accusations.

—In what sense, I say.

Ahearn looks at me sharply.

—In the sense that we know about them. What do you think?

—And what are you doing about them? I say. I feel it happening: my blood is rising to my face, betraying me. In my abdomen, a boiler goes on.

—Mickey, says Ahearn. He puts his hands to his temples and rubs them. He looks as if he's deciding whether or not to continue. Then he says, Look, Mickey. Say you're some lowlife with no money. Say you're out on the Ave, say you're looking for action. What's one way you might get some for free?

I hesitate, just for an instant.

Ahearn is nodding.

—You get it? he says. You say you're a cop.

I say nothing. I look away. It is possible, I concede, that this might happen from time to time. But Paula is smart. I can't picture her being duped in this way.

—Anyways, says Ahearn. Listen. I'll relay the accusation to Nguyen and Internal Affairs if it will make you feel better. Who made it?

—She won't go on record, I say.

—Between you and me, then, says Ahearn. I can't go to IA with an anonymous accusation. They'll laugh me out of the room.

Again, I hesitate.

—Or I don't have to say anything, says Ahearn. Your call.

—Off the record? I say.

—Off the record.

—Paula Mulroney, I say.

The definition of utilitarian ethics, as it was relayed to us by Ms. Powell, is the greatest good for the greatest number. This is what crosses my mind as I give up Paula.

Sergeant Ahearn nods. I know the name, he says. We've brought her in a time or two, haven't we?

—Or three, I say. Or four.

Ahearn rises, still holding his coffee. He puts the lid back on. He stretches leisurely, letting me know the meeting is now over.

—I'll pass on the message, he says.

—Thank you, I say.

—And, Mickey, he says, looking me in the eye. Just focus on your job, okay? You're in the 24th District. You don't have time to do much else.

Back in my car, I radio to Dispatch that I'm done with lunch. Then I sit in my car, fuming.

If I disliked Sergeant Ahearn before, now I revile him. The way he spoke to me was uncalled for. The way he sat there, imperiously, nodding as if he knew it all already. I think of every possible retort I could have made. Then, feeling impotent, I check my phone.

One voicemail from Truman Dawes.

I listen.

—Mick, he says. Call me as soon as you can.

My hands begin shaking. I call him back. As I wait for him to pick up, I head for the Avenue.

—*Answer*, I whisper. *Answer. Answer.*

He doesn't. I call him again.

On the last ring, he picks up.

—Mickey, he says. Where are you?

—Front and Coral, I say. Heading north on Front.

—I'll meet you at Emerald and Cumberland, he says.

I've already almost missed the turnoff for Emerald, and I swerve dangerously to make it. I briefly turn on my bubble gums, causing two cars nearby to screech to a halt.

I hardly recognize myself these days.

—Is she all right, I say to Truman.

—I don't know, says Truman.

He's changed when I pick him up. The only thing I recognize is the backpack he is holding, which now, I presume, contains his undercover attire. He's back in his jeans, his knee brace now visible; he's lost the scarf and the sunglasses and even the down jacket.

He gets in, lowering himself painfully into the passenger's seat. He glances around as he closes the door.

—Why don't we get out of this neighborhood, he says.

Probably a good idea. I drive southeast again, toward Fishtown.

—What happened? I say.

—I bought a syringe off him, Truman begins. I told him I was in from Bucks. I asked if he could tell me where to score.

I nod. This is the beginning of a familiar story: it's how half the overdoses in the district happen. People venture in from the suburbs, looking for a fix, and getting more than they or their bodies bargained for in the process. Potent, deadly fentanyl has found its way into most of the heroin for sale around here, and it's killing even the most experienced users of the drug.

—*Follow me*, he said, says Truman. He started walking north along the Ave.

—Was he talking to you? I ask him. Did he say anything about himself?

—He said, *You're not a cop, are you?* says Truman. I told him, *Fuck that, I hate cops.* He didn't say anything else.

Truman clears his throat and glances at me. Continues.

—He took me down an alley off a little street called Madison. You can get in through the back doors of a couple abandos there. So no one else is around now, and Dock starts talking about what he's got, starts telling me it's the purest stuff I'll ever shoot. Asks me how much I want, what I have to spend. Tells me he's the doctor, he'll shoot me up if I pay him for it. *That's all right,* I say.

He looks at me kind of hard. Says, *You sure? You can do it inside here if you want.*

I'm getting nervous at this point, thinking about ways out. Thinking he knows I'm a cop. When I was on Vice, I'd have a backup team, I'd be wired, I'd have an exit plan.

I'm good, I say.

So I give him some money and he takes it. Tells me to wait there. *You're not gonna run off with that, right?* I say to him.

Nah, he tells me. *I'd be out of business in a minute if I did that.* So he goes inside, pushes aside a piece of plywood that's covering the door and disappears.

I interrupt Truman.

—Did you get the house number? I ask.

—I was trying to figure it out, he says, but I couldn't. It's a house with white siding on it and there's graffiti on a board over one of the back windows that says *BBB.* Three letters.

Anyway, says Truman, as soon as he disappears inside I go up to one of the windows and try to get a look inside. I'm peering through cracks in the boarding. But it's dark in there. I can't see much. I think I can make out at least four people, maybe more. Everyone's in different states of nodding out. One of them looked dead. Might have been dead, Truman says.

I have seen houses like this more times than I can count. To me they look like a circle of hell.

—I'm listening, Truman says, and from inside I hear what sounds like someone pounding up a staircase. A second later he comes back down and suddenly I see this guy Dock walking toward me, toward the back of the house. I jump back, turn around, and pretend to be minding my business.

Here, this guy goes. *You sure you don't want me to shoot you up? Five bucks.*

Nah, I tell him. *I got it.*

He eyes me up. *Don't shoot up near my house*, he says. *And test it first.*

I thank him, go to leave. I'm wishing I could get one more look inside. And maybe he notices me hesitating, because he says to me, *You looking for something else?*

Like what, I say.

A girl, this fucker says.

I get cold. Truman watches me a little before going on.

—I said, *Maybe.*

He says, *You want to see pictures? I got pictures.*

I said I did. He takes out his phone and starts flipping through photos of girls. And, Mick. I saw Kacey.

I nod. I knew this was coming.

—*See anything you like?* this shithead says. I say I do. But I want to get fixed up first. I tell him I'll be back another time. He gives me his phone number. *Call me when you need something,* he tells me. *I'm your guy, okay? I'm the doctor.*

I'm looking straight ahead.

—You okay? says Truman.

I nod. What I am feeling is a loathing that begins very deep inside me.

—How did she look, I ask Truman, but I realize only after I say it that I was too quiet to be heard.

Again I ask.

—What do you mean? says Truman.

—In the photo. How did she look?

Truman sets his jaw. She was, he says. She wasn't wearing much. She was skinny. Her hair was dyed bright red. She looked like she was maybe roughed up. One of her eyes was swollen. I couldn't get a good look.

But alive, I think. But maybe she's alive.

—One more thing, says Truman. Right when I was about to leave, someone comes around the corner. Tough-looking guy, tattoos everywhere, looks like a friend of Dock's. He points right at Dock, happy to see him, and goes, *McClatchie. How you been?*

—McClatchie, I say.

—Right, says Truman.

—Connor McClatchie, I say, remembering the Facebook photo, *Connor Dock Famisall* underneath.

Truman nods. Then nods toward the MDT on the center console.

—May I? he says.

—Go ahead, I tell him. It feels like old times: like my partner, doing the paperwork while I drive.

Truman's login is disabled while he's on medical leave, so I give him mine. Using it, he runs a search in the PCIC.

I keep trying to look while I drive, and I almost swerve into oncoming traffic.

—Jesus, Mick, says Truman. Pull over.

But I don't want to. Not until we're far enough out of the neighborhood so that Truman won't be recognized either. I keep scanning the road ahead of me, glancing in my mirrors, waiting to encounter a colleague. Or Sergeant Ahearn.

—Just read it aloud to me, I say.

Truman reads to himself for a while. Then he says, All right, here we go. McClatchie, Connor. DOB March 3, 1991, Philadelphia. Youngster, he says, glancing over at me.

—What else, I ask him.

He gives a low whistle.

—What? I say. Tell me.

—Okay, says Truman. We've got everything from armed robbery to assault to illegal possession of a firearm. Guy's been incarcerated three— wait, four—five times.

Again, he pauses.

—And? I say.

—Looks like he does have a charge here for promoting prostitution, says Truman.

Pimping. Unusual, actually: most of the women in Kensington work for themselves. But there's always an exception to the rule.

He pauses. He also has a warrant on him, he says. That could be helpful somehow.

—Could be, I say.

I glance at the clock on the dash. It's close to the end of my shift. Almost time to rescue Thomas from Mrs. Mahon, and Mrs. Mahon from Thomas. I also haven't answered a call in too long.

—Where's your car? I ask Truman, and he tells me.

For a while, I say nothing.

Then, at last, I ask him. Do you think she was in that house? I say.

Truman thinks for a long time.

—I don't know, he says. She could have been. I didn't see her downstairs. But there was a second floor, and I know something was going on up there.

I nod.

—Mickey, says Truman. Don't do anything stupid.

—No, I say. I wouldn't.

Truman's phone rings then, and he glances at it before telling me to pull over, saying that he'll jump out where we are.

—I can drive you all the way to your car, I say.

—It's okay, says Truman. It's not far.

He seems antsy to get out. The phone keeps ringing.

He taps the roof of the cruiser, once, as he's leaving.

It's only then that I realize that I never even told him about my meeting at lunch with Ahearn. If anyone would have advice on this front, it's Truman—but Truman has already answered his call.

I watch him for a while as he walks away.

I wonder, again, whom he's speaking to.

At last, the day is over. I worry the whole way home about how Thomas's day has been. I yearn for the release of reconnecting with him after a time apart: a quick hit of dopamine that lowers the shoulders and slows the breath.

It's already close to pitch-black when I arrive at home, and it's not even five p.m. I despise these days: the darkness of the darkest part of winter. Every glint of sunlight feels edible, something sweet to swallow and store for the long cold night.

The first thing I notice when I arrive is that there are no lights on in Mrs. Mahon's house. My stomach clenches, just a bit. I exit the car and trot through the snow, up to the front door. I ring the doorbell. Without waiting long enough, I knock, too.

I press my face to the glass at the side of the door, trying to see anything inside. Where are they? I'm ready to kick down the door. I'm back in work mode, my hand near my weapon.

I'm about to knock again when the door swings open. Mrs. Mahon is on the other side of it, the room behind her dim. No Thomas. She looks at me, blinking through her large glasses.

—Is Thomas here? I ask.

—Of course, she says. Are you all right? That pounding on the door, good lord. You almost gave us a heart attack.

—I apologize, I say. Where is he?

And just then he appears next to Mrs. Mahon, a strip of red above his upper lip. He's been drinking something sugary. He's grinning.

—I hope you don't mind that I gave him Kool-Aid, says Mrs. Mahon. I keep it in the cabinet for when my great-nephews come over.

I have never seen Mrs. Mahon's great-nephews in the entire time we've been living here. No, that's fine, I say. Special treat.

—We've been watching a movie like in the movie theater, Thomas says, his voice shrill with excitement.

—He means we made popcorn and turned the lights off, says Mrs. Mahon. Come in, you're letting cold air into the house.

Inside, while Thomas is getting his shoes and jacket on, I notice a picture hung on the wall of the entryway: it looks like a class photograph, grainy and worn. There are many rows of children, ranging in age from kindergartners to young teenagers. The rear two rows are nuns, dressed in cardigans and skirts and simple head coverings, like the nuns in the parish school Kacey and I used to go to. The photograph is black-and-white and difficult to date. It's hard to imagine that Mrs. Mahon was ever a child, but the image says differently. Quickly, I scan the children to see if I can recognize her, but suddenly Mrs. Mahon touches my elbow.

—While he's off getting ready, she says quietly, I should tell you that the man stopped by again.

My heart sinks.

—Did Thomas see him, I say.

—No, says Mrs. Mahon. I recognized him out the window, so I told Thomas to go upstairs for a moment. And I told him you no longer lived here. Just as you asked.

Relief.

—How did he react, I say.

—He seemed disappointed, says Mrs. Mahon.

—That's fine, I say. He can be as disappointed as he wants. He believed you?

—Seemed to, said Mrs. Mahon. He was very polite.

—He can be, I say.

Mrs. Mahon sets her jaw and nods.

—Good for you, anyway, she says. Most men I have no use for.

She thinks a moment and then adds, One or two of them, I tolerate.

Thomas is full of stories when we enter the apartment.

—Mrs. Mahon let me watch *E.P.*, he says.

—What's *E.P.?*

—A movie. It's a movie about a guy who goes on a kid's bike.

—A guy?

—A monster.

—*E.T.*, I say.

—And he says *E.P. phone home*. And Mrs. Mahon showed me how to do that with my finger, like this.

He extends his little pointer finger toward me, and I touch it with mine.

—Like that, he says again.

—Did you enjoy it? I ask.

—Yes. She let me watch it even though it was scary, says Thomas. He's wired from the movie and, probably, from too much sugar.

—Were you frightened?

—No. *It* was scary. *I* wasn't scared.

—Good, I say. I'm glad to hear it.

But later that night, after I put Thomas to bed in his own room, I am awakened by the pattering of little feet, and there is Thomas, wrapped up in a blanket, looking, in fact, much like the protagonist of the movie he watched today.

—I'm scared, he announces, solemnly.

—That's all right, I say.

—I lied because I am scared after all.

—That's all right, I say again.

He pauses, biting his lip, looking down at the floor. I know what will come next.

—Thomas, I say, warningly.

—Can I sleep in your bed? he says, but in his voice there is resignation. He already knows the answer.

I stand and go to him. I take his hand and walk him back down the hallway to his room.

—You're nearly five years old, I say to him. You're getting very grown up. Can you be brave for me?

In the darkened hallway, I see him nod.

I steer him into his room and turn on the night-light for him. He climbs into his bed and I tuck the blankets over him and put one hand on his head.

—Guess what, I tell him. I talked to Carlotta's and Lila's mothers to invite them to your birthday party.

He's silent.

—Thomas? I say.

He won't look at me. Just for a moment, I hesitate. And then I think of everything I've ever read about how one instills strength and self-sufficiency in a child, how teaching a child confidence and independence young is essential to ensure the child will ultimately be a well-adjusted citizen and adult.

—They said yes, I tell him.

Then I give him a kiss on his forehead and quietly leave the room.

have to go to court the next morning to testify. The trial is for the domestic assault case from last week. Robert Mulvey, Jr., is the accused; it seems his wife has decided, despite her earlier reluctance, to press charges. Both Gloria Peters and I will be called to the witness stand.

It would be a routine case, and a routine day, except for the deep discomfort I experience each time I look at Mulvey. His gaze is unwavering and trained on me, and every time our eyes meet—always against my will—I know I recognize him. Again and again, I try to place him, but I can't.

I don't stay to see whether he's convicted.

Back in my vehicle, I compulsively check the clock on my dashboard.

There are not many things I know about Connor McClatchie, but one of them is that at approximately 2:30 p.m. each day, he is at Mr. Wright's store, shooting up and getting warm. Which means, of course, that he is out of the house at that time.

Don't do anything stupid, Truman said to me yesterday. But it isn't stupid, I believe, to follow through on leads. In fact, it only seems reasonable.

It's eleven a.m. now, which means I have several hours to go until I can safely conduct my own reconnaissance of the place. I do my best not to focus on the time. But I can't help driving, twice, down the little street called Madison—not too many times, not enough to alert or alarm anyone—and craning my neck to see down the alley that Truman described.

If the layout of Center City—all right angles and symmetry—is evidence of the staid and rational minds that planned Philadelphia, Kensington is evidence of what happens when intention is distorted by necessity. Here and there, the landscape is dotted with small parks, many of which are oddly shaped. Aside from the firm and upright line of Front Street, and the diagonal one of Kensington Ave, the rest of Kensington's streets are all vaguely askew, tilted just slightly off the firm equator of Center City streets like Vine and Market and South. Kensington's streets start and stop without warning; they go from one to two lanes with equal abruptness. Madison is different than East Madison; West Susquehanna runs unapologetically below East Cumberland. Most of the small streets in Kensington are residential; on them, brick and stucco-fronted rowhomes stand shoulder to shoulder, except where they have been demolished, leaving behind empty lots that look to me like missing teeth. Some blocks are relatively well kept, and harbor only one or two abandoned, shuttered homes. Other blocks have been ravaged by the misfortunes of their residents; on these blocks, nearly every house looks empty.

Many of Kensington's side streets are intersected by even smaller alleys, which themselves are lined by the rears of houses that look as if they're angry with the passerby, have turned their backs in a huff. These alleys are generally not passable by cars.

It is down one such alley that I now peer, searching for the house with three Bs on it that Truman described.

But if there is such a house, it's not visible from where I am.

When the time draws near, I park my assigned vehicle and enter Alonzo's shop. He looks up and, judging correctly that I'm not there to purchase a coffee, points wordlessly to the closet where he's keeping my change of clothes.

—Thank you, Alonzo, I say to him, and go into the bathroom, and then, with as much dignity as I can muster, reemerge clad in my black, overlarge sweatpants and T-shirt.

I say nothing. Only nod, and place my uniform and its bag back on the shelf, and then disappear out the door. This time, I leave my radio and my weapon with it. I have no way to invisibly holster it under my civilian clothes.

I jog to Madison. It helps to keep me warm. I check my watch: 2:30 exactly.

I slow my pace to a walk as I turn onto the street, and then down the alley that runs perpendicular to it. I try, and most likely fail, to look casual.

There it is, all the way at the end: the back of the house in question. White siding. Three Bs spray-painted onto a board over one of the two back windows. One large, rotting piece of plywood over the place where a back door would formerly have been. It looks like it would be easy to push it to the side, and I imagine that this is how its temporary residents make their way in and out.

I put my face up next to the board that covers the window, try in vain to peer inside through a crack, but the interior is too dark for me to see much. I hesitate for a moment, and then I knock rapidly on the board that covers the door. If Dock answers, I'm not sure what I'll do.

I wait for a while. And then a while longer. I knock again. Nobody answers.

Eventually, I push the plywood covering aside, and, tentatively, I step inside.

Upon entry, I am met with the familiar smell of all such houses, and the deep chill of a shadowy structure in winter. Interior cold, I think, is even bitterer than the cold of the outdoors. No sunlight penetrates the inside of these abandoned homes, not boarded up as they are. The air is still and brutal, like the inside of a freezer.

I take two steps and wait while my eyes adjust. The floorboards creak precariously. I am afraid, in fact, of stepping on the wrong one—or an absent one—and being summarily deposited into the basement.

I wish I had my duty belt, if only so that I had access to my flashlight. Instead, I palm my cell phone and turn on its flashlight application.

I swing it around, shining it toward all four corners of the room I'm standing in. I realize, as I do, that I'm expecting to see human bodies: lifeless ones or living ones, I can't be sure. But I see neither. Only a few mattresses on the floor, heaped with cardboard and trash bags and blankets, and some piles of fabric—clothing, most likely—and other objects I can't identify. This abando appears to be, at least for the moment, actually abandoned.

I think of Truman's description of his encounter with Dock, and recall his saying that, at one point, it sounded like Dock disappeared upstairs. But I don't see a staircase. Not immediately, anyway.

I inch forward and shine my phone toward the front of the house, across from where I entered. I see a front door and a small threshold cut into a wall that ends before a foyer. The staircase, I realize, must be on the other side of that wall.

My eyes have finally adjusted enough for me to walk more confidently, and suddenly I am propelled forward by a new sense of urgency. Get in, I think, and get out.

I mount the staircase quickly, stepping over a few rotten steps as I go, holding the rough banister in my left hand.

When I reach the top, I see a human face staring back at me, wide-eyed.

I drop my phone with a clatter and realize, at the same time, that the face is my own, reflected back to me in a mirror mounted to the wall.

Shakily, I retrieve the phone and begin the old familiar routine of peering into doorways in search of my sister.

I realize that I'm sniffing the air for signs of decaying bodies. It's not a smell one readily forgets. But although the house smells awful, I am grateful to observe that it lacks the distinct and nauseating scent of human death.

A bathroom is missing both its toilet and its tub: there are gaping holes in the floor where both used to be.

A bedroom contains an old sofa, a bunch of magazines, and some used condoms on the floor.

In another, there's a bare mattress on the floor and a chalkboard on the wall, bold markings on it in a childish hand. The windows on the upstairs rooms aren't boarded, and in the daylight they let in I can make out what the artist has depicted: a sort of skyline, a city of tall buildings with innumerable windows represented by tiny dots. I gaze at it, wondering whether the drawing was created before the house's abandonment, or whether a child might more recently have drawn it. There are three stubby pieces of chalk on the wooden rail beneath it, and I can't resist: I reach for one and make a tiny, inconspicuous mark in the right-hand corner. It's been years since I drew on slate.

I'm just returning the chalk to its groove when I hear someone enter the house below.

I flinch. And the chalk makes a slow arc from the rail to the floor, landing with an unmistakable clack.

Who's up there, the person says. A man.

Wildly, I eye the nearest window. How badly injured would I be, I wonder, if I opened it and dropped down to the ground from the second floor?

Before I can decide, I hear loud footsteps pounding up the staircase, and I freeze.

I wish I had my weapon now.

I keep my hands visible. I clear my throat, prepared to speak.

The person pauses on the landing at the top of the stairs. When I entered this bedroom, I closed the door behind me, but didn't latch it. I can almost taste my heart as it hammers in my chest. It feels abnormally high inside me, as if it's trying to escape up through my throat.

The bedroom door opens with a bang. Someone has kicked it open.

At first I don't recognize him.

He's been very badly beaten. His right eye is swollen completely shut. It's black and green. His nose looks out of joint. His ear, too, is swollen, as is his upper lip.

But his haircut is familiar, as is his orange jacket.

—Dock? I say.

I'm shivering now. My knees are knocking. Perversely, I'm embarrassed. It's cold in here, I want to say. I'm shaking because I'm cold.

—What the fuck are you doing here, he says.

—Looking for you, I say.

I'm improvising.

He takes one step forward, slowly.

—How did you find me, he says.

—I asked around, I say. You know. I know people out here.

He gives out a sound that's like a laugh, but painful. He puts a hand to his side. I wonder if his ribs are broken.

—What are you carrying? he says.

I hesitate, just for a minute. There's a very, very small chance that I might convince him I'm armed. And that this might let me make my escape. But I don't know if he is, and therefore it might be foolish to bluff.

—Nothing, I say.

—Raise your hands, he says.

When I've done so, he comes toward me and lifts up my shirt. Then looks down the waistband of my pants. He places his hands all over me. I stand there, feeling helpless.

—I should kill you, he says softly.

—I'm sorry? I say.

—I should kill you, he says, for what your family did to me.

I go very still.

—I don't understand, I say.

—*I don't understand*, says Dock, mockingly. Imitating me.

—One thing Kacey always talked about, he says, is how smart you were. She might have been mad at you. But the way she talked about you, you would have thought you were Alfred Einstein.

I look down at the floor. I stay silent. But it takes all of my strength not to say, *Albert*.

—So I'm not sure I believe you, Dock continues, when you say you don't understand.

I keep my eyes on the floor. I am trying to be as unchallenging as possible. One thing they taught us in the police academy that I have found useful, actually, is how to use your body to convey what you cannot say with your words alone.

Dock points to his face. Look up, he says. Look at me. This wasn't a fair fight, he says. Does this look like a fair fight to you? If you see Bobby O'Brien, you should tell him to watch his back.

Bobby.

I close my eyes. Remember the strange look that passed over his face, upon learning Dock's name at Thanksgiving.

—I apologize sincerely if my cousin did that, I say. You should know that I rarely talk to him. We aren't close.

He scoffs. Right, he says.

—We're not, I say. If he did that to you, he did it on his own. I had nothing to do with it.

Dock pauses, assessing me.

He shifts a little. Scratches his head.

—Why do I believe you? he says at last. It's weird, but I believe you.

—That's good, I say, lifting my head just a little. Glancing up. Then lowering it again.

—Huh, he says, as if surprised.

—Still, he says, you tell him that if you see him. Tell him not to come around the Ave. There are a lot of people here on my side of things.

—I'll convey the message, I say.

He laughs again. Then grimaces. Put your hands down, he says. Your arms must be getting tired.

—What *are* you doing here, he says.

—Looking for Kacey, I say.

I've run out of reasons to lie.

He nods. You love her? he says.

I stiffen.

—She's my sister, I say, carefully. And she's also a citizen of the district I patrol.

Dock laughs again, a little. You're weird, he says.

Then he says, Listen. Get out of here. I don't know where she is. I'm telling you the truth.

—All right, I say. Thank you.

I don't know if he is. I do know I want to leave unharmed. I can still feel his hands on my body. It gives me a crawling feeling, the need to get into a shower.

Before he can change his mind, I walk toward the door and into the hallway. But as I'm about to descend the stairs, he calls out again.

—Mickey, he says.

Slowly, I turn around. Dock is backlit now, framed by the window, a shadow. I can't see his expression.

—You should be more careful, he says. You've got a son to think about.

My muscles tense, as if preparing for a fight.

—What did you say? I say, slowly.

—I said you've got a son, he says. Thomas, right?

Then he sits down on the mattress in the corner and lowers himself painfully until he is prone.

—That's all, he says.

He closes his eyes.

I leave.

Dock's voice as he said my son's name, Thomas, echoes in my ears. If it was meant to be a threat, it worked.

I sit in my car, contemplating my next move. It's obvious, I think, that if my cousin Bobby is the perpetrator of the attack on Dock, then he knows more than he was letting on at Thanksgiving. And yet it's also obvious that he's not prepared to tell me any of it.

My only chance, I think, is to surprise him in some way, or get information about him secondhand.

Without much optimism, I text my cousin Ashley.

Do you know where Bobby's living these days?

While I wait for her to respond, I call Truman. He answers right away.

—Mickey, he says, when I've finished talking. I can't believe you. What were you thinking.

I feel myself growing stubborn.

—Truman, I say, I was simply relying on the evidence I was given to make an informed decision. I knew he'd be out of that house at two-thirty. I knew the house needed to be searched for clues to Kacey's whereabouts. So I made the decision to do it.

Over the phone, I can almost hear Truman shaking his head. Putting his hands to his temples.

—No, Mick, he says. That's not how things work. You could have gotten killed. You understand?

Hearing Truman say it this way, so bluntly, I falter.

—Listen, he says. You're in over your head. Both of us are. Did you even report her missing yet?

I hesitate. I tried, I say. I tried to tell Ahearn. He was busy.

—Then tell a detective, says Truman. A real one. Not us. Tell Di-Paolo.

My resistance to the idea increases with every appeal Truman makes to me. I can't put my finger on why, but distantly a bell is sounding in my brain, and if I could just get Truman to stop talking, perhaps I could hear it.

—Mickey, Truman says, you've got to get serious, now. This guy knows about Thomas. He used Thomas's name. No more messing around.

Finally, the reason for my reluctance presents itself to me. I picture Paula Mulroney's incredulous face as she said to me the words that have haunted me since I heard them. *That's one of your guys,* she said. Your guys. Your guys. Then I picture Ahearn as he received this information. How quickly he shoved it aside.

There it is, at last. The reason I haven't told my colleagues about my sister's disappearance: I am not certain, anymore, that I can trust them.

Truman has gone silent. I've gone silent. The only sound between us is our breath.

—Hey, he says finally. You might not give a shit about your own life. But Thomas does. And I do.

Reflexively, my face reddens. I am unused to such direct statements from Truman.

—Are you hearing me? says Truman.

I nod. Then, remembering that I'm on the telephone, I clear my throat, and say, I am.

After I've hung up, my phone dings once.

A text from Ashley.

Nope.

———

At home tonight, I spend an extra half hour reading to Thomas on the sofa. I listen to him tell me the small tribulations and successes of his day. I count with him as we name the days until his birthday celebration, happy to know there is something in his life he is looking forward to.

CARLOTTA AND LILA, Thomas begins chanting, as soon as he sees them across the McDonald's. CARLOTTA AND LILA. CARLOTTA AND LILA.

We rushed to get here. We're fifteen minutes late for Thomas's own party. South Philadelphia is a half hour from Bensalem, and somehow time got away from me.

The girls run toward Thomas.

—Hello, I say to their mothers, and they both say hi. Lila's mother gives me a hug, which I accept stiffly. I know them both vaguely from Thomas's time at Spring Garden Day School, but I had to look up their first names before I called them.

They are two different types. Carlotta's mother is older than me, probably in her mid-forties, with curly hair and a practical zip-up parka and mittens that look hand-knit.

Lila's mother is around my age, early thirties. She has bangs and long wavy hair and she's wearing a blue coat, clasped with a belt, and both are so beautifully made that I want to reach out and touch them. On her feet are boots with chunky heels and in her ears are delicate golden earrings that dangle almost to her collar. She looks like she works in fashion. Like she smells nice. Like she has a blog.

In my slacks and my white button-down, I probably look like a waitress.

Both mothers, in different ways, seem like they came from good families, went to good colleges.

Both of them, I realize sharply and belatedly, look like they have never eaten at a McDonald's in their lives.

—This is so *great*, says Lila's mom, Lauren. The kids are in *heaven*.

But Carlotta's mother, Georgia, appears mildly concerned. She's scanning the play equipment as if looking for danger.

—I didn't know they had an indoor playground, she says to me.

—They do, I say. It's the draw. It's the only one in the city, and Thomas loves it. I'm sorry you had to come all the way here, though.

—No problem at all, says Lauren. It's not hard to get here. We just took Columbus down. And they have parking, she adds. What a luxury.

—No problem, Georgia agrees, after a beat.

We stand together in silence for a moment, watching the children play. Lila and Thomas have scaled the ladder that leads into a little elevated playhouse, and Carlotta is bathing in the ball pit, flailing her limbs wildly, as if making a snow angel. I glance at Carlotta's mother, who, from the look on her face, seems to be wondering how frequently everything is cleaned.

—So how's work? Lauren asks me. I never spoke to anyone at Thomas's school about what I do, but I imagine both women used to see me picking him up in uniform sometimes, when I didn't have time to change.

—Pretty good, I say. You know. Busy.

I hesitate. I want to ask them what they do, but there's a part of me that imagines they might not work—that they might have the resources to send their children to nursery school for its enriching qualities, not because their livelihoods depend upon it.

I am still struggling with how to phrase this question when Georgia says, What's going on with those murders in Kensington?

—Oh, I say, surprised. Well, there's a lead. But nothing definite.

—Are they connected? says Georgia.

—Looks like it, I say.

—I hope you guys figure it out, says Georgia. I don't like how close that whole business is to the kids' school.

I pause.

—Well, I say. I don't think preschoolers are what this person is after. Both women look at me.

—I mean, yes, me too, I say. I think we're getting close to apprehending him. Don't worry.

More false comfort dispensed. More silence. I cross my arms around my middle, shift my weight from leg to leg.

—I hope everyone's okay, says Georgia, looking at her watch.

—Who? I say. Confused.

—I mean I hope everyone can find this place okay. I got turned around a little bit myself.

—Oh, I say, suddenly realizing. Oh, this is it.

—Keeping it small, says Lauren. Smart.

—This is it? Georgia says, making a circle in the air with her hand.

Thomas comes over, ready with a list of things he wants to order. A shake and chicken nuggets and a hamburger and french fries and another shake. Lila and Carlotta are behind him, ready with their own orders. Clearly they've been plotting.

But Georgia kneels down and places her hand on her daughter's shoulder. Carlotta, she says, we talked about this. We brought lunch, remember?

Carlotta's eyes get wide. She begins shaking her head back and forth, incredulous at the injustice that's about to transpire.

—No, she says. No, I need a hambirder. I need a hambirder and fries.

Georgia glances up at us quickly before standing and steering her daughter, now crying, ten feet away, where she crouches down again and speaks to her lowly, urgently.

I turn away, pretending not to watch, or care. But I can imagine what Georgia is telling Carlotta: This food is not for us, honey. This is not food that is healthy enough or nourishing enough for me to allow you to eat.

I imagine that she thought it would be a large party. That they could slip away unnoticed to eat their healthful, nourishing food.

—What's wrong with Carlotta? Thomas asks, and I say, I'm not sure. Let's give her some space.

Georgia is now leading a wailing Carlotta out of the restaurant by

her arm. She looks back at the rest of us and holds up a finger stiffly:
One minute.

—But will she come back? Thomas says to me, placing both hands on
my folded arms, hanging there, uncertain.

—I think so, I say, but the mistake I made, inviting them here, is set-
tling onto me.

It is Lauren, finally, who claps her hands together, breaking the spell.

—I don't know about you guys, she says, but I'm hungry for a Big Mac.
I look at her.

—I freaking love Big Macs. My guilty pleasure, she says to me seriously, and I want to say to her *thank you, thank you.*

—I love Big Macs too, says Thomas. My guilty pleasure, too.

After we order, the four of us—Lauren, Lila, Thomas, and me—find a
table for six and sit down to eat together. Georgia and Carlotta return
and Georgia furtively hustles her daughter back to the indoor playground, where she will play by herself until the meal is over.

Lauren is sitting across from me, and at first I'm not certain what to
say to her. I've never been good at making conversation, and especially
not with someone like Lauren, who, I imagine, must not know anyone
on earth like me or my family. I have always suspected that people like
Lauren consider people like me and my family trashy, or scary, or too
much trouble and burden to deal with. All of us with our many, many
problems, a line with no beginning and no end.

But Lauren is nonchalant, holding her soda lightly and loosely, teasing her daughter when she spills ketchup on her shirt.

—This shit happens constantly, right? she says, rolling her eyes at me.
I hadn't expected the curse.

Another way I misjudged her: Lauren has a real job, one that requires
her to get up and go to work every day. She's a producer for Philadelphia's public radio station. She majored in broadcast communications,
she says. Thought she'd go into television reporting. (She's certainly
pretty enough.) Ended up, instead, constructing segments for the radio.

—I like it better, she says. Don't have to get up at the crack of dawn to spackle makeup on my face.

For fifteen minutes, we make conversation with remarkable ease, our children next to us, eating contentedly the food that Carlotta's mother has deemed unfit for her daughter. Thomas's little face is lit up with pleasure and excitement, his hands moving quickly over the table to touch his Big Mac, and then his french fries, and then his shake. He is counting his winnings. He is having a happy birthday.

t is only a short time later that I see my son's expression change.

—Thomas? I say.

Before I can stop him, he leaps up and runs across the space between our table and the cash registers.

I stand and turn.

As I do, I hear Lauren say, Does Thomas know that man?

It's too late: Thomas has thrown his arms around the legs of the man in question, whom I can only see from the back.

It's Simon, of course. I knew that it was Simon before I even turned around. Despite everything, despite his behavior, and the way he has treated both me and my son, I am momentarily drawn to him. I suppress some childlike urge to run to him, to follow Thomas, to instantly forgive him of all his sins.

I am battling this impulse when I notice, standing next to Simon, a woman. She has long dark hair, pin-straight. Her stature is small.

On a dime, my emotions lurch toward rage. I watch as the scene plays out across the room: as Simon turns and looks down on Thomas, as he stares at him blankly for too long, not recognizing him, not recognizing his own son, whom he hasn't seen in a year. And then, at last, Simon understands, and he looks at the woman before he looks back at Thomas, more concerned with her feelings than with his.

Thomas is bouncing on his toes, now, his arms stretched up toward his tall and handsome father. Thomas's expression is one I recognize from the last time he saw Simon: adulation, worship, pride. Quickly,

Thomas glances back at Lauren and Lila, and I can read his thoughts: He wants to show Simon off to them. He wants to introduce his friends to his father.

—Daddy, he's saying. Daddy. Daddy.

He thinks, I realize sickly, that his father is here to surprise him.

Thomas can't yet imagine that his father won't acknowledge him, won't reach down his large hands and lift his son up to his chest, the way he always used to do.

I stride toward him. I want to carry him away before he understands.

As I do, Thomas notices me, at last, and turns, his face still full of joy, and says, Mom, Daddy's at my birthday!

The woman next to Simon turns around, too.

I see her face. She is so young that she could be a teenager. She's tiny and pretty, with two cheek piercings that also speak to her age.

And in her arms she is holding a baby, eight or nine months old, a small baby girl in a pink jacket.

Simon is shifting his gaze in a frantic triangle between the three of us: to Thomas, and then to me, and then to the woman next to him.

Thomas has given up on being held, now. He's lowered his hands to his sides. His face is crumbling. He still doesn't understand.

—Daddy? he says, one last time.

—Daddy? the young woman repeats, staring at Simon.

Simon is focused on me now. Michaela, he says. This is my wife, Jeanine.

In a flash, the last year of my life is explained.

Jeanine is gone before Simon can say another word. She has taken the baby with her. Simon stands there for a minute, his arms limp, his gaze on the floor. Thomas stands near him, unmoving.

At last, Simon walks to the windowed entrance of the place and watches as his dark Cadillac backs out of the parking lot too quickly.

It occurs to me, finally, that I need to go to Thomas. I scoop him up, big though he is. He puts his head down on my shoulder.

I don't know what to do next. I want to yell, to scream at Simon, to hit him once, hard, across the face, for ignoring Thomas the way he did. For hurting Thomas's feelings so badly. On his birthday, of all days.

But I won't give him the satisfaction. Instead, I walk Thomas over to the table where Lauren and Lila are seated, and say to Lauren, Would you mind keeping an eye on Thomas for one second?

—Of course, says Lauren. We've got you, Thomas.

Then I walk over to Simon, who's now on his phone, texting furiously, and I stand silently in front of him. He looks up, finally. Puts his phone away.

—Look, he begins, but I shake my head.

—No, I say. I don't want to hear anything from you.

Simon sighs.

—Michaela, he says.

—Just stay away from us, I say. That's it. I don't need anything from you except for you to stay away.

He looks puzzled.

—You found *me*, he says.

—Excuse me?

—At work. You found me. Remember?

I'm shaking my head. I don't know how you got my address, I say, but I don't appreciate the visits.

He crosses his arms.

—Mick, he says. I have no idea where you live.

And for the first time in years, I believe him.

He leaves. Presumably to pick up the pieces with Jeanine, to refocus himself on his new life. At my request, he doesn't say goodbye to Thomas, and Thomas dissolves into sobs. It's better, I think. A clean break. A Band-Aid ripped. No sense prolonging a permanent goodbye.

The party is over.

—I'm sorry, I say, quickly, to Lauren and Georgia. I hand to their children the small bags of favors I bought at the dollar store.

Georgia, who didn't see what transpired, is looking at me in confusion. Lauren is looking at me in sympathy. She'll fill Georgia in, I think. She'll give her the gossip. The situation was, no doubt, clear.

All the way home, Thomas cries.

—I'm very sorry, I tell him. I'm so sorry, Thomas. I know it's difficult to understand right now, but really this is for the best.

—The world is a hard place, I add, after a while.

But my words don't seem to console him.

I am distracted from my attempts to comfort him by a feeling of deep unease that is descending upon me in response to the following question: If Simon has not been the man making visits to my home—who has been?

I'm so lost in thought that when my phone rings, I swerve, and Thomas yelps.

I answer.

—Officer Fitzpatrick? a voice says. Female, older.

—Yes, I say.

—This is Denise Chambers from the Internal Affairs division of the PPD, the person says.

—All right, I say.

—Sergeant Ahearn passed some information on to us that we'd like to investigate. We should schedule a time to meet.

Monday is the day we select. I am both surprised and relieved. Maybe Ahearn, against all odds, is doing the right thing.

At home, I set Thomas up at the TV and then I run down to Mrs. Mahon's front door. I knock.

When she answers, she is blinking, as if she has just woken up from a nap.

—Mrs. Mahon, I say. I was wondering. Can you tell me any more information about the man who's been stopping by for us?

—What kind of information? says Mrs. Mahon.

—Well, I say. Age? Race? Height? Weight? Eye color? Hair color? Any other identifying characteristics?

Mrs. Mahon adjusts her glasses. Thinking.

—Now let's see, she says. His age was difficult to tell. He was dressed very young, but his face looked older.

—How much older? I say.

—I'm bad at that, says Mrs. Mahon. Estimating ages. I have no idea. Thirties? Forties? He was tall, as I said. He was handsome. Well-proportioned features.

—Race? I say.

—White.

—Any facial hair? I say.

—None to speak of, says Mrs. Mahon.

—Oh, says Mrs. Mahon. He did have a sort of tattoo, I think. Something in script on his neck, just below his ear. Very tiny. I couldn't see what it said.

—What was he wearing? I say.

—A sweatshirt, says Mrs. Mahon. The kind with a hood and a zipper.

I flinch. Many people, I remind myself, wear sweatshirts of this variety.

—Both times? I say.

—I think so.

—Did the sweatshirt have any writing on it? I say.

—I can't recall, says Mrs. Mahon.

—Are you sure? I say.

—Very sure, says Mrs. Mahon.

—All right, I say, after a while. Thank you. If you think of anything else, let me know. And Mrs. Mahon, I say.

—Yes?

—If he ever comes back. Have him leave a message. And please call me right away.

Mrs. Mahon looks at me, assessing things. I worry that she's going to be put out by these requests. She doesn't, after all, want 'trouble'—she has always made sure to emphasize this to me.

But all she says is, I'll do that.

Then, slowly, she closes the door.

The Roundhouse isn't the official name of the Philadelphia Police Department's headquarters, but it's the only thing I've ever heard it called.

The building is, of course, round in places, and Brutalist in style, and constructed of a yellowish-gray concrete that darkens in the rain. There is talk of moving out of it soon, and it makes sense to: the PPD is running out of room. The building now looks dated and severe. But I can't imagine the Roundhouse not being the home of the PPD, just as I can't imagine the Tracks not being the home of the people who frequent them. As of last week, Conrail and the city have finally begun to pave the area over. But chaos will always prevail, even when its home is taken away.

Inside, I recognize two officers in the lobby, and nod my hello. They give me strange looks: *What are you doing here,* they imply. I wish I hadn't been seen. Meetings with Internal Affairs are always causes for gossip and, sometimes, for mistrust.

Denise Chambers is friendly, fifty-something, and plump, with gray hair and blue glasses. She welcomes me into her office and tells me to sit down across from her in a new-looking chair that positions me at child height.

—Cold enough? says Chambers, nodding out her window to the thin winter air outside. We're several flights up. From here, I can see Franklin Square, its carousel at a standstill.

—It's not so bad, I say. I don't mind the cold.

I pause, waiting, while Chambers finishes something on her computer. Then she turns around.

—Do you know why I asked you to come here? she says, cutting to the chase. In her question, I hear a faint echo of the way I talk to suspects on the street: *Do you know why I detained you? Do you know why I pulled you over?*

For the first time, a flicker of doubt runs through me.

—You said Sergeant Ahearn passed on some information to you, I say.

Chambers assesses me. Seeing what I know. Yes, she says slowly.

—What did he tell you?

Chambers sighs, folds her hands on the desk in front of her.

—Look, she says, this is a difficult part of my job, but I'm obliged to tell you that you're under internal investigation.

It comes out before I can stop myself. Me? I say, dumbly, pointing to my own chest. *I'm* under investigation?

Chambers nods. I have a sudden memory of Truman's warning to me to get some allies in the district. *Politics, Mick.*

—For what? I say.

Chambers extends her fingers, ticking off items as she speaks.

—On Tuesday of last week, you were seen with an unauthorized passenger in your car. You were also seen outside your assigned PSA. On Wednesday and Thursday you were seen without your radio and out of uniform while on your shift. On Friday, you failed to respond to any calls for a block of two hours. In general, your productivity this fall has decreased by about twenty percent. You've also run searches on two civilians in the PCIC frequently and without cause. Finally, we have reason to believe you've been bribing a business owner in your district as well.

I look at her.

—Who? I ask her, incredulous.

—Alonzo Villanueva, she says. And we believe you've been keeping a change of civilian clothing in his store for unauthorized activities during work hours. And that on at least one occasion, you stored your department-issued weapon there, unsecured.

I'm silent.

Everything Chambers is saying is, technically, true. And yet I am shocked. It's also embarrassing to know I've been watched: I scan my memories of the last week, thinking about what I've said, what I've done, while in a police vehicle. Wondering whether they gathered information through audio or video recording, or simply through having someone from Internal Affairs tag me on my shifts. Anything is possible.

—May I ask what triggered this investigation? I say.

—I'm afraid I can't tell you that, says Chambers.

But I know.

It was Ahearn, without a doubt. He's never liked me. It's true that my productivity has been in sharp decline since Truman went on leave, and my activity logs no doubt reflect that. Sometimes this alone can trigger internal monitoring, a request for surveillance. But I also think, aside from that, he's been looking for a way to get rid of me for years.

—Did Sergeant Ahearn tell you anything else? I ask. Did he tell you about Paula Mulroney? Did he tell you about the accusation she made against at least one officer?

Chambers hesitates. He did say something about that, she says. Yes.

And all of a sudden I know: Ahearn poisoned the well. He played down what I said. He told Chambers that I would be making a complaint, but that I was untrustworthy.

—And what are you going to do about it? I say. Has Detective Nguyen been informed?

—He has been, says Chambers. He's looking into it.

—Look, I say, a little wildly now. Ahearn has never liked me. I'm not his friend. But I'm honest, and I'm telling you that one of our officers—at least one—has been accused of using his power to demand sex from women who are not in a position to say no.

There is silence in the room, briefly.

—And, I continue, emboldened now, that this person was spotted on video following one of our victims.

Chambers's gaze wavers for a second. The fact of our gender—two female officers, one older, one younger, sitting across a desk from one another—lingers in the air between us, just briefly, like smoke.

—Did he tell you that part? I say. Or did he leave it out?

But Denise Chambers will say no more.

walk out of the Roundhouse with paperwork in my hands. It informs me of my rights and responsibilities during the suspension I've been placed on, pending investigation.

At least, I think, I won't have to worry anymore about who will watch Thomas on snow days. At least there's that.

In the lobby, I keep my gaze on the floor.

The only person I wish to speak to, right now, is Truman.

I get into my car and take out my phone. I'm about to call him when a thought takes hold of me. Whether or not this is paranoia, I can't say. But if Internal Affairs knew as much as they did about me, it does not seem out of the question that they have received permission to tap either my phone or my personal vehicle. I glance up at the ceiling, at my dome light, at the backseat, at Thomas's booster seat in the middle. I don't know what actions are within their rights. And I don't wish to get Truman in trouble, too: he's done enough.

I put my phone away and peel out, driving blindly toward Mount Airy.

I feel self-conscious, stopping in on Truman without phoning ahead, but I don't know what else I can do. I hope I don't surprise him at an inopportune time. I keep remembering the woman's voice in the background of my call to him. *Who is that?* the woman was saying. *Truman, who is that?*

Truman's car, a neat and polished Nissan Sentra, sits in his driveway. Truman's personal vehicles are always impeccable. Not a trace of food or dust or dirt anyplace inside or out. Especially since Thomas was born, my car has always been full: full of kids' toys and crumbs and water bottles, full of shopping bags and food wrappers and coins and snacks.

I park on the street again and walk onto Truman's porch. I hesitate before knocking: second thoughts, second thoughts.

I'm standing there, my hand in the air, deciding, when the front door flies open. On the other side of it is a tiny lady, less than five feet tall.

—What are you selling? she says. Whatever it is, I don't want it.

—Nothing, I say, surprised. I'm sorry. Is Truman home?

The lady lifts her eyebrows at me, but doesn't move, and says nothing more.

I weigh my options. The woman before me could be anyplace between sixty and eighty years old. She looks something like an aging hippie. She's wearing a bandanna on her head and a T-shirt that says *Virginia Is for Lovers*. Is this—could this be—Truman's mother? I know he has one, and that she is alive, and that he loves her. I know she was the principal of an elementary school at one time. But last I heard, she was retired and living up in the Poconos.

I try to peer past her, into the house, but the woman closes the door slightly, as if to block my view.

I try again.

—I'm a friend of Truman's, I say. I was just hoping to speak to him.

—Truman, says the woman, as if searching her memory. Truman.

It is then, finally, that Truman himself emerges from the back of the house, wearing a towel around his waist, sort of hopping to get to the door. He's embarrassed to be seen this way, I know: proper Truman, whom I have rarely seen in anything other than a uniform, even after work.

—Ma, he says. This is my friend Mickey.

The woman nods, suspicious, looking back and forth between us. Okay, she says. But she makes no move to let me in.

—Just hang on, Mick, says Truman, and he moves his mother gently out of the way. One second. He closes the door. In the moment before he does, his eyes connect with mine.

Five minutes later, the three of us are sitting uncomfortably in the living room. Truman is clothed now, straight-backed in his chair, his right leg stretched out on an ottoman before him. We all have tea. Truman's mother looks at the cup in her hands.

—Drink it, Ma, says Truman. It's cool enough now.

He looks at me. My mother's been living here for a little while now, he says. He hesitates, glancing at his mother, seeing whether she's listening. She had a fall, he says.

—And she's been forgetting, he adds, quickly and quietly.

—I am right here, son, says Mrs. Dawes, looking up sharply. Right here in this room with you. I'm not forgetting anything.

—Sorry, Ma, says Truman.

—Why don't we go out in the yard? he says to me.

I follow him, watching the sure broad back of him as he leads the way. How many times have I watched him from this angle, leading the way up the steps of a house, leading the way into crime scenes, leading the way as we answered one call after another? Shielding me, in a way, from the worst of it, the first sight of a body or a gruesome injury. Our shared history means that I take strange comfort in following him.

It's freezing in the backyard. Small shrubs, brown from winter, run along a brown wooden fence. We can see our breath as we speak.

—I'm sorry about my mother, says Truman. She's—

He hesitates, searching for the word. Protective, he says finally.

—Don't worry about it, I say—thinking, not saying, that I'm mildly jealous. That it would be nice to have someone in my life who was protective of me in that way.

———

In the backyard, I recount for Truman the story of my meeting with Denise Chambers, and its surprising results. As I speak, he wears an expression of warmth and concern. The words tumble out of me more and more quickly.

—No, he says. Really?

—Really. I'm suspended.

He pauses. Any new info on Kacey? he says.

—Nothing, I say.

For a long time, Truman goes silent, biting his lips as if wrestling with whether or not to say something. Finally, he speaks.

—What about Cleare? he says.

I look at him.

—What do you mean, *Cleare,* I say.

Truman looks at me for a while.

Then he says, Mick. Come on.

When he says this, I sense the crumbling, all around me, of some large and unwieldy pretense, a defensive wall I erected years ago and counted on, along with Truman's sense of discretion and respect, to protect me from any direct questions.

Suddenly, I find my voice has been taken from me.

I rarely cry. I didn't even cry over Simon. I was mad, yes; I punched the refrigerator. I shouted into the air. I hit pillows. I didn't cry.

Now, I shake my head. One hot tear spills down my cheek and I wipe it angrily away.

—Fuck, I say.

I don't think I've ever even cursed in front of Truman.

—Hey, he says. He is gruff. He doesn't know what to do. The two of us have never touched, unless it was in the process of wrestling some perp to the ground.

—Hey, he says again, and at last he extends one hand and puts it on my shoulder. But he doesn't try to hug me. I appreciate this. I'm humiliated enough as it is.

—You okay? he asks.

—Fine, I say roughly.

—How did you know about Simon, I say.

—I'm sorry, Mick, says Truman. It's kind of an open secret. A lot of people know. The PPD is small.

—Well, I say.

I try then to pull myself together. I look up at the cold gray sky until my tears freeze. Then I sniff and wipe my nose once, roughly, with my gloved hand.

—Things started between us when I was very young, I say, by way of explanation, or excuse.

—No kidding, says Truman.

I look away. My face reddens: that old terrible tell. My downfall on the job.

—Hey, says Truman. Hey. What do you have to be embarrassed about? He's the asshole. You were a kid.

But his words only serve to make me feel worse. I dislike the idea that I am a 'victim,' in any sense of the word. I dislike the attention, the sympathy, the hushed tones it elicits. I would prefer, in general, not to be spoken about, by anyone, in any way. And the thought of my colleagues in the PPD gossiping about me and Simon, rolling their eyes and slurping their coffee as they elbowed one another in merriment, makes me want to disappear into the hard earth of Truman's backyard.

Truman is still watching me, measuring his words, assessing the weight of what he wants to say. He puts his hands on his waist. Looks down at the ground.

—You know he's got a reputation, he says, hesitantly.

—Simon?

He nods.

—I don't mean to make you feel bad, he says, or to talk out of school. But you're not the only one. Rumor is there were other PAL kids he targeted. Seems like there was a pattern, but no one ever confessed, or registered a formal complaint. He was suspended for a while, after enough gossip, but they could never nail him on anything certain.

I open my mouth. I hesitate. There's so much more about him, I want to say, that you don't know. But I stay silent. It's all too embarrassing. The father of my son.

We look at each other.

—What were the ages of the victims? says Truman. In Kensington.

—The first was unknown, I say. The second was seventeen. The third was eighteen. The fourth was twenty.

—Mickey, says Truman. Do you still have that video on your phone?

I nod. I don't want to watch it. My stomach feels tight.

Silently, Truman holds his hand out, and at last I bring it up on the screen.

Together, we watch it. It's as grainy as ever, an optical illusion. The figure who crosses the screen first is a shape-shifter, his face inscrutable. And yet—in the figure's height, in his gait—I can imagine Simon.

—What do you think? I say, unwilling to make the pronouncement myself.

Truman shrugs. Could be, he says. You know him better than I do. I've always steered clear. He's a scumbag.

—No offense, he says, glancing up at me.

We watch it again and again.

And then, finally, Truman takes stock of our evidence.

—Listen, he says. The good news is you're free tomorrow. I'm free tomorrow. What leads do we have at this point? Who are our suspects?

—Connor McClatchie, I say. And Simon, I guess.

—We'll split up, says Truman. I'll take McClatchie. I don't want you going near him after what he said to you. You take Simon, he says.

We plan to switch cars, since Simon knows mine. I'll leave my car in Mount Airy, and drive Truman's home to Bensalem. I apologize, pre-emptively, for the mess.

Before I leave, Truman puts his hand on my shoulder one more time.

—We'll find her, he says. You know, I actually believe that we'll find her.

t is odd to be spending the first day of my suspension engaged in police work.

When I wake in the morning, I put on a dark sweater and a plain baseball cap. When Thomas sees me, he looks suspicious.

—Why are you wearing that, he says. Where's all your stuff?

—What stuff?

—Your bag, he says. Your duty belt.

—I'm off today, I say.

I still haven't determined what, exactly, to tell Thomas, and I need to buy a little bit more time until I decide. I don't know how long my suspension will be, so I can't tell him I'm on vacation.

—No Bethany! says Thomas. But he knows better.

—Bethany, I say.

After Bethany arrives and takes over, fifteen minutes late as usual, I drive toward South Philadelphia.

There was a time in my life when I was frequently a passenger in Simon's personal vehicle. In fact, if I try, I can still imagine myself inside of it: it smelled of leather, and faintly of cigarettes, which Simon smoked only occasionally, but usually on nice days, when he could roll the windows down. He kept it clean and polished it on the weekends. The Caddy, he always called it, with affection. He liked cars: his father had taught him about them, he said, prior to his death.

Now, regarding it in its place outside the headquarters of the South Detectives, I am reminded, against my will, of the many times we were intimate together in that car. Just as quickly, I turn my thoughts away.

In Truman's car, I park not far away. I lower both visors. I need to stay alert, so I have brought an audiobook to play: this way, I can keep my gaze on the door of the building. I've also brought along some food and water. The latter I'll ration very carefully to avoid the need for a restroom.

All morning, the front door swings open and closed, admitting various personnel, most of whom I don't recognize. Once or twice I think I catch a glimpse of Simon, only to discover it's a lookalike.

At eleven a.m., however, I spy him: he emerges from the building and, glancing to his left, turns right, toward his vehicle. He's wearing a nice overcoat. Gray dress pants and shiny black shoes are visible beneath it. His hair is slicked back. It's a typical look for him since he became a detective.

Instantly, I'm on high alert. The street we're on is a relatively quiet one, so I'll wait to start the engine of Truman's car until after Simon has already departed.

I follow him. He may be on assignment, I think, going to interview someone in the South Division, a person of interest or a victim or a witness. Or he may just be taking an early lunch. He starts out going north on Twenty-Fourth Street. At Jackson, though, he suddenly does a U-turn, and heads south.

He makes a right on Passyunk. And suddenly, I find myself following him onto the highway.

I suppose I know where we're going even as we go there, but it still takes me by surprise, the way things happen just as you predict them to. The inevitability of the moment.

He takes the exit for 676 East, and then takes the Allegheny exit off 95.

I could close my eyes, practically, and still drive the rest of the way.

The neighborhood is crowded today, and it occurs to me that it's the beginning of the month. Paychecks have arrived. Customers are out. To my right, a distraught young woman throws her bag to the ground and then sinks into a crouch, crying.

One block from the Ave, Simon pulls over abruptly and parks. I'm forced to drive past him so as not to alert him to my presence. I'm keeping an eye on my rearview, and I'm almost sideswiped by a car emerging from a small street to my right. I turn right onto the Avenue and park as soon as I can find a spot: out front of a soup kitchen, today, where thirty or forty people stand in line, waiting for the doors to open. I exit my vehicle. Then I peer around the corner of the building I'm in front of, seeing whether Simon's walking my way.

He's not.

I can see, from here, that his Cadillac is empty. This means he went on foot in one of three directions, all of them away from me.

I jog toward his car.

What is he doing in Kensington at this time of day? His work is in South Philadelphia. All of his cases are there. It is possible—unlikely, but possible—that he's doing undercover work. But if he were, he'd have dressed down for the day.

When I reach Simon's car, I look down the side street it's closest to, and then I jog until I reach another side street half a block away. But I don't see him on either. I keep going, running now, picking up steam, peering down every small side street I come to, looking for his gray dress coat, scanning houses for open doors. Five minutes go by.

I've lost him, I think.

At last, I stop on a side street called Clementine, one of the blocks in Kensington that's relatively well taken care of, only a couple of abandos, the rest of the houses kept up. In the middle of the block, I put my hands on my hips, winded, disappointed that I've lost my chance. Truman, I think, would probably not have lost him. His years of vice training have made him good at tailing people.

When I look up, I find myself in front of a house that, for some reason, looks familiar to me.

Have I made an arrest here before? Have I done a welfare check?

Eventually, I focus on the metal silhouette of a horse and carriage that adorns so many storm doors in this part of Philadelphia. The horse, I notice, is missing its front legs. And suddenly I'm seventeen again, waiting outside this door with Paula Mulroney, trying to get inside, trying to get to my sister.

I close my eyes, only briefly, just long enough to will myself back to that moment: one in which the question of whether Kacey is alive is still unanswered but the answer to it will turn out to be *yes*. One in which, though I didn't know it then, I was about to find my sister and bring her home.

At the sound of the front door swinging inward, I open my eyes.

A woman is staring at me. I can't remember if it's the same woman who opened the door all those years ago; in my memory, that woman had black hair, and this woman's hair is entirely gray. But it's been well over a decade. It could be her.

—You okay? says the woman.

I nod.

—You need something? she says.

I don't want to waste my money—I don't have much to spare these days—but I fear the woman will be suspicious if I don't. Maybe, too, she has information I can use.

Maybe she still knows Kacey.

So I say yes, and the woman opens the storm door with the metal silhouette on it, and then I am back, suddenly, in the first house my sister ever died in.

The last time I was in here, there was hardly any furniture. There were people in the shadows everywhere I looked.

Today, the house is warm and surprisingly well kept. It smells something like cooked pasta. Pictures on the wall: Jesus, Jesus, Mary, an Eagles poster signed by somebody whose signature I can't read. There are tidy throw rugs on the floor and there's plenty of furniture, cheap-looking but new.

—Sit down, says the woman, gesturing to a chair.

I'm momentarily confused. I have my made-up order ready: as many Percocets as the twenty in my pocket will buy me. Three, maybe, depending on dosage. One if the woman suspects I'm an amateur. I'll get outside, I think, and throw them in the gutter. I'm going to spend twenty dollars, basically, for any information the woman can give me.

I keep my hands in my pockets, warming them up, while the woman disappears briefly into the kitchen and then reemerges, holding a glass of water in her hands. She hands it to me.

—Drink that, she says. You don't look good.

I do as I'm told. Then I wait. I feel as if there's been some misunderstanding.

—How'd you hear about me? the woman says.

I pause. A friend, I say.

—What friend?

I hesitate, deciding. Matt, I say.

A safe gamble of a name, in this neighborhood.

—You're a friend of Matty B's? says the woman. I love Matty B!
I nod.

—Drink that, she says again. Obediently, I take a sip.

—You sober today? says the woman.

—Yes, I say. It's the first truthful thing that's come out of my mouth since I've been here. I'm starting to feel bad.

At this, the woman reaches out and puts a hand on my shoulder. Good work, honey, she says. I'm proud of you.

—Thank you, I say.

—How many days you have?

It's only then that I notice the framed *Twelve Steps* print on the wall behind her head, small enough so it would only stand out to someone who was looking for it. Jesus's head, in the picture next to it, is tilted mildly in its direction, as if he's contemplating the steps alongside the viewer. I wonder if this is by design.

I cough into my hand. Um, I say. Three days.

The woman nods seriously. That's great, she says. She looks at me. I bet it's your first time getting clean, she says.

—How'd you know? I say.

—You don't look too tired, she says. People who've been at it for years just look more tired out. Like me, she says, and laughs.

I feel tired, though. I have felt tired since Thomas was born. I have felt overwhelmed since moving to Bensalem. And I have felt exhausted since Kacey went missing. But I know what she means: I've seen the same people the woman is referring to, people who have been in and out of sobriety for a decade, for two decades, for more. In sobriety, they often look like they just want to go to sleep and stay there for a while.

—Anyway, says the woman. Are you going to meetings? Do you have a place to stay?

She glances at the stairs.

—I got about six people staying with me right now or I'd give you a bed. Actually, she says, let me think. Wait here a second.

The woman marches over to the bottom of the staircase and calls up it. TEDDY, she says. TED.

—It's okay, I say. I have a place to stay.

The woman is shaking her head. No, she says, we can get you in here.

A man calls down the stairs. What's up, Rita?

—Really, I say. I have a good place to stay. My grandmother's house. No one's using there.

The woman, Rita, looks at me doubtfully.

Still watching me, she calls up the stairs. When you going to West Chester?

—Uh, says the invisible Ted, Friday?

Rita says to me, There. We can get you in here Friday if you want. Maybe Thursday night if you don't mind the couch.

I begin shaking my head, and Rita says, I know, I know, you have a place to stay. Just keep it in mind, she says. Then her face changes. I'm not gonna charge you anything, honey, she says. Is that what you're worried about? Oh no, this is something I do for myself. Pay it forward, that kind of thing. Only thing I ask for is that you bring in food to share when you can, toilet paper, paper towels, that kind of stuff. And if I think you're using again I'll kick you out.

—All right, I say.

I'm starting to feel terrible, misleading this woman.

She looks at me.

—You've got a funny way of talking, she says. You from around here? I nod.

—Whereabouts?

—Fishtown, I say.

—Huh, she says.

All I can think about is how to gracefully leave. But I still haven't gotten a chance to ask her about Kacey.

—Here, says Rita, let me give you my number. You have a phone?

I take it out. Rita recites the digits of her phone number, and I enter it. While I'm looking at the screen, a text comes in from Truman.

Where are you?

Not far from K and A, I write back.

Then I pull up a picture of Kacey, and I hold the phone out to Rita.

—What's that? says Rita.

—I'm just asking people in the neighborhood if they've seen her around, I say. I'm her sister and she's been missing for a while.

—Oh, honey, says Rita. I'm sorry to hear that.

She takes the phone from my hand and holds it at arm's length from her face, trying to focus. She brings it a little bit closer. Her brow furrows.

—That's your sister? she says, looking up at me.

—It is, I say. Do you know her?

In an instant, a cloud passes over Rita's face. She is calculating something, realizing something, making connections that I can't understand.

—Get the fuck out of my house, she says to me suddenly. She is pointing to the door. Leave.

receive no further explanation. By the time I'm walking down the front steps, the door has slammed behind me. I turn back once to look at the horse-and-carriage silhouette before picking up my pace and heading back toward where Truman's car is parked.

I can see my breath. I tuck my chin down inside my jacket. My eyes water.

I watch for any more sightings of Simon. No luck.

Truman texts me again.

How fast can you be at Kensington and Somerset?

2 mins, I respond.

A moment later, another text comes in.

K and Lehigh now, he says.

He's moving. Not wanting to stop. Wanting to lose anyone who's tailing him.

It's faster for me to walk, actually, than to get in the car and drive. I beat Truman there, and I wait for a while on the corner. I wish I had something warm to drink. The cold has gotten its claws in me, and I can't stop shivering.

I jump when Truman says my name.

—Come on, he says. I parked near here. Let's talk in your car.

Inside, I get behind the wheel, and I tell Truman to start talking.

I do and don't want to hear what he's discovered. I glance at him out of the corner of my eye. He looks grim. He's thinking of how to tell me something: I know it.

—Truman, I say. Just tell me.

went to the house off Madison, he begins. The one with three Bs on it. I rapped on the plywood covering the back door. A minute later, Mc-Clatchie appears. Looking really bad, really strung out. Nodding a little, you know. Which, okay, I think is maybe gonna work in my favor. His guard is down.

Who are you? he says.

I texted you about a girl, I say.

He's really high, I'm noticing. Can barely hold his head up.

Okay, he says.

I wait. *So what's the story,* I say. *You got a girl for me, or what?*

He goes, *Yeah. Come in.*

So I follow the guy into this boarded-up house. Inside there's a bunch of people nodded out, and a couple shooting up. Nobody says anything to me.

McClatchie leans up against a wall, spacing out, and practically goes to sleep. I'm freezing, and the house smells like shit, and this guy seems to have forgotten that I'm there. So I say to him, *Hey. Hey.*

He wakes up a little.

Where's your phone? Show me the girls again.

He finally takes it out of his pocket, pulls up some photos, hands me the phone. I start flipping through them and I recognize a lot of the girls that were on there last time he showed me. But no Kacey.

I look at him. Now I know, in that moment, that if I ask about Kacey, he'll peg me. He'll connect me to you.

But what do I have to lose, I think. Besides, I thought there was a small chance that he'd be so out of it he wouldn't even put two and two together.

So I go, *Where's the redhead? I saw a redhead on here last time.*

And McClatchie goes, real slowly, *Aw, that's Connie.*

I said, *I want that one.*

And he said, *Connie's out of commission.*

Then he raises his head up and looks at me, and I swear it's like a hawk zoning in on something. His whole expression changes. He stares at me. His eyes get really focused.

Two guys across the room rise from the dead, lift their heads up off the floor and start looking at me, as if I'm causing trouble, and suddenly the mood in the room starts changing.

Why, McClatchie says. *Why do you want her so bad.*

I don't know, man, I say. *I like redheads.*

I'm already backing out of the house. I'm facing him, still, in case he's packing.

He comes toward me. Perking up now. Looking more alert. *Who sent you?* he's saying. *Her sister? You a cop?*

That's when I turned and booked it. Turns out my knee works pretty well these days.

But I heard him calling after me, all the way down the block.

You a cop? he was saying. *You a cop?*

Truman looks at me, scratches his cheek.

I'm getting a feeling: like cold water is spreading through my veins and arteries.

—What does that mean, I say. *Out of commission.*

Neither of us can answer.

t's my turn, now, to tell him about Simon.

—He drove straight to Kensington, I say. He didn't hesitate. Just got into his car and drove straight there. I lost him when he got out on foot.

—No kidding, says Truman.

—He has no business in this neighborhood, I say. He's in the South Division.

Abruptly, I pull into a parking lot. A small, sad strip of stores is in front of us: Chinese restaurant, laundromat, shuttered hardware store, Dunkin' Donuts. I put my visor down, not wanting to be seen by anyone exiting these shops. Someone gets into the car next to mine. I keep my gaze down.

—I think it's time, says Truman.

—For what?

—We've gotta bring this to Mike DiPaolo, he says.

But I'm already shaking my head. No way, I say.

—Come on, Mickey, says Truman. He's a good person. I've known him since we were kids.

—How do you know? I say.

He looks at me.

—What are your other options? he says.

—Keep doing it on our own, I say.

—And then what? says Truman. Say you find out who the killer is.

What do you, take him out yourself? Go to jail for the rest of your life? No. At a certain point, Mickey, he says.

He trails off.

—You really trust him, I say.

Truman thinks. Then he says, He never cheated at sports.

—Excuse me?

—When we were kids. He never fudged the scores, says Truman. I trust him, he adds, clarifying.

—What about you, I say. Are you sure you want to be linked to this? You might be risking your job. We haven't exactly been following protocol.

Truman says, Mickey. I'm not going back.

There it is. I've been wondering.

—Why not, I say.

—I don't want to, says Truman plainly. Look. I get along with people. Keep my head down. People like me. It's too easy, you know? It's easy to forget that the system isn't right. I'm not just talking about Philadelphia. I'm not just talking about these particular homicides. I'm talking about the whole thing. The whole system. Too much power in the wrong hands. Everything out of order.

He pauses. Takes a breath.

—I can't sleep, he says. You know what I mean? People dying. Not just the women. Innocent people. Unarmed people. I can't sleep.

This is probably the closest Truman will ever come to disclosing his politics.

I'm silent for a while.

—I can get out now, says Truman. Get my pension. Get a different job if I want it. Go to bed at night with an easier mind.

—People are dying, he says again. All over, people are dying.

—I understand, I say.

And, more and more, I agree.

Truman calls Mike DiPaolo while we drive, in my car, to his.

—Got a question for you, says Truman. Probably not something you can get into at work. Can you meet at Duke's tonight?

Duke's is a bar in Juniata, near where the two of them grew up. It's Truman's favorite—someplace that's been in the neighborhood for decades. He knows all the bartenders. I've only been there once, for Truman's birthday, with a group of other officers. But never aside from that. It's not a police hangout, which makes it a good place to meet when one wants to talk shop.

I can't hear DiPaolo's reply, but apparently the idea works for him.

—Eight o'clock? says Truman, and then, Good. He hangs up.

—Think you can get there then? he asks me, and I say, I'll make it work.

Happily, surprisingly, Bethany comes through for me. She can stay late, she says. No problem.

Duke's, when I arrive, is quiet and uncrowded. Wood-paneled walls, dark lighting, a pool table in the back. It's one of the few places in Philadelphia where one can still smoke, and although no one is exercising that right at the moment, the place still reeks of stale tobacco.

Truman is sitting in a booth in the corner, away from everyone. DiPaolo hasn't arrived yet. A Corona is on the table in front of Truman: the only kind of alcohol I have ever seen him drink. The one lowbrow vice he has. He's almost finished with it. I ask him if he wants another.

—Sure, he says, and at the bar I order two. One for him, one for myself. I have never been a drinker—I suppose when Simon and I were together, I would partake on occasion—and now I try to remember the last time I had anything alcoholic at all. Maybe a year ago. Tonight, it tastes wonderful.

DiPaolo walks in. He's Truman's age, early fifties. But while Truman could pass for someone a decade younger than he is, DiPaolo wears his years heavily, and he walks heavily, too. He's pouchy and tired, perpetually a benevolent crank who, every once in a while, really lets loose. At Truman's birthday party here, DiPaolo got drunk and set the jukebox to 'Livin' on a Prayer,' by Bon Jovi, and then led everyone in song. I like him.

—Looks like you needed that, he says to me now, gesturing at the Corona, not saying hello.

—I did, I say. Would you like one?

—You're kidding, he says. What are we, at the beach? Jameson on the rocks, he says to the bartender. And another Corona for the lady. How you doing, Pete.

The three of us settle in: Truman and I on one side of the booth, DiPaolo on the other. Truman thanks DiPaolo for coming, somewhat formally, and DiPaolo grins.

—I know this is gonna be good, he says. What kind of trouble are you two getting into?

Truman glances at me, and I look at DiPaolo for a moment. Too long. The smile on his face fades.

—What? he says.

—Do you know Simon Cleare? I say.

He studies my face before looking down at his Jameson and taking a sip. He doesn't grimace.

—I do, he says. Yes.

—How well? I say.

DiPaolo shrugs. A little, he says. Met him at some all-bureau meetings. He's in South, though, he says. So it's not like I see him every day.

I measure my words. It's important, I think, to be calm.

—Does he have any reason to be in Kensington during his workday, I say. That you know of.

DiPaolo looks at me hard.

—Why, he says.

I sit back. I saw him there today, I say. Middle of the day.

DiPaolo sighs. He looks at Truman, seeking his gaze, but Truman won't return it. He turns back to me.

—If this is some sort of, he says. He puts his hands in the air, making circles. If this is some sort of lovers' quarrel, I really can't get involved.

I pause.

—What do you mean, I say.

—Look, says DiPaolo. I don't want to be presumptuous. But everyone knows about you and Simon Cleare. And I just don't want, he says.

He trails off. Sighs.

—I don't know why he was in Kensington, he says, but he might have had his reasons, you know?

I wait for my temper to settle before responding.

—This has nothing to do with me, I say. I'm trying to give you some information you might be able to use in the case of the Kensington murders. Because no one else is listening.

—What does that mean, says DiPaolo.

—I don't know how much of this you know already, I say. I take a long drink, and then I begin.

I tell him about Paula Mulroney, and Paula's accusation. I tell him Paula won't go on record saying it. I tell DiPaolo about Kacey, that she's missing. I feel like I'm rambling, and every so often I look up at DiPaolo to check his expression, but it's difficult to read.

—I started by telling Sergeant Ahearn this, I say. I went straight back to the station and told him I needed to talk to him. I felt it was information he should have, and I wanted to follow procedure. He said he was aware of the accusations and that he would relay them to the right people.

I pause.

—But I don't know if he did, I say. And a few days after I told him what I'd heard, I got a call from Internal Affairs, asking to meet. When I went in, they said I was under investigation. Put me on suspension.

Saying it aloud for the first time, all at once like this, I am suddenly jolted by the injustice of it all.

DiPaolo's face is still blank. I have no idea how much of this he knew in advance. He's good at his job.

—Okay, he says finally.

I wait.

—What I'm saying is, I say, it may be someone on the force who's killing these women. Simon's on the force. And I just saw him in a neighborhood he's always told me he hates.

DiPaolo waits. It seems like a leap to him. I can tell.

—Anything else? he says.

—He likes young girls, I say. And he's not—ethical. When it comes to his relationships.

DiPaolo keeps his face still.

It hits me, suddenly, how insane it all sounds. The facts don't favor me. I'm operating, I know, on a hunch, a suspicion, a gut feeling that doesn't translate to the outside world. And yet, saying it aloud, my conviction grows stronger.

I'm looking down at the table, but in my peripheral vision I see DiPaolo looking at Truman. Trying, again, to gauge what he thinks. DiPaolo clears his throat. I know what this looks like. Here I am, on suspension for unclear reasons, coming in with some pretty serious accusations against someone I used to date, with very little evidence. He must think I'm a crazy woman. A crazy ex-girlfriend.

—I'm not crazy, I say, though I know it's futile. I look at Truman. Tell him I'm not crazy, I say.

I suddenly realize I'm getting drunk. I'm at the bottom of my second beer.

—No one's saying that, Mick, says Truman. Now he shakes his head at me, just as subtly. *Stop talking.*

DiPaolo puts his hands on the table.

—Look, Mickey, he says. I hear you, okay? But you need to let this go, all right?

Against my will, I let out a sound that isn't very polite. *Hah*, I say.

DiPaolo looks at me levelly.

—You're out of your depth here, he says.

—In what sense, I say.

—I'm not at liberty to tell you. Just trust me.

He stands. Prepares to leave.

—I'll go to the press, I say, suddenly. I have a friend who's a journalist for a local radio station. She'd be very interested in a story about police corruption in Kensington.

I think of Lauren Spright. Imagine her expression if she heard me calling her a friend. She'd probably laugh at me.

DiPaolo keeps his face straight. Under the table, Truman puts his hand on my knee and squeezes, just once. *Stop.*

—Really, says DiPaolo.

—Really, I say, at the same time that Truman says, Mick.

—Go ahead, then, says DiPaolo. Do it. You know what she'll tell you? I'm silent.

—She'll tell you we've got our man, says DiPaolo. Because as of 4:35 p.m. today, we do. And as of—he checks his watch—ten minutes ago, he continues, a press release went out to local and national media outlets, saying as much.

I feel my mouth open.

—But if you want to talk to her about police corruption, DiPaolo says, go ahead. You might want to start by telling her what you were suspended for.

He takes a final swig of his Jameson. This time, he does make a face.

I don't want to give him the satisfaction of asking. But I can't help myself.

—Who is it, I say.

—Robert Mulvey, Jr., says DiPaolo. I think you're acquainted, actually.

As soon as DiPaolo leaves, I get on my phone. I can't look at Truman. He says nothing either. He is embarrassed, no doubt, by my behavior.

I navigate to the website of one local news station after another. Over and over again, I refresh them.

Within minutes, the story pops up.

Suspect Arrested in Connection with Kensington Homicides, reads the headline.

Robert Mulvey, Jr., looks out at me from my phone, his mug shot nearly as menacing as his expression the last time I saw him, in court.

Mulvey, the article says, was arrested today in connection with the murders after an anonymous tip placed him at the scene of the first crime. Video footage from a nearby business confirmed his presence there. And a state police DNA database linked him to the second and third victim, as well.

I look up quickly.

—That's how, I say.

—How what, says Truman.

The first words he's spoken in a long time.

—I recognized him, I say. I knew I recognized him. I saw him on the Gurney Street tracks when we discovered the first victim's body. I said to him, You're not supposed to be down here. He ignored me.

I remember him. Ghostly and defiant, a strange expression on his face, receding into the brush.

I look at Truman, finally. His expression is serious.

—What's wrong with me? I say. What have I done?

At last, Truman exhales. Aw, Mick, he says. I get it. Believe me, I do. You're missing your sister. You're worried. It's hard to think straight.

—She's probably laughing at me, I say. Kacey. She's probably off with some new boyfriend. She's probably laughing at me right now. Thinking about me searching for her and laughing.

I'm shaking my head. I am perhaps more disappointed in myself than I've ever been. For not making the connection to Mulvey myself. For not recognizing him when he recognized me, when he was practically taunting me to my face. For letting my emotions get in the way of hard evidence.

I've always thought I'd make a good detective. I think the last several weeks have proved to me, definitively, that on this point I've been deluded.

I order another Corona. And then, remembering DiPaolo's, I order a shot of Jameson, and then another, and then a third.

—Want one? I say to Truman, but he declines.

—Slow down, Mickey, says Truman, but I don't want to slow down. I want to speed up, to speed past this moment in my life and out to the other side.

—All right, I say, chastened. I can feel my tongue growing heavy in my mouth. I drove here, but I know I shouldn't drive myself home. I want to put my head on the table and go to sleep.

He hesitates for a while.

—It's my fault, he says at last. I'm the one who put that idea in your head. I've never liked the guy. And there are enough rumors about him that I just thought . . .

He trails off.

—It's easy to get carried away, you know? says Truman. After what he did to you. I never liked him, he says again.

Both of us are silent for a while.

—It still doesn't explain what he was doing there, I say, finally.

He shrugs. Maybe he was undercover, he says. This thing has become a high-profile case. It's all hands on deck. Maybe they're sending in guys they think will be new faces in the neighborhood.

I shake my head. He's a detective, I say. He's not on Vice.

—Who knows, says Truman. Neither you nor I is exactly in the loop right now.

I look at him in the stark light of the lamp hanging on a chain above our booth. It's a Tiffany lamp. Louis Comfort Tiffany, interestingly, spent some time here in Pennsylvania when he attended the military academy in West Chester. The lamp above us, though, does not look well made. It looks like an interrogation light in an old detective movie. And it occurs to me then that my job has taken over my life completely, that everything I do and think and see is filtered through the lens of my work. My work, which I might not have anymore, when DiPaolo sends word back to IA about what I've been doing. I start laughing.

—We can't escape, I say. We really can't escape.

Truman doesn't seem to know what I'm talking about. He's looking at me, concerned. In fact, he looks almost tender. Like he might reach out and put a hand on the side of my face.

—Are you gonna be okay, Mickey? he says. I'm worried about you.

—I'm gonna be great, I say.

I keep laughing, a little frantically now.

Truman says, Come on. I'm giving you a ride home.

stumble just a little on my way out the door. Truman catches me around the waist and keeps his arm there as we walk down the sidewalk toward the car. I am aware of his strength, of his hand on my side. I tense the muscles there. I am aware of the very faint scent of what I imagine to be his laundry detergent. This is the closest I've ever been to Truman, and it's not unpleasant. In fact, it's nice. Very nice to have another person holding me up. I put my arm around him, too, and I lean my head against his.

He's parked on the street, a block away from Duke's. He brings me around to the passenger's side and I stand in front of the passenger-side door, facing him as he double-clicks a button on his key. The car beeps twice. The noise echoes through the quiet street.

He leans past me to squeeze the door handle. I don't move.

—Mick, he says, I'm gonna open that door for you.

I look at his face. And suddenly I understand something new about the world, and about Truman and me. It seems so obvious in this moment that I laugh, just briefly: he's been here this whole time, right next to me for nearly a decade. How have I never noticed? Truman is breathing in time with my breath. Quickly now. Both of us.

I kiss him on the cheek.

—Mick, says Truman. He puts a hand on my shoulder.

I put a hand on his face, as I imagined him, earlier, doing to me.

—Hey, says Truman. But he doesn't move away.

I kiss him on the mouth. He stays there, just for a moment. Responsive. But then he pulls back.

—No, says Truman. Mickey, that's not right.

He takes a couple of steps backward, puts some space between us.

—That's not right, Mick, he says again.

—It is, I say. It is right.

He sets his jaw. Look, he says. I'm seeing somebody.

—Who? I say, without thinking.

But I know the answer before he says it. I think of the portrait on Truman's end table, a happy family. His beautiful girls. His beautiful wife. I think of Truman's mother, skeptical when she opened the door for me. *Protective,* Truman said.

Truman hesitates.

—It's Sheila, Mickey, he says at last. We're getting back together. We're trying to make it work.

On the ride home, we're both silent. I say nothing, even when I get out of the car.

Bethany watches me as I enter the apartment, her eyes appraising. I try very hard not to get too close to her, but I'm certain, when I pay her, that she can smell what's on my breath.

wake up feeling more ashamed than I've ever been in my life. Memories return to me, first slowly and then quickly. I put my hands over my face.

—No, I say. No, no, no, no, no.

Thomas, who has apparently crept into my room in the night, wakes up at the foot of the bed. What, Mom? he says.

I look down at him.

—I forgot something, I say.

Bethany, as usual, is late. While I wait for her, I allow myself to indulge in a particularly delicious fantasy: Maybe I'll fire her on the spot when she walks in the door. I'm on suspension now, anyway, and therefore not actually in need of her services at the moment. But two things prevent me from acting on this impulse: The first is that I have to go retrieve my car in Juniata today, and I'd rather not explain to Thomas how it got there in the first place. The second is that, presuming I get my job back, I'll need childcare—and finding a second person, quickly, with Bethany's flexible schedule sounds daunting, if not impossible.

So when she arrives, at last, I pretend to be leaving for work. And she actually apologizes, for the first time in our acquaintance, for her tardiness. She hasn't done her makeup today, for once, and she looks very young without it.

I am caught off guard by her sincerity.

—Well, I say. That's all right. Don't worry.

—Thomas can watch one show today, I add. You can decide when.

It turns out that a taxi from my apartment in Bensalem to Juniata costs $38.02, not including tip. A fact I never needed to know.

After the taxi drops me off, I get into my car and drive.

The day is mine, I realize, to do with what I wish. It's been a very long time since I've had this luxury. It's been a very long time since I felt so aimless, no work, no child to watch, no self-assigned mission.

I cruise through Kensington, through the 24th. Off duty, I can afford to notice things about it that I never do at work: the way certain small and empty lots have been converted by neighbors into improvised playgrounds, old donated slides rusting in a corner, haphazard basketball hoops mounted to chain-link fences. The secondhand appliance stores that set their wares out on the sidewalk, dented and dismayed-looking washing machines and refrigerators, upright soldiers in a line.

I'm not in my cruiser, for once, and the women I pass don't even glance at me. A young boy on a three-wheeler pulls up next to me, at a light, and then eclipses me when it turns.

I have the sudden urge to see my old house in Port Richmond, and I drive toward it. It belongs, now, to a preppy young man in his twenties (or, more accurately, to his parents, according to the paperwork I signed). Then I drive toward Fishtown, where I drive past Gee's house, the house I grew up in. Today, it looks uninhabited. Dark inside.

It's time to head home. But, driving past Bomber Coffee, I decide impulsively to stop in. I'm out of uniform today, and when I walk in, no one blinks. Briefly, I let myself imagine a different life for me and Thomas: coming here on the weekends to read the newspaper. Having the time to teach him everything he's curious about, to give him a light and peaceful existence, to serve him a fat five-dollar muffin from the glass case in front of me, or the fresh fruit and yogurt in a blue ceramic bowl that the boy at the counter is now handing to a customer. I imagine being friendly with this boy, with all the people who work here. I imagine going to other restaurants, too, on my days off, lots of them, sitting for hours at them. Bringing a sketchbook, maybe, and sketching my surroundings. I used to like to draw.

I'm standing in line, formulating my order, when someone calls my name from behind.

—Mickey? someone says. A woman. Is that you?

Immediately, I tense. I do not like the feeling of being caught unaware. Being watched when I'm unprepared to be looked at.

Turning in place, I see that the voice has come from Lila's mother, Lauren Spright. Today she's wearing a loose knit cap and a sweatshirt with stars all over it.

—Hey! says Lauren. It's so good to see you. I've been wondering how you were, since.

She pauses, thinking of how to phrase it. Since the party, she says.

—Oh, I say. I shift my weight back and forth. Put my hands into the pockets of my pants. Yes, I'm sorry about that, I say. It was a scene.

—How's Thomas doing? Lauren says.

—He's fine, I say, too quickly. *None of your business,* I want to say. But I sense in Lauren something genuine: hers is not a superficial or prurient concern.

—I'm glad, says Lauren. Meaning it.

—Hey, she says. Do you guys want to come over to our place sometime? Lila talks about Thomas every day. It would be nice to get them together again.

—Help you? says the boy behind the counter, impatiently. I did not realize I had reached the front of the line.

—All right, I say to Lauren. Yes. That would be great.

Lauren is retreating, letting me order. I'll call you, she says.

Coffee in hand, I drive south on Frankford, and then north on Delaware Ave. Then, surprising myself, I turn into the parking lot that borders the pier that Simon and I used to go to. The waterfront has changed since those days: SugarHouse Casino now looms to the south. New parking lots have sprung up nearby, and new condo buildings look out on the river.

But our pier is unchanged: still decrepit, trash-strewn, largely abandoned. The same stand of trees, bared by the winter, still obscures the water from view.

I park and get out of my car. I walk between leafless trees, push aside branches, step over weeds. On the wooden pier, I put my hands on my hips. I think of Simon. I think of myself, sitting here, eighteen years old, half a lifetime ago. I think about what kind of man, what kind of person, would work so hard to win the affections of a child. Because that's what I was, in the end.

By one p.m., I'm tired, and probably hungover, and starting to feel sick. I'll let Bethany go early. Give her the afternoon off. I pull out of the parking lot, merge onto 95, and drive north.

When I open the door to the apartment, it's quiet. Thomas still, occasionally, takes an afternoon nap around this time of day, though that's rarer and rarer.

I take off my jacket and hang it on a hook. I eye the kitchen as I pass it. It's littered with dishes from breakfast and lunch, and Bethany is nowhere to be found. I take a deep breath. Let it out. This is another conversation I've been meaning to have with her: *If you could tidy up throughout the day* . . .

Then I tell myself, Choose your battles.

I walk down the hallway. Thomas's door is closed. If he's sleeping, I don't want to wake him up.

The bathroom door is closed too. I stand outside it for a moment, listening. Thirty seconds go by, and I hear no running water, no sounds from inside.

Finally, gently, I knock on it.

—*Bethany?* I whisper.

I try the door handle, at last, and open it a crack.

—*Bethany?* I repeat.

Finally, I open the door wide. No one is inside.

I spin around. Open the door across the hallway. Thomas's room. His bed is unmade, but empty.

I call out, now. Hello? I say. Thomas? Bethany?

The apartment is still silent.

I run into my own bedroom, and then turn and run back to the front of the apartment, looking frantically for a note, for any clue to where they might be.

Bethany's car was in the driveway. And it's too cold out for them to have gone for a walk, I think—not that Bethany was ever one for walking, even when it was nice out.

I run outside, then down the back stairs, not bothering with a jacket. I leap over the landing and do a U-turn at the base of the stairs, running fast around the house. The wind bites through my sweater.

I look inside Bethany's car as I pass it. But it, too, is empty. The booster seat I bought for Thomas, I notice, is still not installed.

I pound on Mrs. Mahon's front door. Then I ring the doorbell, too.

I think wild and horrible thoughts. I imagine the body of my own son, splayed out, lifeless, a version of the many victims I have seen in my years on the job. Somehow, I have only ever seen one child after death, a little girl, six years old, hit by a car on Spring Garden. I wept. Her image has never left my mind.

I ring the doorbell again.

Mrs. Mahon answers, finally, blinking through her large glasses, wearing a brown fuzzy bathrobe and slippers.

—Are you all right, Mickey? she says, taking in my expression.

—I can't find Thomas, I say. I left him with his babysitter this morning and now they're gone. There's no note.

Mrs. Mahon's face goes pale. Oh no, she says. Oh no, I haven't seen them today.

She peers out the front door. Her car is still here, isn't it? she says.

But I'm already gone, rounding the house again, running back up to

the apartment, where I grab my phone and call Bethany—no answer—
and then text her.

Where are you, I say. *Please call me. I'm home.*

It's then that the words of Connor McClatchie arrive in my mind like a
fire alarm. *You've got a son*, he said to me. *Thomas, right?*

It takes me ten seconds to consider my options.

At the end of it, I call 911.

have never before interacted with Bensalem's police force. They are
small, but very professional. Within minutes, the house is a crime
scene. Two patrol officers arrive first, a young man and an older woman,
and they interview me quickly.

Downstairs, Mrs. Mahon is being interviewed separately.

It feels strange to be working with a police department outside of
Philadelphia. It seems reasonable to me that being an officer myself
would be helpful to me in this moment, and yet I can think of no one
right now on whom I might call. Every connection I have—Mike Di-
Paolo, Ahearn, Simon, even Truman now—feels lost to me, for different
reasons. Even my own family is lost to me. I can think of no one at all to
call, and in an instant, the depths of my solitude are made real to me.
The world closes in around me, one notch tighter, one notch tighter,
until my breathing turns shallow and quick.

—Easy, says the female officer kindly, noticing this. Easy. Deep
breaths.

I have never, in all my life, been on this side of an interview. I do as
she instructs.

—What do you know about this babysitter? the female officer asks.

—Her name is Bethany Sarnow, I say. I believe she's twenty-one years
old. She does makeup in her spare time. Occasionally she takes classes at
CCP. Online, I think.

The officer nods. Okay, she says. Do you know her home address?

I blank. No, I say. I don't, actually.

I pay Bethany in cash. Under the table. Twice a month.

—Okay, says the officer. How about any of her friends or family members? Anyone you can think of to contact?

Again, I shake my head. Berating myself. I had exactly one reference for Bethany, her instructor at the makeup academy, and even she, if I am being honest with myself, had sounded lukewarm.

—I'm worried about something, I say, my throat catching. Something in particular.

—What's that? says the officer. Her partner, the young man, has joined her now, after taking a cursory look through the apartment. I know what it must look like to him: shoddy, run-down, messy. Not the kind of place one has guests to.

—My sister is missing too, I say. At least, I don't know where she is. And there are people who know that I'm looking for her and may not be happy about it. And also, I'm a patrol officer in the 24th District of the PPD, but I'm under investigation right now. But it's due to a misunderstanding. Or maybe foul play.

The officers exchange a quick look, but it doesn't escape me. I've been in their shoes. I know what I sound like.

—No, no, I say. It's not like that. I'm an officer. I'm a cop. But I'm on suspension right now, because.

I trail off. Stop talking, I think. Just stop talking. I hear Truman, too, saying it in my ear.

—Because? says the young man. He scratches his nose.

—Never mind, I say. It's not important. I'm just worried about a possible abduction.

The female officer shifts again. What gives you reason to believe your son might have been abducted? she says. Is there anyone in particular who concerns you?

—Yes, I say. Connor McClatchie. But there are other possibilities too.

The male officer walks down the hallway to radio to Dispatch. I can't hear exactly what he's saying. The female officer continues to interrogate me, and slowly, more and more people arrive on the scene.

Just then, a terrible pounding begins on the door.

Through its glass window, I see Mrs. Mahon's face, her hair wild, her expression unreadable.

—Let me in, she is saying through the door.

They're back, Mrs. Mahon says, once I have opened the door. She is looking right at me, ignoring everyone else in the room.

It takes all of my effort not to collapse to my knees, to put my head in my hands, to burst into tears.

—Where are they, I ask.

—In the driveway, says Mrs. Mahon. A man's with them.

I run out the door, ignoring the male officer as he says, Just a moment, ma'am, please.

I fly down the stairs, followed more slowly by Mrs. Mahon, and around the house, and there is Thomas, looking serious, standing off to the side with a detective who is squatting down next to him, her face inches from his, talking to him.

I go to Thomas. I lift him into my arms. He buries his face in my neck.

I scan the driveway.

There is Bethany, crying. Next to her is a young man I don't recognize. He's been handcuffed. His face is red and furious.

Later, I will find out that this is Bethany's boyfriend. That the two of them thought it would be a good idea to go to the mall, to take Thomas with them in the boyfriend's car, unequipped with any child seat, a car in which the backseat does not even have functioning seat belts. The two of them thought it would be a good idea to do this without so much as a note or a text. (*I thought you might be mad,* Bethany will say to me, and I will say, *Correct.*) In half an hour, I will fire Bethany, and Bethany will ask me, with no irony or compunction, for a reference.

For this moment, though, I close my eyes. I know people are speaking to me, but I cannot hear them. I hear only my son's breath, feel nothing but my own heartbeat, smell nothing but, around me, the clean air of winter.

L ater that night, another knock at my door makes me jump.

Again, I see Mrs. Mahon's face peering in at me between the lace curtains that cover the window, too close to the glass, her breath fogging it.

I am tired. I just want to rest, now, to curl up on the sofa with Thomas and watch television.

But Thomas, when he sees Mrs. Mahon, springs up excitedly.

—Hi! he shouts. Since the snow day he spent with her, he has had a special reverence for Mrs. Mahon, and has excitedly waved to her each time we've crossed paths.

Now, he runs to the door and throws it open for her, and I say, Come in.

The cold air that gusts into the apartment slams a door in the back.

Mrs. Mahon is carrying, in her hands, two objects: one is a bottle wrapped up in brown paper, and one is a rectangular object in Christmas paper. A little bump protrudes from the center of the latter.

—I just came to check on you both, she says. After your ordeal. And to bring you these.

Stiffly, she holds the bottle toward me, and the present toward Thomas. She speaks formally, and seems nervous.

—That's very nice of you, I say. You shouldn't have.

But I take the bottle into my hands.

—It's only lemonade, says Mrs. Mahon, before I can open it. I just make it for myself. I just bottle it and keep it in the fridge. If it's too tart you can add sugar, she says. I like mine tart.

—As do I, I say. Thank you so much.

Thomas opens his package next. When the wrapping comes off, I see that it's a chessboard and a plastic bag that contains all the pieces. And, for a moment, I falter.

Thomas looks up at me, rather than Mrs. Mahon.

—What is it? he says.

—It's chess, I say, quietly.

—Chest? says Thomas.

—Chess, says Mrs. Mahon. It's a game. The best game there is.

Thomas is now delicately removing all the pieces from the bag, in order of size: first kings, then queens, then bishops, then knights, then rooks, then pawns. Mrs. Mahon names them as they emerge. At the sound of these words, I tense. I haven't heard them said aloud since my adolescence. Since Simon.

Thomas picks up the bishops, holds one up to Mrs. Mahon.

—Is he a bad guy? he says.

He does look menacing: opaque and eyeless, the slit in his hat like a frown.

—They're bad and good both, all the pieces, says Mrs. Mahon. Depending.

Thomas looks at Mrs. Mahon, and then at me. Mom, he says, can Mrs. Mahon have dinner with us?

I had been looking forward to a quiet night at home with my son. Now, of course, there is no option but to say yes.

—Of course, I say. Mrs. Mahon, will you join us?

—I'd be glad to, says Mrs. Mahon.

—But you should know that I'm a vegetarian, she says.

Mrs. Mahon is full of surprises.

I look in my cabinets, my refrigerator, and my freezer. There is almost nothing to serve. Finally I determine that I can offer her spaghetti and tomato sauce from a jar, slightly past its suggested use-by date. Frozen broccoli will round out the meal.

Conversation, unfortunately, does not flow easily, and I serve dinner as soon as I can.

The three of us sit around my small table. I give Mrs. Mahon the seat at the head, and offer the bowl of pasta to her first. Thomas and I sit across from one another. All three of us have glasses of the lemonade Mrs. Mahon has brought. It has fresh mint in it, which Mrs. Mahon says she grows indoors. It tastes like a long-overdue reminder that there is a season called summer. Thomas finishes his in three gulps.

Long silences between bites fill the room, and in them I can sense Thomas growing anxious. He wants the adults in the room to get along.

I clear my throat.

—Mrs. Mahon, I say, finally. Have you lived in Bensalem all your life?

—Oh no, she says. No, I grew up in New Jersey.

—I see, I say. New Jersey's a very nice state.

—It is a nice state, Mrs. Mahon agrees. I grew up on a farm. Not many people think about farms when they think about New Jersey. But I do.

All of us resume eating then. Mrs. Mahon has a large dot of spaghetti sauce on the front of her reindeer sweatshirt, and I feel somehow responsible. I pray Mrs. Mahon won't notice it, now or later, that it won't cause her embarrassment.

Thomas looks at me. I look at Thomas.

—What brought you to this area? I say to Mrs. Mahon.

Mrs. Mahon says, The Sisters of St. Joseph.

I nod. I am remembering the class photograph on the wall of Mrs. Mahon's house, the one I noticed while picking Thomas up at the end of his snow day.

—Did you go to a school they ran? I say.

—No, says Mrs. Mahon. I was one.

—You were one, I repeat.

—Yes, she says.

—A nun.

—For twenty years.

Why did you leave, I want to ask her, but I sense that this might be rude.

After dinner, Thomas sidles over to the chess set that Mrs. Mahon bought for him, and begins to place the pieces on the board.

—Come here, says Mrs. Mahon, patting the sofa, and she teaches him where all the pieces go, and how they move.

As they play, I clear the table and then wash the dishes, slowly, doing them by hand. My shoulders sink and suddenly I realize that I've been carrying them up by my ears for months. I feel the specific relaxation of knowing one's child is being well cared for by someone else. A moment of pure and peaceful inwardness, unencumbered by any guilt.

Afterward, I let Thomas teach me what he has just been taught, pretending not to know already. And then Thomas and Mrs. Mahon play against one another. Mrs. Mahon coaches him through every decision— *Are you* sure *you want to do that?* and *Take that back* and *Wait, wait, think a minute*—until at last, and under entirely false pretenses, Thomas is able to pronounce, *Checkmate.*

He celebrates, his little hands going into the air in the touchdown pose his father once taught him.

—I win! says Thomas.

—With help, I say.

—Fair and square, says Mrs. Mahon.

Later, Mrs. Mahon waits on the sofa while I walk Thomas to his bed. At Thomas's request, I leave a light on low in the corner and hand him a superhero compendium that I gave him for his last birthday.

—I love you, says Thomas.

I stiffen. This is not a phrase I regularly use. Certainly Thomas must know how much I love him from my actions, from the way I care for him, from the various ways in which I attend to him and his well-being. I have never trusted words, especially not words that are used to describe internal emotions, and something about the phrase feels artificial to me. Phony. The only person who ever said it to me in my life, that I can recall, was Simon, and well. Look how that turned out.

—Where did you learn that, I say.

—On TV, says Thomas.

—I love you too, I say.

—I love you three, Thomas says again.

—All right, I say. Enough. Go to sleep. But I am smiling.

Back in the living area, Mrs. Mahon is dozing lightly. I clear my throat loudly several times, and she sits up with a start.

—Oh dear, she says. Long day.

She puts her hands on her knees as if to stand, and then looks at me, changing her mind.

—Mickey, she says. You know, I've been meaning to tell you. I'm happy to watch Thomas from time to time. He's a nice boy. And I know you're having a hard time at the moment.

I shake my head. That won't be necessary, I say.

But Mrs. Mahon is looking at me in a steady, calm way that tells me she is serious, and also that she doesn't want to hear excuses. She reminds me suddenly of some of the stricter sisters from the first grade school I attended.

—He needs consistency, says Mrs. Mahon. It doesn't seem like he has much, right now.

For the first time all night, I bristle. There she is: the Mrs. Mahon I expected, the one who tells me how to bag my groceries and how to parent my son.

Mrs. Mahon begins to speak again, but I cut her off.

—We're fine, thank you, I say. We've got it under control.

A silence settles over the room. Mrs. Mahon looks down at the chessboard. She rises, painfully, and brushes at her pants.

—I'll leave you alone now, she says. Thank you for dinner.

As she opens the door, I surprise myself.

—Why did you leave the order, I say. I've been wondering since Mrs. Mahon mentioned it. And apparently we're getting personal now.

—I fell in love, says Mrs. Mahon, simply.

—With who? I say.

Slowly, she closes the door again.

—With Patrick Mahon, she says. A social worker. A very good person.

—What was your name before it was Mrs. Mahon? I ask.

She smiles. Looks down. She walks to the sofa and, with effort, sits down. I join her there.

—I was born Cecilia Kenney, she says. Then I was Sister Katherine Caritas. Then I was Cecilia Mahon. Am, she says.

—How did you meet Patrick Mahon? I say.

—He worked for St. Joseph's hospital, she says, which our order helped to run. He shepherded families who came in with sick children. Poor families, you know, she says. Or families who didn't speak English, or parents suspected of abuse or neglect. Those were the hardest cases, she says. He worked around the clock there. I got to know him while I was assigned to care for the babies in the NICU. My training was as a registered nurse. A lot of us Sisters were nurses.

She pauses.

—We fell in love, she says again. I left the order. We got married. I was forty years old.

—That was brave of you, I say, after a pause.

But Mrs. Mahon shakes her head. Not brave, she says. Cowardly, if anything. But I don't regret it.

I am afraid to ask what happened to him. To Patrick.

—He died five years ago, says Mrs. Mahon. In case you were wondering. We lived together twenty-five years, there in that house below you. This, she says, gesturing around at the apartment, was his studio. He painted, you know. Painted and sculpted.

—I'm sorry, I say. I'm so sorry for your loss.

She shrugs. So it goes, she says.

—Are those his paintings downstairs? I say.

She nods. She puts a finger on a rook and moves it two ahead. Two back. She looks at me over the top of her glasses.

—They're very nice, I say. I like them.

—Do you have family, Mickey? she says.

—Sort of, I say.

—What does that mean? says Mrs. Mahon.

So I tell her. There is less at stake, somehow, with Mrs. Mahon. I tell her about Kacey and Simon. I tell her about Gee. About my mother and father. About my cousins upon cousins who live both near and not near. Who do and don't know me. I tell her everything that I have always been afraid will scare people away. The burdens I carry that are almost too much for anyone to bear.

Mrs. Mahon is motionless as I speak, her eyes focused, her posture alert. I feel more heard than I have ever felt.

I have a memory of making my first confession as a six-year-old, before making my First Holy Communion: the terror of it, Gee telling me to be quiet, to calm down, to just shut up and invent something; and then being shoved inside a little booth, confessing my nonexistent sins to a disembodied voice. The ordeal of it. The shame.

This version of confession, I think, would have been much more appropriate. Every six-year-old should have a Mrs. Mahon to speak to on a comfortable couch.

By the end of my story, I am so at ease, so wonderfully understood, that it's as if I've entered another dimension, almost. It has been many years since I've felt so calm.

—Mrs. Mahon, I say. Do you still believe in God?

It's a silly question, a frivolous one, something I've never asked anyone except for Kacey, when I was younger, and Simon.

But Mrs. Mahon nods slowly.

—I do, she says. I devoutly believe in God, and in the work of the Sisters. It was the great tragedy of my life to leave the convent. But it was the great joy of my life to marry Patrick.

She waggles her hand, looking first at the front, and then at the back.

—Two sides of the same story, she says.

I do as she does, inspecting my hand. The back of it is hard, weathered, scaled by the cold of the season. This happens every season, working the streets. The palm is tender and soft.

—You know, says Mrs. Mahon. I'm not a nurse anymore, but I still volunteer at St. Joseph's. Ever since Patrick died. I go every week, twice a week. I cuddle the babies, she says.

—You what?

—The babies born to addicted mothers, she says. More and more babies in this city are being born to mothers who never stopped using. And then they don't come around. The mothers and fathers, I mean. They go back to the street the minute the baby is born. Or they aren't allowed to come around, in some cases. So the babies go into withdrawal, and they need holding, she says. Being held reduces their pain.

I am silent for so long that Mrs. Mahon puts a hand on my shoulder.

—All right? she says.

I nod.

—It might be nice if you came sometime, she says. Would you be interested?

I say nothing.

I am thinking of my own mother. I am thinking of Kacey, as a baby.

—Sometimes helping others gets the mind off its own problems, says Mrs. Mahon. I find, at least.

—I don't think I can, I say.

Mrs. Mahon looks at me appraisingly.

—All right, she says. Let me know if you ever change your mind.

Every day for a week, I stay home with Thomas. I haven't been home with him for so long since my maternity leave. I am happy to have this time with him. It has been too long, I realize, since I've devoted whole days to him, and he seems to blossom: We read books and play games. I take him to the Camden aquarium and the Franklin Institute. I teach him all the small things I know about the city.

Also, I've recently made a decision. Now, when he comes into my room in the night, I don't turn him away. I let him crawl into bed, pretending not to notice. In the morning, when I wake, I watch him: in a shaft of sunlight, his little-boy face, which is changing each day; and his hair, disheveled from sleep; and his small hands, tucked under his pillow, or folded over his chest, or raised above him in a gesture of surrender.

It's getting close to Christmas, so I take him to a Christmas tree lot and buy two: a small one for us, and a slightly larger one for Mrs. Mahon, which I leave propped against her door with a note saying we are upstairs if she needs help with it.

As it turns out, she does.

I think every single day of apologizing to Truman. But my shame prevents me from picking up the phone. I am cut off, therefore, from my source of information about the force as well. I hear nothing from him, and nothing from Mike DiPaolo. There is nobody I can ask for an update.

Each morning I expect a phone call from Denise Chambers, calling me in. I'll be fired, I assume. But every day passes without incident.

Christmas Day is freezing cold and sunny. Ice has made its way, in curling tentacles, across my windshield, and I put Thomas in the backseat before tackling the situation with a scraper. Mrs. Mahon is with her sister for the day.

Now, in the backseat, Thomas says, Where are we going?

—To Gee's house, I tell him.

—Why?

—We always visit Gee on Christmas, I say.

This isn't quite true: we always visit Gee *around* Christmas, because typically I've had to work on the day itself, which means I've had to leave Thomas with his former babysitter, Carla. I've always told myself that he's too young to notice. Last year, I'm not sure that this was true. Conveniently, no such obligations exist for me this year, during my interminable period of suspension. To Gee's house we go, then, bearing two small gifts that Thomas and I selected for her from the King of Prussia mall.

It's not that I miss her. It's that I miss the idea of family, in general, I suppose. The day that Thomas went missing, the fact that I had no one to call for support troubled me deeply. And I told myself, Michaela, it is your responsibility to create a greater network of friends and family than what you currently have. If not for yourself, then for Thomas.

Yesterday, therefore, I called Gee to let her know we would be coming. She sounded at first reluctant—protesting that her house was a mess, that she had not had a chance to buy anything for Thomas, due to how many shifts she had been picking up around the holidays—and then resigned.

—Gee, I said. You don't have to worry about that. Thomas has been asking to see you. That's all.

She paused.

—He has? she said.

In her voice, I heard the faintest smile.

—Well, she said. All right then.

—How's the afternoon? I said. Four o'clock or so?

—That'll be fine, said Gee, and then she hung up without saying goodbye, which, for her, is standard.

This morning, Thomas and I spent some quiet time together. I made him waffles: a favorite of his. I gave him four presents to unwrap: a Transformer figure that comes up to his waist; a ukulele (he has been telling me he wants to learn guitar); a collection of *Grimms' Fairy Tales*, the same ones that I loved, too, as a child; and a pair of light-up sneakers with Spiderman on them.

Now he is wearing the last, and from the backseat I hear small thuds that indicate he is tapping his heels together and watching the result. When I glance in the rearview mirror, I see he is looking out the window, his face grayed by the dim light of winter.

I exit at Girard and make my way toward Fishtown. The streets are quiet. On Christmas Day, everyone's either in the suburbs or bundled up inside their homes.

I turn onto Belgrade, my childhood street, and park easily. I let Thomas out and take his hand as we walk.

I press the bell once, then wait. It gives off the same sound it's given for thirty years: a ding followed by an electronic wheeze. It's never been fixed.

When enough time goes by, I take out my own key—several times, over the years, Gee has had the locks changed to prevent Kacey from stealing anything, but she has always made sure I have an up-to-date copy—and put it in the lock.

Just before I turn it, Gee flings the door open, blinking into the sunlight. She's taken some care with her outfit: her hair, short and dyed brown, is combed neatly, and she's wearing a red sweater and blue jeans, rather than her usual outfit of a sweatshirt and leggings. She has put earrings in her ears that are meant to look like small spherical Christmas ornaments, red and blue. I don't think I've ever seen Gee wearing anything but silver studs, the kind you get at nine years old from piercing stations in the mall.

—Sorry, says Gee, moving aside so we can enter. I was on the john.

It's chilly inside. Gee still keeps the heat turned down to save on her gas bill, apparently. Thomas starts shivering. I can hear his teeth.

But I can see, too, that Gee has put some effort into the place: there is a Christmas tree in the corner, tiny and scraggly (Got it yesterday down the corner, says Gee, the last one on the lot); and there are three little music boxes on the mantel of the fireplace, which has never worked. The music boxes support a dancing bear and a nutcracker doll and a figure of Santa Claus that jackknifes its legs and arms as it turns on a round base. Kacey and I loved them and made them go around and around every day, often all at once, which made a terrible racket that Gee deplored. Thomas, too, is drawn to them, and he approaches them and takes the bear down and looks it over, inspecting its gears. He is tall enough, I notice, to reach the top of the mantel.

—Do you mind? I say, standing near a light switch.

—Go ahead, says Gee. I was gonna do that anyway.

I flick it, and the strand of lights on the Christmas tree turn on.

I nearly ask her if I can turn the heat up a little, too, but instead I opt to simply leave my coat on. I'll leave Thomas's on, too.

I hand Gee a loaf of cranberry bread that I picked up from a bakery in Bensalem yesterday, and she takes it wordlessly and brings it into the kitchen. I hear the refrigerator door open and then close. For as long as I can remember, Gee has been waging war on the mice that come and go seasonally in her house, and this means never, ever leaving food out on the counter.

She comes back into the living room, and suddenly I notice how small she has gotten over the years. She was always petite—Kacey and I both outsized her profoundly from the time we were about ten—but now she is childlike, very thin, perhaps too thin. She still moves quickly, always jittery, her hands always searching for something I can't quite identify, moving to her jaw and then her waist and then into her pockets and then out again. She paces to the tree and extracts from it two packages, hastily wrapped, one for Thomas and one for me.

—Here, she says.

—Should we sit down? I say.

—Whatever you want, says Gee.

Thomas and I take seats on the sofa—unchanged since my childhood, fraying at the seams—and I let him open his present first. The box is large and unwieldy, and I have to hold it for him while he tears at the paper.

It's a Super Soaker, a neon water gun with a pump on it that acts as the trigger. I am certain that Gee bought it on sale, off-season. I would never have gotten such a thing for him. I've never allowed him to have any gun-shaped toys. I keep my face neutral.

Thomas inspects it silently.

—You loved those when you were a kid, Gee says to me, suddenly.

I don't think this is true. I have no memory of ever even using a water gun.

—Did I? I say.

Gee nods. The neighbors had one, she says. They played with it all day long, every summer. You wanted to get your hands on that thing, boy. Stood by the window and watched them. Couldn't drag you away.

I know, now, what she's referencing. But it was the children I was watching, not the gun. I was watching them and making a record of all of their small actions and exchanges, all their mannerisms, so that I might steal them and use them myself.

—What do you say? I say to Thomas.

—Thank you, Gee-Mom, says Thomas.

—Thank you, I say, after a beat.

My gift to Gee is a picture frame with the word *Family* on it, into which I put the most recent school picture I have of Thomas, taken over a year ago, now. Thomas's gift to Gee is a pin in the shape of a butterfly. Gee's gift to me is a sweater, very light blue, which she says she saw at Thriftway and thought would look nice on me.

—Paid good money for it, too, says Gee. Even with my discount. It's cashmere.

Gee turns the television on, then, to something Thomas will like, and I follow her into the kitchen to help her put out food.

It is then that I notice that a panel of glass in the window on the back door has been knocked out. A sheet of Saran wrap has been inexpertly taped over it, but a draft is coming through nonetheless.

I walk over and inspect it. No glass on the floor. No indication that it was a recent event. Still, the fact that the glass pane is the one closest to the doorknob gives me pause.

—Gee, I say. What happened?

She glances at me, and at the door.

—Nothing, she says. Hit it with a broom handle on accident.

I pause. I put a finger to the Saran wrap. Trace its edges.

—Are you sure? Because, I say, but Gee cuts me off.

—I'm sure, she says. Here, come help me with this.

Gee's lying. I know she's lying. Her insistence, her abruptness, her eagerness to change the subject tell me this. I don't know why she's lying. But I also know enough not to press her. Not yet.

Instead, I help her set out cheese and crackers, and I help her roll pepperoni and cheese into Pillsbury crescent rolls, and then I excuse my-self, saying I forgot something in the car.

—I'll be right back, I say to Thomas as I pass him.

On the television, the stop-motion version of *Rudolph the Red-Nosed Reindeer* is playing, very soft.

Outside, I stand in front of the house, inspecting it. Between Gee's house and her neighbor's is a shared alley through which they take the garbage. It leads to their small concrete back patios. And off these patios are the back doors to both houses.

A blue-painted alley door, usually bolted from the back, prevents any intruders from entering the alley. But the door is old and rickety, and the wood is splitting. I put my hand on the door and push.

It gives easily. I walk around to the other side. The bolt lock, never well secured to begin with, has been torn off of its screws. As if someone kicked the door open.

A tingling sense that I'm on the verge of knowing something impor-tant is beginning at the base of my neck. My nose fizzes with adrenaline.

I go back inside. Back into the kitchen.

—Gee, I say. I noticed something.

She turns to me. On her face is an expression of defiance and guilt.

—What, she says.

—The alley door, I say.

—Yeah, she says. Tried to get someone out here yesterday to fix that when you called. No one would. Christmas Eve.

—Who kicked it in, I say slowly.

Gee sighs. All right, she says, resigned. All right. All right.

We had a fight, says Gee. Me and Kacey. We got into it. She came around here asking for money and I told her, once and for all, that I was done. She got very mad.

—When was this, I say.

Gee looks at the ceiling. Two months ago, she says. Maybe longer. I don't know.

—Why did you lie to me? I say. When I asked you if you'd seen her lately.

She points at me.

—You, she says, have enough to worry about. I know how you meddle. You're softer on your sister than I am. Wouldn't be able to say no to her the way I can.

I'm shaking my head.

—Gee, I say. Do you know how worried I've been? You've heard about those murders. You must have known I was worried about Kacey.

Gee shrugs.

—I guess a little worry now, she says, is better than a lot of worry later.

I turn my head away from her.

—Anyway, she says. Next day, I come home, someone's broken into my house. I don't think it was a coincidence. Do you?

—Did you call the police? I say, and Gee laughs, not kindly.

—Now why would I do that, she says, when you're the police.

She pauses. Then she says, Besides. I don't know what all she took from me. Can't figure it out. Wouldn't know what to report, if I did.

A theory is beginning to form in my mind.

—Looked all over the house, says Gee. Money was there. TV was there. Jewelry was there. Silver was there.

She continues, naming items on the mental list she keeps of her meager possessions, after I've left the kitchen and headed for the staircase.

—Where are you going, she calls, but I can no longer see her.

—Bathroom, I reply.

At the top of the staircase, I turn instead into my childhood bedroom: the room that Kacey and I used to share. I haven't been in it in years. I have no reason to go in there when I visit Gee; I keep my visits short and formal and mainly stay on the ground floor, only going upstairs to use the facilities when necessary.

Gee, I notice, has stripped this bedroom of any sign of us. All it contains now is the full bed we shared as children, and even that has been remade, with a calico bedspread that looks like it's made of polyester. There is no other furniture in the room. Not even a closet. Not even a lamp.

In the corner of the room, I get down on my hands and knees and lift the edge of the wall-to-wall carpeting. Beneath it is the loose floorboard, and under that, our childhood hiding place. Our home for notes and treasured objects. Our sacred space—the one that Kacey later co-opted for her paraphernalia when darkness first crept into her life.

Maybe, I think, Kacey didn't break into this house to take something, but to leave it.

Holding my breath, I lift the floorboard.

I reach into it. My hands touch paper. I pull some out.

I don't understand, at first, what I'm looking at. It's a check from the Commonwealth of Pennsylvania for 583 dollars, dated February 1, 1991. I look through the rest. It seems that there's one a month for a decade, in amounts that slowly increase.

More: three documents processed by the Pennsylvania Department of Human Services on behalf of Daniel Fitzpatrick. Our father. The beneficiaries of the agreement are listed: Michaela and Kacey Fitzpatrick. Support services, it says, will go to Nancy O'Brien. Our guardian. Our grandmother, Gee.

Gee always kept a PO box, so we never got mail at our house. Now, suddenly, I understand why.

I reach back into the hollow. There's more. Dozens of Christmas and birthday cards. Dozens of letters. Halloween cards. Valentines. All of them signed, *Love, Daddy*. Some contain references to money, to dollar bills included and, presumably, extracted by Gee.

The most recent one I can find is from 2006, when I was twenty-one years old, and Kacey was nineteen.

The realization arrives with a thump in my gut: This is after I thought he was dead.

descend the staircase, still holding the papers and cards in one hand. Thomas glances up at me as I pass him in the living room.

—Stay there, I say to him.

In the kitchen, Gee is holding a beer in her hand. Leaning against a counter. She looks at me, pale-faced, resigned. She knows, I think, that I know something new. Her outfit, which pleased me when I first saw it, has become sad to me: a sad attempt to cover over many years of wrong-doing.

For a moment, I say nothing. But the hand that's holding the evidence I've gathered is shaking slightly in anticipation.

—What's that, she says. What are you holding there.

She's looking at the paperwork.

I walk to where Gee is standing and put the stack on the countertop forcefully. Standing next to her, I notice again that I tower over her. I wait, but Gee doesn't pick up the documents.

—I found these, I say.

—Don't waste your time looking for your sister, says Gee. When Kacey goes missing, she wants to be missing. Don't waste your time, she says again.

—Look at them, I say.

—I know what they are, Gee says. I can see them all right.

—Why did you lie to us? I say.

—I never lied to you.

I laugh. How do you do that math, I say. You complained about child support every day of your life.

Gee looks at me sharply.

—He left you, she says, simply. He got my daughter hooked on that shit and then he left when it killed her. I was the one who raised you. I was the one who took over when everyone else left you girls behind. A couple hundred bucks a month doesn't change that.

—Is he alive? I say.

—How should I know, says Gee.

—Gee, I say. Was your life ruined by having us?

She scoffs. Don't be dramatic, she says.

—I'm not, I say. I'm serious. Did we ruin your life?

Gee shrugs. I guess my life was ruined when my daughter died, she says. My only child. I guess that's what did it.

—But we were kids, I say. Kacey was only a baby. It wasn't our fault that she died.

Gee whips her head around. I know that, she says. You think I don't know that?

She points to the refrigerator suddenly. Look at that, she says. What's on it? Just look.

For years, the front of it has looked something like a collage. Yellowing, curling papers are taped to it everywhere: notes from our teachers, the one good report card that Kacey ever got, school photos. A card Thomas made for Gee last Christmas.

—I've always cared for you, Gee says. Cared for you, cared for Kacey. You're my family.

—But you didn't love us, I say.

—Of course I did, Gee says. She nearly shouts it. Then settles down. But talk is cheap, she says. I cared for you with what I did. Spent my life on you. Every paycheck. Spent it on you.

I wait.

—I was soft, I say, and you made me hard.

Gee nods. That's good, she says. The world is a hard place. I knew that was something I had to teach you, too.

—You did, I say.

She looks away. That's good, she says again. That's what I wanted.

I have nothing more to say.

—Gee, I say, changing my tone, adding into it a sweetness that she very occasionally responded to when we were children. Please. Do you have any idea where Kacey might have gone?

—You'll leave her, Gee says. Her face has hardened into something impenetrable. You leave her alone if you know what's good for you.

—I'll do what I want, I say.

I have never in my life spoken to Gee in this way.

Gee pauses for a long time, as if she's been slapped.

Then she looks at me, hard.

—She's expecting, she says at last.

The word is so old-fashioned that I try for a moment to make it mean something else. Anything else. Expecting what, I want to say.

—That's why we fought, says Gee. Now you know. Might as well hear it from me.

Gee is watching me, measuring my reaction. I keep my face still.

Then she looks past me, over my shoulder, and I follow her gaze. Behind me, Thomas has quietly entered the room. He is standing still, looking worried.

—There's your baby, says Gee.

THEN

Let me say this. I have tried, to the best of my ability, to live my life in an honorable way.

The idea of living *honorably* has guided my behavior both professionally and personally. For the most part, I am proud to say that I have stayed true to my sense of what is right and just.

Nevertheless, like all people, I have made one or two decisions in the past that, today, I admit I might reconsider.

The story of the first of these begins around the time that Kacey relapsed while living with me in Port Richmond.

Swiftly, I asked her to leave.

The idea of her staying with me was always contingent upon her sobriety. When she arrived on my doorstep, I told her that there would be no second chances. And I knew, always, that in order for her to believe me on this point, I would have to know, in my heart, that I'd do it.

So when I came home to find her using, and when I found all of the evidence of her use in a drawer of her dresser, she said nothing to me, and I said nothing to her. She only packed up her things, in silence, while I wept in the basement of my home, hoping that she wouldn't hear me.

I had so loved having her there.

She left without a word.

The first time I ever saw my sister working, I didn't know for certain that that was her intent.

It happened one morning soon after she moved out. I was on a shift, and a priority call came in that drew me out of district, northeast, toward Frankford. Truman was with me on that day, and he was driving. I was in the passenger's seat.

Driving high up on Kensington Ave, I caught a passing glimpse of a woman who was standing on the sidewalk in shorts and a T-shirt, her purse slung over her shoulder. A moment later, I thought: That was Kacey. But it had happened so quickly that it felt like a mirage. Was it really Kacey? I couldn't be sure. I whirled in my seat to look back at her, but she was already out of sight.

—You okay? said Truman, and I told him I was.

—I just thought I saw someone I knew, I said.

Truman had never, at that time, met my sister.

On the way back from the call, I asked Truman to let me drive, and I intentionally steered our vehicle past the same intersection.

Yes: it was Kacey. She was bent at the knees. High. She was leaning down now, into the window of a car, the driver of which pulled away when he noticed our cruiser, attempting to look nonchalant, nearly taking Kacey's arm with him in the process. She straightened abruptly, stumbled a few steps backward, annoyed. She hoisted her purse up on her shoulder. Crossed her arms around her middle, dejected.

I was driving so slowly that Truman again asked if I was all right.

This time, I didn't reply.

I didn't plan to, but when the car was directly in front of my sister, I slowed to a halt right there in the middle of the road. Nobody beeped. Nobody would beep at a police vehicle.

—Mickey? said Truman. What are you doing, Mickey?

A long line of cars was forming behind us. Several cars back, someone sounded their horn at last, unable to see what the holdup was.

And this, finally, is what drew Kacey's gaze upward. She saw me. She straightened her posture.

We looked at each other for a long time. Time, in fact, seemed to slow and then stop. What passed between us in that moment was an unbearable sadness, the knowledge that nothing would ever be the same, the crumbling to dust of all the ideas we ever had as children about the better life we'd one day make for one another.

From inside the car, I lifted my hand and put one finger to the window, pointing in her direction. Truman leaned forward to see past me.

Kacey looked her worst that day, as bad as I've ever seen her: already too skinny, her skin marred with red dots where she'd picked at it, her hair unwashed, her makeup smeared.

—You know her? Truman said. But there was no snideness in his voice, no disgust. In fact, I heard in the phrase he used a great tenderness, a readiness to embrace her if she was any friend or relative of mine. Yes, Truman, I thought. I know her.

—That's my little sister, I said.

That night, I was inconsolable. I called Simon over and over again, but he didn't answer.

At last, he picked up, sounding peeved, as he always did when he didn't want to be contacted.

—What's the emergency? he said.

I asked very little of Simon. I was always hesitant to seem too demanding, too desperate. That night, though, I was lost. I need you, I said.

He told me he would be by soon.

In an hour, when he arrived, I told him what I'd seen.

To his credit, he was extremely attentive as he listened, and extremely generous in his dispensation of advice.

—You don't want to do this, he said to me, when I told him I had cut her completely out of my life.

I told him that I did. That I had to.

He shook his head. You don't, he said. Not really.

—Let me talk to her, he said.

We were sitting side by side on the sofa. His leg was crossed ankle to knee, so that from above, his body would have looked like a four. Absentmindedly, he touched the place on his calf where the letter X was tattooed.

—One last try, he said. You owe her that much. And yourself. I don't think you'd be happy with yourself if you didn't give it one last try. I can help.

At last, feeling tired, I acceded.

—I have a history with this, he said. Don't forget I have a history with this. Sometimes you just need to hear it from someone who's been there.

Within a week, Simon had located Kacey at the abandoned home in which she was squatting with friends. He had put his detective skills to use, he told me: as he phrased it, he asked some of his contacts on the ground.

She was resistant at first, he told me, but he persisted.

Each day he interacted with her, he reported back to me: Kacey looked bad today. Kacey looked good today. I took Kacey out for lunch. I made sure she ate something.

For a month, he narrated his experience of seeking her out. And it made me feel better, feel cared for, to know that someone else in the world was watching out for her in this way. Someone else was helping me to shoulder the responsibility I felt I had been assigned at four years old. Simon still seemed to me so capable, so reliable, so *adult*, in some unquantifiable way.

—Why are you doing this, I asked him once, marveling at his generosity.

And he told me, I've always liked to help people.

After two months or so, one day, he called me and said: Mickey, I need to talk to you.

Which I knew sounded bad right away.

—Just tell me now, I said.

But he insisted.

He came to the house in Port Richmond. He sat down next to me on the sofa. Then, taking my hands in his, he said, Mickey. Listen. I don't want to scare you, but Kacey's bad-off. I think she's delusional. She's started ranting about things I can't make sense of. I don't know if it's just the drugs, or something else. Either way, it's something to be concerned about.

I furrowed my brow.

—What's she saying? I said.

He sighed. I can't even make it out, he said. I know she's angry about something, but I can't tell what it is.

Something about what he was saying sounded strange to me.

—Well, I said. What words is she using?

It seemed, to me, like a reasonable question, and yet Simon looked annoyed.

—Just trust me, all right? he said. She's not herself.

—All right, I said. What should we do?

—I'm going to try to get her help, said Simon. I know some folks in social services who might be able to help her if we can get her a diagnosis of psychosis, or something like that. The first step is getting her seen by them.

He looked at me. Yes? No? he said.

—All right, I said again.

That night, I couldn't sleep. I lay in bed, awake, counting the hours until my morning shift began. It occurred to me that I had not seen my sister on the street in all the time Simon had been reporting on her—a development I took to be a sign of progress.

It was one in the morning, and I was due to start work at eight. But, discovering that no amount of self-hypnosis could coax me toward sleep, I at last gave up the chase and rose from my bed.

I put on clothing. I located the most recent picture of Kacey that I had.

I walked outside, got into my car, and drove to Kensington.

I had a vague idea of where Kacey might be living, based on certain things that Simon had said.

So I went to the nearest intersection, and began to ask around.

Overnight, Kensington is usually fairly active—and never more so than on warm and balmy evenings close to the summer solstice, as that one was. It was early May, and the few flowering trees Kensington boasts were in full bloom, waving their white, heavy branches in the wind. They looked uncanny, lit up by streetlamps, sun-seeking flowers in the darkest part of night.

Plaintively, I held out Kacey's picture to several people standing on the street.

Right away, someone recognized her, a man I eyed suspiciously, wondering if he was a client of hers. Yeah, I know her, he said. Then he asked me, What do you want with her?

I didn't want to tell him any more than I needed to, so I only said, She's a friend. Do you know where she's living these days?

He was hesitant.

In Kensington, though it often seems like everybody knows everybody else and all of their business, it is difficult to get anyone talking. For most, it's a matter of convenience: Why butt in when you don't have to? Why invite trouble your way? *Keep my name out of your mouth* is a common refrain, one that might be emblazoned on Kensington's crest, if it had one. Besides, it was possible that this man remembered my face from seeing me around the neighborhood, dressed in uniform. Perhaps he thought I was undercover, and had a warrant for her arrest.

There is, fortunately, a relatively easy way to get people talking, and it's green.

A five—the price of a nickel bag of heroin—most likely would have done the trick, but I'd come prepared with a twenty, which I offered to him if he could lead me to where she was.

I also had a weapon strapped to my back, under my shirt, in case he tried to take the money from me. I did not tell him this.

The man glanced left and right. I didn't like the look of him. I sensed he was so hungry for a fix that he'd do anything to get it. A person in this state is loaded like a spring. Their minds are often disconnected from whatever innate code of ethics they otherwise might have.

The man led me down two streets—farther and farther away from witnesses, incidentally—and I kept my body tight and ready, prepared to unholster my weapon if I needed to. I walked several paces behind him so I could keep an eye on him and scan my surroundings as well.

At last, he stopped outside a house.

To me, it didn't look abandoned. No boards were covering the windows. No graffiti marred its siding. Two planters outside, in fact, were well maintained, and red geraniums sprouted from the dirt inside them.

—She's been staying here, said my guide, and he held out his hand for the money.

I shook my head.

—How do I know she's in there? I said. I can't pay you until I know.

—Aw, man, he said. Really? I feel so rude knocking this time of night.

But he sighed, and complied, and I felt bad, actually, that I had underestimated him.

He rapped twice at the door, first gently, and then firmly.

The woman who answered, after about five minutes of knocking, was not Kacey. She looked annoyed, blinking at us sleepily, but she looked well, and didn't look intoxicated. She was wearing pajama pants and a T-shirt. I didn't recognize her.

—What the hell, Jeremy? she said to the man. What's going on?

He stuck out his thumb at me. She's looking for Connie, he said.

I could see inside the house: it was well kept, neat, with clean carpet on the floor. It smelled of fresh garlic and onions inside, as if someone had recently prepared a wholesome meal.

I noticed, after a moment, that the woman was staring at me, annoyed. She snapped her fingers at me. Hello? she said. Can I help you?

I turned so my back was to the woman. I handed the money to Jeremy as subtly as I could. He departed. Then I faced the woman again.

—She's my sister, I said. Is she in here?

Reluctantly, the woman stepped aside.

I found Kacey asleep in a twin bed in a tidy room. She was breathing lightly. She'd always been a heavy sleeper, ever since we shared a bed as children; it did not surprise me that she could sleep through Jeremy's pounding at the door.

—Thank you, I said to the woman, expecting her to leave. But she waited there, unmoving, one eyebrow raised. She was staying, I realized, to gauge Kacey's reaction to my presence. She wanted to make sure I was welcome. And I felt certain she was prepared to intervene if I was not. She had a tough, determined expression on her face—a look she shared with many of the women I grew up with, including Kacey, including Gee. Over the years, I have manufactured a facsimile of that look to wear when on the job, but it still does not come naturally to me.

I placed a hand on Kacey's shoulder and I shook her gently, and then firmly.

—Kacey, I said. Wake up. Kacey. It's Mickey.

When, at last, she opened her eyes, her expression changed quickly from disorientation to confusion to surprise to shame.

And then, just as rapidly, her eyes filled with tears.

—He told you, she said.

I said nothing in response. I wasn't certain, yet, what she meant.

She sat up and lowered her head into her hands. Her roommate shifted slightly in my peripheral vision.

—I'm so sorry, Mickey, Kacey was saying, over and over again. I'm so sorry. I'm so sorry.

sensed even in that moment that the two of us were at a crossroads. The map of our lives stretched out before us, and I could see, quite clearly, the various paths I might choose to take, and the ways in which this choice might affect my sister.

In retrospect, of course, the path I chose was wrong.

Dishonorable, even.

—I'm pregnant, said Kacey.

—It's Simon's, said Kacey.

—It was during a bad streak for me, said Kacey. I didn't know what I was doing. He took advantage of me.

—I've been trying to get clean ever since, said Kacey.

And I said, No.

That's the first word that came out of me. I felt in my body the same lightheadedness that sometimes felled me as a child, and I wanted to stop it, and so I said, again, No.

As I said the word, I sensed that some decision had been made for me. It was difficult to turn back. If I could have, I would have put my hands over my ears.

I should have left. I should have taken more time to think.

—Mickey, said Kacey.

I turned my face away sharply.

—Mick, I'm so sorry, Kacey said. I'm sorry. I'd take it back if I could.

———

Today, when I consider the list of the worst things I've ever done and said to Kacey, at the top of it is the lie I once told her, in anger, about our mother: that she once said to me that she loved me more than Kacey. It was a child's fantasy, the sharpest knife I could wield, a moment of real cruelty in the middle of an otherwise ordinary spat between siblings. Kacey's reaction, the horrible wail that came out of her, made me remorseful enough to swear to myself I'd never say anything so unkind again.

And yet I did, that night.

—You're lying, I said, calmly.

She looked briefly confused.

—I'm not, she said.

—Anyway, I said. How would you even know.

—I don't understand, said Kacey.

—Who the father is, I said. How would you even know?

She looked, for a moment, as if she might hit me. I recognized the tightened fist, the tightened arm, from her childhood, when she regularly brawled. Instead she absorbed the shock of my words in silence, and looked away from me.

—Leave, she said.

Her roommate—a woman I had never before met—echoed the word to me, pointing at the door. It occurs to me now that her loyalty to my sister—this relative stranger, this person I did not know—was greater, that day, than mine was.

made it so easy for Simon. I did not even require him to issue a denial to me. Instead, when he came to see me the following day, I told him that I agreed with his assessment, and that it was imperative that we find help for Kacey.

—She told me that she was pregnant, I said, and that it was yours.

He was silent.

—Can you believe that? I said.

—I told you, he said.

—Is she really pregnant? I said.

—She may be, said Simon. I guess we'll have to wait and see.

That spring and summer, I did see her, more and more. She returned to the street, with vigor. I saw her working, on my shifts.

And I saw that, sooner or later, she was beginning to show.

If she'd been clean when I found her at the house with the geraniums outside it, she was very clearly using, now. Her eyes were glazed and bloodshot. Her skin bore red marks on it. Her stomach was the only thing protruding from her body, which otherwise was gaunt. I am sad to say that this did not seem to deter her clients. Very often, I saw them stop for her. Sometimes doubling back to do so.

—I can't watch this, I said once or twice to Simon.

I was thinking of the baby, and the baby's welfare, and I was thinking of our own mother, and the choices that she made.

I began to research lawyers.

The first of them told me that third-party custody was not out of the question. It happened frequently in cases where one or both parents were addicted. She had personally handled several cases just this year. But even if custody is wrested from the mother, she said, the mother would have to testify that she did not know who the father was. If she named a father, then he would have to sign paperwork agreeing to give over the child, as well.

—What if, I said, the mother is delusional? What if she falsely names a father, but it isn't true?

—Well, said the attorney—Sara Jimenez was her name—then a paternity test would be recommended by most judges.

I told this to Simon, who went silent.

In fact, that whole year, he had been suspiciously silent every time the subject of Kacey came up. He stopped seeing her, stopped trying to help her. When I brought her up he changed the subject.

But when I told him, at last, that a paternity test would be necessary to disprove Kacey's assertion—and when his only response was further silence—then I began, finally, to acknowledge aloud what I suppose I had known all along.

By then, of course, it was too late to take back what I'd said to my sister.

Thomas Holme Fitzpatrick was born on December 3, 2012, at Einstein Medical Center. Of course, Thomas was not the first name he was given. Kacey called him Daniel, after our father. But I knew right away that that couldn't be his name.

I was not present for his birth. But I learned, after the fact, that Kacey entered the hospital drowsy and intoxicated, clearly high. And I know that within minutes of being born, Thomas was taken from his mother and placed in the care of the nurses in the NICU so that they could monitor him for signs of withdrawal—which, within hours, he began to show.

At home in Port Richmond, I was ready to receive him, to welcome him into the better life that, for months, I had been planning. I had turned one of the bedrooms in my house—Kacey's old room, in fact—into a soothing nursery. I decorated it in shades of pale yellow, a sunny color I hoped would presage a cheerful life for my new son. I framed favorite quotations from books I loved and hung them on the walls. I went to bookstores and bought for him the books that, as a child, I was never read. I'd read them all to him, I thought: as many times as he wanted, and then more. I'd never say no, I thought.

By that time, Simon and I had stopped speaking, but had come to an arrangement. He would give over the rights to Thomas, but he wanted to remain in the boy's life. (Why? I asked him, and he said he always prided himself on finishing what he started.) I told him he could do so if he would fund Thomas's education. Nothing else: just the money I needed to ensure for him a respectable education.

All of this was off the record.

In our arrangement, two threats were implicit, a careful equilibrium we orchestrated and maintained: I held over Simon the threat of my telling his superiors about the beginnings of our relationship. He held over me the threat of seeking custody of Thomas.

We were cordial with each other, but we rarely spoke. Once a month, after his birth, a check came for Thomas: his tuition for Spring Garden Day School, and nothing more.

In exchange, once a month, Simon took Thomas out on an excursion—something Thomas at first resisted and then began to look forward to more and more as he got older, something he counted on for weeks in advance and narrated the story of for weeks after.

The person who was left out of this arrangement, of course, was Kacey.

She didn't give Thomas up voluntarily. She wanted to keep him. In her hospital room she promised, over and over again, that she'd get clean. But Thomas's NAS score at birth was very high, and his withdrawals from the many narcotics that had been running through his mother's body were severe. As my attorney and I expected, the baby was taken into the custody of the Philadelphia DHS, where he remained for one night while they assessed him and located the baby's closest relatives. The next day, they telephoned Gee, and they telephoned me.

Gee told me I was crazy to get involved. You don't know what you're doing, she said. You don't know how hard it is to raise a child alone.

But I had already decided.

Yes, I told the social worker; I have a place for him.

My plan was to seek full custody of the child. With my attorney, I decided against requesting a complete termination of Kacey's parental rights. I left the door open, always, for her to get into recovery, for her to begin to see Thomas. But at my instruction, my attorney requested a caveat: Kacey would not be allowed to see her son until she began to pass court-ordered drug tests.

She never could. Despite her protests, despite her many attempts to regain visitation rights, she failed every test that she took.

She has never, therefore, been allowed to see Thomas, and I have retained full custody over him. The court has deemed this arrangement to be in the best interest of the child—an easy decision for any respectable judge.

This is, I suppose, exactly what I offer: Respectability. Decency. Sobriety. A stable home. A career. A chance for Kacey's son—now my son—to be educated.

told the PPD, and Truman, I had adopted a child.

No one asked questions.

Even Truman, with whom I had already been partnered for five years, only said, Congratulations. He brought me a present: a beautiful gift bag of books and clothes, so carefully selected that it must have taken him ages to compile. I wrote him a thank-you note and mailed it to his home.

The PPD's parental leave policy is not generous. It is unpaid, for one thing. But they do grant new parents up to six months off, which is better than nothing. With the small amount I had saved, I determined that I could afford three months and one week. After that, I would enroll Thomas in day care.

Those first months of Thomas's life were among the most difficult of mine. I do not recommend attempting to tend to any newborn for months on end alone, without some relief—familial or paid—let alone a newborn in withdrawal from a daily narcotic regimen as active as Kacey's. But I did so.

In the hospital, he had been given morphine.

He was sent home with a prescription for phenobarbital.

Neither spared him completely from the pain of withdrawal, and so I watched in sympathy as his small body trembled and sometimes convulsed, and placed a hand on his chest to feel it rise and fall more rapidly than I sometimes thought possible, and listened in agony to his cries, which were at times unstoppable. He vomited so much after his feedings that every ounce he gained was a small victory. He was unable, often, to be consoled.

Still, I held him, and in the short-lived moments of peace that presented themselves like oases when I thought I could no longer go on, I fell in love with the baby, watched as his lit-orb eyes opened slowly, in wonder, to take in his small world. Cheered him through each physical accomplishment, through the vowels that poured out of him fluidly, and then through each new consonant pronounced.

Who on earth can explain, in words alone, the great gutting tenderness of holding your child in your arms? The animal feeling of it—the baby's soft muzzle, the baby's new skin (which throws into relief the wear your own has endured), the little hand reaching up to your face, searching for family. The quick small pats, light as moths, that land on your cheek and chest.

The strongest grief I've ever felt in my life arrived one afternoon as I was feeding him. I was sitting on my bed, Thomas in my arms, and as I looked down at my son—the soft tiny wisps of hair on his scalp, the balloon-animal arm, its new plumpness segmented at the wrist and elbow—a sudden storm of disbelief and sorrow burst about me, and I opened my mouth and—I am embarrassed to admit it—I wailed aloud.

Because for the first time I understood the choice my own mother had made to leave us—if not by design, then by her actions, her carelessness, the recklessness with which she sought a fix. I understood that she had held me—us—in her arms, and gazed at us as I was then gazing at Thomas. She had held us like that and had decided to leave me, to leave us, anyway.

In that moment, I made a promise to myself, one that has become the guiding principle of my life: I would protect my son from the fate that befell Kacey and me.

———

Thomas's struggles continued for the better part of a year. Watching him, my anger with my sister rose and rose in my throat. How could she, I thought to myself. How could anyone.

Nights blended into days and then back again. I often forgot to eat and to use the bathroom.

Gee was the only person, aside from Simon, to whom I revealed the particulars of our arrangement. And although she was diligent at first in stopping by, soon her visits became less frequent.

The one time I ever mentioned to her how difficult it had been since Thomas's birth, she looked at me and said, Imagine two of them.

I never complained again.

Those months made me determine one thing with certainty. I would never let Thomas's beginning hold him back. I'd never let him use his history as a crutch. In fact, I promised myself, I wouldn't even tell him, until he was ready to receive the information without allowing it to negatively affect his self-perception.

It is for this reason that, today, Thomas believes me to be his biological mother.

thought that Kacey would return to the street and forget.

I thought she'd be angry with me but quickly move on: the routine of seeking and finding and seeking a fix is immersive and hypnotic, and it's difficult to emerge from that cloud for long enough to care.

And yet, several times during my maternity leave, I peered out my upstairs window to see Kacey outside, sitting on the stoop of the house across the street, or on the curb, her legs stretched out before her, dejected. She turned her face up, squinting toward the house, her gaze darting rapidly over its facade, from window to window, seeking a glimpse of her son, I imagine. My son.

Once or twice, she even went so far as to ring the doorbell.

I never answered.

On these occasions I made sure the rooms inside the house were darkened, and I gave Thomas a bottle so he wouldn't cry, and I stayed far away from the door as she pounded on it, as she rang the bell, over and over again, wailing for the baby.

Once, toward the end of those months, I walked outside with Thomas in a carrier I used to wear strapped to my body. I intended to walk to the corner store. As always, I had checked out the window before walking outside, ensuring that my sister was not present.

But ten yards from the front of my house, I heard the footsteps of someone quickly approaching, and I turned, shielding Thomas's head protectively, and there was Kacey, wild-eyed, her hair a mess, an angry ghost. She had been hiding, I suppose.

—Please, Mick, she was saying. Please let me see him. I just want to see he's okay. I'll never ask again.

I don't know what came over me. I should have said no.

Instead, after hesitating, I turned wordlessly in her direction, allowing her to gaze upon Thomas's small face. He was sleeping. His cheek was pressed into my sternum. He was—is—a beautiful child.

Kacey smiled, just a little. She began crying, which made her look even wilder. She swiped at her nose with the back of her hand. A neighbor passed and looked at us both, goggle-eyed. Then she tried to catch my eye to ensure I was all right, presuming, I'm certain, that I was in the midst of being harassed by a crazed stranger. I didn't look back at her.

Tentatively, Kacey stretched out one hand, as if to put it on Thomas's forehead—a benediction—but I jerked away, instinctively.

—Please, she said again.

It was the last word she would speak to me for the next five years, aside from our occasional encounters on the job.

I shook my head. I walked away. She stood in place behind me, as still and as sorry as an abandoned house.

To this day, I sometimes have nightmares about Kacey returning to claim Thomas.

In these dreams, Kacey is well, a vision of health, and her demeanor is exuberant and jolly, just as she was as a child, and she looks very beautiful, and Thomas runs to her across a crowded place—a store, usually, or a school, or sometimes a church, and he says to her, *I've missed you,* or sometimes, *I've been waiting,* or sometimes just *Mother.* Very simply. Claiming her too. Naming an object, stating a fact. *Mother.*

NOW

There's your baby, says Gee, in the kitchen. And in her voice I hear a hint of a reproof.

—You've got him already, says Gee. Don't need to worry about another.

—Stop talking, I say.

Behind me I hear the faintest gasp from Thomas, who has never heard me say such an impolite thing in his life.

I look at my surroundings, and I have difficulty believing, suddenly, that this is where I spent the first twenty-one years of my life. This cold and unwelcoming house. This house that is no place for children. Every part of me begins, then, to send a simultaneous signal: get out, get out, get out. Get Thomas out. Don't ever come back to this house, to this woman.

Wordlessly, I touch Thomas on the shoulder and signal to him that we have to leave. He picks up the Super Soaker, and I almost tell him to leave it, but at the last minute I change my mind.

As we walk out the door, Gee's words echo in my head. *The world is a hard place. The world is a hard place.* She said that to us all the time when we were children. And I realize, suddenly, that these are the words I use with Thomas, too, when explaining all the difficulties he has faced this year.

Behind us, Gee is calling down the block.

—You'll leave her alone, she says, one final time. You'll leave her alone if you know what's good for you.

Thomas and I sit for a while in the car. He is pensive and worried. He knows enough to know that something strange is happening.

In my right hand is one of the birthday cards our father sent us. I snatched it up before I left. This one is to Kacey. In the upper left-hand corner of the envelope is an address in Wilmington, Delaware.

I need to get someone to watch Thomas for a while. At the moment, the person it feels safest to leave him with is Mrs. Mahon.

Once I'm in the car, I call her landline, and pray she will be back from her sister's house.

Mrs. Mahon answers quickly, as if she had been waiting by the phone.

—It's Mickey, I say.

And I ask her whether I might take her up on her offer to help, and I promise to explain everything tonight. Of course, says Mrs. Mahon. Knock when you're home.

I notice, when I hang up, that Thomas has gone silent. When I look into the backseat, I see that he's started to cry.

—What's wrong? I say. Thomas, what's wrong?

—Are you leaving me with Mrs. Mahon again, he says.

—Just for a little, I say.

I turn in the front seat and regard him. He looks very old and very young at once. He has seen too much lately.

—But it's Christmas, he says. I want you to help me play with my new toys.

—Mrs. Mahon can help you do that, I say, and he says, No. I want you.

From the front seat, I reach my arm into the back, put a hand on his sneaker, and squeeze it. Beneath my grip, it lights up. Briefly, he smiles.

—Thomas, I say. I promise I'll be around tomorrow, and every day after. Okay? I know it's been a difficult winter. I promise things will be better soon.

He won't look at me.

—Let's do something fun with Lila soon, I say. Would that be nice? I can talk to Lila's mom.

He smiles at last. Wipes a tear from his cheek.

—Okay, he says.

—Would that be nice? I say again.

He nods bravely.

The length of time it's been since I've seen my father is greater than the length of time I knew him. I was ten years old when he disappeared from our lives. Kacey was eight.

After dropping Thomas off at Mrs. Mahon's, I enter into my GPS the address I have for my father, in Wilmington, and begin to drive.

The envelope on the passenger's seat is over a decade old. It is possible, I realize, that my father no longer lives at the return address. But with no other leads, this is the one I have to follow.

In my memory, he is tall and skinny, like me. He has a low, slow voice and is wearing baggy jeans and an Allen Iverson jersey and a backward baseball cap. At that time he would have been twenty-nine years old—younger, in this memory, than I am now.

Because I was fiercely loyal to my mother, and because Gee always implied that my father was to blame for her death, I hated him. I didn't hug him. I didn't trust him.

Kacey did. Kacey never wanted to believe what people said about him, including me. She took it much harder than I did when our father didn't come around. When he did make an appearance, she hung on him, followed him from room to room, never more than a foot from him, talking in her breathless, gulping, unstoppable way, demanding his attention. I was quieter. I watched.

The last time we saw him, he took us to the Philadelphia Zoo. It was supposed to be a treat for us; we'd never been. We knew for weeks ahead of time that he was taking us there. I told Kacey not to get her hopes up.

He did show up, but what I mainly remember about the day is that he wore a pager that kept going off, and that he looked nervous every time it did. We saw some giraffes and then we saw some gorillas and then he said we had to leave.

—But we just got here, Kacey said, furious. We haven't even seen the turtles.

Our father looked confused.

I knew why Kacey wanted to see the turtles: it was because our neighbor, Jimmy Donaghy, had made fun of her once for never having seen one. An arbitrary thing, casual cruelty, just an easy way to tease Kacey. I don't remember now how it came up between them, but there it was: Kacey wanted to see a turtle so she could tell Jimmy Donaghy she'd seen one.

—Aw, Kace, said our father. I don't even know if they have turtles here.

—They do, said Kacey, emphatically. They definitely do.

Our father glanced around. Well, I have no idea where they are, he said, and we have to leave.

His pager was buzzing and buzzing. He looked at it.

The drive home was silent. I let Kacey ride up front, for once. Our father dropped us at Gee's house and she opened the door for us, her mouth set, as if she'd been expecting this.

—That was fast, she said, smugly.

A week later a package arrived at the doorstep. In it were two stuffed animals: a turtle for Kacey, a gorilla for me. I was careless with mine, and lost it almost immediately. Kacey kept hers, carried it with her everywhere, even to school. She might still have it, for all I know.

We never again heard from him, after that. Gee made it seem as if she didn't, either. She told us with frequency that she should really take him to court for child support, but she didn't have the time or money for a thing like that. She was too busy trying to keep a roof over our heads, she said, to go after our good-for-nothing father for the pennies he could afford to pay her.

After he disappeared, we spent our teenage years avoiding discussion of him. We never wanted to get Gee started on him. We'd never hear the end of it. Once or twice, I heard rumors from neighbors or relatives regarding his whereabouts: Wilmington, Delaware, was the consensus. He'd gotten another girl pregnant there. Two more. He had six other kids, I heard once. He was in jail, I heard a lot.

He was dead, I heard later.

When I heard that one, I searched for him online. There it was: a death record for a Daniel Fitzpatrick from Philadelphia, born the same year as our father. But I did not know the day of his birth, and I didn't ask Gee, who probably wouldn't have known it herself.

Still, I assumed it was him.

I never told Kacey. I started to, many times, but I couldn't bear to break the news to her. I suppose I believed, on some level, that our father was one of the few glowing embers of goodness that existed in Kacey's life, a perennial secret hope, just out of sight. Something to live for, in other words. Someone to make proud. I didn't want to take that from her. I didn't want that small light to go out.

My GPS brings me to a small house: the right side of a brick duplex across from the Riverview Cemetery. It's a decent-looking structure, in good shape. Both halves are decorated for Christmas. The right half has electric candles in the windows and a plastic Christmas tree on the front porch. It's seven at night now, and it's been dark for hours.

I park on the street, fifty feet away, and turn off my car. As soon as I kill my headlights, the road becomes impossible to see. The only light comes from the windows of the houses, the Christmas decorations they bear.

I sit for a while. I turn back to look at the house in question. Face front. Turn back.

Could my father live inside that house? It's hard for me to reconcile my last memory of him with my ideas about the resident of 1025B River-view Drive.

After five minutes, I get out of my car and close the door, careful not to slam it. I walk over the ice patches that dot the road, slipping once. Then the darkness becomes overwhelming, and I feel the presence of the graveyard behind me, and I quicken my pace.

I walk up the four front steps of the house. I ring the bell and then take several steps back, waiting on the porch. I think of all the other times in my life, in my career, that I've knocked at houses whose residents weren't expecting me. Out of habit, I keep my hands by my sides, in sight of whomever opens the door.

There is a faint rustle at the window to my right: a curtain being pushed aside and then dropped back into place.

A moment later, a girl answers, a young teenager. She's skinny, with black curly hair and glasses. My immediate impression of her is that she is shy and studious, perhaps somewhat nervous around strangers. She looks me over.

She says nothing. Waits for me to speak.

Suddenly it feels absurd to assume that my father still lives at an address that was his so long ago. In my experience, it's Gee's generation that has stayed rooted in place, still living in the homes they grew up in. Our parents' generation is transient.

So it is with a certain amount of embarrassment that I begin.

—Hello there, I say to the girl. I'm sorry to disturb you. I was wondering if Daniel Fitzpatrick lived here.

The girl frowns slightly. She hesitates. Looks worried.

—It's all right, I say.

The girl is maybe thirteen or fourteen years old.

—It's nothing urgent, I say. I was just hoping to speak with him, briefly. If he lives here.

If he's alive, I think. I don't say it.

—Hang on one sec, says the girl. She retreats into the house, but leaves the front door open.

Is it possible, I wonder, that that was my father's daughter? My half sister? There's something about her mouth that reminds me, the slightest bit, of Kacey's mouth.

I lean forward a little, peering into the house, looking around. Everything looks tidy. There's a staircase in front of me and a living room to my right. The furniture is old but well cared for. A little dog, some kind of terrier, comes over and sniffs at my feet, ruffs once or twice. I give him a nudge with my foot, make sure he doesn't attempt to escape. A radio is on in another room. On it, pop songs about Christmas play quietly.

The girl is gone a long time, long enough so I wonder if I was supposed to have followed her. Cold air is still rushing into the house. I begin blowing into my hands to keep warm when I see someone descending the stairs right in front of me. Bare feet, and then legs, hidden by gray sweatpants.

It's a man, someplace around fifty, dark-haired.

It's my father.

—Michaela? he says. Is that you?

I nod.

—I'm so glad you found me, he says. I've been looking for you.

He glances behind him, slides his feet into shoes, and then palms some keys on a table beside the front door. He steps onto the porch and closes the door behind him.

—Let's go for a drive, he says.

I hesitate for a moment. He's been redeemed in my mind, in a way, by what I discovered at Gee's. And yet I still don't know his motives. And I still don't know where my sister is.

He registers my hesitation, perhaps.

He says, Or you can drive. Up to you. You have a car with you?

—I do, I say.

We get in.

—I thought you were dead, I say, before he has even fastened his seat belt.

At this, he laughs a little. I don't think I am, he says. He puts one finger to the back of the other hand. Nope, he says. Not dead yet.

I feel self-conscious around him for reasons I can't explain. Suddenly I wonder what I must look like to him after this many years of absence. I want him to think well of me, and just as quickly I'm angry with myself for caring.

I tell myself that I won't talk until he does.

Finally, he begins.

My father tells me that he's been looking for both of us, me and Kacey, for a long time.

He got sober, he says, in 2005.

At that point we were both adults, and he assumed, he said, that we hated him, because we never responded to any of his letters or cards.

For years, he let this be his excuse for not seeking us out.

—Then my daughter Jessie, he says, but he stops.

—That was my other daughter, he says. Jessie. She's twelve. This year she starts asking me about you guys, why I don't see you. Wanting to meet her half sisters, I guess. And I realize, maybe enough time has gone by so you all are ready to talk to me again. I know I messed up in a lot of ways, he says. I know that's on me. But I'm sober now, so I figure, it's worth a shot. I've always felt badly about the way things went down with you girls. But at this point I have no idea where I'd even find you, and I know your grandmother isn't gonna help me out. So I hire a guy I know, ex-cop, now does private work. Mostly gets hired by people looking to catch their husband or wife in the act, but, you know. Gets the job done.

—He found you both, he says. Pretty quick, too. He found Kacey where she was living in Kensington, and he found you in Bensalem. He comes back and reports to me on what he saw. Gives me both addresses. Tells me that now it's in my hands.

My father puts an elbow on his armrest. He's nervous, I can tell. He clears his throat several times in a row. Coughs, one hand politely over his mouth. Continues.

—I went to see Kacey first, he says, because my friend told me she was in a pretty bad way. That got me worried. This was three, four months ago. I went to find her at a place she was staying, some abando. She barely recognized me. I would never have known her.

—We had a long conversation, he says. Made plans for her to come stay with me. I just need one more day, she says. *Listen,* I say. *I'm an addict too. I know what that means.* I don't like it. Sure enough, the next day, I went to pick her up and couldn't find her.

—Meanwhile, he says, I go to visit you at the address my buddy gave me in Bensalem. This nice old lady answers the door, says you're not home, no other information. Asks me if I want to leave a message.

I glance at my father now, in the passenger's seat. I remember Mrs. Mahon's description of the visitor who came to see her twice in Bensalem. Yes: my father does, I suppose, look like Simon, at least very generally. He fits the same description, anyway. He is tall, as Simon is; he has dark hair. There, just below his left ear, is indeed a tattoo, just as Mrs. Mahon said. In the dark, I can't make it out.

He goes on.

—So I think I'm striking out, he says. I tried. With both of my daughters. I tell myself I'll try you again soon, but life got in the way, you know. Somehow, a month passes.

—Then, he says, out of the blue, Kacey shows up at my door. She won't tell me where she was or how she got there. She's got a broken wrist, he says, but she won't tell me how it happened.

—And, he says, she tells me she's pregnant. That she wants to keep the baby. That she wants to get clean.

———

I'm driving aimlessly, taking arbitrary rights and lefts, not sure where I'm headed. If you paid me, I wouldn't be able to find my way back to the house.

My father clears his throat.

—As you can imagine, he says, this was a lot to process. But I figured, This is my chance to make up for what I did wrong in the past. Besides, I've been through it, he says. I know what it's like to get sober. I know what it's like to try to stay clean. I still go to meetings two or three times a week, he says. I figure I can take her with me. Get her a sponsor and everything. Be there for her, I guess.

—I have a good job now, too, he says. Got my diploma from ITT Tech a while ago. I do IT now. I make pretty good money. I can help get health care for her and the baby.

In my peripheral vision, I see him glance at me, gauging my reaction. Does he want me to be proud of him? I'm not, yet.

—Anyway, he says. Kacey says she's already started to taper off. She says she's been using Suboxone when she can get it. I take her to the doctor, who says the recommendation is, if you're pregnant and using, you need to get on to methadone and stay on it. So the doctor helps get her into a methadone maintenance program. She's been going ever since.

—So she's with you, I say at last.

—She's with me, my father says. She's right back there in that house.

—She's alive, I say.

—She's alive.

I pause for a long time.

—Can I see her? I say, finally.

————

Now it's his turn to go silent.

—Thing is, he says, I'm not sure she wants to see you.

—She told me about her son, he says, and I flinch.

My son, I think. My son.

—As soon as she got to my house, she told me about that, and she told me she didn't want anything to do with you, he says.

—But it's funny, he says. The longer she's been sober, the more she's been talking about you.

—Doesn't sound sober to me, I say.

It's a bitter thing to say.

He nods. I see his face, silhouetted against the dim light outside the window of the car. Behind him, streetlights tick by.

—I hear you, he says mildly. A lot of people don't think being on methadone is the same thing as being sober.

He doesn't say anything else.

—But you do, I say at last.

He shrugs. I don't know, he says. I don't know what I think. I've been off methadone a while now. But I know I needed it at the start. Would never have stayed in recovery without it.

Neither of us speaks after that.

I keep driving. I'm on a larger road now, driving straight. Not turning. And suddenly, ahead of me, I see a glint of water, and realize I've found the Delaware again. The same dark river that has followed me since birth.

—Might want to turn right here, says my father. Or you'll end up underwater.

Instead, I pull over and stop the car. Its headlights shine out into the blackness. I turn them off.

————

—She's been talking about you more and more, says my father. She misses you. She needs her family.

—Hah, I say.

It's the noise, I realize, that I make whenever I'm uncomfortable. Making a joke out of something serious.

—After Kacey showed up, I went a second time to try to find you in Bensalem, he says. But that time, the same lady told me that you'd moved.

I nod.

—I thought I'd lost you again, says my father.

—I told her to say that, I say. I thought you were someone else.

I turn on the dome light, abruptly, and look at him.

—What's up? he says. He looks back at me, blinking in the sudden brightness.

I'm inspecting him, trying to make out the tattoo beneath his ear.

L.O.F., it says, in curlicued script.

It takes me a second to understand. They are our mother's initials.

He sees where I'm looking and puts a finger to it, presses on it tenderly, as if it were a bruise. Then he turns away.

—I bet you miss her, he says. I do too.

It's nine o'clock when I finally drop my father back at his house. We have made no plan. He has my phone number now, and I have his. That will suffice until Kacey and I both determine our feelings on a potential reunion with one another.

My father says he will talk to her. Try to convince her.

—You girls need each other, he says.

—You don't have to convince Kacey of anything, I say stiffly. If she doesn't want to see me, that's just fine.

—Okay, says my father. All right. I hear you.

But I can tell, from his voice, that he doesn't believe me.

After I drop him off, I wait for a while, watching as he runs up the steps. The shades on the house have been lifted, and I can see inside it. Each lit-up window contains within it the possibility that Kacey will pass by.

But she doesn't, and doesn't, and finally I drive away.

My phone, after a long day of being out of the house, has died completely, which adds to my sense of unease. I don't like being out of contact with Thomas.

No one is on the road. It's snowing lightly. A fat yellow moon sits in the sky. I try to picture Thomas and Mrs. Mahon, and I try to tell myself that they are tucked in and cozy, watching something to do with

Christmas on television. Maybe, I think, Thomas will still be awake when I get home. It will make me feel better, less guilty for leaving, if I can at least say good night to him.

When I park the car and walk up the back stairs, I see a low flickering light through the window next to the door. I turn my key as quietly as I can, in case Thomas is sleeping already. But the door stops an inch from its threshold. I push it again, more frantically. There's something blocking it.

Through the window at the top of the door, I see Mrs. Mahon's round concerned face. She looks past my shoulder for a moment, too, as if making certain I haven't been followed.

—Mickey? she says through the door. Is that you?

—What's going on? I say. It's me. Are you all right? Where's Thomas?

—Just hold on, she says. Hold on one second.

A scraping sound as she drags something away.

At last, the door swings open, and when I enter the apartment I scan the room quickly for my son.

—Where's Thomas? I say again.

—Asleep in his bedroom, says Mrs. Mahon. Then she says, Thank God you're home. They've been looking for you.

—Who has? I say.

—The police, says Mrs. Mahon. The police came here about an hour ago and rang your doorbell. Poor Thomas was terrified. I was terrified, Mickey. When they turned up in your doorway, I thought they were going to tell me you'd died. They said they'd been trying to call you but couldn't get through. They came to find you at home.

—My phone's dead, I say. Who was it? What officer?

Mrs. Mahon fishes in her pocket, takes out a card. Hands it to me. *Detective Davis Nguyen*, it says.

—There was another one too, she says. Another man. I can't recall his name.

—DiPaolo? I say.

—That's the one, says Mrs. Mahon.

—What did they want? I say.

I move to the corner of the room, where I keep a charger on an end table, and plug in my phone.

—They didn't tell me that, says Mrs. Mahon. Only said to have you call them when you got in.

—All right, I say. Thank you, Mrs. Mahon.

—I wonder, though, says Mrs. Mahon, if it has anything to do with the news.

—What news?

Mrs. Mahon inclines her head toward the television, and I follow her gaze. It's not a Christmas movie playing in the background: a correspondent is standing on Cumberland Street, near an empty lot that's been taped off. The same light snow that's falling on Bensalem is falling there.

Christmas Day Murder, says a caption below the reporter's pale face. She's bundled into a purple parka. Into her microphone, she's saying, Two weeks ago, the Philadelphia Police Department was assuring the public that they had a suspect in custody. Today, however, there is speculation that this homicide may be connected to the string of homicides that took place in Kensington earlier this month.

Mrs. Mahon is shaking her head, making small disapproving noises. Poor girl, she says.

—Who, I say. Have they named the victim?

—No, says Mrs. Mahon. Not yet. Only said it was a female.

—Anything else? I say.

—Said she was discovered around noon today. Seems like she'd only been dead a short time.

I'm still holding my phone in one hand. At last, it is sufficiently charged, and it comes to life at my command.

—Mrs. Mahon, I say. Would you mind staying here a moment while I make this call? I don't want to send you away if they're going to need to bring me to the station.

—That's what I was thinking, Mrs. Mahon says. I don't mind at all.

t's DiPaolo I phone, not Nguyen. I know DiPaolo better.

He answers right away, sounding alert. He's outside someplace: I can hear traffic in the background.

—It's Mickey Fitzpatrick, I say. I heard you stopped by my house.

—Glad you called, he says. Where are you right now?

—At home, I say.

—And where's your son? says DiPaolo.

I begin to answer, then change my mind. Why? I say.

—We just want to make certain you're both accounted for.

—He's fine, I say. He's sleeping.

But suddenly I feel the need to know this for myself. As I speak to DiPaolo, I walk swiftly to Thomas's room and open the door.

There he is.

He has bunched all the blankets into a nest at the center of his bed. He's hugging them tightly. His jaw is tense. Softly, I close the door again.

—Okay, says DiPaolo.

—What's going on? I say. Is Mulvey still in custody?

DiPaolo breathes for a bit.

—He was, he says. Until today.

—What happened? I say.

—He has an alibi, he says at last. He's got a sober friend says he was with Mulvey for two days straight around the time the Walker girl was killed, and Mulvey's claiming that the reason his DNA was on two of the girls who died was that he was a client of theirs. Nothing more. Both of them, Mulvey and his friend, they swear he didn't kill them. He law-yered up. We had to let him go.

—What time was he released? I say. Was he in custody at the time of today's homicide?

I don't know what I want the answer to be.

—He was, says DiPaolo.

In his voice, I hear there's something more he has to say.

—Listen, says DiPaolo, I'm sending a patrol car your way. Rookie from the 9th District. He'll be parked in your driveway tonight, okay? Don't be surprised when you see him there.

—Why? I say.

DiPaolo pauses. In the background, I hear a siren go by. He coughs once, twice.

—Why, Mike? I say.

—It's just a precaution, he says. Probably an overreaction. But the name you gave me when we met at Duke's—the woman you said made an accusation to you against someone in the PPD?

—Paula, I say. Paula Mulroney.

DiPaolo's silent. Waiting for me to connect the dots.

—She was the victim today, he says finally.

tell Mrs. Mahon to sleep in my bed for the night. I'll sleep on the couch, in the room closest to the front door, where anyone entering would encounter me first.

I want us all under the same roof.

All I tell Mrs. Mahon about the cruiser that inches quietly up our snowy driveway and parks there is that my colleagues are being extra cautious because of some information I was able to give them.

—It's nothing to worry about, I say, and Mrs. Mahon says, Do I look like I worry about much?

But I know she's only putting on a brave face, just as I am. And while Mrs. Mahon is using the bathroom, I sneak quietly down the hall and take down, from the lockbox, my weapon.

Now I can't sleep. I'm thinking about the cruiser in the driveway, wondering why, if DiPaolo is afraid that Paula was killed to silence her, it's a PPD officer who's been assigned to guard us. I would feel safer with a member of the state police, an outsider. It's true: DiPaolo took pains to tell me that he was assigning a rookie to the watch, someone from a different district—and therefore someone, presumably, without many ties to the 24th. Still, I lie awake on the sofa until four a.m., watching the second hand of the wall clock tick in the dim light from the outdoor lamp. Shadows segment it, cast by the slatted blinds. I'd climb into bed with Thomas if I weren't worried this would wake him up. I want to be close to him, to know I am protecting him, to know he's right next to me in the world.

Another feeling begins slowly to take over, joining forces with my worry: it's sadness, terrible sadness for Paula, whom I can still picture clearly as an eighteen-year-old with a sharp tongue and a quick laugh. Someone who always stood up for Kacey, just as Kacey always stood up for me. I suppose I always liked knowing Paula was out there, watching over my sister, watching over all the women of Kensington.

Last, and worst, comes guilt. If the person we're looking for is in the PPD; and if I am the one who first spoke Paula Mulroney's name—to Ahearn, and then to Chambers, and then to DiPaolo—then, yes. It is possible that I am the one responsible, indirectly, for her death.

I close my eyes. I put my hands to my head.

Off the record? I said to Ahearn.

Off the record, he said to me.

By the next morning, the PPD still hasn't released Paula's name to the news.

I spend a little while searching for information about her online. Quickly, I come across a Facebook page, set up by friends in her memory.

On it, I find information about a mass for her. It will be at Holy Redeemer this Thursday.

There's no viewing. The implications of this settle queasily onto me.

I intend to go.

All day, I wait for more information about the circumstances of her death. I want to watch the news, to see whether they've apprehended anybody, but I don't want to frighten Thomas. Instead, I listen to local radio, using my cell phone and an old pair of headphones that I find in a box in the closet. I wear them around the apartment, doing laundry, organizing, while Thomas builds his wooden train tracks into an elaborate maze.

—What are you listening to? he says several times.

—The news, I reply.

The cruiser in the driveway has departed, but a new one comes by our house every so often, driving slowly down the street. I can see it from my bedroom window. Sometimes, I find it comforting; others, I find it threatening, foreboding, predatory. I try to keep Thomas away, but he's quite observant, and he knows something is afoot.

The station I'm listening to is the local public radio affiliate that Lauren Spright works for. At the end of a one-hour show, I hear the host say her name.

I remember, suddenly, our encounter in Bomber Coffee, and her offer to host a get-together for Lila and Thomas. It occurs to me, in fact, that I might ask Lauren whether she could do this during Thursday's funeral for Paula. Spring Garden Day School is closed for the week between Christmas and the New Year, which means that Lauren, too, might be at home.

I retreat again into the bedroom, call her, and leave a message, telling her I have a funeral to go to and asking if it might work for Thomas to come over at that time. A minute later, she calls me back.

—Sorry, she says. I didn't recognize your number. That sounds great. I've been looking for stuff for Lila to do. This break is never-ending.

Lauren laughs briefly, and then stops. I'm sorry about your friend, she says.

—Thank you, I say. She wasn't, I say, she wasn't a close friend. She was a friend of my sister's more than mine.

—Still, says Lauren. A friend of the family. No one likes for anyone to die young.

—No, I say. That's true.

Paula's funeral is underattended, despite the fact that the PPD has finally released her name. I walk in ten minutes before the mass is due to begin, and seat myself in a pew toward the back, genuflecting out of habit before sitting.

I have two reasons for being here: The first is to pay my respects. I am not certain whether or not I believe in an afterlife, but I do believe in trying to do what is right during one's own life, and if I don't know with certainty, yet, that my mention of Paula's name to the PPD led directly to her death, what I do know is that it was, at least, a betrayal of her trust. I am here, therefore, to make my amends.

The second reason: I feel it is possible that I might overhear something useful while I'm here, may hear speculation about the cause of her demise.

This morning, I dressed myself in black pants and a black shirt and realized, suddenly, that I looked like Gee in her catering uniform. So I put on a gray shirt instead, and kept my hair and face as plain and inconspicuous as possible.

Now, from my pew in the back, I can see that the first few rows on either side of the church are full, but the rest of the room is empty. I recognize most of the people in the church, either from working in the 24th or from high school. All of the attendants seem to me to be in varying degrees of sobriety today. A handful of men sit together, one of them coughing outrageously, another nodding out. A dozen women, some of whom I know I've brought in.

The parish, Holy Redeemer, is the one we went to as kids, and the one affiliated with the first grade school we attended. It's a big stone church, cool in the summer even with no air-conditioning, cold in the winter, as it is today. I have many memories from this church: I made my First Holy Communion here, and then Kacey did two years later, wearing the same dress. I can still see her, dressed as a tiny bride, trying to remember to walk slowly.

It is not out of the question, I know, that Kacey herself might be here. Surely she has heard by now of Paula's death, and I thought perhaps she might make the decision to come. But I don't see her anyplace. Not yet. Every so often, I turn back to check the door.

The service begins. The priest—Father Steven, who has been here so long that he also led our mother's service—speaks quickly, intoning the rites. I imagine, morbidly, that funeral masses in this neighborhood have increased in number in the past two decades. Father Steven seems quite accustomed to his role.

From here, I can see the profile of Paula's mother, in the front row on the side opposite mine. She's wearing jeans and sneakers. She doesn't take her puffy jacket off, but keeps it wrapped around herself, another layer of protection. She has her arms crossed about her middle in an odd way, so that the palms of her hands are facing the ceiling. She is gazing down into them, as if cradling the memory of her daughter, recalling the weight and the warmth of the baby Paula. Wondering what went wrong.

Fran Mulroney, Paula's older brother, delivers a eulogy that's mostly about his own anger with the perpetrator. *Whoever did this,* he says, over and over again, wagging his head back and forth with as much menace as he can muster in a church. Father Steven clears his throat. Toward the end, Fran hints at his anger with Paula, for being in the situation she was in. He remembers her sense of humor, how sweet she was as a child. I just don't know what happened, he says, several times.

—I wish she made better decisions, says the person who introduced everyone around him to the pills that would eventually undo them all.

———

The service ends. A receiving line is forming at the back. Fran Mulroney and his mother and someone else, a grandfather, maybe, are standing at the front of it, near the main doors.

Kacey never came.

I slink down a side aisle, and then I position myself in line behind a group of women I recognize from working the 24th. They are friends of Paula's, and were friends of my sister's, too.

I look down at my phone, trying to be casual, in case they turn and see me. Most of them, I imagine, would recognize me, despite my lack of a uniform today.

They're speaking in near whispers, but I can hear snippets of what they're saying, one word every so often that gives me an indication of their views.

—That fucker, says one, and another repeats, That fucker.

At first I think they are talking about Fran Mulroney. They're looking in his direction, at least. But then the conversation shifts, slightly. At one point I hear, distinctly, the word *cop*. At another I hear *wrong guy*. *Bail,* I hear. My view is mainly of the back of their heads, but every so often one of them turns to another and inclines her head to whisper something, and I catch a glimpse of her face and her expression, in quarter-turn.

Suddenly, one of them—she is standing at the front of the pack, turning back to listen to something her friend is saying—spots me and freezes.

—Yo, she says to her friend. Yo. Shut up.

All four of them, seeing where she is looking, turn in my direction. I keep my eyes on my phone, pretending not to notice. But I see, peripherally, that no one is turning back around.

The woman closest to me is short and strong looking. She's wearing purple jeans. She points her finger right at me, almost touching my chest, so that I am forced to look up.

—You've got some fuckin' nerve, she says. Showing up here.

Her hair is slicked back into a low ponytail. She wears earrings that come almost to her collar.

—I'm sorry? I say.

—You should be, says another woman.

All four of them are moving toward me now, menacingly, hands in pockets, chins thrust forward.

—Get the fuck out of here, says the woman in purple jeans.

—I don't understand, I say.

She snorts.

—What are you, she says. Stupid?

It's a word I've never liked. I frown.

The woman is snapping her fingers in my face now. Hello? she's saying. Hello? Go home. Leave.

A sudden movement, behind my aggressors, catches my eye. Someone is entering the church, moving in the opposite direction as the departing crowd.

I don't recognize her at first.

Her hair is light brown, as close to her natural color as I've seen it since she was a child. Her complexion is pale. She's wearing glasses. I've never seen her wear glasses before.

Kacey. My sister.

Despite looking healthy, she also looks frazzled, running late, her belly protruding through an unzipped jacket. Under her coat, she wears a white shirt and gray sweatpants. Perhaps the only pants that fit her at the moment, I think. She is weaving, now, past the receiving line.

The woman in purple jeans glances back at her friends and then, wordlessly, two of them come toward me and take me by both elbows.

—Don't say a fuckin' word, one of them mutters into my ear. Be respectful. You're at a funeral.

But instinctively, my police training kicks in, and I spin hard enough to knock one of them over onto her hands and knees. The other lets go.

—Oh, no, says the one who's still standing. She did not just do that.

I hold up my hands. Listen, I say. I think there's a misunderstanding here.

Suddenly, Kacey is at my side.

—Hey, she says, looking at the four women, not me. Hey. What's going on?

—This bitch just put her hands on me, says the woman who was knocked to the floor—forgetting, I suppose, who actually laid hands on whom first.

Kacey won't look at me.

—She's sorry, says Kacey, about me. Mickey, tell them you're sorry.

—I don't, I begin, and Kacey elbows me, hard. Say it, Mickey. Say you're sorry.

—I'm sorry, I say.

The woman in purple jeans is looking not in my eyes but at my forehead, as if a target were painted there.

She turns to Kacey. She shakes her head. No disrespect to you, Kacey, she says. No disrespect, I know she's your sister. But you should watch your back. You don't know everything about her.

Kacey is quiet for a second, looking back and forth between me and this woman, and then—as if a decision has snapped into place in her brain—she flips the woman off and puts her hand roughly on my shoulder, steering me out of the church, past Fran and his mother, who are watching us, confused. I think suddenly of Kacey as a child, rising over and over again to my defense, just waiting for someone to cross me.

A chorus of jeers follows us out of the church, down the steps, to the street.

From inside, the woman calls out to Kacey one more time. *Watch your back.*

My sister says nothing to me for a while. I walk toward my car, parked just around a corner, and she walks next to me, her breathing heavy.

I don't know what to say to her either.

—Kacey, I say at last. Thank you.

—No, she says, too quickly. Don't do that.

We're at the car already and I pause, embarrassed, uncertain how to proceed.

She looks me directly in the eye for the first time.

—Dad says you came looking for me, she says.

—I wasn't, I begin. I am about to deny it. *I wasn't looking for you.*

Instead I say, I was worried.

She folds her arms over her middle defensively, above her belly. She doesn't respond.

—Mickey, she says finally. What were they talking about? Those girls?

—I have no idea, I say.

—Are you sure? she says. Is there anything you want to say?

I swallow. I think of Paula. Of my betrayal of Paula's response, when I asked her to make a report. *No fucking way,* she said. *Get on every cop's shit list in this godforsaken city.*

—No, I say. Kacey, I don't know what they're talking about.

She nods, assessing me. For a long time, we're quiet. On the street, a pack of kids goes streaking by on dirt bikes, popping wheelies, and Kacey doesn't speak again until the noise of them is gone.

—I trust you, she says.

Kacey declines a ride.

—I took Dad's car, she says. He's expecting me home.

So I walk her to his car, and then I say goodbye, on the side of the road, feeling so racked with guilt that my stomach hurts.

It's time to pick up Thomas at Lauren Spright's house in Northern Liberties. She invites me in. The house itself is big and modern, across from a park that bad kids used to frequent when I was small. Back when this neighborhood was still ours.

The kitchen, which looks like it was built for a show on the Food Network, is on the ground floor, in a big open room with a sliding glass door that leads out to a patio. There's a Christmas tree out there, a real one, covered in white lights. I've never seen this before: a Christmas tree on someone's back patio. I like it.

—The kids are upstairs, says Lauren. What can I get you to drink? Do you want some coffee?

—Sure, I say. I'm still shaken from what happened at Paula's mass. Holding something small and warm in my hands would be nice.

—How was the funeral? says Lauren.

I pause.

—Strange, actually, I say.

—How come?

Lauren is pouring hot water directly onto ground coffee in a tall glass cylinder. She puts a lid on it that has a kind of stem at the top, and lets it sit there. I've never seen coffee made this way before. I don't ask questions.

—It's a long story, I say.

—I've got time, says Lauren.

From upstairs, the sound of a crash, and then a pause, and then smothered giggles.

—Maybe, says Lauren.

I consider her. It is tempting, actually, to unburden everything I know to Lauren, who's a good listener, who seems to have an organized and happy life. Lauren Spright and her people seem to have everything figured out. There is a part of me that thinks, looking at her, *I could have had this*. I could have had a different career, a different house, a different life. When we first became involved, Simon and I used to talk about making a life together, after his son Gabriel was grown. I want to tell Lauren about all the plans I had. I want Lauren to know that I did well in school. I want to pour out the facts of my life into the open, friendly vessel of Lauren Spright, whose broad, pretty face is turned toward me welcomingly, whose very name sounds like something innocent and charmed.

I don't. I hear Gee's voice in my ear, telling me, *You can't trust them.* She never said who *they* were, but I'm certain that Lauren Spright qualifies. As wrong as Gee was about everything else, there is a large part of me, maybe all of me, that still agrees with her on this point.

That night, after I put Thomas to bed, my phone rings.

I look at it.

Dan Fitzpatrick cell, it says. When my father gave his number to me, I couldn't bring myself to save it under *Dad*. Nothing so chummy as that.

I answer.

He doesn't say anything at first, and then I hear soft breathing that I recognize as someone else's.

—Kacey? I say.

—Hi, she says.

—You okay?

—Listen, says Kacey, after another pause. I'm going to tell you something important. And it's up to you to decide whether or not to believe me.

—All right, I say.

—I know you haven't always believed me in the past, says Kacey.

I close my eyes.

—I asked around today, says Kacey. I called some friends. Tried to figure out what people are saying about you.

—All right, I say again.

Waiting.

—Are you with Truman Dawes? she says.

—What do you mean? I say.

Hearing his name like this, so suddenly, is jarring. I haven't heard from him since I clumsily tried to kiss him. Out of guilt and embarrassment, I've been trying to avoid thinking about him.

—I mean right now, says Kacey. Is he with you. In the same car. In the same room.

—No, I say. I'm at home.

Kacey goes quiet.

—Why? I say. Kacey?

—They think he's the one, says my sister. They think he killed Paula and all the rest of them. And they think you know about it.

E very part of me rebels.

No, I think.

This can't be true. It isn't possible. My fundamental understanding of Truman does not permit me to believe what I've just heard.

I open and close my mouth. I breathe.

On the other end of the phone, I hear Kacey breathing too. Waiting for me to respond. Measuring, in my long pause, my trust in her.

I think of the last time I doubted her: how I took Simon's word over hers; how profoundly incorrect I was. The ways in which that one word, *No*, affected the course of our lives.

And so instead I say to her, Thank you.

—Thank you? says Kacey.

—For telling me.

And then I hang up the phone.

A churning, uncomfortable dissonance roils inside me. My belief in my own instincts conflicts with my belief in Kacey's words. The only solution, it seems to me, lies in allowing Kacey's assertion to be a theory that must be proved—or disproved—with evidence.

I'm down the stairs, knocking at Mrs. Mahon's door, in a hurry.

When Mrs. Mahon opens it, I've already got my jacket on and my purse in my hand.

—I know, she says, before I can say anything. Go do what you need to do. I'll stay with Thomas upstairs. I'll fall asleep there if I need to.

—I'm so sorry, I say. I'm so sorry, Mrs. Mahon. I'll pay you.

—Mickey, she says. This is the most useful I've felt since Patrick died.

—All right, I say. Thank you. Thank you.

Then, cringing, I ask something else of her. I don't think I've ever asked so much of anyone in my life.

—How would you feel if we swapped cars? I say. Would you mind if I borrowed yours for a while?

By now, Mrs. Mahon is laughing. Whatever you need, Mickey, she says. She fetches her keys from off the hook in her entryway, and I hand Mrs. Mahon my own.

—It's got good pickup, says Mrs. Mahon. Just so you know.

—Thank you, I say again, and Mrs. Mahon waves a hand dismissively.

Then she follows me upstairs. She sits down on the sofa and takes a book out of her purse.

I go to the closet and reach toward the top shelf, toward the lockbox where I keep my weapon, a department-issued Glock with a five-inch handle. I've never had any desire for an alternate personal weapon before today. Today, I wish for something smaller, more compact, something I could easily carry undetected.

Instead, I'll have to put on my duty belt and fit the bulky weapon into it. I have a jacket big enough to conceal the whole thing, but it still feels cumbersome.

Back in the living room, Mrs. Mahon looks up from her book.

—Mrs. Mahon, I say, don't open the door for anyone.

—I never do, says Mrs. Mahon.

—Not even the police, I say.

Mrs. Mahon looks suddenly worried. What's going on? she says.

—I'm trying to figure that out, I say.

I pull out of our driveway so quickly that the tires on Mrs. Mahon's Kia squeal. It does, indeed, have good pickup. I have to remind myself that I'm not on duty, not in a cruiser. The last thing I need is to be pulled over. I slow to a more reasonable speed.

At this time of night, going slightly above the speed limit, it only takes me half an hour to get to Truman's house in Mount Airy.

I park on his street, half a block from his house, and quietly get out of the car.

It's eleven at night now. Most of the houses are dark. Truman's is still light inside, though, and from the street I can see his bookshelves and the many volumes they contain. I don't see Truman. I walk unseen to his porch.

Tiptoeing now, I ascend the stairs and look through a window. Both Truman and his mother are in the lit-up living room, Truman reading, his mother dozing in her armchair.

I look hard at him. He seems very interested in whatever he's reading: I can't get a look. He's prone on the couch, barefoot, and with one foot he scratches the other.

He says something to his mother that I can't make out. Maybe *Go to bed, Ma. Wake up, time for bed.*

Then his gaze shifts from his mother to the window. For a second, it seems like he's looking right at me. I drop to the ground. I huddle there, my back against the wall of the house. But the front door doesn't open, and finally my breathing slows down.

Eventually, I creep back down the steps, staying low. I head to Mrs. Mahon's car. Get inside.

From this vantage point, I watch the house.

Five minutes go by. Ten. Then, at last, Truman rises from the sofa. In the window, he is silhouetted by the lamp behind him. He walks across the room. There is still, I notice, a slight hitch in his step.

That's when the first glimmer of doubt settles into my stomach. And a question occurs to me that, perhaps, I should have been asking all along. Was the attack that sent Truman out on disability random, as he led everyone to believe?

Or was his assailant motivated by something else?

More questions occur to me, one after another.

Was he telling me the truth about visiting Dock? He went to find him twice, and each time reported back to me about his day. But I have no evidence, in fact, that either of these visits actually happened.

Was any of it true?

Abruptly, the lights in Truman's house go off.

It's then that a final thought occurs to me, sickly. One that I can't push aside. It was Truman who first suggested to me that Simon might be the culprit. Standing on the other side of his house, in the backyard, he asked me to make that leap with him. And then he left me hanging out to dry when Mike DiPaolo told me I was crazy.

It's getting cold now. I can see my breath. Every so often, I turn the car on, run the heat, and then shut it off again. I turn on the radio.

My goal: to stay awake until Truman Dawes leaves his house. And then to follow him, just as I followed Simon, at Truman's urging.

At 7:30, I wake up with a jolt. I'm freezing, so cold that I can't feel my fingers or toes. I rub my hands together quickly. I will my stiff joints to move. I turn the key in the ignition and let it run for a while, waiting for it to warm up.

Truman's car, I am glad to see, is still in his driveway.

Slowly, the blood returns to my hands and feet, throbbing as it does. The car is warm enough to blast the heat now, and I do.

I check my phone. No messages, no calls.

I know I'm going to be hungry soon, and I also have to use the bathroom. I look at Truman's house, calculating. There's a Wawa only five minutes from here. If I go, there's a chance I might lose him, but I might have a long day ahead of me, and I doubt I can hold it.

Impulsively, I pull out and head for the convenience store, still going just a little too fast.

When I get back to Truman's street a little before eight—bladder relieved, water and coffee and breakfast and lunch obtained—his car is backing out of his driveway. I pull over, nervous that he's going to drive right by me and see me in the car. But he drives in the opposite direction, and after a few beats, I pull out and follow him.

Mrs. Mahon's Kia is a very forgettable white sedan, nothing that will look familiar to Truman. I wish again that I had some undercover training. Without it, I do my best to drive on instinct: following him a couple of car lengths behind, praying that I hit the same lights he does. Once, I run a red to keep up with him. A nearby driver honks incredulously, flips me off. *Sorry,* I mouth.

Truman follows Germantown Avenue southeast for several miles. All roads, I think, lead to Kensington. I know where we're headed, and I'm not surprised, but a feeling of dread is growing inside me.

I don't want to know the truth.

He makes no stops. He drives slowly, ambling, not rushing. It takes all of my willpower to do the same, to refrain from passing him. Truman used to make fun of me for being a speed demon, for driving recklessly, when we were in the car together.

When he gets to Allegheny, he turns left. So do I. He follows Allegheny east, and then parks abruptly just before Kensington Ave.

I pass him and park slightly ahead. I watch him in my rearview, now, and then my side mirrors, not turning around.

He gets out of his car.

He's walking slowly, maybe because of his knee. He turns a corner onto Kensington.

Only when he's out of sight do I jump out of Mrs. Mahon's car and run in the direction of the Ave. I don't want to lose sight of him.

I'm relieved to see the back of Truman when I turn the same corner he did, but now I'm too close on his heels. My jacket has a hood, and I pull it up over my head and lean against a wall for a minute, trying to put some distance between the two of us while not looking suspicious. I'm probably failing.

I glance at Truman sideways as he slowly recedes. A hundred feet away from me, he turns left and opens the door of a shop. Before going in, he glances to his right and left, and then disappears out of sight. And at last I realize where we are, where Truman is going.

The window display in Mr. Wright's shop hasn't changed in the slightest since we first went in. The little sign that says *Supplies* is still tipped over on its side. The same plastic dolls gaze at me, dead-eyed; the same dusty plates and bowls and cutlery are arranged the same way on the same rack. The display is so crowded that I can't, in fact, see the inside of the store, and for this reason I'm now standing outside, at a loss for what to do.

If I follow him in, I might show my hand too early. He'll have the chance to invent some excuse about why he's in Kensington.

If I wait until he comes back out, I could risk missing important information, miss seeing some transaction that I should be aware of.

I make a deal with myself: I'll wait ten minutes. If he's not out again in ten minutes, I tell myself that I'll go in.

I position myself thirty feet away from the front door, then check my phone for the time. I put it back in my pocket. Start counting.

Less than half the time I allotted myself goes by before Truman emerges. Now, he's dragging something behind him.

It's a large black suitcase on wheels.

From the way he's maneuvering it, it looks like there's something heavy inside it.

He walks south along the Ave and I begin again to follow him. This time, he turns left on Cambria, and he walks another few hundred feet before turning down an alley I don't believe I've ever encountered before. There's no foot traffic on these small streets, and I fear that Truman's going to turn around at any moment and see me a hundred feet behind him. I try to walk as quietly as I can. I try to float, so that he doesn't hear my footsteps.

When I get to the alley Truman turned down, I don't see him. But I hear something: the banging of a door.

There are only six structures in front of me, and two of them are open shells with no roof. The other four look abandoned to me, but intact.

I get close to the side of one of them, ready to duck into an empty lot if anyone comes out. I listen for a while, trying to hear any other noises that might give Truman's location away. But all I hear is my own breathing, my own blood as it rushes in my ears. Beyond that, traffic from the Avenue. The El shuttling by on its tracks.

I advance. I peer into the boarded-up windows of each house, one after another. I see nothing through the windows of the first two on my left. When I peer between two boards blocking a window in the third house, I catch a glimpse of movement, some shadowy figure crossing the room. I cup my hands around my eyes, trying to darken the outside world so I can see what's happening better.

Everything inside is still.

Then I hear a voice. Truman's voice, very quiet.

I can't hear exactly what he's saying, but I can see that he's talking to someone on the ground. Truman bends down, and then I can't see him anymore, or what he's doing.

I think of Kacey. Of all that she endured for a decade on these streets. I think of Paula. Before I change my mind, I draw my weapon and pull open the unlocked door of the house.

edge in through the doorframe sideways, trying to make myself a small target, as I have been taught.

My eyes, as usual, are slow to adjust inside the dark house. A figure—Truman—raises his head abruptly.

—Don't move, I say, aiming my weapon at his chest. Don't move. Put your hands up.

He complies. In silhouette, he raises his arms.

I look around wildly. There's a second person in the room. In the dark, I can't make out any identifying characteristics. She's lying on the floor, in between Truman's legs.

Truman's suitcase is closed and lying on the floor beside him.

I keep my weapon pointed at him.

—Who's on the ground? I say.

—Mickey, says Truman.

—Who is it? Is she hurt? I say.

—Tell me, I say.

But I can hear my voice getting weaker, losing its authority.

Truman speaks, at last. What the hell are you doing here, he says quietly.

—I'm just, I say, but I hesitate, and then find that I can't finish.

—Put your weapon away, Mickey, says Truman.

With the Glock, I gesture to the suitcase. What's in there? I say.

—I'll show you, says Truman. I'll open it and show you.

The woman at his feet hasn't moved an inch.

Truman crouches next to the suitcase. He says, I'm just going to take out my phone, all right?

Slowly, he reaches into his breast pocket and removes it. He shines the phone's flashlight toward the suitcase, and unzips it. He flips open the lid.

I can't, at first, see what's inside. I take two steps forward, peering into it. What I see are sweatshirts, gloves, hats, woolen socks. Hand warmers and foot warmers, the chemical kind that last for eight or ten hours. Energy bars. Chocolate bars. Bottles of water. And, zipped into the netting on the underside of the suitcase's lid: a dozen or so doses of Narcan nasal spray.

—I don't understand, I say.

In my peripheral vision, the figure on the ground moves slightly. I swing back, aim my weapon in her direction briefly before turning it once more on Truman.

—He's still conscious, says Truman. But we shouldn't wait much longer.

—What do you mean, I say, *he?*

Truman shines his phone toward the figure. And suddenly I see my mistake.

—Who is that? I say.

—Name's Carter, I think, says Truman. That's the name he gave me, anyway.

Slowly, with a dawning sense of shame, I walk toward the person on the floor. It's not a woman at all. It's a boy, a young boy, sixteen or so, the same age Kacey was the first time I ever saw her in this state. He's skinny, African-American, dressed vaguely like a punk, eyeliner on his eyes, trying hard to look older than he is. The childish slightness of his frame betrays him.

He's gone completely still again.

—Oh no, I say.

Truman says nothing.

—Oh no, I say again.

—Do you want to dose him, or should I? says Truman flatly, gesturing down toward the Narcan in his suitcase.

Later, on the street, we wait together for the ambulance to arrive.

The victim, Carter, is revived, sitting on the ground, crying, dismayed. I don't need an ambulance, he's wailing, ineffectively. I gotta go. His sleeves come down over his fingers; he holds them there. I try to place a hand on his shoulder and he shrugs it off.

—Sit still, says Truman sharply, and the boy listens, finally resigned.

Truman is off to the side, not looking at me.

Several times, I try to speak, to consider how best to apologize. For today. For what happened at Duke's. In general. But no words come to mind.

—What are you doing here? I say, finally.

Truman looks at me for a long time before responding. As if deciding whether I deserve an explanation.

At last, he speaks. For a while, he says, he's been volunteering with Mr. Wright. Every day he can get to Kensington, he stops into Mr. Wright's store and picks up a suitcase that Mr. Wright has filled with supplies, and then he roams around the neighborhood, doing what he can to help. Giving people food and supplies. Administering Narcan when necessary. It's something Mr. Wright's been doing, he says, for a decade, ever since his sons died. But now Mr. Wright is getting older, less mobile, and someone has to fill his shoes.

—That's really nice of you, I say, uselessly. Weakly. But my heart is sinking. Apologize, I think. Apologize, Mickey.

But a new thought is occurring to me, distracting me.

—The attack, I say with something like sadness. The man who attacked you.

—What about it?

—It wasn't random, I say. Was it.

He looks down the block.

—People don't like me poking around here, he says.

—You knew him?

—I'd pulled him off his girlfriend a day or two before. Found him beating the shit out of her. Pulled him off.

—Why didn't you say anything to me? I ask.

He looks at me impatiently. How was I supposed to explain what I was doing in some abando off duty? he says. To you or anyone?

I have no good answer.

I look away.

—Well? says Truman finally.

—Well what?

—Your turn, he says. His mouth is a line. There is no warmth in his voice.

—I was following you, I say.

I feel helpless and resigned. I have no capacity at the moment to tell him anything but the truth. My eyes are focused on the cracks in the pavement, on the little weeds and pebbles that have made their way into each crevice.

—Why, says Truman quietly.

I exhale. I say, They said you were the one.

—Who?

—Kacey's friends.

Truman nods.

—And you believed them, he says.

—I didn't, I say.

Truman laughs, but his voice is hard. Ah, he says. And yet here we are.

I say nothing. I look down at the ground a while longer.

—It was an unhappy coincidence, I begin, but Truman interrupts me.

—Why do you talk like that, says Truman. Mickey. Why do you talk like that?

An interesting question, actually. I think for a bit. Ms. Powell used to tell us that people would judge us based on our grammar. *It's not fair,* she said, *but it's true. Your grammar and your accent. Ask yourself, how do you want to be perceived by the world?* said Ms. Powell.

—I had a teacher, I begin, and Truman says, Ms. Powell. Ms. Powell. I know.

—Mickey, he says, you're thirty-three years old.

—And? I say.

He doesn't reply.

—And? I say again, raising my head. Only then do I see that Truman isn't beside me anymore. I look to my right and see only the back of him, a lifted heel as he disappears around a corner at the end of the block.

realize, suddenly, how long it's been since I've checked my phone. When I do, I see I have three missed calls.

All of them are from my own landline.

I have one voicemail, as well.

I don't listen to it. I call the house.

—It's Mickey, I say. Are you all right, Mrs. Mahon? Is Thomas?

—Oh, now, everything's fine, says Mrs. Mahon. It's only Thomas seems to have come down with something.

—What does he have? I say.

—Well, says Mrs. Mahon, unfortunately, there's been some throwing up.

—Oh no, I say. Mrs. Mahon, I'm so sorry.

—Don't worry, says Mrs. Mahon. I got to put my nursing degree to use. He seems a bit better already, though. He's eating crackers now. You might want to pick up something hydrating on your way home.

—I'll be home in forty-five minutes, I say.

On the drive, I call my father.

—I need to talk to Kacey, I say.

A second later, my sister is on the line.

—Hang on, says Kacey.

In the background, I can hear her footsteps as she walks someplace. Seeking privacy, probably.

A door closes.

—Go ahead, says Kacey.

Quickly, I give her a summary of my day.

—I really don't think it could be Truman, I say, at the end. No matter what your friends said.

Kacey pauses, considering this.

—Why would they lie? she says. Why would they lie about something like this? That doesn't make sense. Everyone in the whole neighborhood has the same idea.

A thought is beginning to occur to me. That old sensation: holding a puzzle piece I know will fit precisely.

—Kacey, I say. Kacey. What were their exact words.

—God, Mick, I don't know, says Kacey.

—Please try to remember, I say. Do you remember anything?

Kacey exhales.

—Something like, she says. Something like, *Everyone in Kensington knows about your sister's partner. You think your sister doesn't know it too?*

I fall silent.

—What, says Kacey.

—Truman hasn't been my partner since last spring, I say.

—He hasn't? says Kacey. Who has?

The huge quantity of information that I know about Eddie Lafferty now seems to me, very improbably, like a blessing.

We were only partnered for a month, and I mainly spent that month listening to him as he talked about himself, at length, in the passenger's seat.

But recently, I've heard nothing at all about him.

After I asked Ahearn not to partner us anymore, I generally avoided him. And since my suspension, I've been even more out of the loop.

The person I want most in the world to talk to about this is Truman. Right now, unfortunately, I don't think he's an option.

Instead, I give Kacey Lafferty's name, and she goes quiet for a long time.

—That sounds familiar, she says. I feel like I've heard that name before.

—Give me a second, she says, just give me a second.

But when I reply, I find she's already hung up on me.

At home, Thomas is lying on the sofa, a glass of water on the table before him. He's watching a show he likes on TV. He looks pale, but otherwise all right.

—I puked, he announces.

—I heard, I say.

I put a hand to his forehead, testing for fever. It's cool.

—How many times? I say.

He holds up one hand, dramatically, all five fingers extended. Then he raises the other hand into the air too. Ten.

Subtly, across the room, Mrs. Mahon shakes her head.

—He feels better now, she says. Don't you, Thomas?

—No, says Thomas.

He is looking at me, worried.

—I still feel sick, he says.

Mrs. Mahon opens her mouth. Closes it. Then nods, with her head, toward the back of the apartment.

I follow her.

In my bedroom, Mrs. Mahon gently closes the door.

—I hate to butt in, she says. But I'm not sure how else to say it. I think Thomas might be worried about you.

—What do you mean? I say.

Mrs. Mahon hesitates. I think he's fine, she says. He did throw up, once, in the early morning. But since then, I think he's been faking. He runs into the bathroom, runs the water, makes some noise, and flushes. Then comes out, says he's been sick. I caught on after a couple of episodes. I think, says Mrs. Mahon, that he might just need some attention.

—I've been home with him all week, I say. All week, until yesterday.

—Children are very perceptive, says Mrs. Mahon. He can tell that something's not right with you, I think. Maybe he thinks you're in danger.

—Hah, I say.

—He'll be fine, says Mrs. Mahon. He's a good boy. Very polite.

—Thank you, I say.

Mrs. Mahon smiles.

—Well, she says. I'll get going. Leave you two to catch up.

—Thank you, I say again.

I do as instructed. I spend the day with Thomas, curled up on the couch. He sinks into me gratefully. I keep waiting for Kacey to call me back. She never does.

When, at bedtime, he falls asleep on me, I keep holding him. Like I'm applying pressure to a wound. Keeping the blood inside him. His small body softens and relaxes. I don't let go. I should do research on Lafferty. I should call somebody. I should do my job, I think. Instead, I hold my son, and gaze at the miracle of his face, which is a small version of Kacey's, a constellation of tissues, perfectly arranged.

—Don't go anyplace, he says suddenly, startling himself awake.

—I won't, I say. I promise.

At nine o'clock in the evening, I hear the distinct sound of a car in the driveway. I don't believe Mrs. Mahon has left her house since she went downstairs, and I am certainly not expecting anybody.

Gently, trying not to wake Thomas, I wriggle out from under him and stand.

I turn off all the lights in my apartment. I leave on only the outdoor light: all the better for viewing whoever might approach. I slide the chain lock into place.

Then I regard Thomas, out cold on the sofa. I don't like having him so close to the front door. Abruptly, I scoop him up, bring him into his bedroom, and tuck him into his bed.

I want him out of sight.

Back in my darkened living room, I stand, frozen, listening. In a moment, I hear footsteps walking slowly up my wooden stairs. Outside my door, the visitor pauses. Doesn't knock.

I wish I still had my weapon on me. I consider going back to the linen closet to remove it from the lockbox.

I crawl instead on my hands and knees to the front door, then kneel next to it. I raise my head to the window and move the bottom of the sheer curtain a fraction of an inch.

It's Kacey.

I stand up and unlock the door. I crack it open. Cold air from outside hits my face.

—*What are you doing here,* I whisper.

—I have to show you something, she says. It can't wait.

I step aside awkwardly, turn on the lights, and let her into the apartment. She looks around appraisingly.

—This is nice, she says, kindly.

—Yes, well, I say.

I pause. She pauses.

—How did you find this place? I say.

—Dad gave me the address.

I look at her. You told him what's happening? I say.

She nods seriously. I tell him everything, she says. It's the only way to stay sober that I know of. Total honesty. Otherwise I start lying about little things and then.

She trails off. Turns her hand into an airplane and mimes a nosedive.

—Can I call him, actually? she says. I promised I would call him when I got here.

Once she's finished, she turns to me and says, Do you have a laptop?

In my bedroom, we sit side by side on the bed. Kacey is holding the computer.

She navigates it expertly. She opens Facebook and enters, as a search term, *Edward Lafferty.*

Together, we look at the screen. Of the seven Edward Laffertys who appear in the results, one of them seems to be him. There he is, wearing sunglasses, his bald head uncovered. He's grinning and he has an arm wrapped around a dog that looks like a pit mix, which I can recall him talking about.

Before I can point him out, Kacey touches a finger to his face, on the screen.

—That's him, she says.

It's not a question.

I nod. That's him.

—He's Connor's friend, she says. I've met him before, she says.

Connor. It takes me a second to process.

—Dock? I say, without thinking, and Kacey says, How do you know that name?

—I know that, I say, because I was looking for you, and I came across him. Unfortunately.

Kacey nods.

—Yeah, she says. Yeah, he's tough.

—*Tough?* I say. That's one way to say it.

Kacey twitches suddenly, straightens up on the bed, puts both hands on her belly. Oh, she says softly.

—What's wrong, I say.

—She's kicking, says Kacey.

—She, I say.

Kacey shrugs. She looks as if she wishes she hadn't said anything. Again, she hugs her stomach. Protecting it.

—Maybe I better start from the beginning, she says.

Last summer, says Kacey, I started seeing this guy. Connor. That was his name. People call him Dock but I never did. He was nice to me. First boyfriend I'd had in a long time. Came from a good family. I never met them but he told me stories about them. Told me he missed them. We were gonna get clean together, he told me, and I wanted that too.

Of course it never happened. We'd get clean together and then one of us would cave, me or him, and we'd bring the other one down with us.

—You don't want to be alone, is the thing, she says. Whether you're clean or you're sober, whichever one you are, you want the person you love to be there with you too. So we couldn't stay straight.

—In September, says Kacey, I realized I hadn't had my period in a while. Now, I don't know how long, because I wasn't keeping track of stuff like that. I tried to use condoms until I got together with Connor, and then we just slipped up, you know. It happens. So all of a sudden I notice it's been a while, and I go to the free clinic, and I get a pregnancy test. They do an ultrasound right there. And there's a shape in me, I could see it on the screen. The second time in my life that I'd seen something like that. *That's your baby,* they said.

———

Kacey is starting to cry. She wipes her nose on her sleeve. Tucks her hair behind her ears with both hands, just as she did when she was a child. I have the sudden urge to comfort her. I don't.

—They told me I was eleven weeks along, says Kacey. That was in September. They asked me if I'd been drinking or using any substances. I was honest with them. I told them yes, I'd been using heroin, I'd been using pills. I'd been drinking. Yes to all of it.

So the nurse, really nice nurse, says to me that she's going to refer me to a methadone clinic, that the recommended course of action was to get on methadone, because if I quit cold turkey that could have a really bad effect on the baby. You know. I'd heard that before. I have other friends on the Ave who've gotten pregnant while they were still using, so this wasn't news to me. But I still felt, I felt awful, Mick, because I just, if I ever got pregnant again I wanted to do it the right way. It's something Connor and I used to talk about sometimes, having a baby after we got clean. It was a nice thing to think about. But I never wanted another baby taken away, says Kacey, looking at me.

I knew it would kill me, she says.

—I told Connor the news, says Kacey. He was happy, really happy. I started going to the clinic and he came with me. The two of us were really motivated for the first time.

For two weeks, I went to the clinic every day. So did Connor. We found a decent place to stay, it was abandoned but it was clean, and it was still warm enough out so it wasn't a problem to sleep there at night. We knew we had to find something better when it got cold, but for the time being we were happy.

One day I went to the clinic at our regular time, and Connor was supposed to meet me, but he wasn't there. So I get my dose, and I go back to where we were living, and I find him high.

That's when I knew I had to make a change. I prayed, she says. I'm not religious but that night I prayed to God for help.

—The next day, she says, Dad showed up at the door. Like a sign, she says. Or an answer. Crazy, right? Connor was out. Dad offered to take me to Wilmington right then and there, no questions asked, but I couldn't do that to Connor. He was the best guy I'd ever known. I know you think I'm crazy, but at the time, I thought that it was true.

I told Dad I needed a day. Just a day. I told him to come back to get me tomorrow, and I'd be ready. I could tell he didn't believe me.

—Connor got back from wherever he was, says Kacey. I waited until he was awake enough to talk to me, and I told him I was leaving for a while, that I needed to leave him so I could get better, stay clean for the baby. I didn't tell him where I was going. He didn't take it well. We got into a terrible fight. He hit me, strangled me, said he was going to kill me. He pushed me down so hard I broke my wrist.

I walked out. I slept in a park that night, and the night after. I didn't meet Dad.

I missed two doses. I was too embarrassed to show up at the clinic looking beat-up. They ask you questions, make you talk to a social worker.

I started getting shaky. Feeling bad. I know I'm withdrawing. So I figure, if I can just find subs on the street, I can treat myself for a while and taper off.

She pauses for a long time. She is looking at the ground. She's quiet for so long that I wonder if she's sleeping. Then she begins again.

———

—I went right back to it, says Kacey. Right back in, like I never stopped. I was sleeping outside the whole time, sleeping on the street, going on a bender. I was picking up clients on the Ave.

After a few days, says Kacey, I'd had enough. I came to my senses.

Again, she goes quiet.

—What did you do, I say. Where did you go?

—I've never stopped being in touch with Ashley, says Kacey. I think you know that. She's always asking after me, always checking in. Sometimes she even gives me money, Kacey says.

So I found her. I showed up at her house, and she took me in.

I shake my head. Incredulous.

—Ashley knew? I say. She saw you? She knew you were alive? She didn't tell me?

But Kacey is frowning.

—It's my fault, she says. I made her swear. I told her the one person she could never tell was you.

—So she lied to me too, I say.

—She saved me, Mickey, says Kacey. She fed me and gave me a shower. She gave me a bed in her house. She or Ron drove me down to the methadone clinic twice a day. They watched out for me. She talked to me about the pregnancy all the time, got me excited about meeting the baby.

You know she's religious now, goes to church, her and Ron. They're raising their kids in the church. And she was so supportive of me, brought me to church with them on Sundays. They even gave me work there, like cleaning the basement and the bathrooms. They paid me in food that I brought home to Ashley. Everyone was nice there. I felt really at home. Everyone there knew about the baby, too, and they were always telling me they were proud of me, that I was doing the right thing. I felt like they respected me. When I was there, in the church, it was nice. I felt almost like a hero to them.

But I was scared, Mick. Every night that I went to sleep I thought about the baby, and what I had done to the baby already. I was scared I had hurt it. I was ashamed. I hated myself. Every dose of methadone I took, I hated myself more. I know what it feels like to withdraw. I've had fifteen years of knowing that, and I'm grown.

She takes a quick breath.

—I thought of Thomas, she said. I couldn't stop thinking of Thomas.

It's the first time, in my memory, that she has ever used the name I gave him.

Kacey is crying hard now, her voice cracking and high. I stay where I am, watching my sister.

Finally, Kacey calms down a little. Continues.

—Aunt Lynn's birthday party was at the beginning of November, says Kacey.

—Don't tell me you were there, I say.

Kacey looks confused. She furrows her brow. Why? she says.

———

—I saw them two weeks after that, I say. At Thanksgiving. They all knew I was looking for you, I say. All the O'Briens knew it. Why did they lie to me?

Kacey inhales, deeply. She is measuring her words. Deciding whether or not to say something. I can still read her face.

—Look, she says, they don't trust you.

I laugh, once, harshly.

—Me? I say. It's *me* they don't trust? That's the most backward thing I've ever heard.

—You never come around, says Kacey. You're a cop. And, she says, but she stops. Pulls her punch.

—And what, I say.

—Say it, I say.

—And everyone knows you took Thomas.

I laugh.
    —Is that what they say?

———

—That's the truth, says Kacey. Whatever the circumstances. They know you took Thomas.

I think of the looks on their faces, that day at Ashley's. All the O'Briens. Shifting and formal and strange. Stiff when I approached them. All of them knew about Kacey. None of them let on. A slow humiliation spreads from the center of my chest outward, a sensation I recognize from childhood, so potent that it almost makes me cry. This is the feeling that being around the O'Briens has always given me. That I'm an outsider, a foundling, someone who doesn't belong.

I stand up, abruptly, and walk to the edge of the room. I face away from my sister.

—I'm their family too, I say at last.

I hear Kacey breathing. Considering what to say next. When she speaks, her voice is delicate.

—I don't think any of them knew you cared, she says.

I clear my throat. Enough of this, I think. Enough.

—Was Bobby there, I say.

—Where?

———

—At Lynn's party.

I turn to face her. She nods.

—Bobby was there, she says.

—And what did your face look like?

She winces. Perhaps I was too blunt.

—You mean, she says. You mean was I still beat-up-looking? Yeah. I was. I told him it was an ex. I didn't say who.

—That explains it, I say.

—What?

—I told Bobby you'd been dating someone named Dock. He must have put two and two together. Because apparently Bobby took matters into his own hands after that.

Kacey fights a smile. You're kidding, she says. Bobby did that for me?

———

I shrug. I don't approve of her reaction, of her satisfaction.

—I've always liked Bobby, says Kacey.

—I haven't, I say.

The whole time we've been talking, Kacey has been sitting up on the bed. Now she lies down awkwardly on her side. Head on pillows. She's tired.

—What happened at the party, I say finally. At Lynn's birthday party.

—Ashley asked me how I felt about inviting Gee, says Kacey. Lynn and Gee see each other, you know. I hadn't seen Gee in years but I said sure, why not. One of the steps is about making amends, and I have a lot of amends to make, and I figure I could start with Gee.

That night, at Lynn's party, Gee was great. I mean, she was ornery, she was herself, but she was pretty nice. She said I looked good. Asked what I was up to. I told her I was on methadone maintenance but that I'd been clean besides that. She said I was doing good. Told me to keep trying. *Just don't fuck it up,* she said, because Gee is Gee.

By the end of the night I had decided to tell her about the baby. She was going to find out sooner or later, I figured. Might as well break the news. I walked outside with her and stood there with her while she waited for the bus.

Gee, I said, *I have to tell you something.*

She turned on me with this look of absolute horror.

Oh no, she says. *Please tell me you're not gonna say what I think you're gonna say.*

I started to feel nervous. My hands were shaking, I was sweating.

What do you think I'm gonna say? I said.

Gee's got her eyes closed now. She's just saying, *No, no.*

I'm pregnant, I say.

And Gee actually starts to cry. Have you ever seen her cry in your life, Mickey? I've never seen her cry in my life. She puts her face in her hands. I don't know what to do. I put my hand on her back.

But as soon as I touch her she whirls around on me and brushes my hand off her. She lost it, Mickey. She screamed so loud. I thought she was going to hit me. She told me she was through with me. She goes, *Who's gonna be this baby's mama when you start up with that same old shit?* She told me she was done taking care of other people's babies. And that you were too. She told me you had enough trouble on your hands without taking in another little bastard of mine. She used that word. *Bastard.*

Kacey pauses for a second, waiting for me to react, before continuing.

—She said, *I'm not gonna watch you do to this baby what your mother did to you.*

—Did you hear me? Kacey says to me.

I nod.

—No, Kacey says. No. Do you understand?

—Understand what? I say.

———

—I knew you wouldn't notice it, Mick. But I've always wondered. *To you,* is what Gee said. Not *you and Mickey.* Not *you girls.* Not to us both. To me.

I said to Gee, *What do you mean, to me?* And she said that Mom had been getting high when she was pregnant with me.

But not Mickey? I said.

Mick, I swear to God she smiled.

Not Mickey, she told me, like she was satisfied to be telling me this. *Lisa started that shit after Mickey was born.*

I wait a moment, letting the information settle.

Then I say, Oh, Kacey. She could have been lying to you. She could have been trying to scare you. I wouldn't put it past her.

But the question lies there, between us, hovering.

Kacey shakes her head.

—I wanted to believe that, she says. That she was lying.

I thought about it while I was walking away from Gee. She was still shouting at me. She was saying, *I feel sorry for that baby. I feel sorry for that child.*

I thought about it all night. I couldn't sleep.

Ashley didn't know what had happened between me and Gee. She didn't know any of this. In the morning, I left a note for Ashley, saying I was safe. Then I snuck out before anyone was awake.

I took the bus to Fishtown. I walked to Gee's house. I figured she'd be at work. I was right. I knocked a few times, but she didn't answer.

I haven't had the keys to her house in years, but you know the alley door comes loose if you hit it hard enough, so I popped the lock and walked through the alley to the back of the house. I checked the back door and it was locked. I broke the glass and let myself in.

I know it was wrong of me. I don't care.

I went down into the basement. I just wanted to know if it was true, what she said. It had become important to me to know.

You know that filing cabinet Gee has in the basement? There was this folder in it, in the bottom drawer, called *Girls*.

I pulled it out. There was a big stack of documents in it. Your birth certificate was in it, Michaela Fitzpatrick, and a photo of you from the hospital, and your birth weight and length and all, and a few papers certifying that you were healthy. That was it.

Mine was different. My birth certificate was in there, just like yours. But my discharge papers were like an instructional manual. *Care for the substance-dependent newborn*. It said I might be more irritable than other newborns. That I might cry more. There was a prescription for phenobarbital. So I guess I've been using since I was born.

I know that paperwork, I want to say. I received a similar packet when I took custody of Thomas.

I stay quiet.

Kacey goes on.

—I kept looking through the filing cabinet. And I found other stuff, too. I found this whole folder marked *Dan Fitzpatrick*, says Kacey.

I nod.

—You know this part, says Kacey.

I nod again.

————

—You found them. The cards and the checks.

—I did, I say.

—That's good, says Kacey.

She pauses, thinking.

—I guess I left them there on purpose, she says. I guess I thought you might find them there, if you were ever looking for me.

—I needed to leave, says Kacey. I needed to get out of that house. I took all the paperwork from the hospital where I was born, and I took one of the cards from Dad. A birthday card he sent to me when I turned sixteen.

I left Gee's house a mess. I didn't try to hide from her that I'd gone through her things. I didn't care. I walked back through the alley and left. I walked all the way down Girard to the on-ramp to 95 South, and I stuck out my thumb, and I hitchhiked to the return address on the card I was carrying with me. I didn't even know if he lived there anymore. But I was desperate.

That was at the beginning of November. I've been at his place ever since. He's been taking care of me, Kacey says. Making sure I have what I need. Making sure the baby will have a good home when she's born.

She looks at me, and for the first time I register the presence of fear in her expression.

—We'll have everything we need, she says.

And I tell her, Kacey. I believe you.

This is not something Kacey asks for. But I have the notion, suddenly, that I should bring her to see Thomas.

Quietly, the two of us walk toward his room. Quietly, I open the door. Low light from the hallway spills in. By that light we can make out his shape in the bed, a landscape of covers and sheets and pillows and, curled inside them, my son.

Kacey looks at me, asking permission, and I nod.

She walks to the foot of his bed and kneels down before it. She puts her hands to her knees and gazes upon him. She stays like that for a long time.

We had five books in the house as children. One was the Bible. One was a history of the Phillies. Two were Nancy Drew books that had been Gee's when she was small. And one was an ancient compendium of *Grimms' Fairy Tales*, wildly illustrated and frightening, full of witches and woods. The same one I gave to Thomas, this year, for Christmas.

In this volume, the story I liked best was the one about the Pied Piper of Hamelin. It frightened me: the way he came from nowhere to lure the children away. I was frightened, too, by the helplessness of the parents, the way the town failed them, the way they, in turn, failed their children.

Where did those children go, I wondered. What was their life like after they left? Were they hurt? Was it cold? Did they miss their families?

I have thought of this story every day of my life on the job. I picture the drug as the Piper. I picture the trance it casts: I can see this trance quite clearly every day that I work, everyone walking around, charmed, enthralled, beguiled. I imagine the town of Hamelin after the story ends, after the children and the music and the Piper have gone. I can hear it: the terrible silence of the town.

Now, looking at Kacey as she kneels at the foot of the bed, repentant, I see the possibility, very faintly, that one day she might return.

Then I look at Thomas, and I am reminded, as always, of the ever-present threat of departure, of permanent loss. It hovers there, foreboding, a faint, high melody that only children can hear.

Kacey and I return to my bedroom, and to my laptop, on the bed.

She points to Eddie Lafferty again.

—This guy, she says, used to come around all the time while I was living with Connor. It was before I got sober. It's hazy. I remember him, though, because he talked to me. He was friendly. He talked to me and kind of eyed me up. I thought maybe he was looking for a date, but he never asked me for one. He and Connor usually went off someplace together. I don't know what they were doing. I thought he was just there to get high. Connor dealt. Still deals, I guess.

—Try to remember more, I say.

Kacey looks up at the ceiling, then down at the floor.

—I can't, she says.

—Try again, I say.

—There's a lot in my life I can't remember, says Kacey.

Both of us go quiet for a while.

—We could just ask him, Kacey says suddenly.

I look at her, incredulous.

—Connor? I say. Dock? You want to ask Dock for help after what he did to you?

—Yeah, says Kacey. I know it's hard to believe, but he was a pretty good guy. Treated me better than any other guy has treated me, at least.

—Kacey, I say. He attacked you.

She pauses, considering this.

—But I bet I could get him to talk, she says, finally.

I'm shaking my head now.

—Absolutely not, I say.

Kacey turns away.

—We'll figure it out in the morning, I say. Both of us need sleep.

Kacey nods.

—All right, she says. I guess I'll get going.

She doesn't move, though. Neither do I.

—Do you mind if I just take a nap? she says.

I turn off the light. Both of us lie down, awkwardly, next to each other on the bed. There's silence in the room.

—Mickey, says Kacey, suddenly. It startles me.

—What, I say, too quickly. What.

—Thank you for taking care of Thomas, she says. I've never said that.

I pause. Embarrassed.

—You're welcome, I say.

—It's funny, she says.

—What is? I say.

—All the time you were trying to find me, she says. I was trying to hide from you.

—Funny is one word for it, I say after a while.

But I can hear, by her breathing, that she's already asleep.

It's been sixteen years, half of our lives, since we slept next to each other in the back room of Gee's house. I picture us, just children then, telling each other stories to get to sleep, or reading books, or looking up in the dark at a domed ceiling light that rarely contained a working bulb. Below us, the hoarse voice of our grandmother, complaining on the phone, or chanting to herself in anger about somebody's misdeeds. *Put your hand on my back,* Kacey would say, and I would comply, remembering tenderly the way my mother's hand felt on my own skin. In retrospect, I believe it is possible that I was trying to bestow some sense of worth upon her; to be the vessel through which our mother's love poured, posthumously; to immunize her against the many hardships of the world. In that position, my hand on her back, we'd both drift to sleep. Above us was a flat tar roof, poorly engineered for winter. Beyond the roof, the night sky over Philadelphia. Beyond the sky, we couldn't say.

When I wake up, it's sunny out, and my phone is ringing.

Kacey isn't next to me.

I sit up.

I lift the phone into my hands. It's my father.

—Michaela? he says. Is Kacey with you?

I check everywhere. No Kacey. I look out a window. Her car is not in the driveway.

—Maybe she's on her way to your place, I say.

But both of us are quiet. We know the odds of that.

—I'll find her, I say. I think I know where she is.

Then I remember Thomas.

I promised him. I told him last night that I would stay with him. I think of him as Mrs. Mahon described him yesterday, running into the bathroom, running the sink, feigning illness in a misguided attempt to bring his mother home to him, and my heart nearly shatters.

Then I think of my sister—who may be at this very moment putting her life on the line—and the life of her unborn child—in the interest of protecting others. And I think of those others, countless other women on the streets of Kensington, whose lives are also at risk as long as Eddie Lafferty is at large.

Suddenly, surprisingly, I am met against my will by a strange quick sympathy for Gee, and the lengths she went to procure stable childcare for us. What must it have been like for her, I wonder, to work so hard, to constantly fear the closure of our schools?

I think. I think.

And at last I decide that what's happening today feels bigger than just the two of us, bigger than just the needs of our small family. There are lives at stake, I tell myself, and then I steel myself and call Mrs. Mahon.

Once she's arrived, I walk into the bedroom to say goodbye to my son.

He's still asleep. For a while, I watch him. Then I sit down next to him. He opens his eyes. Closes them tightly again.

—Thomas, I say, and he says, Don't leave.

—Thomas, I say again. I have to go do something. Mrs. Mahon is here with you.

He begins to cry. His eyes are still closed tightly. No, he says. He shakes his head.

—I'm sick, he says. I'm still so sick. I think I'm going to throw up.

—I'm so sorry, I say. I have to. I wouldn't leave unless it was really important. You know that, right?

He says nothing. He's gone still now, breathing lightly, as if he's feigning sleep.

—I promise I'll be back soon, I say. I promise I'll explain someday. The reason I've been gone so much. When you're grown up, all right? I'll tell you.

He turns over. His back is to me. He won't look at me.

I kiss him. I put my hand on his hair and leave it there a moment. Then I stand up. What if I'm wrong, I think. What if I'm making the wrong choice?

—I love you, I say.

I leave.

When I arrive in Kensington, I park on a side street not far from Connor McClatchie's makeshift abode.

Quickly, I walk east on Madison. Then I turn down the alley that leads to the back of the house with three Bs on it.

As I round the corner, I'm greeted by a little group standing about halfway between me and the end of the alley. There are three men: two of them in construction gear, work boots and helmets. One in a long overcoat and nice jeans.

I can see the house they're standing in front of: it's McClatchie's place.

I don't know what they're doing there, the men. I walk toward them, slightly less certain than I was a moment ago.

They notice me. They pause in their conversation and turn toward me.

—Can I help you with something? says the man in the overcoat. Friendly. He's got a thick Philly accent, like he's from the neighborhood. But he looks like he's come up in the world recently.

—I was, I say. But I'm uncertain how to proceed. I'm looking for my sister, I say. I think she might be inside there.

I nod to the white house we're standing in front of.

—No sisters in there, says the man cheerfully. He has no idea how familiar this phrase has become to me. Better not be, anyway, he says. We're starting demolition tomorrow. Just did our last walk-through.

Sure enough, the door to the place is standing open.

—Hey, are you okay? says one of the construction workers, when I have been silent for long enough.

—Fine, I say vaguely. I turn around and face Madison Street once again, putting my hands on my hips, uncertain what to do next. Behind me, the men resume their discussion. It's condos they're building. Soon to be populated, perhaps, by the Lauren Sprights of the world, the kids drinking coffees at Bomber. The city is changing, unstoppably. The displaced, the addicted, shift and reorder themselves and find new places to shoot up and only sometimes get better.

It's then that my phone dings.

I take it out of my pocket and inspect it.

On the screen is a message: *cathedral on Ontario*

The sender—the number has been saved, unused, in my phone since November, when I first met him at Mr. Wright's—is *Dock*. Connor Mc-Clatchie.

The cathedral on Ontario is technically called Our Mother of Consolation. But from the time I was a child, its size and grandeur meant that everyone just called it the cathedral. I've only been in it once, when I was about twelve. A friend of Kacey's took us there after a sleepover. It's massive: materials brought over from Europe, we always heard, the high-ceilinged interior built to remind people of God. It closed several years ago. I read about it in the paper; at that time, I didn't think anything of it. It's one of many churches that have closed in Philadelphia in recent years.

The cathedral is only a short drive from where my car is parked. I get in and take off.

When I pull up, I look at the cathedral closely for the first time in a while. It's technically part of the 25th, so I have little reason to go past it on my patrol. It looks nothing like it did in its prime. Most of the windows are broken now. The front doors have *Condemned* signs on them. A bell tower rises from the eastern side of the church, but there's no bell inside. I wonder who salvaged it.

I park and walk up the front steps. I try all the doors, but they're locked. I circle around the side of the building and find one of the back doors ajar, a chain ineffectively roping it off. Quietly, I duck under it and enter.

———

I hear a low murmuring as soon as I'm inside, and instinctively I stop to listen, to see if I can hear Kacey's brassy hoarse cadence. But all of the voices I hear are unfamiliar to me. Nobody's speaking loudly, and yet their words echo forcefully off the broken tile floor, off the walls and high ceilings. Whispered phrases float toward me through the cold.

It's only. I said so. The other day. Until.

There are two smells here: one I recognize from years of churchgoing, the smell of the thin paper of holy books, the dusty velvet of the cushions that cover the kneelers. This is a warm smell, a good smell, the smell of a Christmas bazaar, a nativity pageant, the sign of the cross. The other is the distinct smell of a place overtaken by the transient, people with few resources and no other place to go. I know the second smell well. As neatly as pins, two sharp shafts of light from holes in the roof spear the main area of the church. The nave, it's called. The word comes back to me quickly, along with a vision of Sister Josepha, my favorite grade school teacher, diagramming the parts of a church. *Nave. Altar. Apse. Chapel. Baptistery.* And my favorite: *ambry.* I remember them all.

The light in the church becomes diffuse, slowly. I begin to see people in the pews. They're sitting there, patiently, as if waiting for a mass to begin. Some are sleeping. Some are moving. Some are standing. Some are sitting in the throne-like chairs reserved for the choir. There must be twenty or thirty people in this church. Maybe more.

The wail of a baby cuts through the place sharply, and everyone quiets. After a moment, their murmurs resume. I am distracted, momentarily, by wanting to find and remove this child, to take it into my arms and leave and never return.

A woman brushes past me on her way someplace, startling me.

—Watch yourself, the woman says, and I say, I'm sorry.

Then I say, Excuse me. May I ask you something?

The woman stops, her back to me, and pauses there for a moment before turning around.

—Have you seen Kacey? I say. Or Connie? Or Dock?

We're still in the darkest part of the church, and I can barely make out this woman's face. I can see her body, though. I see how she freezes when I say these names. She looks at me, assessing.

—Check upstairs, says the woman finally. And she points in the direction of a door that's been taken off its hinges. It's resting against a wall to the right of a dark threshold. Beyond it, I can vaguely make out a staircase.

As I climb the steps, the voices in the main room of the cathedral fade. I don't know where I'm going, but the air gets colder as I move. I take out my phone and use it to illuminate the steps in front of me. Occasionally, I see small movements to the right and left of my feet. Mice, or roaches, or perhaps it's just four years of accumulated dust.

The staircase is covered in decaying carpet, and it lets me move in silence. I count the steps as I go. Twenty. Forty. I pass a landing. I pass a locked door. I try it several times, and give it a nudge with my shoulder for good measure, but it doesn't give way.

After sixty steps, faint light begins to enter the stairwell. A double door to my left has two openings at the top that I assume used to contain stained glass, as that's what's now lying shattered at my feet. On the other side of the doors, I hear voices.

I try the doorknob. It turns.

When I open it, as quietly as I can, the first person I see is Kacey.

She's leaning against a waist-high railing, and the open expanse of the cathedral is behind her. She's standing, I see, in the choir loft: presumably, they came up here for privacy.

Connor McClatchie is speaking to her. I see his face, in profile; he doesn't seem to notice me. There's another figure, too, a man, I think, who also has his back to me.

I catch my sister's eye.

know the other man is Eddie Lafferty before he turns around. I see his bald head, his stance, his height. I remember the slight stoop he had. *Bad back,* he told me.

I have my hand on my weapon. Before I can think, I draw it. I hold it before me.

—Hands, I say, loudly and clearly. Let me see your hands.

I recognize that I'm using my work voice, the particular cadence I borrowed from Kacey, from Paula, from all the girls I grew up with, a toughness that served them at school, at work, in life. And it occurs to me suddenly that it might not be natural to them, either. That they, too, may have adopted it, out of a different kind of necessity.

The two men turn toward me. Lafferty and McClatchie.

I can tell that it takes Lafferty a second to place me. I'm out of uniform and out of context. I am unshowered and wild-looking, my hair pulled back into a low knot. I'm tired and strained.

—Whoa, says Lafferty. He smiles, or tries to. Obediently, he raises his hands into the air. Is that Mickey? he says.

—Get your hands up, I say to McClatchie, who finally complies.

—Move away from her, I say to McClatchie, nodding toward Kacey.

I don't like how close he's standing, an arm's length from my sister, who herself is leaning against a ledge. I don't know how far the drop is to the floor of the nave, but I know I don't want her going over. Below us, there is still the low murmur of footsteps and coughs and voices, nonsensical now, echoing indecipherably.

—Where to, says McClatchie, dryly. He's even skinnier than the last time I saw him.

—Against that wall, I say, gesturing, with my head, to my right.

He walks to it. He leans back against it. Puts a foot up.

Eddie Lafferty is still smiling at me, sickly, as if racking his brain for some funny explanation, a reason we all came to be standing here together.

—You undercover too? is what he comes up with.

I say nothing. I don't want to look him in the eye. I also don't want to look away from him for an instant. I'm not sure whom to focus on: McClatchie or Lafferty. Kacey is standing behind the latter. And I realize, suddenly, that she is mouthing something to me.

Looking past Lafferty's right ear, I squint at her. Kacey nods toward McClatchie. Her lips are moving, forming words I can't parse. *He's* something. *I.*

I'm still focused on Kacey's mouth when I notice Lafferty's body tense in that particular manner of a police officer about to give chase. And then he charges at me and knocks me to the ground. My weapon discharges once, shattering a section of ceiling, and then it goes skittering across the carpeted floor of the choir loft.

Below us, a woman screams, and then the cathedral goes silent.

Lafferty is standing over me, one foot on either side of my torso. McClatchie leaves his post and picks the gun up.

lie very still. I'm panting. From the ground, I study the arched ceiling of the cathedral. Dimly, I can make out where the bullet found its mark. A little cloud of plaster dust descends slowly in a shaft of light. The ceiling, once painted celestial blue, is peeling now. A bird's nest, I notice, occupies the nearest corner.

The shot is still echoing in my ears. Otherwise, the cathedral is silent as a tomb.

I picture my son. I wonder what will become of him, if today is the end for me. I think of the choices my own mother made—and realize, painfully, that I am not so different from her after all. It's only the nature of our respective addictions that diverged: Hers was narcotic, clear-cut, defined. Mine is amorphous, but no less unhealthy. Something to do with self-righteousness, or self-perception, or pride.

Thomas, I think, uselessly. I'm so sorry I left you.

When a few long seconds have passed, I glance over at McClatchie. He's clutching my weapon, the one he retrieved from the floor, but he's not holding it right. It occurs to me, suddenly, that he has no idea what he's doing. I'm considering how I might use this to my advantage when he suddenly says, to Lafferty, Kneel down.

Lafferty looks at him for a moment.

—You're joking, he says.

—I'm not, says McClatchie. Kneel down.

With a certain amount of incredulity, Lafferty does so.

—Keep your hands in the air, says McClatchie.

He glances at me where I lie on the ground.

—Is that right? he says to me.

I lift my head. My forehead got knocked pretty badly when Lafferty plowed into me, and I'm still seeing stars. My neck aches.

—You stand up, McClatchie says to me.

I glance at Kacey, who nods quickly, and I comply.

Then McClatchie does something I don't understand: still aiming at Lafferty, he edges toward me until we're standing shoulder to shoulder, side by side. He hands me the weapon.

—You're better off with this, he says. I have no idea what the fuck I'm doing.

As soon as I take the gun and turn it on Lafferty, McClatchie puts his hands behind his head, takes a big breath of relief. He walks to the railing at the edge of the choir loft, leans on his elbows, and looks out at the church below.

I hear footsteps coming up the staircase behind us. For a tense moment, I aim back and forth between Lafferty and the stairs.

The door flies open. I see Mike DiPaolo and Davis Nguyen emerge, guns drawn.

—Drop your weapon, DiPaolo says to me calmly, and I put it on the ground.

I don't understand.

I think, for a moment, that it was Lafferty who called for backup, which will make the job of explaining my case much harder.

—He's dangerous, I say, about Lafferty, and Lafferty starts to protest, but suddenly Kacey's raising her voice above all of us.

—Did Truman Dawes send you? she says to DiPaolo and Nguyen.

—Who's asking? DiPaolo says. He and Nguyen are still stiff-arming their weapons, aiming them at all of us in turn. I can imagine their confusion.

—My name is Kacey Fitzpatrick, says Kacey. I'm her sister, she says, nodding at me. I'm the one who contacted Truman Dawes. And that, she says, nodding toward Eddie Lafferty, is the man you're after.

Nguyen and DiPaolo call for backup. Then they take all of us down to the station—me and Kacey and Lafferty and McClatchie—all of us in separate cars.

We're kept apart, and then we're interrogated.

I tell the two of them everything I know, from start to finish. I leave nothing out: I tell them about Cleare. I tell them about Kacey. I tell them about Thomas. I tell them about Lafferty, and what Kacey told me about him. I even tell them about Truman, and my embarrassing behavior in that regard.

I tell them the truth, the whole truth, for the first time in my life. Then the two of them leave.

Several hours go by. It occurs to me that I'm starving, and that I have to go to the bathroom, and that I've never wanted a glass of water so badly in my life. I shift uncomfortably. I've never been on this side of things before.

Finally, DiPaolo enters the room I'm being held in. He looks tired. He nods at me, pensive, his hands in his pockets.

—It's him, he says. It's Lafferty.

Wordlessly, he holds forth a printed picture of a young woman, smiling, wearing a pretty dress.

—You recognize her? he says.

It takes me a moment, and then suddenly I'm back on the Tracks in

October, leaning over a log, peering toward the first victim. Next to her, in my memory—I shudder to think it—is Eddie Lafferty. I think of the face of the victim, on that day: pained and unpeaceful. I think of the spattering of red dots near her eyes. The violent way she died. I think of Lafferty's reaction to her. Impassive. Aloof.

—Who is she? I say.

—Sasha Lowe Lafferty, says DiPaolo. Eddie Lafferty's most recent ex-wife, he says.

—No, I say.

DiPaolo nods.

I look at the picture again. I remember Lafferty talking about his third wife, about her youth. *She was immature. Maybe that was the problem.*

—She was badly hooked herself, says DiPaolo. Using every day. The rest of her family had cut ties with her over a year before. They've had no contact with her since then. Her only contact was with Lafferty.

He pauses.

—Why she was never reported missing, I guess, he says.

—Jesus, I say.

I'm still looking at the photo. I'm glad to see this woman at a different moment in her life. I close my eyes quickly. Open them again. I let the image of the smiling woman before me replace in my mind the pained, deceased version of Sasha Lowe Lafferty that I've been carrying around in my mind since I found her.

—Guess where they met, says DiPaolo.

I know before he says it.

—Wildwood, I say.

DiPaolo nods.

—Jesus, I say again.

DiPaolo looks like he's hesitating for a moment. Then he continues. You asked about Simon Cleare, he says.

I steel myself. I nod.

—I want you to know, he says, I looked into it. I wasn't trying to blow you off. After we met, I assigned a guy to tag him a few days in a row.

Sure enough, on day two he heads up to Kensington, middle of a work-day, no assigned reason to be there.

—Okay, I say.

DiPaolo looks at me. He's got a problem, Mickey, he says. He was there for the same reason everyone else goes to Kensington. Bought a thousand MGs of Oxy off a guy we know. No heroin, that I know of, but that's probably next. How he affords that much Oxy on a detective salary . . .

DiPaolo trails off. Whistles.

I look down at the table.

—I see, I say. That makes sense.

I think of Simon's words to me when I was young. The tattoo on his calf. *I went through a phase of it myself,* he told me, when I was frightened for Kacey.

At the time, it had brought me such comfort.

After Kacey and I are released, the two of us leave together through the front door of the station. My car is all the way back at the cathedral, two miles from the station. So is the car Kacey borrowed from our father.

Speaking of our father: I call him as soon as I can. Tell him Kacey's okay. That she'll be home soon.

—And you? he says.

—Excuse me?

—Are you okay too? says my father.

—Yes, I say. I'm okay.

I am, in fact, feeling quite relieved. As Kacey and I walk, side by side, I look at our surroundings. Kensington itself looks different, somehow changed, or perhaps I am simply noticing things about it that I never noticed before. It's a lovely neighborhood in many ways, and several of its blocks are quite nice, well maintained, blocks that have managed to stave off the encroaching chaos, blocks with grandmothers who have never left and never will, who sweep their stoops each morning, then sweep all the stoops of their neighbors, and sometimes the street itself, even if the city doesn't come around. We pass a street, on the right, with white lights strung across it for Christmas.

At last, Kacey recounts her morning to me.

She, too, went first to the house with three Bs, the last place she knew

Connor McClatchie to be living. When she found the house vacant and condemned, she went back to the Ave to ask around. Fairly soon, she learned where McClatchie had gone.

She drove over to find him. She wanted to tell him what was going on. Ask what he knew about Eddie Lafferty.

—I can't believe you did that, I say, interrupting. Why would you do that?

—I told you, says Kacey. I knew when he found out that Eddie Lafferty might be the one killing those women, he wouldn't stand for it. I know him.

I shake my head. I notice, suddenly, that Kacey looks unsteady and pale. She has her hands on her stomach. She is six months pregnant, now, and seems to feel it. I don't know if she'll make it the whole way. She keeps insisting she's fine, but she's bent forward slightly. How long has it been, I wonder, since her last dose of methadone?

—Are you okay? I ask her.

—Fine, Kacey says, tightly.

We walk in silence a little longer. Then she goes on.

—Connor can do bad things, Kacey says, but he's not all bad. Almost nobody is.

I have nothing to say to this. I picture Mrs. Mahon, her hand tipping back and forth in the air above the chessboard. *They're bad and good both, all the pieces.* It is possible to acknowledge, on some level, the truth of this. And yet I hate Connor McClatchie for what he did to my sister. And I know, without a doubt, that I'll never forgive him.

—Anyway, Kacey says, Connor told me that Lafferty approached him last summer, told him he was a cop. Told him he'd keep him protected in exchange for a cut. That's why I recognized him, she tells me. And that's why they went off to the side to do their business. Lafferty was taking kickbacks from Connor.

—That fucker, I say suddenly.

—Which one?

—Both of them, I say. Both fuckers.

A thought occurs to me then: Did Ahearn assign Lafferty to my car so that he could dig up some dirt on me? Six months ago, I would have said that was absurd. Now, I don't know.

—And Ahearn's a fucker too, I say. I bet he knew. Maybe got a cut too.

Kacey, I notice, is laughing.

—What? I say. What?

—I don't think I've ever heard you curse before, says Kacey.

—Oh, I say. Well, I do now.

—Well, says Kacey. You're right. Connor told me Lafferty wasn't the only one. Taking payment, I mean. Said it happens more regularly than you know.

—I believe it, I say.

—Connor didn't know about the women, Kacey says. That's the one thing he didn't know. He didn't know that Lafferty had been seen with the four victims. He didn't know people were talking in Kensington. When I told him, he freaked. Punched a wall.

—Noble, I say.

—He can be, says Kacey pensively.

—Anyway, she says, he had Lafferty's phone number, and he called him right away. Told him he had a business proposal for him, and he wanted to see him in person at the cathedral. Once Lafferty got there, I texted you from Connor's phone. And I texted Truman Dawes, too.

—How did you have Truman's number? I say.

—Oh, says Kacey. He gave it to me years ago. I don't think you were even there that day. He came across me on the Ave when I was pretty bad off, looking down and out, and he gave me his card. Said if I ever needed anything, if I ever wanted to get clean, to give him a ring. I memorized it.

—Oh, I say. Yes. He does that.

—He's a good person, she says. Isn't he.

—He is, I say.

She smiles, unaware.

—Well, she says, I'm glad it all worked out.

And suddenly I can't believe her: the danger she put us all in. Truman. Me. Thomas. Herself. And the baby she's carrying, too.

I stop walking and turn toward her. Goddammit, I say. Goddammit, Kacey.

She flinches, slightly. What? she says. Don't shout.

—How could you do that to me? I say. Put me in the position you put me in today. I have a son to think about.

Kacey goes silent. Both of us turn away from one another and start to walk again. In my peripheral vision, I see Kacey begin to shiver, her teeth chattering.

We reach an intersection and I stop at the crosswalk to let the cars go by. But Kacey continues. She walks out into traffic, blindly. A car screeches to a halt. The one behind it nearly rams into it. Horns go off in all directions.

—Kacey, I call.

She doesn't turn around. I toe the ground in front of the sidewalk. The cars don't slow. I wait until, at last, I have the right of way, and then I break into a trot. Kacey is fifty feet ahead of me, walking fast. She turns the corner onto the Avenue, and I lose sight of her momentarily.

When I finally reach the Ave, I turn left, like Kacey did, and I see her twenty yards away, squatting on the ground, elbows on her knees, head in hands. Her belly points down, toward the sidewalk. I can't tell from here, but it looks like she's crying.

I slow to a walk. I approach Kacey carefully. We're at the intersection where she and Paula used to work, right in front of Alonzo's store, and I have the feeling, now, that if I say or do the wrong thing, I'll lose her: the Avenue will take her back, away from me. Kacey will sink into the ground and disappear.

I stand over my sister for a minute. She's shaking with sobs. She's crying so hard that she's gasping for breath. She doesn't look up.

—Kacey, I say.

I put a hand, finally, on my sister's shoulder.

Violently, Kacey windmills her arm.

I bend down, get to eye level with her. Pedestrians move around us.

—What's going on? I say. Kacey?

She lifts her head up, at last, and looks at me. Looks me right in the eye. Says, Get the *fuck* away from me.

I stand again. What the hell, Kacey, I say. What did I do?

Kacey stands up, too, chest out, belly out. I brace myself.

—You knew, Kacey says. You might not have known about Lafferty, but you knew this shit happened. You must have. You'd been told before.

I bristle.

—I didn't, I say. Nobody ever told me.

Kacey laughs loudly, once.

—*I* told you, says Kacey. Me. Your own sister. I told you that Simon Cleare took advantage of me when I couldn't say no. You didn't believe me. You said I was lying.

—That's different, I say. I was wrong about that. But it's different.

Kacey smiles, sadly.

—What's Simon? she says. What is he? Is Simon a cop?

I close my eyes. Breathe in.

—Because I thought he was, says Kacey.

Kacey looks at me for a long time, searching my face.

Then she looks past me, toward the corner, toward Alonzo's store. She's frozen. I turn, finally, to see what she sees, but no one is there. And I know, without asking, that Kacey is picturing Paula Mulroney standing there, one leg propped up against the wall, cocky, smiling, her usual stance.

—They were my friends, says Kacey, quietly now. All of them. Even the ones I didn't know.

—I'm sorry, I say at last.

She doesn't reply.

—Kacey, I'm sorry, I say again.

But the El train is going by now, and I don't know if my sister can hear me.

LIST

Sean Geoghehan; Kimberly Gummer; Kimberly Brewer, Kimberly Brewer's mother and uncle; Britt-Anne Conover; Jeremy Haskill; two of the younger DiPaolantonio boys; Chuck Bierce; Maureen Howard; Kaylee Zanella; Chris Carter and John Marks (one day apart, victims of the same bad batch, someone said); Carlo, whose last name I can never remember; Taylor Bowes's boyfriend, and then Taylor Bowes a year later; Pete Stockton; the granddaughter of our former neighbors; Hayley Driscoll; Shayna Pietrewski; Pat Bowman; Sean Bowman; Shawn Williams; Juan Moya; Toni Chapman; Dooney Jacobs and his mother; Melissa Gill; Meghan Morrow; Meghan Hanover; Meghan Chisholm; Meghan Greene; Hank Chambliss; Tim and Paul Flores; Robby Symons; Ricky Todd; Brian Aldrich; Mike Ashman; Cheryl Sokol; Sandra Broach; Lisa Morales; Mary Lynch; Mary Bridges and her niece, who was her age, and her friend; Mikey Hughes's father and uncle; two great-uncles we rarely see. Our cousin Tracy. Our cousin Shannon. Our mother. Our mother. Our mother. All of them children, all of them gone. People with promise, people dependent and depended upon, people loving and beloved, one after another, in a line, in a river, no fount and no outlet, a long bright river of departed souls.

NOW

Some days, I spend hours on my laptop, visiting online memorials for those who've died. They're all still there: Facebook pages, funeral home websites, blogs. The deceased are digital ghosts, the last posts they ever made buried beneath a tidal wave of grief, of commands to Rest In Peace, of in-fighting between friends and enemies who claim that half the people on the page are *fake*, whatever that means. Their girlfriends still posting *happy birthday baby* two years after they're gone, as if the Internet were a crystal ball, a Ouija board, a portal to the afterlife. In a way, I suppose, it is.

It's become a habit of mine to look at these pages, and at the pages of the friends and family members of the deceased, first thing in the morning. How is the mother holding up, I wonder. And I check. How is the best friend? The boyfriend? (Usually, it is the boyfriends who move on first: down come the profile pictures of the happy couple, posing in a mirror; up goes a picture he has taken of himself; next will come the new woman in his life.) Sometimes, friends are bitter. *u promised kyle. i swear if one more person dies. why kyle. rip.* People in the throes of addiction are hardest on others like them. *THA WHOLE NTHEAST IS FULLA FUKN JUNKIES,* one of them rants, and I know I've pulled him in before for dealing. In his pictures he's glazed and dreamy.

When I think about Kacey, when I wonder whether she will find the strength and luck and perseverance to get and stay clean, it is these souls

I think of first. How few ever seem to make it out. I think of the Piper, the whole town of Hamelin, shocked in his wake, abandoned and condemned.

But then I look at Kacey—who comes to visit most Sundays now, who at this moment is sitting on my couch, who on this day has 189 days clean—and think, maybe she'll be one of the few. The veteran of some war, wounded but alive. Maybe Kacey will outlive us all, will live to be a hundred and five. Maybe Kacey will be all right.

Letting hope back in feels right and wrong all at once. Like letting Thomas sleep in my bed when he really should sleep in his.

Like letting him meet the woman who brought him into the world.

Like breaking an oath of loyalty when you know a secret needs telling.

turned in my uniform. Thomas was happy to see it go. The day I did, I worked up some courage and called Truman Dawes, holding my breath until he answered.

—It's Mickey, I said.

—I know who it is, he said.

—I just wanted to tell you I quit, I said. I quit the force.

Truman paused for a while. Congratulations, he said finally.

—And I'm sorry, I said, closing my eyes. I'm so sorry for the way I treated you this year. You deserve better.

I could hear him breathing. I appreciate that, he said. But then he told me he had to go tend to his mother, and in his voice I heard that he was through, that I had lost him forever.

This happens, I tell myself. Sometimes, this happens.

The PPD, nationally embarrassed, is denying that they have a widespread problem. But I know differently, and Kacey knows differently, and the women of Kensington know differently. So I called Lauren Spright, and told her that I wanted to give her some information on condition of anonymity. The story was on public radio the next day. *Police sexual assault is not uncommon in Kensington*, the reporter began, and I turned the radio off. I didn't want to hear.

Some days, I still wake up with the sick feeling that I've done something terribly wrong. I worry I've sold out the people who've protected me all these years, who've always had my back—sometimes literally.

I think of the many honorable people who work for the organization. Truman was in the PPD. Mike DiPaolo still is. Davis Nguyen. Gloria Peters. Even Denise Chambers, who recently phoned me personally to apologize.

Then there are the Laffertys, the evil ones. They're few and far between, but everybody's met one.

The hardest cases, I think—perhaps the most dangerous ones—are the friends of the Laffertys'. People like Sergeant Ahearn, who has possibly known for years about what goes on in Kensington. Maybe he even participates himself—who knows. And he'll never be fired, never be questioned, never even be disciplined. He'll go on with his daily routine, showing up for work, casually abusing his power in ways that will have lasting effects on individuals and communities, on the whole city of Philadelphia, for years.

It's the Ahearns of the world who scare me.

I still don't have a job. I probably could have gotten a lawyer and sued the PPD, given all that happened, but I don't have the inclination.

Instead, I live on unemployment. I work at my uncle Rich's car dealership in Frankford, doing paperwork and answering phones, being paid under the table, all cash. With a more regular schedule, I have found a regular babysitter, someone I trust, to watch Thomas two days a week now. Mondays and Wednesdays, I bring Thomas with me to Rich's. And Fridays, Mrs. Mahon watches him.

The system isn't perfect, but it's working for now. Next year, Thomas will go to kindergarten, and everything will change again. Maybe I'll sign up for classes at the community college. Maybe, eventually, I'll get a degree. Be a history teacher, like Ms. Powell. Maybe.

When I get it, I tell myself, I'll frame it, and then send a copy to Gee.

On a Tuesday morning in the middle of April, I open all the windows in my apartment. A rainstorm has just come through, and the air outside has that plump spring smell, wet grass and new earth. A pot of coffee is on in the kitchen. Thomas's new babysitter is due to arrive soon. He's in his room now, playing with his Legos. I've taken the day off work at the car dealership.

The babysitter arrives, and I say goodbye to Thomas, and then I go downstairs and ring Mrs. Mahon's doorbell.

—Ready? I say, when she opens the door.

The two of us get into my car. We drive toward Wilmington.

The outing has been long anticipated.

The seeds of it were planted one day back in January, when I had both Kacey and Mrs. Mahon over for dinner. That first dinner turned into a weekly one. Now, every Sunday, we put Thomas to bed and then we watch TV, the three of us, something silly, whatever new comedy is on demand. Kacey likes comedies. Other times we watch a murder show—the term Kacey still uses, despite recent events—a show that is almost always about a missing woman, who was almost always murdered by her abusive husband or boyfriend. The host narrates the whole thing with alarming calm. *That would be the last time the Millers would see their daughter.*

—He did it, Kacey usually says, about the husband. He definitely did it, my God, look at him.

Sometimes, the victims are poor. Other times they are rich women, blond and impeccable, with husbands who are doctors or lawyers.

The rich women look, to me, like grown-up versions of the girls at *The Nutcracker*, the one time Kacey and I ever went, decades ago. All those blond girls with their hair in buns. All of them wearing different-colored dresses, like rare birds, like the dancers themselves. All of them loved.

Each Sunday dinner, Kacey has made the two of us swear that we'll visit her in the hospital when her daughter is born.

—I want visitors, she says. I'm afraid no one will come. Will you visit me, both of you?

We will, we tell her.

Today, Mrs. Mahon and I turn into the parking lot of the hospital.

The child was born yesterday. She still doesn't have a name.

Our father has told us she's in the NICU for now, until her condition is better assessed.

Kacey can see her as much as she wants. She's been cooperative with the doctors. Everyone knew, going in, to monitor the baby for signs of withdrawal.

Mrs. Mahon looks at me, before we get out of the car. She puts a hand on my hand. Holds it there firmly.

—Now this will be hard for you, she says. It will make you think of Thomas, and remember the pain he was in. You're going to be mad at Kacey all over again.

I nod.

—But she's doing her best, says Mrs. Mahon. Just think: She's doing her best.

There is one memory I have of my mother that I've never shared with Kacey. When I was small it felt too precious: speaking it aloud, I feared, might make it disappear.

In this memory, I can't see my mother's face. All I can recall of her is a sweet voice talking to me while I took a bath. We were playing a game. Someone had given us plastic eggs one Easter, and I was allowed to take them into the tub with me. They were yellow and orange and blue and green, and they were split down the middle into two halves. I could take them apart and put them back together again so they didn't match: yellow with blue, green with orange. Everything out of order. *Oh no oh no,* my mother would cry, teasing me. *Put them back together again!* And for some reason, this was the funniest thing in the world to me. *Silly,* my mother would call me. The last time I was ever called anything so young-sounding. I remember the smell of my mother, and the smell of the soap, like flowers in sunlight.

When I was younger, I used to think it was this single memory that saved me from Kacey's fate, that made me the way I am and Kacey the way she is. The sound of my mother's voice, which I can still hear, and its gentleness, which I always took to be evidence of her love for me. The knowledge that there was once a person in the world who loved me more than anything. In some ways, I still think this is true.

In the hospital, Mrs. Mahon and I are given visitor badges. We ring a small bell, and we're admitted into the ward. We're following a nurse named Renee S.

We see Kacey, first, at the end of a hallway. She's out of bed already. Our father is standing next to her. The two of them are looking through a glass window at what I presume is the NICU.

—Visitors, says Renee S., brightly.

Kacey turns.

—You came, she says.

Renee swipes her badge through a reader and opens the door. A doctor greets us quickly on her way out.

Inside the NICU, it's dark and quiet. White noise is on in the background.

There are two basin sinks to the right of the door and a sign over them instructing us to wash our hands.

We comply, all of us. While Kacey is scrubbing, I look around. The room has a central aisle that divides two rows of plexiglass bassinets, four on either side. Machines and monitors flash steadily but silently. At the opposite end of the room there is another nurses' station, slightly removed, lit more fully.

There are two nurses in the room, both at work: one diapering a baby, another entering something on a computer that sits on a rolling, waist-high stand. An older woman, a volunteer or a grandparent, sits near us in a rocking chair, moving slowly, a newborn in her arms. She smiles at us but says nothing.

Which one of these babies, I wonder, is Kacey's?

My sister turns off the water. Then she turns around and walks across the room to one of the bassinets.

Baby Fitzpatrick, says a name tag at the head of it.

Inside is a baby girl. She is sleeping, her eyes closed and swollen from the work of being born. Her eyelids flutter a little, and she turns her perfect face from left to right.

All four of us stand around her, looking in.

—Here she is, Kacey says.

—Here she is, I repeat.

—I don't know what to call her, Kacey says.

She looks up at me, plaintively. She says, I just keep thinking, *That's what she'll be called for the rest of her life.* And it stops me.

The room is very quiet, all of the sounds in it faraway, as if underwater. And then, from behind, there comes a high-pitched cry, a wail of pain.

Thomas, I think, reflexively.

All of us turn toward it. The cry comes again.

It's a sound I'll never forget: the newborn cry of my son. How many times a night did it drag me from sleep? Even in his waking hours I would flinch, in anticipation, every time his small brow furrowed.

I glance at Kacey and see that she's a statue, unmoving, eyes fixed.

—Are you all right? I whisper, and she nods.

The crying child is five feet away from us. We watch as a nurse materializes, leans down into the bassinet, and lifts into her arms a tiny baby in a blanket and cap.

Where, I wonder, is his mother?

—There, says the nurse. Oh, now, there.

She places the baby on her shoulder, begins to sway. I think of my mother. I think of Thomas. My body remembers both being held and holding.

The nurse pats the baby firmly on the diaper. She puts a pacifier into his tiny mouth.

But his crying continues: little hiccupping wails, high as a birdsong, that can't be soothed.

The nurse lowers him again into his bassinet and unswaddles him. She checks his diaper. She swaddles him tightly again. Lifts him into her arms. Still, he cries.

Another nurse walks past her and reaches for the chart at the end of the bassinet.

—Oh, she says. He's due.

—I'll bring it, she says, and walks away, toward the other end of the room.

My sister, beside me, is still frozen in place. I hear her breathing, light and quick and shallow. Gently, instinctively, she places a hand on the head of her sleeping, unnamed daughter.

The second nurse returns with a dropper.

The first nurse places the child, still crying, into the bassinet.

The dropper is lowered. The child turns his head toward it, toward the medicine, seeking it. He remembers it.

He opens his mouth. He drinks.

Acknowledgments

Thank you to those who have spoken to me over the years about their personal experiences with a variety of the subjects covered in this novel, especially India, Matt, David, José, Krista Killen, and the women of the Thea Bowman Center.

Thank you to photographer Jeffrey Stockbridge, who has dedicated a large part of his life to photographing Kensington, and who first introduced me to the neighborhood in 2009. Without his introduction, this novel would not have been written.

Thank you to Natalie Weaver, Father Michael Duffy, and the staff of St. Francis Inn for your friendship, your service to the community, and the opportunity to get to know your organization. Thank you also to Women in Transition and Mighty Writers, two other organizations that provide indispensable aid to the city of Philadelphia and its residents.

Thank you to Zoe Van Orsdol, Signe Espinoza, Dr. Charles O'Brien, Nathaniel Popkin, Marjorie Just, and Clarence for your help with the research that informed this novel and related writing projects, and to Jessica Soffer and Mac Casey for reading and discussing early drafts.

Thank you to the authors of the following books, which provided useful information as I wrote: *Voices of Kensington: Vanishing Mills, Vanishing Neighborhoods*, by Jean Seder, with photography by Nancy Hellebrand;

Acknowledgments

Silk Stockings and Socialism: Philadelphia's Radical Hosiery Workers from the Jazz Age to the New Deal, by Sharon McConnell-Sidorick; *Work Sights: Industrial Philadelphia, 1890–1950*, by Philip Scranton and Walter Licht; *Whitetown USA*, by Peter Binzen; and the *WPA Guide to Philadelphia*.

Thank you to Seth Fishman and the Gernert team; to Sarah McGrath, Jynne Dilling Martin, Kate Stark, and the Riverhead team; and to Ellen Goldsmith-Vein and the Gotham team, for your professional guidance and your friendship, too.

Thank you to the many family members, friends, and providers of childcare who facilitated the writing of this book. Every day, I'm grateful for you.